THE CRIMSON COIL

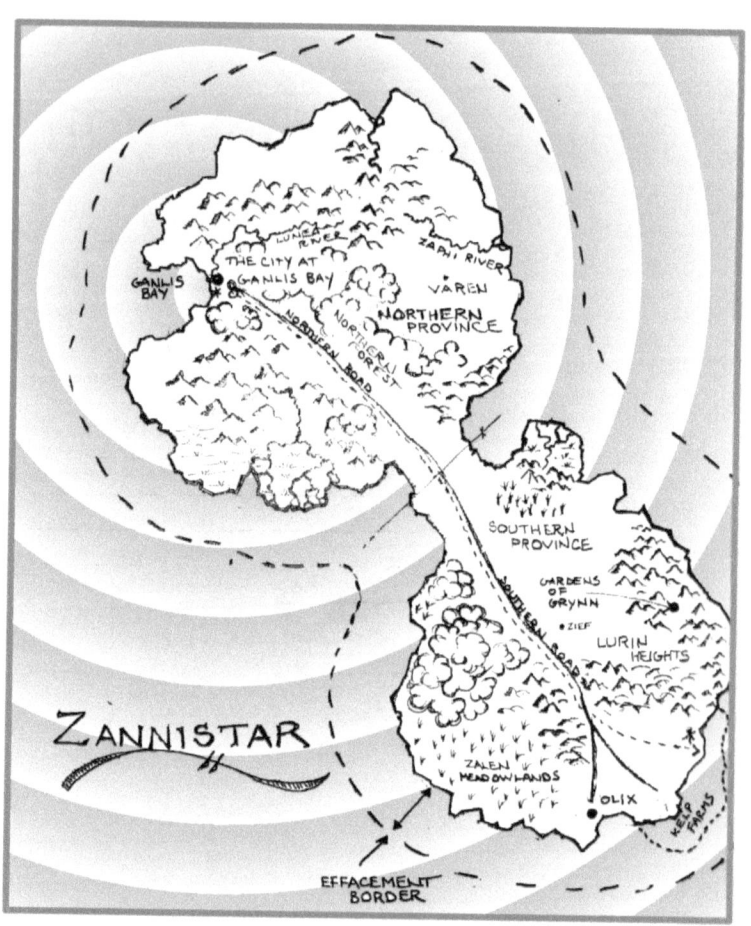

THE CRIMSON COIL

LEO RIÁN

Gearwood
Press

Lines from "Night and Day" by Virginia Woolf written in 1919, originally published by Duckworth, UK. Reprinted without permission as work is in the public domain.

First paperback edition April 2019

Cover illustration by Ron Bowman
Map by Leo Rián

Printed in the United States of America

ISBN 978-1-7338957-1-2 (paperback)
ISBN 978-1-7338957-0-5 (ebook)

Published by Gearwood Press
www.gearwoodpress.com

For Cherish

"I see you everywhere, in the stars, in the river, to me you're everything that exists; the reality of everything."
–Virginia Woolf, *Night and Day*

ACKNOWLEDGMENTS

I would like to first thank Titus ONeill, whose boundless enthusiasm invaded my thoughts and took root, reminding me of the possibilities. I am grateful to Ron Bowman for his generosity, humility and technical expertise.

A special thank you goes to the book's Beta Readers, without whom this work would have remained a hot mess:

Jennifer Babineau, Cherish Cart, Zander Cart, Dannie Ceballos, Matt Estrada, Jon Frye, Steve Keryo, Adrian Martinez, J. M. Murdoch, Shavone Payne, Nigel Pick, Sylvi Ramundo, Tara Shafiei, and Nancy "Bug" Uliano.

Additional thanks go to the larger community of writers and readers whose kind counsel and genuine encouragement have inspired me to be better.

PROLOGUE

"AERION! YOU'RE TOO CLOSE!" yelled Corwyn.

Argus cupped his hands over his mouth and joined in. "Listen to your Uncle, you boar-blooded whelp! You'll meet death today for all your stupidity, boy!"

Both men were towering, wild-haired hunters clad head to foot in a patchwork of leather and fur. As was tradition, each carried two-days provisions along with a longspear of worked bronze and decorated gearwood. They had been on the move since morning.

Just ahead of them past the treeline, a boy of hunting age stood knee deep in fresh snow, holding his longspear at the ready.

"I can take him!" screeched the young Aerion. "The beast has nowhere to flee!"

Corwyn and Argus pressed through the frozen thicket and emerged onto a small, snow-covered clearing that ended in a cliff.

A massive rock stag with black fur paced near the edge. It snorted steam and desperation. Aerion kept his spear trained on the agitated game and renegotiated his footing.

"Back away, Aerion," warned Corwyn through labored breaths. "or we'll lose the beast to the lake."

"But, his neck is in the path of my spear!" called back the youth.

Himself somewhat winded, Argus hunched. "The stag! It will run you down before it bleeds out!"

Aerion became even more determined. He pumped his spear back and forth.

"Listen to my words, Aerion," reasoned Corwyn. "You've tracked and engaged your prey with skill. The other hunters will accept you. You've proven yourself. There's no shame in yielding now. Let the beast go!"

The stag ceased pacing and faced Aerion's direction. Its massive head was as high two men combined. It sniffed the air, calculating its chances. Aerion's heart raced as the beast lowered its eyes, revealing the full splendor of its deadly antlers.

Aerion surveyed his surroundings. He figured there were only two options for the stag, and neither one of them was without sacrifice.

"Yield the path!" howled Argus. "And live to tell of it!"

"No, we finish this!" answered Aerion, taking aim.

Argus grunted. "Think of your mother, boy!"

Corwyn gripped Argus' shoulder, signaling him to be quiet. Aerion's courage intrigued him.

Snow descended in large flakes while Aerion made his final calculations. Opposite him, the stag stopped pacing. Then, as if beckoned by an unseen disturbance, the beast raised its ears and turned its head toward the sky behind it.

Aerion saw his opportunity.

"I've won," whispered Aerion, pulling back his spear for the throw.

In that moment, the snow clouds in the northwest skies darkened. Then a ball of blue fire trailed by a vast column of red smoke exploded through the clouds, passing overhead with great speed. The ground quaked as the hurling object carved a great, fiery wound across the forested landscape to the east, where it crashed in the distance. The impact was so violent, it threw the hunters to the ground. Fire was everywhere.

When Aerion came to his senses, the odor of burning wood mixed with his own fear assaulted him. He spat at the ground. Though the other hunters had returned to their feet, Aerion fumbled for the longspear buried in the snow beside him.

"Aerion, the stag!" cried Argus, pointing.

Aerion turned around and saw the rock stag standing over him. Fear pushed his muscles, and he crawled away from the beasts as fast as he could. Despite creating distance, he still expected the stag to rush and trample him but it did not. Instead, the stag gazed past him toward the fires and sniffed the air. It was here in this vulnerable position that Aerion realized the great power and majesty of the rock stag. If it wanted to trample him, he could not stop it. Aerion prepared to dodge.

The beast snorted as if expelling an unpleasant stench. It looked into Aerion's eyes. With a gentle, purposeful movement, the beast threw itself off the cliff into the freezing depths of Mirlandis Lake.

"Gastwyrd protect us," whispered Argus.

Corwyn shook his head. "We're stricken, Argus." He spun toward the fires. "This is an unnatural fate. We must warn the village."

Aerion stared at the empty spot where the rock stag had been. He found his senses and crawled toward the edge and searched the lake. There was no sign of the beast except for a small, concentric ripple in the water hundreds of feet down. Aerion knew the stag would have perished on impact. A sense of emptiness and failure welled up within him. The lake stole the kill. Frustrated, Aerion thrust his fist into the snow. Had he returned with the beast, the people would have respected him.

The village bell tolled in the distance. Aerion trained his eye in that direction, but movement on the cliffs across the lake diverted his attention.

"Come!" Aerion wailed.

Corwyn and Argus labored through the snow to the edge, joining Aerion on their bellies. Corwyn found Aerion's longspear.

"Are you hurt?" asked Corwyn, handing him the weapon.

Aerion aimed it across the lake. "No, but look!"

"What is it?" asked Argus.

Corwyn removed his spyglass from his hunting pack. He wiped the lens on the fur of his coat and aimed it west.

"Nature has abandoned hope," he said, handing the spyglass to Argus. "We must get to our families."

Argus gasped. "What evil can cause such a thing, Corwyn?" he pleaded. "Are we forsaken?"

Aerion snatched the spyglass from Argus and leveled it westward. Argus lunged at him.

"Leave him!" Corwyn snapped. "He shares our fate. Let him see for himself."

Aerion reeled at the sight. He thought he was seeing a waterfall at first. But he soon realized that the surge was not water at all but an endless stream of forest animals. Dumbfounded, Aerion watched as the beasts ran themselves over the cliff by the thousands.

"We hurry," said Corwyn, scanning the surrounding area. "The forest burns and the village alarm warns of danger." He motioned toward the village on the lakeshore where distant lines of smoke rose from cottage chimneys.

Shaken, Argus could not turn away from the spectacle before him.

"Now, Argus!" warned Corwyn.

Argus gave his attention to Corwyn and nodded.

Time was even shorter than they realized. They attempted to rise, but the ground shook, accompanied by a distant rumbling sound. The hunters grabbed at the snow for handholds.

"Listen!" cried Corwyn.

The clamor of an approaching stampede grew. At this, the two elder hunters shot each other a knowing glance.

"Move!" shrieked Argus, too late as the frenzied horde of animals exploded through the wooded barrier into the clearing.

The men rolled to opposite sides. Aerion tried the same, but became trapped on his back while the maddened throng leapt over him to their deaths. Time seemed to slow. The beauty of their flight mesmerized him.

Argus was screaming something, but Aerion could not hear over the deafening roar of the beasts' thunderous footfall. He knew he would die if he stayed here. Refocused, he lifted his head enough to see past his feet toward what approached. He rolled once to the side, stopping on his back to survey his options. He repeated the move. The second time, he gasped at what he saw.

Covered in flames, a giant, howling redbear tripped on a slower tangle of animals and crashed to the ground, launching nearby beasts this way and that. The redbear tried to gain control but continued to slide across the clearing toward Aerion. There was no time so Aerion closed his eyes and braced himself. But death did not come. He felt the shoulder straps of his hunting pack become taught then he realized he was in the air.

Aerion opened his eyes. Corwyn had used his longspear to hoist Aerion in a giant arc over the water and dropped him in the snow out of the way of the stampede. The burning redbear jettisoned over the side, taking most of the snow with it. The remaining beasts changed direction, swarming to the north around the clearing instead of through it. They found another path to the cliff. Argus jumped to his feet and thrust his own spear into the freezing air above, letting out a cry of victory.

Corwyn rushed toward Aerion. "Did I pierce you?"

"I'm fine!" Aerion retorted. He was still angry about the rock stag's denial. The inexperienced hunter arose, brushing off snow and humiliation. He failed the hunt.

Corwyn squeezed Aerion's shoulder, staring him in the eye. "I thought I'd lost you, Aerion," he said. "The village needs us. We must hurry."

Aerion pulled away from Corwyn. "But you didn't lose me," Aerion snapped. "I'm saved because you are always there to rescue me. Are you going to follow me around like a dog the rest of my life?"

The words cut Corwyn. He took a serious tone. "We don't have time, Aerion. The forest burns, the animals are killing themselves and the village calls. We leave now."

"No! I won't return empty-handed!"

"Stop this! Where is your gratitude? If your father were here, he would ban you from the hunt for acting this way."

"What?" Aerion returned, tears forming. "And where were you when he died? Why didn't you save him?"

In a sudden burst of rage, Aerion bolted past the men toward where the fireball landed.

"Wait!" Argus shouted, but the boy was already among the trees.

"We must go for him, Argus," said Corwyn.

"He's your sister's son!" retorted Argus. "And we can't have the Quarrymaster's nephew disappearing on a routine hunt, now can we? Let's be swift before this calamity finds us jumping to our own deaths, eh?"

Corwyn gave a sharp nod and together they bounded after Aerion.

Aerion was not sure what he was doing or why, but he knew he needed to run. He pushed his muscles their limit. He was accustomed to sprinting but not for long distances. Flames danced on the trees around him as he passed, heat filling his lungs. Like a wild hare, Aerion leaped over burning logs and brush, following the trail the fireball had made.

As he sped along, Aerion allowed thoughts of his father's death invade his mind. He had been killed during the hunt two years prior. That day, Aerion lost the innocence of his childhood belief in the Great and Venerable Spirit—The Gastwyrd. He recalled the memory of watching his inconsolable mother as the elders of the village pushed the blazing funeral barge away from the lake-shore. In that hollow moment, Aerion decided to never believe again. And it was from that time forward that Aerion devoted himself to mastering the art of the hunt—and to slaying the beast that took his father from him. Stealth, spear and determination had become Aerion's new pursuits, not ancient spirits who favor beasts over men.

At last, Aerion discovered a long, mud-filled trench cut in the ground. The surrounding snow had melted. He tested the mud which was hot but bearable. Aerion jumped into the waist-high trench and plodded toward the smoldering hole. With each step, the trench deepened making passage difficult. As he drew closer to the end, Aerion had to exert more effort just to keep moving. It was as if an invisible force was slowing his progress. It pressed first against his chest, then into his mind. The blood in his veins erupted in pain.

"I won't stop!" Aerion resolved. With renewed vigor, he pressed on to the pit. Aerion searched its depths with his hands. The mud was hotter here. Aerion felt the ground beneath him collapse, causing him to lunge forward.

Something jabbed his right hand. Cursing in pain, he pressed the wound against his chest. Careful, he reached into the mud with his other hand. It took a few moments, but he found the object that had wounded him and explored its dimensions. He found a place to grip it and pulled it free of the mud.

It looked like a piece of smooth, sharpened obsidian about the size and shape of a spearhead. Aerion wiped it on his tunic and examined it. It was beautiful. Even in the grayness of the snowfall, it gave off a brilliant shine unlike any stone he had ever seen. Aerion decided that fate brought this to him. Nobody owned such a tool, not even the Quarrymaster. Perhaps he succeeded in the hunt after all. As he pondered, he heard the approaching footsteps of the other hunters.

"Aerion! Aerion, where are you?" called Corwyn.

"Uncle! I've found something!"

The boy slogged his way back through the mud and climbed out where he had first entered. Blood from his wound flowed, staining his tunic dark red. Remembering what his uncle had taught him, Aerion held his punctured hand high to slow the bleeding.

Aerion examined the mysterious stone and felt a wave a sadness wash over him. He wondered why the stag and the other beasts of the forest ended their own lives.

The pursuing hunters emerged from the burning treeline into the elongated clearing made by the object from the sky. Patches of fire and smoke stretched in every direction. Corwyn could see the outline of his nephew through a cloud of ash and cinder.

Corwyn called out. "Aerion! We're here!"

Corwyn stopped in his tracks. Something was wrong.

Argus approached. "What is it, my friend", he gasped, clutching his longspear. "We're cursed!"

Aerion stood before them, one hand high above his head and in the other a sharpened piece of obsidian. He was still, as though he were dead, but his presence felt alive. Corwyn noticed the blood on the boy's tunic and located its source. What he saw on Aerion's hand gave Corwyn a depth of unease that caressed the bottom of his spine with a finger of ice.

In the center of Aerion's raised palm was a swirling vortex of crimson smoke that twisted inward far beyond the depth of Aerion's hand. Blood dripped, but appeared likewise motionless. Corwyn swallowed hard, deciding this was sorcery.

"Argus, he's lost," said Corwyn, surveying the scene from different angles. "We must gather everyone in the village and leave this place to its dark destiny."

"Aerion's your kin!" pleaded Argus.

Corwyn threw down his longspear, seized Argus and shook him.

"You think I don't know?" Corwyn grabbed Argus' face and forced it toward the boy. "Look at him! He's gone, taken by the abyss!" Corwyn trembled as tears flowed from his eyes.

Argus, saw the pain in his companion's face and softened. "I'm sorry, Corwyn."

Corwyn released Argus and patted his shoulder. "Go. Warn the village. I won't be long."

Argus nodded. He regarded the boy, then disappeared into the charred trees.

Corwyn fell to his knees near Aerion. This was dark sorcery. "I am not worthy of your care," he said aloud through clenched teeth.

He removed a glove and reached out to touch the boy. Yet, an invisible force blocked him; made him sick, filling his veins with fire. As he moved his hand closer, he felt the air around Aerion push back. He pushed harder but doing so only caused more burning in his blood. The pain became unbearable. He pulled away. There was nothing more he could do.

He rose from his knees and beheld Aerion one last time. With sadness and regret, Corwyn followed his companion toward an uncertain future.

CHAPTER 1

"I DO NOT LOVE YOU, CHARLES. I NEVER DID."

Charles stared at Nissa, the blood gone from his face. He considered himself a good husband: honest, loyal, hardworking—the basics. Yet, his attempts at worthiness over the course of their marriage failed. He feared this moment would someday come.

Charles noticed Nissa searching him for some sign of protest.

Nissa folded her arms. "Will you say nothing? Where is your mettle?" These were fair questions.

She was in a darker mood than usual. Some days he was ready for it, but not today. She attacked him the moment he returned from the counting house.

"Nissa, everything you asked of me, I have given to you."

"You have given me nothing!" Nissa's vibrant eyes grew wet as she regained composure and checked her dark tresses for the platinum clasp that restrained them. She raised a trembling finger to Charles and bared her teeth. "I deserve more than this, Charles. Don't you see that? Look at me! I am wasted on you."

Charles winced at the jagged words.

Nissa flowed toward the west window where the final remnant of the sun made its escape below the horizon. Charles figured her patience was dying with the daylight.

Charles searched his heart. He was not fond of the unfairness of arranged marriages, but they were lawful. Anyway, he loved her, even if she did not return the sentiment. He resolved long ago that just being with her was enough though he felt challenged during moments like these. But still, Charles marveled at her fierce beauty and impeccable bearing. She was a striking woman who had grown accustomed to second glances. He knew she reveled in the attention most times.

Her skin was pale, offsetting a thick shock of black hair pinned atop her head. She commanded a slight physique though she had strong hands. Her eyes were large, aquamarine and captivating. Still, Charles was not without physical merit himself. Tall and lean, he refused to fatten, regardless of how many brierberry dumplings he ate. His straight, light-brown hair was ear-length, typical of male courtiers of Secondary status. He was dark-eyed, square-jawed and wielded a generous nose. His looks were not his problem.

Confidence, courage and presence were the things that eluded Charles and everyone knew it. The other courtiers often gossiped about his weak affect and lack of self-esteem. Despite this, Charles carved out a place for himself through the quality of his work, not the strength of his pomp. He was a skilled accountant with a perfect record. Managing the King's holdings was a difficult task for which Charles had no equal. But no matter how adept one was, all

Secondaries who worked for the court reported to a Primary. That was the agreement.

Charles reported to the Treasurer, Duke Osric Branlin, the King's nephew. Most of the other courtiers disliked Osric, but Charles tolerated him. Osric was disinterested in the details of the counting house so he left them to Charles. This pleased Charles, who enjoyed the autonomy. Besides the occasional inspection, Charles never saw Osric. But Osric did little else when he visited but nod and stroke his pointed beard. He stayed long enough to receive a good report, which Charles always gave. The arrangement satisfied them both.

Charles felt a sudden burst of spirit. "Nissa, I can improve. It is possible for a Secondary to succeed a Primary. Osric has no other successor. Yes, it would require extra effort and a little cunning but I can make sure I am the obvious choice when the time comes. The King knows me."

Nissa did not turn from the ocean. "Cunning? You are about as cunning as a whore is chaste. Besides, Osric has many seasons of service left in him."

The oversized, burgundy sleeves of Nissa's black velvet gown teased the slate floor as she placed her hands on the window sill. "I understand Osric will soon scout a new accountant."

"And why would he do that, Nissa?"

"Because, husband. You stole from the King."

Charles laughed. "Ridiculous!"

Nissa raised her finger in the air. "It is believable, you know. All those hours, spent alone in the counting house. Maybe you grew tired of being Osric's dog. Then again, maybe you resented the King for not making you a Primary when your parents died. Or maybe you finally realized you would never be significant. So, you did the noble thing and sabotaged yourself."

Irritated, Charles stiffened. The sound of crashing waves gave him some solace.

"Oh Charles, what important thing have you accomplished in your life?"

Charles flashed hot. "I have done my duty to Zannistar!"

Nissa raised a preened eyebrow. "Is that a glint of pride I detect?" She looked to the sea and sighed. "I am sorry it comes to this," She turned to face him, waving her hand in his direction. "Is there a proper husband buried under all that fear and hesitation? Too little too late, I should think."

Charles lowered his face. Nissa's words stung, but he had grown used to her belittling long ago. She was skilled in her cruelty, but very careful to avoid such behavior in public. Nissa was special.

In all Zannistar, none were as refined as Nissa Warfield. She set herself apart from the other courtiers with her demure and dignified demeanor. She outperformed all, even the Primaries. Even the King. This was no accident. Charles watched her practice the ways of the court since they first met as young adolescents. Charles remembered how she obsessed over the chance of becoming a courtier. Now she was a celebrity, drawing attention from the younger courtiers who emulated her every move.

Charles was amateur. Everyone knew when Charles used the wrong honorific, ate with the wrong utensil or wore the wrong clothing, Nissa stifled urges to rebuke him. But here, in their private quarters? *That* was different altogether. Nissa berated Charles for many things behind closed doors, most often their status as Secondaries.

There were three levels of nobility in Zannistar: Primaries, Secondaries and Tertiaries. Nissa started life as a Tertiary, the lowest caste. She was the daughter of famous crossbow makers from the Southern Province whose craft caught the attention of the Marshal Atherton Kell during his travels. The Marshal was so impressed with their crossbows, he offered to search the palace for a Secondary of similar age for Nissa to marry in exchange for a steady supply. This was amenable since a Zanni citizen could marry one level of nobility up or down, but Primaries never married Tertiaries. It was too great and rapid a social bridge to build between families. Pedigree was important. Nissa's parents jumped at the chance because it meant she would transcend Tertiary life.

Charles reflected on Nissa's cleverness. Had she discovered a legal way to bury their arranged marriage? The Kingdom of Zannistar grew from a simple idea: Agreements were binding under the law as long as they did not violate the original Kingdom Charter. An agreement was an agreement. The most common way to prove it was by drafting a contract, including for arranged marriages. And breaking a contract was the same as breaking Zanni law. Charles could only think of one reason the King would negate a marriage contract: treason.

As Charles regarded the crafted slate tile of his great-room floor, Nissa's moccasin-laden feet appeared. Charles smelled the spiced tinctures in her hair.

She spoke in a small, sweet voice. "Imagine it, Charles. Imagine what the King will do when he discovers that you have stolen from him."

Charles sneered, remaining downcast. "Unthinkable! Why are you doing this? No one will believe this—this lie of yours."

Nissa placed warm hands on his shoulders. "Oh? The Marshal's men make their way now to verify my report."

"What report? What have you done, Nissa?"

She knelt, so she was looking up at him. "No, Charles. *You* are the criminal here."

Charles felt hopelessness rise inside him. "I love you. That is my crime."

"Touching, but wrong again. You stole the King's nombit, Charles. I found it in your drawer. What was I to do?"

Charles imagined the King's nombit, a plain, coin-sized piece of bone engraved with two hands grasping one another in agreement. Only the King and his family had a legal right to it. Stealing was bad enough. But stealing the King's nombit? That was treason. The King of Zannistar would erase him from history, kill or banish him then strike his name from the Book of Nom forever. Charles saw how Nissa planned to end this.

Nissa ran a scarlet nail the length of Charles' cheek to chin and lifted his face to hers. Her spacious eyes traced the contour of his features.

Nissa whispered in Charles' ear. "I fear our time together is at an end." She brought his lips to hers. Within the softness of her genuine gift, Charles forgot Nissa's treachery. As she withdrew, Charles refused to open his eyes. He thought of the time they spent together as betrothed adolescents, when things were simpler, when she sought his company and thoughts. He pinpointed their return from wedding sabbatical as the moment she became cold.

Overcome with loss, Charles hung his head and sobbed. Offering nothing more, Nissa rose, turned her back to him and stood silent.

That moment, the carved door to the Warfield household flew open. The air clamored with the sounds of many armed men. The next pair of feet Charles saw were in polished plate armor.

"Where is it?" The voice was thunderous.

Charles gave no answer. Three people knew the whereabouts of the King's coin: the King, Charles and Osric.

The voice boomed again. "Search this place! It is here, somewhere."

As the soldiers rifled through his palace quarters, Charles had the strangest sensation. It felt like an open hand pressed on his soul. Charles could not figure its origin or nature, but he understood its intention: It wanted him and it was coming soon.

"We have found it, My Lord!" A different man's voice from the back room.

"Bring it Guardsman," ordered the Marshal.

A gloved hand thrust into Charles line of vision. In it was the King's Nombit. Charles closed his eyes and acknowledged the cruel brilliance of Nissa's betrayal.

"Treason!" yelled the Marshal. He pulled Charles' head back by the hair just before another helmeted soldier bludgeoned him with the oversized pommel of his long-sword.

Charles swam into darkness.

CHAPTER 2

OSRIC BRANLIN, TREASURER OF ZANNISTAR, nephew to the King and first in the line of succession, leaned against the polished granite wall of the Great Hall. He watched as the Marshal's men absconded with Charles, who seemed unconscious. Osric stifled a smile that threatened to usurp his entire face. He waited many years for this day. Until now, he had been powerless to satisfy his wish to have Nissa Warfield. It was a problem that ate at his every waking thought.

At thirty-eight, he was pushing the social boundaries of acceptable age for marriage. Arranged or otherwise, if a Primary did not marry by their fortieth year, they risked great ridicule at the least. The court expected Primaries to marry and provide successors. Most entered a betrothal by their fifteenth birthday but not Osric. He did not know his parents, and he convinced his uncle, the King, to abstain. Osric was not interested in matrimony.

Not until recent years. But it had to be someone special. It had to be Nissa.

Osric took great pains to make sure his succession was unchallenged when the time arrived. This was necessary because he was not a court favorite. But Osric knew all his political positioning, backstabbing and kissing of rings would pay off one day. He imagined himself the only logical choice.

Still, Osric could not help brooding like an anguished adolescent. He hated skulking about, hiding his feelings for Nissa. Every night, he waited for Charles to leave for the counting house, then stole into Nissa's room by way of rope, hook and ocean window, a skill he had since mastered. Love reduced him to a common footpad in his own Duchy.

When the Marshal's men disappeared, Osric straightened and tended his beard with manicured hands. He grabbed lengthy ebon locks of curled hair emerging from a wide-brimmed, blue silk hat, and laid them along his shoulders. He pulled the wrinkles out of his purple and gold doublet, then stepped across the Great Hall toward a large door of reddened oak and alabaster trim. Beauty and bliss awaited him on the other side.

He stopped halfway to reconsider the wisdom of such a bold move. A young Secondary passed in front of him, bowing her head in deference. Osric thought her familiar, but there were many new courtiers.

"Glorious day, Duke Osric," she said in a practiced tone.

With one hand on his hip and the other resting on the jeweled pommel of his rapier, Osric placed his right foot forward and nodded. "Pleasant day to you, good Lady."

She swept past him, on her way to indulge in whatever business Secondaries attended. Then Osric remembered he did not care. She was beneath him.

And there it was—Propriety. Since the beginning, it was the social force that gave everyone purpose and place. It drew lines and determined fates. It was beautiful and Osric was among those few who benefited most. Osric regained his courage. He was a Primary and Nissa was a Secondary. She needed him and he tired of sneaking.

He looked around at the many colorful doors lining both sides of the ancient Great Hall. Artisans crafted them centuries ago from the rarest materials available. Each entryway led inside the home of a courtier. Some were like Osric, born and reared on the palace grounds. Others came from the farthest reaches of Zannistar to fulfill a particular duty. Regardless, the King required all to live in the palace quarters until he discharged them, regardless of their responsibilities elsewhere in Zannistar.

Above each door hung a rectangular, pewter plate engraved with the name and arms of the courtier living within. Osric regarded Charles' arms, an open book with a raised, nautical compass on the left page. He felt the emblem simple, even for most Secondaries.

"How uninspiring," said Osric aloud. He peered down the Great Hall.

"You were a loyal and effective assistant but, you were not enough for her. It is better this way. Good bye, Charles."

Emboldened, he licked his thumb, smoothed his thick eyebrows and resumed his pace. This time, Osric decided he would use the front door.

CHAPTER 3

NISSA GAZED AT THE EMPTY CHAIR where the Marshal's men pummeled Charles unconscious. She regarded the pooled blood on its ivory-white, silken cushion with something like the beginnings of remorse.

She seldom experienced such feelings. Yet, deep in the marrow of her ambitious bones, she believed progress sometimes required sacrifices. She reminded herself that she vowed to accept whatever consequences came from this treacherous course of action, no matter how dire. But still, Nissa thought the cost unbearable. The Martial's inept cronies ruined her chair.

The pale, wooden seat was borne of the Southern Province; crafted by a master carpenter long since dead. It was one of a kind, precious, irreplaceable and worth ten useless husbands. Now it was ruined, stained by the blood of a man unworthy of its artful achievement. She huffed at the thought of discarding it.

Nissa awoke from her thoughts by the sound of someone knocking at the door. She realized she appeared much too composed for a grieving wife. She mussed her hair, forced tears and formed a distressed expression before opening the door. A smiling Osric Branlin stood in the entryway. He removed his hat.

Nissa's sorrowful expression morphed into a visible panic.

"Duke Osric," she began through nervous laughter. "To what do I owe this very rare and unexpected visit?" Nissa spied a group of young Primaries passing by, along the Great Hall.

Osric beamed and bowed deep, hat in hand. "Glorious day, Lady Nissa," His curls nearly touched the floor.

Nissa craned to peer over Osric's shoulder. The young Primaries had stopped to catch a peek inside.

"Please, My Lord," Nissa beckoned with refined urgency. "Come. Refresh yourself with Zannistar's finest brierberry tea."

"Sounds splendid," Osric returned with optimism. He raised his bearded chin and passed through the doorway.

Nissa curtsied toward her gawking audience, shut the door and stood seething and motionless.

Osric honed his voice to a throaty whisper and spoke to the back of Nissa's neck. "Your beauty is without equal."

Nissa spun to meet his eyes. "And you sir, foolishly wager what we have labored to do! You coming here now, was not part of our plan. You risk too much!"

"But Nissa," Osric explained. "He is gone. I cannot wait a single minute longer!"

"You must!" She snapped. But, sensing her own loudness, Nissa lowered her voice. "You must. If the King uncovers the truth, he will kill us both, or worse—banish us!"

Nissa calmed somewhat and placed a strategic hand on Osric's chest. "Soon, my love. Soon. For now, we continue with the plan. Once the King condemns Charles, I will invoke the Right of Retention, after which you come forward to claim me as your own, saving me the disgrace of returning to Tertiary status. The court will adore you for it; celebrate you. That is the moment we are safe to display our love."

Osric stared into Nissa's blue-green eyes with devotion. "A turn of good fortune, starting life as a Tertiary. And here you are, a Secondary by marriage ready to climb to the life of a Primary, even Queen of Zannistar someday. You garner more than your share of the spoils. Tell me Nissa, what do I get out of this dangerous deception? Do I not have the most to lose?"

Nissa encircled Osric's body with lithe arms. "Yes, you do. And you have the most to gain, Osric."

Osric raised both of his sharp eyebrows. "Oh?"

"Me. You get me."

"Ah, yes. Now, I remember."

"Well, dear Osric, let us not waste a visit."

She pulled away and headed toward the bed-chamber, looking back to find Osric's eyes fixed on hers. He stirred and took after her with light feet. On the way, he stopped himself from tossing his hat onto the blood-stained chair. "Blessed Anvil! That chair was worth more than the entire town where it was made . You are ruthless aren't you?"

Nissa beheld the chair and turned her eyes back at Osric. "Come. It pains me but there are much greater things in our future to consider than rare furniture or the filth that defiles it.

"Indeed."

CHAPTER 4

"WHY AM I HERE, MOTHER?" *asked Charles.*

"Because, my son, you chose to be."

High atop the obsidian tower, Charles and his adopted Mother surveyed the mottled clay and wooden rooftops that rose from an opaque blanket of morning-mist. It began to rain.

Charles leaned out, looking down the length of the tower. "Is this where you found me?"

"Over there," she answered, pointing toward an obscured cluster of silent masts where Charles knew the docks to be.

"I do not remember."

"You were small and very frightened."

"But this day is different; the day you died."

Charles drove a wave of grief back down into the pit of his stomach. He angled his head south, scanning the remote coastal cliffs for the palace. Like a great watcher, the ancient structure loomed high above the turbid waters of the Western Sea.

"It can not be undone," Charles said half-hearted. He closed his eyes and melted at the warmth of his mother's hand on his shoulder.

"It is no small cruelty that has befallen you, my son," she said. "But, you must brace yourself for what lies ahead. It will not be simple for you."

Charles leaned against a rapid rush of wind arriving from the west. He opened his eyes and gasped, powerless to break away. In the sky, many leagues out to sea, a vast cloud front swirled, filling the heavens. A pillar of dark-red smoke, rotting human corpses and animal carrion spilled from the eye of the giant maelstrom with a deep rumble that spoke doom to Charles' bones. As the foul effluent crashed into the sea, Charles saw that an enormous wave appeared and was heading toward them.

"What is happening?" Charles yelled over the relentless wind and the now heavy rains.

"Your journey home is just beginning, child," said Charles' mother, now standing atop the battlement, her back to the ledge. Her long, crimson hair whipped about in the storm, and her gaunt face was as Charles remembered. "You must take flight to the north. Emptiness comes to claim you."

"Let it come!" cried Charles in defiance. "I welcome it, we are kindred!"

"Perhaps more than you realize," she warned. "But your destiny weaves into the marrow of the world itself. You must forge ahead." Charles' mother smiled. "Do not despair. All pass to the world-after, but it is not yet time."

Charles watched below as the black wave struck the city. The tower shook against the might of the storm surge, but stood firm. Charles turned to his mother with sorrow in his eyes.

"I did not understand," he began. "So many lost, so many gone. Who did this? Who took you from me?"

"Your enemy."

"My enemy? But I have no enemies!"

Charles' mother turned to the churning sea and sighed. "Time is short, child," She reminded him.

Charles was about to say he loved her when an enlarged malevolent hand of blood-tinted smoke crept over the ledge and curled around his mother's waist.

"And I love you, Charles. Always," The hand yanked her from the tower's edge.

"Wait!" Charles screamed, lunging forward to grab her, but was too late.

Charles watched helpless as she plummeted. More hands of smoke emerged from the mist to quicken her descent. Stricken, Charles fumbled backward, toward the center of the tower. He managed a few steps before he realized there was another presence, behind him. Charles stopped and waited, fear dancing in his veins. It was his mother's hand, again resting upon his shoulder. But, this time, it was cold and bloated, as the fisherman's lifeless bounty.

"I came back for you, Charles," announced three separate voices: his mother, a little girl and an old woman. "Such a lovely a boy. Always, Charles. Always."

The hand pressed into Charles' flesh.

"You are no mother of mine!" screamed Charles. Unable to move, he stared in horror as crimson smoke billowed from bloodless holes in his mother's swollen, rotting hand. The smoke climbed up Charles' neck, searching for a way inside.

"I have a special place prepared for you, my son," the voices cooed, as the smoke found Charles' nose and mouth.

16

Wide-eyed and shaking, Charles labored to scream, but could not prevail against the darkness that filled his throat; fetid tendrils seeking his inmost parts.

"Always, always, always!" screeched the voices.

A pair of cold but strong hands shook Charles awake.

"Wake up! You're choking!" bellowed a gritty, masculine voice. Charles clutched his throat and kicked his legs as the hands tried to steady him. His bearings returned, and he relaxed. The smell of filth and death assaulted him while the evil voices still played at the distant hovels of his consciousness.

Always, Charles. Always.

"In the grip of dark imaginations, I see," reassured the roughened voice, breaking the silence. The freezing hands released him. The sounds of feet on stone echoed against the walls.

Charles strained to see in total darkness while memories of being betrayed and imprisoned formed in his mind, along with a nagging hunger. He rotted in this wretched, stinking oubliette for days but no one had yet spoken to him. Charles had assumed he was alone.

"Who are you?" Charles asked, searching the darkness in utter futility.

"I am your friend."

"I have no friends," Charles said. "Not anymore."

Charles crawled over to a crack in the wall from which river water was seeping. He figured, based on his knowledge of the palace, he was against the northern wall; the one that sat near the Lunea river. He also calculated that he was some distance underground, due to the faint sound of running water above and somewhat away from him. Not only that, he also heard Lunea Falls to the east, dumping into the ocean.

Charles slurped at the breach for some time before slumping against the damp wall. He puzzled over how he spent a lifetime in the palace without ever visiting the King's legendary oubliette. But then Charles Warfield was not so much given to bravery as he was to avoiding most anything that caused him discomfort.

His head ached where the Grand Marshal's men struck him. He reached up to touch the wound, but touched something small, segmented and many-legged, which darted down the back of his neck. Charles jumped to his feet and flailed his limbs in a panic, trying to rid himself of the creeping thing. Satisfied, Charles slid back down the wall into a squatting position.

"Anyway, I am Charles. Or, at least I was," said Charles, being unsure of why he bothered.

Other than the distant sounds of water, the room remained silent. He grew impatient. Charles offered unseen hand gestures in the blackness. "Well, friend, what terrible crime has delivered you to into the bowels of the King's oubliette?"

As Charles waited for an answer, he focused on separating the different water sounds. It reminded him of the musicians at court; each instrument adding its own uniqueness to the overall composition. But just like Nissa and even his name, the music abandoned him. Only darkness, a battered skull and a stranger with no manners remained. Charles grew tired of drawing breath.

"I bring a message," said the man.

Charles woke. "He speaks! A message, you say? And what sort of message would earn you a stay in this place?"

"The King doesn't realize I'm here."

"Oh, and yet here you are." Charles' words dripped with contempt. Charles was in no mood for word-play. Frustrated with his present company, he rested his head against the wet stone and worked again to hear only the sea. He wished to gauge its distance relative to his position, and it did not take long for him to decide that it was below him and a long way down at that.

Charles thought about the hole in the middle of the floor he had found earlier. Though meant for matters of hygiene, it was just big enough for a person to fit, should they decide that starvation was too grueling a death to endure. It led to a long chute that emptied into the ocean, twisted just right, so no outside light would enter the room. Anyone attempting escape this way would dash against the cliff-bound rocks. It was knowledge passed between Zanni children during gatherings on long, stormy nights.

Charles considered the choice, but decided against it. His sense of cleanliness was much too powerful. Instead, he opted to stay in the damp corner where he first awoke, dreading when nature would once again demand he search for it.

"You won't survive," warned the voice. "The fall's too great." Charles remained indignant. "Perhaps I do not want to survive, sir. Had you considered that?"

"Yes, yes. But, you're a fighter, Charles."

"A fighter? Oh, I see," said Charles. "And how is it you have such esoteric knowledge? No friends, remember?"

"I know you, Charles," The voice returned. "Believe it."

"Oh, I doubt it. I think I would remember a voice like yours. Prove it, then."

"Brierberry dumpling's are your favorite food."

"Anyone could find that out. Try again."

"Well then," said the man, up to the challenge. "You can't swim. The water terrifies you."

Startled, Charles silenced himself as images of the storm from his dream assaulted his mind. It was true. He feared the water and Nissa was the only other who knew. He supposed it was possible Nissa told someone, given her recent treachery.

Charles applied pressure to the wound on his head to verify that he was awake. He was. He pondered the absurdity of his situation and shame washed over him. What kind of noble was afraid of water? But he was afraid of many things. Nissa was right all along. She was more than justified. The only thing left they had in common was how much they both hated Charles Warfield.

Charles' heart sank as despair flowed through him in a way he never knew was possible. It was deep; encouraged and amplified as if by some distant enemy of his being. As it took hold of his capacity to hope, Charles tried to conjure even a single reason to continue his existence. He realized the immutable truth that his life meant nothing. It was a mistake on the canvas of eternity that devalued the larger masterpiece. Every comfort he ever enjoyed and every breath he ever drew was the stolen property of others more worthy. He was a criminal stowaway of the worst order, undeserving of even death.

Defeated, nauseous and no longer concerned with cleanliness, Charles inched forward on his hands and knees in search of the hole. As his final willful action, he would assign himself to the deep where perhaps he would join with his mother. And though he did not deserve such comfort, he decided he was coward enough to accept it.

Yes, Charles, that's it. Such a good boy! Always.

Charles shook his head as the stench of rotting seaweed pushed to the surface of his awareness. He continued forward until, at last, he came to the corroded edge of a hole in the stone floor. He traced along the edge of the pit with his hand. It was the perfect size. Charles sat himself on the edge, his feet dangling inside the pit.

"This isn't your end, Charles," said the man through the darkness, who now seemed somewhat closer. "Your purpose lies elsewhere."

Though the voice's words promised hope, Charles knew there was none. "No, I am a condemned criminal with no future save for the few remaining moments spent with you in this darkness. Who would remember me? Who would believe I was ever here." The words rang with finality.

"It's you who doesn't remember," said the man. "You don't belong here."

"Enough!" spat Charles, trembling. "Enough of your cruelty! Have you not tortured me to your satisfaction? Now, you entice me with the sweet promise of being someone else? If only it were true." Charles lost his composure and tears flowed. "Then perhaps she would have loved me!"

The bright sound of a small metal object hitting the stone floor interrupted Charles' sobbing.

"Take it," said the man. "It'll lead you to the truth."

Charles did not understand the impulse, but he ran his hand across the slimy stone until he found the object. He picked it up deciding it a small coin of some type, silver perhaps. He may not have been a perfect courtier or a model husband, but he was an excellent judge of coinage, even here in this damp and darkened place.

"A silver coin?" Charles asked.

"In your case, most of the time, yes."

"In my case? You sound insane."

"There isn't much time, Charles. Listen to me."

"No, you listen to me! Seems as if you have donated a trifle amount of silver to the depths of the sea. But thank you for such a sharp reminder of how I have squandered my life; locked away in a room, counting others' silver and gold, while the Duke Treasurer enjoyed the comforts of my wife. And as you have mentioned, I can not swim so if the rocks do not end it, the water will. This time I will do what is right on my own terms. Good day to you, whoever you are."

Resolute, Charles eased himself partway into the hole. He cursed himself for not having the courage to dive in headlong.

Oh, you are a coward, Charles. Always.

"Laedenor!" yelled the man.

The sound of the word sliced through the dark and stopped Charles in mid-task. A distant familiarity brushed against Charles' mind—enough to pique his interest, if only for a moment.

Charles had already lowered himself half-way down the hole. "I am sorry. What did you say?"

"Your true home, Charles. You birthed in Laedenor, not Zannistar."

Charles grabbed at his churning stomach. "Laedenor?"

"Yes," the man said.

Charles threw his head back, releasing an outpouring of laughter. "Me? A savage from beyond? You *are* insane!"

"Believe it," the man said. "The people there need you, your people."

Charles allowed himself to entertain the thought. He conceived it possible. His mother did not birth him but found him wandering around the docks when he was a toddler. Anyone could have dumped him there. But did it matter? He stuffed the notion and returned to the surety of despair.

"I am still here in this place, condemned to suffer a traitor's fate. I can never go back. There is nothing left for me here. The sea awaits, sir."

"People are coming to free you," said the man. "You'll do well to be ready to join them when they arrive."

Charles huffed. "Yes, I know. They are the August Guard and they will parade me around court during the Grand Assembly. King Lidig will try me for treason and the Effacer will erase my existence. I assure you, I am not worth the effort. Now, if you will excuse me—"

"Hear me! The folk I speak of are your allies. They'll aid your escape to the north, beyond the shores of this accursed, mockery of a kingdom, past the growing reach of the Neverwall, and into the truth of who you are. You must go with them, lad. If you don't, we'll all die—all of us."

Again, Charles' mind touched an already fading familiarity, just out of reach.

"What do you mean, *all* of us?"

"I mean everyone, Charles."

"Everyone in Zannistar? And is that so bad?"

"Everyone who's ever lived, past or future."

"You are a lunatic! What is a Neverwall? And go beyond Zanni borders? I'll end it here, thank you. The outside world is chaotic and squalid. No, I began as nothing and I will end as—"

"You are a king!" bellowed the voice. "And you are acting like a spoiled child having no regard for anything but his own petty sorrow! Now, stop this endless complaining, remove yourself from that hole and make ready for the guards."

Perhaps it was the authority in the man's voice, but the scolding startled Charles to the point of obedience. Chastened and curious, he began his ascent from the hole. Almost there, the overwhelming hopelessness in his mind waned to a manageable level.

"A king, eh? Ridiculous! You claim to know me. We have never met, I am sure."

"Charles! He is here! He pushed through!"

"What now?"

From the darkened depths, something grabbed Charles' legs and coiled around them. He kicked hard, but could not break free. Whatever it was, it pulled Charles downward.

"Something has ensnared me!" screamed Charles.

"Fight it, Charles! It's him!"

"It is pulling me!"

Let Go, Charles. I love you. Always.

"Don't give in, whatever the cost!" yelled the man.

Driven by the fear of meeting the creature from his dream, Charles held his arms straight out, preventing the thing from pulling him further into the hole. It wrenched on him.

Be good, Charles and let go. You wanted this. Yes. Worthless coward. She hates you. But I love you.

Charles' armpits numbed. He wouldn't be able to hold on much longer. The thing was strong, yanking on him in waves. It relaxed and pulled, then relaxed and pulled again.

"Whatever your name is, help me!" The pulling was too much to endure. With a sickening sound, sinew ripped in one of his shoulders. Charles let out a guttural groan with every pull.

You always wanted this.

That moment, a shaft of light exploded into the room from the high ceiling, illuminating the scene at the hole. The thing released its hold.

It is all right, Charles. We have plenty of time. Always.

Blinded by light, in unbelievable pain and exasperated, Charles clung to the rim with his strong arm, seeking to gain purchase on the slippery stone, the coin still in hand.

"What are you doing down there, you traitorous pig?" called a gruff voice from overhead. "Thought you could escape justice, eh? No such luck today. You have an appointment with the Effacer. Afterward, none of us will have to remember your stinking face, now will we?"

The squeak of a rusted pulley heralded the lowering of a bucket, big enough in which to sit. Despite his near blindness, Charles found the outline, but only just. He let out a yelp when the bucket smashed into his injured shoulder.

Charles braced with his elbow, freed his legs then placed the small coin in his mouth. He then made a grab for the rope, succeeding. He mustered all of his remaining strength and pushed through bright sparks of pain to pull himself from the hole, with some help from the guards. Charles liked sitting on solid ground.

"Get in the bucket, worm!" hollered the guard.

Something warm, wet and slimy struck his face as he lifted his head to respond. Charles heard a chorus of cruel laughter from the guards.

Sighing, Charles obliged and sat in the bucket, holding on to the rope with his good hand.

One guard giggled. "Are you in yet, pig?"

Charles maneuvered the coin to the inside of his cheek to decrease its effect on his speech. It tasted of silver, and something else.

"Yes," Charles called back through his teeth.

The guards pulled him upward. Charles' eyes adjusted to show the general dimensions of the oubliette, which were just as Charles imagined them to be. There was a problem—a problem that struck Charles' sense of reality.

Besides three corpses reclining against the opposite wall, there was no sign of another human being ever having been here, much less a living and breathing person. Charles scanned the room for the man. Was he hiding? Did he, somehow, fall in the hole?

"Where is he?" Charles called to the guards.

"Where is who?" one of them returned.

"The other prisoner! A man!"

The guards cackled. "You're the only one down there who lives!"

Charles' mind raced. Nothing seemed real anymore. Perhaps he had imagined everything: the man, being someone else—and a king, no less. Yet, he couldn't explain the coin or his hurt shoulder.

Charles then decided the Effacer's ceremony seemed a welcome alternative to the perils of this surreal, bewitched pit. It was even more sinister than the old childhood stories. Charles pushed it from his mind. The pain from his shoulder was immense, and he guessed that he had a long day ahead of him. Well, whatever the case, he had one final bit of meaning to look forward to. It would be enough. He couldn't wait to get a proper look at that coin.

CHAPTER 5

BLOOD DRIPPED FROM AERION'S up-stretched arm as he stood awed at the surrounding scene. Nothing appeared as it should be. It was as if everything had lost its normal shape and color. Blurred, silvery masses writhed around him, colliding with other shapes before dividing again.

The ground below rippled and surged as a turbid lake, yet it did not disturb his foothold; a concern that left Aerion's stomach unsettled. The sky moved closer, curving around him into the fashion of a tunnel.

Clouds gathered into vaporous outlines of tremendous, shifting faces, whose only distinguishable features were vague smiles and pulsing swirls of crimson smoke in place of proper eyes. They followed Aerion's injured hand, as if they lusted for it. Distant and arcane whispers caressed his ears though he did not detect their meaning.

Aerion shrank back. "Bless the Venerable Spirit, I am dead."

He reeled at the words flying out of his own mouth. But here, in this shaft of unnatural wonder, Aerion questioned his assumptions. Had he been mistaken? Was the Gastwyrd real? He suddenly realized there was no pain in his hand, a curiosity that provoked him to inspect it. Inside the oozing puncture, Aerion beheld a wondrous spiral of crimson smoke and vapor twisting inward on his palm. It had no end. The boy found neither spiral nor wound on the back of his hand. Aerion panicked at the sight.

With sudden desperation, Aerion shook his hand, yet the spiral remained. He yelped and tried to wipe it away; first on his fur tunic and then on the ground. Again, nothing. At last, he pressed the accursed spiral against his chest, obscuring it from view.

Immediately, the whispers grew loud and the grinning faces above pushed into the tunnel, accompanied by giant, clawed hands intent on reaching him. In a mere moment, the faces surrounded him. With no other alternative, Aerion dropped to his back on the odd ground and brandished the black shard as a weapon. He was determined to at least wound these creatures; whatever they might be.

As they closed in, Aerion felt the purity of their hatred and the extent of their dark intentions for him. The over-sized claws opened and closed in the way an infant communicates its want for a favorite object. Aerion swung the fragment back and forth, but it only increased the whispering.

"Show them the Coil!" It was a man's voice coming from elsewhere in the tunnel.

"Is that you, Uncle?" Aerion shrieked.

"No," responded the man. "But I *am* an ally! Now hurry! Show them the Coil on your hand!"

Aerion knew what the man meant. He forced his bewitched, open hand in the air.

The faces and claws receded back into the tunnel's curved ceiling. So too did the whispers subside to a bearable level; a most welcome blessing.

Aerion just lay heaving for air and staring at his raised hand as the man approached him.

"Whatever you do," warned the man, "do not lower your hand."

Aerion did not intend to.

CHAPTER 6

KING LIDIG BRANLIN FLINCHED as his golden-robed valet plucked a final hair from his brow.

"You look radiant, Majesty," said the seasoned attendant. "Well suited for today's Grand Assembly."

"Let me see, Jacent," said Lidig. "Let me see!"

The Baron Lord Jacent Ferris, personal servant to the King of Zannistar and accomplished courtier, raised a jewel-encrusted, silver hand mirror to Lidig's level of vision.

Lidig huffed and gestured. "It's missing something, Jacent. More vermilion on the cheekbones. Quick!"

"Ah yes," agreed Jacent. "My mistake, Majesty."

Lidig glanced at Ferris in the mirror. "Of course it's your mistake, Jacent. You've been my helper for how long now? Get it right, will you?" he snatched the mirror from Jacent's hand.

Lord Jacent bowed, cocking his head to the side, before reaching for a fine-tipped brush and a small tin of red cream from the gilded vanity.

As Jacent worked, Lidig stared at the reflection, his mind unsettled. He feared this year's Grand Assembly to be unpleasant. There was always conflict among the Primaries. But this year, border disputes and family dynamics were the least of Lidig's worries.

Nothing distressed him more than having to try a member of his own court; and for treason? It was madness. Treason lurked elsewhere in the world, true enough. But not here; not Zannistar. The King wished he could be someone else today—anyone else. He was fond of the accused; close even.

Having finished, Jacent withdrew and awaited.

Lidig examined the work and signaled that it was correct: His face was hairless, powdered ghostly white, with vivid pink circles on his plump cheeks. Painted black eyebrows arched over optimistic brown eyes and a thin, false mustache of the same color ran across his top lip.

"Well done, Jacent. Well done," said Lidig. He admired the result.

"Thank you, Majesty," Jacent said. His own makeup mimicked Lidig's, only less grandiose.

"My wig. Is it ready?"

"Yes, Majesty."

Jacent clapped his hands and in response, a pair of oaken double doors opened into the hall. Two young men in ordinary, blue silk tunics and matching haircuts entered, carrying Lidig's wig between them. They maneuvered the formidable mass of golden curls around Lidig's shoulders, then rested it atop his bald head before retreating backwards to a safe distance.

"Magnificent!" Jacent announced, whilst shooing the wig-bearers out of the room. "It is time, Jacent," said Lidig. "I will find you at court in one hour."

"As you wish, Majesty."

As the Lord Jacent Ferris bowed at the waistline, King Lidig and the ornate wooden bench upon which he reclined vanished from the bedchamber, leaving behind a wisp of pale red vapor smelling of pine needles and sap.

Satisfied, Jacent marched out and through the hall in search of the morning meal.

CHAPTER 7

THE KING TREMBLED as he stood aside the magic wooden loveseat he used for his throne, while members of the palace's entire complement of over one hundred noble families entered the immense throne-room through the south entrance. Of the customs that Zanni tradition required, the King hated this one the most. He loathed to be in the same place as nobles he would rather pretend did not exist. That was most. Besides, he could not stand on his feet for too long before his legs curved under the strain of the weight they carried. He became soft over these many years. Such was the price for commanding the fabled Bekrot Chair and with it, the power of teleportation.

The King managed an insincere smile as each representative bowed and placed their family nombits on the Anvil of Ages in the middle of the chamber before again bowing and retreating to their respective places.

Arminius Morlund, the High Scrivener, verified the authenticity of each nombit, by checking them against the Book of Nom—an old tome that never left his side—and then announcing the family name in as loud a manner as a frail, silver-haired, clean-shaven man of eighty-three years could. His attire was modest, comprising a pleasant, but plain brown cotton robe with flared sleeves, covering everything from his neck to his feet. His only adornment was a modest gold chain around his waist attached to a likewise golden swivel and plate on the book's spine.

Arminius made an impressive spectacle of reading the names. And even though he paused for effect as he referenced each nombit, everyone knew the old goat had every symbol committed to memory and had no need of the Book of Nom. He looked in its pages only for the sake of tradition.

Legend told they remembered most everything. But not even the revered memory of a Scrivener could withstand the compelling force of Gyldred the Effacer's thought-pillaging witchery—though the people believed the effects would only last as long as an Effacer lived. But there was no real promise of the Effacer meeting his end soon. Gyldred had outlived every Scrivener, king and citizen in Zannistar since its founding.

Arminius professed many times he had made peace with that long ago. He had held the position as High Scrivener from adolescence and he knew the job well, but he seemed tired these days. Soon he would need a successor. The process of succession among Scriveners remained a mystery. In fact, not even a presiding High Scrivener knew how to do it until the situation required it, an age-old fail-safe meant to protect the knowledge from being plundered by effacement. No Effacer hoped to steal a memory that did not exist, not even the powerful Gyldred.

34

The King glanced across the room, meeting eyes with Gyldred, who stood motionless near the east wall in his tattered, ceremonial robes. It had always disturbed the King that Gyldred kept every part of himself covered, except for his black, deep-set eyes. Only the mysterious sorcerer's acolytes were privy to what lay beneath. Lidig hated when Gyldred stared. He wondered which of his own secrets Gyldred concealed behind those dark orbs. Lidig suffered a shiver and looked away, pretending to notice someone else.

The procession continued, and the Primary nobility found their seats to the left of the throne opposite the Secondary nobility. Any Tertiaries in attendance took their places in the back with the musicians, who were busy weaving a lovely accompaniment.

The scene was a testament to the kingdom-wide pursuit of opulence. Standing in front of their seats, the men sported tight-fitting and deep-waisted doublets of colored patterns and paned sleeves above billowing, puffed breeches gathered under the knee, revealing hose of silk or knee-high boots. Some presented grandiose neck-ruffs from which their painted, sometimes-wigged, heads emerged—not unlike ripe melons atop lace pillows. Others still, wore small, embroidered capes. All kept a rapier on the hip, carried a wide-brimmed hat accented with ostrich plumes in one hand and a jeweled cane in the other.

Statuesque ladies displayed colorful, flowing gowns that split in the front, revealing matching petticoats topped by fitted, square-necked bodices. The most senior ladies wore impressive, conical hennins on their heads, from which long veils of gilded silk tied in a bow under the chin. The younger ladies offered towering hairstyles complete with hairnets of gold and diamond mesh. Most strained to move, burdened by rings, brooches, necklaces and earrings, all represented to excess. This was court, the essence of civilized society.

Despite the serious, capital business to tend to, few attendees were half as interested in the King's judgment of a traitor as they were in what the lovely Nissa Warfield was wearing to this year's Grand Assembly. Many stole glances at her, trying to gauge her demeanor. If the Zanni Royal Court was the firmament above, then Nissa would be its most magnificent star. And as always, she inspired and out-shined all others.

Nissa displayed the appropriate yet delicate balance of humility and pomp expected of a noblewoman whose husband was to be judged for treason. She opted to wear a modest country maiden's dress, of Tertiary design cut from a single piece of strong-quality black cotton; a gesture of honor toward her humble beginnings. Her head hidden by a hooded cape of the same shade, bearing only the most subtle hints of embroidery. She wore no jewelry and her face was untouched by the artist's brush. This ensemble put her in stark contrast to the other courtiers who were exhibiting the excess and exuberance of their best livery. She enjoyed the distinction. And though she stood next to Charles' empty seat, she was careful to appear hopeful but not proud. She was beyond compare— exuding simple beauty and an air of practiced humility—and she knew it. She relished in yet another calculated gambit of social manipulation.

The throne-room was massive and divided by a broad, central walkway of polished silver tiles that ran under the Anvil of Ages, all the way from the south entrance to the the royal platform. The remainder of the floor was a jeweled mosaic depicting every creature of land and sea native to the kingdom. Overhead was a vaulted ceiling of sculpted stone and stained glass, showing the many birds of Zannistar in flight; an historic masterpiece by the famed glass-smiths of the Southern Province, where the purest sand lay in abundance on vast, sub-tropical beaches.

Smooth columns of white, reflective marble lined the path. Each column enjoyed the company of an inward facing member of the August Guard, clad in silvery ceremonial chain mail and blue surcoats embroidered with a lone silver anvil in the center.

Once the Scrivener verified the final nombit and found his place, the King lumbered to the front of his wooden loveseat and paused while his wig-bearers readied themselves and the musicians finished up. Lidig motioned his intent and the entire room sat in unison, save for Lord Jacent Ferris, who circled the King, ensuring that the sovereign's enormous golden gown draped across the floor. The valet's footsteps echoed throughout the otherwise silent chamber as he scurried to his seat behind Lidig, near the wig-bearers.

After, a balding man, dressed in fine white silk and lace, rose from his seat on the right side of the King to address the room. His movements and voice dripped with academic elitism.

"Welcome, worthy nobles of the realm," he said, scanning the room. "to the regular Grand Assembly of the Sovereign Kingdom of Zannistar. Included in this year's business, we have gathered to witness King Lidig's perfect judgment upon Charles Warfield, a full member of Secondary stature who now stands accused of high treason against crown and kin."

A predictable ruckus erupted from the crowd which the Chamberlain Nolan Haspeth quelled by raising his hands, revealing the splendor of his flowing, lacy sleeves.

"Yes! It is unthinkable, I know," continued the Chamberlain. "The Grand Marshal will now present the accused." The

Chamberlain Haspeth gestured toward the south entrance causing all in attendance to turn around in their seats. Some nobles lifted dazzling, feathered masks to their faces.

Atherton Kel, Grand Marshal of Zannistar, entered the chamber with his cape flowing and his helm tucked under one arm. He wore the polished, silver-colored plate armor of the Zanni August Guard. A wreath of shoulder-length, dark gray hair skirted his bald scalp, accenting his usual grim expression. He marched toward the Anvil of Ages, bowed and added his own nombit to the pile in front of him: a steel disk embossed with three broadswords, blade to pommel, forming the shape of a triangle.

"Your Majesty," he announced in a telltale rasp wrought from thirty years of martial service. "I present the prisoner Charles Warfield for your review and judgment."

Not moving anything else, the King waved his plumped index finger in approval. Atherton Kel nodded and stepped aside as two of his men escorted Charles Warfield into the chamber.

Covered in a smock of itchy brown burlap, girted by twine, Charles stood slumped before the Anvil, before the King—before Nissa. He harbored no desire to lift his shaven head; why break old habits now? Rhythmic spikes of pain stabbed at his shoulder even though the Court Healer had forced his dislocated arm back in its proper place hours earlier. The taste of silver was strong in his mouth where he still concealed the mysterious coin. Charles managed the impressive feat of hiding it from the guards; even while they were ramming their fists into his belly and face earlier. He so wished he could look at that coin, now. He thought the beating earned him the right.

The Chamberlain took center stage. "His Royal Majesty and Benefactor of the Realm, King Lidig!" He bowed, and retreated backwards, in a swath of expensive lace and self-importance.

The King shifted in his loveseat to a lounging position. He lifted his palm to the height of his shoulder as if waiting for someone to place something in it.

"Oh, yes," said Jacent Ferris, caught daydreaming. He popped from his seat and dug into his belt-pouch, producing a small object. He smiled and placed it in the King's waiting hand.

The King examined his nombit, rolling it between his thumb and forefinger. He kept his eyes locked on the object as he addressed his subjects.

"It is by the sublime ideals of tradition, agreement and propriety I am afforded the honor of sovereign rule; to act as benefactor and judge for every one of my subjects, from the desolate ruins of Ganlis Bay, here in the Northern Province, to the lush barley fields of the Southern Province." His voice was high and he spoke in a sing-song manner. "And today, I sit in melancholy judgment of a member of my court, a man upon whom I have lavished my love and trust; a man I have known from the time of his youth and, a man I have since considered as worthy of appointment to the Primary nobility." At this last, unexpected admission, Nissa's composure threatened to waver, but remained steadfast. There was no turning back, now.

The King turned his face to the crowd. "You may wonder why I would do such a thing! Who is he that he should receive such a gift? Well, year after year, he has performed the duties of his royal office in an exemplary manner; never seeking praise or recognition. He has endured the Treasurer's neglectful absences, time and time again, only to speak well of him at court."

Osric Branlin wriggled in his chair, which was in the front row of Primary nobles. The King locked eyes with him before continuing. "Such was Charles' loyalty, I even entrusted him with the use of the Bekrot Chair for his wedding sabbatical, that he might treat his lovely bride to a few nights in the unreachable Gardens of Grynn in the Lurin Heights in the great Duchy of Virk. They, and the throne, returned on time, undamaged. Not the actions of a traitorous thief!"

The seasoned and demure Lydia Mirette, Duchess of Virk, swelled with pride at the mention of the natural wonder that lay within her Duchy to the south. Like most tenant nobles, she missed home.

"Yes, yes. Charles is unrefined and somewhat aloof," the King posited. "But, he is no traitor. He is incapable. I am sure."

Nissa tried to look hopeful and sad in the same expression. It was convincing. Once they noticed it, the younger noblewomen mimicked her expression.

Charles was not even aware that the King was defending him. He lost himself in the beautiful variety of the kingdom's many nombits piled on the Anvil. He identified his own among them; a piece of copper with an engraved depiction of an open book and nautical compass. Nissa placed it there on her way in. The King would destroy it. Sadness deepened within him at the thought. His entire life, he regarded the book and compass as an inseparable reflection of his own identity.

The gasps of the audience and the overpowering smell of pine needles broke his speculation.

"Charles," said the King who had teleported from the platform to the Anvil of Ages, near Charles. "It was not you! Will you not defend yourself against the charges brought against you by this assembly? Will you not attest to your own goodness?"

Charles' gaze remained low. He was tired and bitter. He shook his head. Scathing images of Nissa and the Duke Treasurer flooded his mind, increasing his despair. His life belonged to someone else now.

"Charles, you are not my blood, and though you are of Secondary origin, I still consider you kin. When your parents found you, a boy of only five years, wandering around the docks without your memory, I was skeptical of your origins. But I took pity on them, for they had no children of their own. It was an absolute pleasure to watch your friendship with my nephew, Osric, grow. Even when you were children, you were always kind to him even when he was not kind to you."

"And when your parents died at Ganlis Bay, I took you in and watched you come into your own. Even in my care, you never complained about being a Secondary noble, not once. You accepted your family's name and station. So I tell you Charles, I know you well. Thievery is not in you. Now, defend your honor before the anvil so we can discover the true thief and forget this foolishness!"

Charles made no verbal reply, choosing only to shake his head again, refusing to make eye contact with the King.

King Lidig paused for a final moment. "Then you leave me no choice," he resolved with genuine sadness. He and the Bekrot Chair teleported back to the platform. Red vapor hung in the air where he had been. The King acknowledged the Chamberlain. "Proceed," the King ordered.

The Chamberlain stood, once again, and hurried to the steps of the platform. "For five hundred years, we have lived apart from the savagery of the world that exists beyond our shores. This was due to the miraculous craft of the Royal Effacer. On that day, and every day since, we have recognized our very own Gyldred as the Sublime Hero of Zannistar; our deliverer—the man who caused the entire world to forget that Zannistar ever existed, thus hiding us from our enemies. Fate has rewarded his sacrifice with long life well-beyond normal." The Chamberlain gestured toward the dark, hooded figure, who bowed in kind with unnatural fluidity while the crowd clapped.

The Chamberlain continued, pacing and gesturing. "We all know the Scrivener's tales of our journey to recovery. Where once there were blood-soaked wastelands, now there are fields of flower and plenty. Once, lawlessness and anarchy ruled the land, now there is the simple harmony of process and order. There was ignorance and indiscretion, now we enjoy knowledge and propriety."

Most of the nobles nodded. The Chamberlain ran at the Anvil of Ages and pointed to it, fiercely.

"This is the heart of Zannistar!" He yelled, making a fist. "Trustworthiness, integrity and accountability! It was upon this anvil the leaders of the first families signed the Charter. That was almost five hundred years past. From that day forward, they promised to cooperate. No war, no deception and no uncertainty. Instead, we would live by the rule of agreement; everyone in their proper capacity, working toward the benefit of all Zanni people."

The Chamberlain looked down at the Anvil of Ages, searching for Charles' nombit. He reached down and plucked it from the pile. He presented it in triumph.

"My brethren, there is one in our midst who has dishonored the fabric of our society by allowing envy and petty greed to dictate his actions. For all of his life, Charles Warfield enjoyed the special favor of the King. Yet, it was not enough. He took the property of another."

Osric again jostled in his seat, fighting the urge to turn and meet eyes with Nissa, who he was sure was staring at the back of his head.

The Chamberlain showed his disgust, then resolve. "According to Zanni law, theft of the King's property makes up a crime of considerable weight, causing a charge of high treason, which calls for permanent banishment from the land into the wild, following the name effacement ceremony. The entire history of the Warfield family stricken from memory and public record; known only to the Effacer." The Chamberlain looked at Gyldred, who tilted his head in acknowledgment.

The King struggled to stand prompting everyone else to rise. "It is my sublime judgment based on evidence found in your dwelling and your refusal to deny your involvement in the same, that you are guilty of the unredeemable crime of theft. For this, the Effacer will erase you from all memory then release you to your fate among the wretched and depraved denizens of the outside world— forgotten for all time."

Banishment into the savage world. Charles preferred the horrors of the hole in the oubliette to this.

The King sat, followed by the rest. All, that is, except for Nissa.

"Your Majesty," Nissa said. Every eye trained on her. "Please do not think me a churlish and unfeeling wife while I speak, for I am sick over the fate of my husband. However, considering His Majesty's wise and supreme judgment, I wish to invoke the Right of Retention as set forth in our venerated Charter."

There was a quiet, general murmur developing in the crowd as the King stared at Nissa. His gaze spoke mistrust.

The Chamberlain sauntered over to the King and whispered something into his ear. It was the reminder that Nissa would have to retreat to the status of a Tertiary noble, unless someone of Secondary or even Primary status stepped forward to claim her.

After a thoughtful moment, the King straightened his posture as best he could. "This is your right, Nissa Warfield," the King said. He motioned toward the audience. "Are there Secondaries who will accept?"

Duke Osric Branlin vaulted from his chair. "I will, Your Majesty! I accept!"

In an uncommon and useless flash of jealousy, Charles raised his head to scowl at Osric, then Nissa.

The King looked puzzled. "But Duke Osric, you are of Primary status. There are several eligible secondaries that—"

"There are none," Osric interrupted.

The King furrowed his painted brow.

Osric shook his head. "What I mean, Your Majesty, is that there are none who feel as responsible as I do for the tragedy that has unfolded. It is only proper I should see to the Lady Warfield's well-being, myself. The traitor was under my direct supervision. It is the least I can do, Sire." Osric bowed, feigning humility.

The King regarded Osric. It pained him to do this to Charles. But preserving the tradition of law was most important. "Yes, Duke Osric, Charles was, in fact, under your direct supervision; a detail that warrants further investigation. But for today, I will grant your acceptance of her petition, provided there are no secondaries who wish to step forward. In such an event, they shall enjoy preference."

Osric looked about. "There, you see? No one else. Good. I accept the honor of—"

"Wait!" A voice rang out from the Secondary ranks.

Everyone turned their attention to the young Sir Tavist Upland, an unproven officer in the Grand Marshal's use, standing at attention; the image of youthful potency. What he lacked in experience, he made up for in eagerness. Among his peers, he gained notoriety for accepting challenges without regard for the consequences and making vows before understanding the cost. Every recruit believed a member of the August Guard did not to spread his honor too thin. Tavist Upland never learned that bit of wisdom; a malady of character that brought him constant strife. It would seem that he was at it yet again.

His voice wavered as he spoke through his nervousness. "I, Sir Tavist Upland, a sworn officer and noble of Secondary status, accept Nissa Warfield's petition for noble retention, Your Majesty."

Surprised, intrigued and infuriated, Charles tilted his head toward Sir Tavist; perfectly dressed, perfectly groomed, perfectly young Sir Tavist. Charles could remember when Tavist was still at his mother's breast. This was too much humiliation to bear; first the Duke Treasurer's obvious betrayal and now this: The rutty enthusiasm of an over-privileged upstart, vying for Nissa's hand.

Also surprised, Nissa raised her eyebrows in satisfaction, before remembering she should maintain a more saddened countenance, to which she returned.

Osric tried to mask his anger. "Ridiculous! You are but a pup," he said, shrugging and stretching out his hands. "You don't have the stature or the experience necessary to compliment a lady of such...sophistication."

Without the concealing benefit of cosmetics, Nissa's blushing was obvious.

"I am an officer of the Zanni August Guard, My Lord," Tavist replied in a bratty tone. And I carry the right to answer any lawful petition given in the sanctity of the King's court." Sir Tavist committed himself. There was no going back. "Whether it be twenty days or twenty years of service, a Guardsman's rights remain the same."

Osric, now distressed, turned to the King, who looked impressed; if that were even possible. "Your Majesty, I must express my objection to the insolence of this—this boy," Osric complained through clenched teeth. "He has no lands, no decorations, no sense at all!"

The King raised his hand above his head, an indicator that Osric cease speaking.

"Young he may be, but Sir Tavist Upland is a Secondary noble, within his right to answer the petition and, unless you challenge him to combat before the Anvil of Ages, he will win the honor of taking Nissa Warfield as his wife."

Tavist failed to hide his prideful self-satisfaction from Nissa as he looked in her direction. She did not avert her eye contact.

"And remember, dear Osric," the King continued. "We do not get to choose which laws we heed."

Osric frowned and lifted his chin. His speech was slow and acrid. "Then I challenge Sir Tavist Upland to combat."

The room erupted in chaos as attendees voiced their various opinions regarding what was about to happen. The Chamberlain tried his best to quiet the crowd while Osric and Tavist made their way to the floor between the King's platform and the Anvil of Ages where they faced each other. Osric oozed calm conceit and unfastened the leather strap that secured his priceless, jeweled rapier. He drew it with precision and grace; the sound of its movement rang out—an anthem to a lifetime of practice.

"Does your mother know where you are, boy?" goaded Osric.

"I swear, I will dispatch you!"

"You should know by now you should not make vows you cannot hope to keep."

Sir Tavist, removed his surcoat to reveal a suit of shined, ceremonial plate mail; an emblem of his gained authority. With little delay, he lunged forward and freed his long sword with violence and power. The room's occupants jumped in their seats.

It rattled Nissa. She had expected complications, but not this. Sir Tavist was a blonde, virile treat, to be sure; no doubt malleable and eager to please. She drank in his magnificence but soon realized the problem in this situation. He was a Secondary noble. If he won, she would remain a Secondary. Still, she became flattered and maybe aroused by the young man's ambition, whom she decided she would like to visit later, when this was over. But if she had to choose, then she would have to choose status above all.

She had no control in this matter. She could only wait, allowing combat to decide her fate and hoping that Osric was as skilled at swordplay as he was at sneaking into the rooms of other men's wives. Curious, Nissa brought herself to steal a peek behind her, at Charles, who was staring back at her, with unreachable pain in his eyes. She felt a tinge of guilt, but forced it to die. Charles watched it happen. She returned her attention to the pending melee.

The Chamberlain approached the two duelists and bowed to each of them. "You have committed to the legal tradition of combat before the Anvil of Ages. You will duel as gentlemen, to the end of life. The best man will marry Nissa Warfield at once. That is all."

"To the end of life?" Osric questioned.

"Yes, My Lord, the end of life," said the Chamberlain. "Well, Mr. Haspeth," said Osric. "We both know I am no upstart!"

Pleased, the robed Master Musician nodded in agreement and readied his troupe. Many of the seated nobles expressed their approval by clapping. Again, some of the nobles raised masks.

The Master Musician gave a count of four and then signaled the troupe to begin.

The sweet pampering of strings and woodwinds caressed the chamber in tones dark, alluring and pensive. After an additional count of four, Osric and Tavist touched swords and danced to the music.

Their movements were fluid and expressive. They mirrored each other with precision. In unison, they raised one leg and spun around, simulating a sword clash. Then, they spun in the opposite direction, simulating another collision of metal. They lunged; arms high. They lunged; arms low. They circled and bowed, then circled again. Every movement was astonishing. Every pose was symbolic.

Meanwhile, Charles closed his eyes, allowing the music to permeate his soul, knowing full well that this might be the last time he would hear it. He wished he could stop time and capture this moment. But stopping time was an impossible idea. Just like the lie he was a king, or he was so important that all of creation would perish without his help. Nothing but delusions. At least he had this moment while it lasted.

Before too long, however, Charles realized that something was wrong. In his head, the music soured, becoming warped and dissonant. The smell of ocean water and seaweed filled his nose. He felt a cold wisp of breath push into his ear.

Worthless coward. Always. You are a good boy. I am coming to see you soon.

Charles pulled on the guards, who were holding him. "Leave me alone," he said to the voices. The Guardsmen tightened their grip. As quick as the ordeal had started, the music sounded normal again. Charles opened his eyes to see Gyldred the Effacer looking at him. His eyes were smiling.

The music quickened, and the duel followed. They danced, keeping pace and expecting one another. The ballet was a spectacle of unmatched elegance. The two dancers increased their speed and the complexity of their movements. Telling them apart became difficult. But, the younger participant wavered, allowing Osric to touch him on the neck with his sword, drawing no blood. The duel was over. Tavist cursed out loud and stepped back to bow to the victor.

The attendees of the Grand Assembly burst into praise for the Duke Osric Branlin, who sheathed his sword and patted Sir Tavist on the shoulder. The musicians bowed, pleased with such a rare opportunity.

"Excellent effort, young man," Osric said through the smile of victory. "The End of Life is a difficult dance, requiring many years' practice to master. Well done, all the same." Osric meant every word. He knew The August Guard received only the most rudimentary education in the dancing arts. But he rather appreciated Tavist's ability. The youngster had practiced outside his station.

Tavist boiled with rage, but he forced himself to yield to the Treasurer's words. "Thank you, My Lord," he said, turning to the crowd. "I withdraw my claim to the Lady's petition! The Duke Treasurer has won the day!"

There was clapping and celebration throughout the chamber. But, The Grand Marshal refrained from celebrating. Instead, he stood still, frowning in consternation. He loathed this mockery of a ceremony. Swords were for killing your enemies, not dancing with them. It was disgraceful.

Nissa touched her folded hands to her forehead, in a show of relief; tears of joy streaming down her cheeks. Osric made his way to where she stood and he offered her his open hand, which contained his family nombit; a large piece of platinum with a rose surrounded by seven equidistant caltrops etched on it. She grasped the coin and held it high, causing the cheering to increase to a deafening roar.

As the King's proxy, the lace-laden Chamberlain raced to the new couple and kissed them both on the left cheek, then pronouncing them married. They then kissed the Chamberlain's outstretched hand who, likewise, ran up the platform and kissed the King's offered hand. The designated Duchess Nissa Branlin bowed to the room while Osric clapped next to her.

Devastated beyond his capacity to endure, Charles tried to remember the music. When that failed, he wrenched on his own injured shoulder, trying to increase the pain there. It helped somewhat.

With a saddened expression, the King nodded at Atherton who then signaled the Guardsmen on either side. The two young men grabbed under Charles' arms and dragged him, backwards, out of the chamber. Pleased to be leaving, Atherton Kel snatched up his nombit and followed them, as did the Effacer Gyldred. No one else even noticed that Charles had left. There had been an important wedding. However, it was now time for the name effacement ceremony in the solitude of the Effacer's keep.

As the acolytes forced Charles down the hall, he could hear the Chamberlain calling the room to order, for the next matter on the royal agenda. Something about the very important matter of increasing taxes on fine furniture imported from the Southern Province.

CHAPTER 8

CHARLES NOTICED, PERHAPS FOR THE FIRST TIME, just how gorgeous the Great Hall was as Gyldred dragged him through it. Despite the tremendous stabbing in his shoulder, bloodied heels scraping along the floor and the sting of a broken heart, he allowed himself to appreciate the many works of art that lined the walls.

Paintings, sculptures, bas-relief and pottery told the story of a kingdom raised from the chaos of the Sixteen Generations War. The walls boasted heroic depictions of immense battles between blue-caped Zanni Guardsmen and endless hordes of large, armored men brandishing savage expressions and eldritch weaponry.

Charles knew the story. Zanni schoolmasters taught that, before the war, Zannistar had enjoyed a thousand-year reign over a world-wide network of prosperous sub-kingdoms located across massive oceans. History further surmised that two of the more powerful sub-kingdoms, Arom and Laedenor—lands to the southeast and north—had become entrenched in a political struggle over money, religion and magic. Corwyn XVII, then the High King of Zannistar, made many tries to bring peace, but the other kings were staunch in their positions. The two outlying kingdoms conducted small skirmishes and raids on each other's coastal towns. All-out war soon followed.

The scientific superiority and martial ingenuity of the Aromites in the south-east came against the religious devotion and magical might of the Laedenorans to the north. And despite the stark differences in their war engines, they matched overall. As a result, both sub-kingdoms sought the favor of the High King, whose military forces and vast natural resources would have most likely tipped the balance. However, he tried to remain uninvolved, admonishing the lesser kings to cease hostility and engage in diplomacy instead. This advice went unheeded and, as the war progressed, Aromites and Laedenorans alike, came to blame Zannistar for the devastation the war brought to their people, accusing the High King of not taking a more active role in its course. Bitterness morphed into action when, twenty-three years after the start of the war, Aromite raiders sacked the Zanni city of Olix in the Southern Province Duchy of Virk.

Infuriated at the loss of so many of his own, the High King declared total war on both countries to force the peace, and for the next four hundred and fourteen years, war devastated the known world.

It became the purpose of every man, woman and child in existence to see their enemies crushed under foot. Whole communities and entire generations evolved and crumbled under the constant shadow of global war. Peace was a vaporous legend that nobody believed was possible. And while each of the three kingdoms enjoyed sometimes-long periods of advantage, none would ever emerge victorious.

Instead, hunger, savagery, depravity and dark magic permeated every corner of society. Evil itself—like a living, palpable scourge—blanketed the heart of every living thing, wanting only for itself. With each life lost, hopelessness increased its grip on the people of the world until they became little more than scandalous creatures driven by dark, fleeting passions, paranoia and hunger. Thievery became an acceptable, even respectable occupation and murder was no longer seen as a crime but as a tender mercy.

Legend told that, for a week's food, fathers sold their sons into the service of enemy military forces and mothers sold their daughters into prostitution to serve those same forces. Cannibalism became commonplace in some remote parts of Arom as villages flailed under the weight of starvation. The world festered.

During the final few years of the war, Zanni provincial lords fought amongst themselves over scarce provisions and arable land; a course that would lead to civil war. The cost in Zanni lives was unimaginable. Zannistar could not fight a war on two fronts when her own people were fighting amongst themselves.

With her population decimated to near annihilation and most of her cities razed to the ground, the once great Kingdom of Zannistar was on the brink.

It happened, four-hundred and fourteen years after the Sixteen Generations War had begun, the reigning King, Feol II, sent messengers throughout Zannistar, calling for a secret meeting of the heads of the remaining noble families.

Some weeks later, under cover of a moonless night, the nobles met in the shop of a trusted smithy in the northern city of Ganlis

Bay, the last known bastion of true civilization left in the world. There, the King introduced them to Gyldred, a young Effacer and defector from Laedenor who would offer to conceal Zannistar's existence from the rest of the world, in exchange for asylum. They would heal their broken land. All agreed to it.

So, on that night, amidst the grit and the miscellany of a commoner's craft, the nobles signed the new royal charter atop the smithy's anvil, thus ending the civil war and marking the start of Zannistar's ensuing five hundred years of peaceful isolation from the outside world.

Charles turned his gaze to Gyldred who glided behind. Gyldred's eyes showed they knew Charles' thoughts. Gyldred turned his hooded head toward the art on both sides of the Great Hall, then back. Charles thought it strange to see paintings with Gyldred in them; paintings of events some of which took place five hundred years prior.

Without breaking pace, Gyldred motioned toward the east wall ahead of Charles, with a sleeved arm, coaxing him to look. Disturbed but curious, Charles stretched his neck to see.

Charles realized that he was looking at the open door of his own palatial suite. There were at least a dozen or more pale, hooded figures removing all of his belongings from his home and transporting them down the hall, to the Effacer's abode, which Charles then knew was his own destination. They reminded Charles of a line of foraging ants. There were another two acolytes on ladders working hard to pry away the coat-of-arms above the door with a hammer and chisel. All evidence of the family Warfield's existence would soon vanish forever.

Sensing the proximity of the Effacer, the acolytes ceased their bustle and bowed in unison while the group passed by. Charles saw workers chuckling. He felt sick. His whole life would disappear. No one would remember that he, or his mother and father had ever existed. He palpated the coin in his mouth with his tongue and pondered what had happened in the oubliette earlier. Charles considered how preposterous the whole ordeal was and feared that total madness would soon find him. He wished it would happen before they arrived at Gyldred's room of horrors.

The keep at the end of the Great Hall had been Gyldred's home since the beginning. In those early days, it stood separate from the main palace. But over time, the succession of kings grew more dependent on Gyldred's talents. Two-hundred-fifty years into Zannistar's isolation, stonemasons from the Southern Province connected Gyldred's keep to the main palace via the Great Hall. The builders constructed individual living quarters lining the length of the hall. Thus, the tradition of tenant nobility began.

Despite its proximity to the palatial suites, tenant nobles did not venture too close to the keep. So unsavory was the consensus regarding the place that the two closest dwellings, on either side of the hall, remained empty. It was useless for the King to assign them, for no sane noble would accept. The Effacer's keep was terrible or worse than the oubliette, according to rumor. How fitting Charles should experience both in one day. He supposed he should just allow the inevitable to play out. No more fantasies about a secret, grand fate. Just let it happen.

Yes, Charles. That's it. Just let it happen. Like you did with Nissa...like you did with everything. Always.

The Grand Marshal, Duke Atherton Kel was now ahead of the group, guiding the way while Gyldred maintained a respectable distance in the back. Charles avoided further eye contact with the Effacer. The sorcerer's gaze disturbed him. Everything about

Gyldred was unnatural: His age, his dress and his walk. Sometimes, it looked as if he floated across the ground, without touching it. However, his robes concealed his feet, making it impossible for Charles to confirm his suspicion. No matter. Charles concluded that he would find out soon enough.

A quarter hour passed, and the group made their way to the end where a door of solid rosewood was open, revealing a stone-encased closet, containing an ascending spiral staircase of similar stone, attended by one of Gyldred's acolytes; a tall, robed shell of a man who sported a grin that hinted at secrets dark and unsavory. Several eroded areas of his ebon robe revealed a pale, gangling physique.

There were more hooded acolytes streaming passed the doorman, and up the stairs with Charles' belongings. The Grand Marshal stopped, stepping off to the side. His men did the same, allowing Gyldred to glide to the front.

Atherton Kel displayed distrust and discomfort on his face. Common sense and logic told him he had likely seen the Effacer's acolytes before, though he could not remember it. This put him at great unease. There were many. Where did they all come from? Who were they? The Grand Marshal and everyone else knew Gyldred had servants, but he could not have imagined their sheer numbers. In fact, Atherton wondered just how many times he had made this same journey before. How many people had he escorted to their doom? Charles Warfield could not be the only criminal effaced in over thirty years of service. The odds were against it.

"I've made preparations," announced the towering doorman, in a voice that crept like nocturnal insects. Gyldred said nothing, nodding at the doorman in approval, before heading up the spiraling stairs.

Out of nowhere, two more acolytes relieved the guards and dragged a defeated and compliant Charles up the stairs, after Gyldred.

A moment passed, and the Grand Marshal engaged the ashen-faced servant at the door. He was terse. "How many of you are there? Speak!"

"Now, now Atherton," he answered. "You ask me that every time, you know. We have become such good friends over the years, you and I—yes, good friends."

"Who are you?"

The strange servant placed a large, yet emaciated hand to his own breast. "Oh, you are persistent."

The doorman's eyes glinted like firelight. Within them, lived a distant hint of gathering clouds and swirling smoke. Atherton took a step back, his hand poised to draw steel. "Do not play me, cur," he warned. "I have no reservations about thinning your ranks and, unlike the Treasurer, I am no dancing idiot! My sword craves real blood, not the applause of the court."

A sigh passed between the servant's pale, grinning lips. "I never tire of your attempts to frighten me, friend," he said. The doorman's face twisted into the likeness of the Grand Marshal, except its eyes became swirling, black pits.

Atherton spun around in a whirlwind of long, gray hair and pointed to one of his Guardsmen with a gloved finger. "The King must know of this! Hurry!" The designated Guardsman broke into a run.

"Oh, he will not make it, friend," said the doorman through pouting lips. "He will forget.—and like always—so will you." He smiled, offering a generous spread of jagged, yellowed teeth, set in black gums. The teeth—they were vibrating; each one quivering as though loose.

"I am not your friend." Atherton backed away, tightening his grip on the handle of his sword. "You are a creature of darkness! Where did you come from? Not even Gyldred the Great Effacer keeps such company."

The doorman laughed. "Gyldred is not my master."

"Then who is?" Atherton braced himself for a melee.

"Goodbye, Atherton."

Before Atherton or the other Guardsman could react, the mysterious servant slid backwards through the threshold; the door slamming shut after him. The sound of laughter and locks being bolted did little to rouse Atherton from his stunned state.

CHAPTER 9

ON HIS WAY UP THE SPIRAL STAIRWELL, Charles counted each step as his lower back struck them, despite his tries to abstain. This was no small feat owing to the overpowering stench of rot that saturated the air, making him retch. Bile mixed with the tang of silver was a flavor he could have lived without.

Ominous shadows flew back and forth, up and down on the curved wall, making it difficult to focus. The two acolytes that were dragging him were strong and silent.

He counted forty-seven by the time they reached the landing; a peculiar number of steps. But before Charles could ponder it further, the acolytes dragged him through the threshold of another rosewood door, into large circular room—a room with several points of conversational interest, including a man-sized slab of stone in the middle of the room, circled by acolytes with Gyldred in their midst. The Effacer regarded Charles with smiling eyes and pointed to the slab.

After closing the door, they placed Charles supine on the slab where he could see the high-domed ceiling, decorated with an authentic representation of the night sky. It captivated Charles.

Anonymous hands secured Charles to the stone with leather belts. This is how it would end: effaced under a canopy of false stars; the just wages for having lived a false existence with false friends and a false wife. Somehow, erasing such a worthless life did not seem cruel, but kind. Let them forget. So be it.

So be it, coward. I'm coming now.

Gyldred stood at Charles' head, holding outstretched arms; looking to the ceiling. Charles noted that the stars pulsed. Great clouds of color shimmered and undulated as oil in water. They collided and formed new and fascinating shapes. Gyldred waited. Then a star shot across the ceiling. The Effacer made a reeling motion as if astounded by what he was seeing. Gyldred leaned over Charles, interrupting his amazement and replacing it with horror. Then being free from the wrappings that covered his lower face, Gyldred revealed his secret.

Where a nose and mouth should have been, was a swirling vortex of red smoke and shadow, spinning into oblivion. A low, dissonant hum filled Charles' head as the vortex reversed, emitting a cone of twisting doom into the room. Gyldred's black eyes sparkled, reflecting Charles' horrified look. The cone then erupted into dozens of small, moist fingers that palpated Charles' face. His eyes darted in their sockets as they sought to avoid the smarmy digits that pressed their way around them, looking for a way in. Fetid smoke billowed from Gyldred's sleeves into Charles' nose. Invasion and pain consumed his being.

Charles opened his mouth to scream, revealing the coin between tooth and cheek. He heard shrieking, but not his own. It was the vortex, or perhaps Gyldred. No, it was both. Gyldred clawed at his own eyes and backed away, before detonating in a flash of heat and white light. Red-hot ashes floated to the floor. Terrified, Charles closed his eyes and awaited sweet death. After a time, he opened his eyes, expecting to see Gyldred's acolytes moving in to throttle him, but nobody came. Except for the rhythm of Charles' heaving breaths, the room was quiet.

Charles' bearings crept back. What had just happened? Could it have been the coin? He tried to stand, but leather straps bound him. He struggled in vain for a few moments until a long, feral roar echoed from the bottom of the spiral staircase that lay just beyond the closed door; the sound of ascending footsteps soon following —at a tremendous rate of speed.

Adrenaline burst into Charles' veins. One, two, three... Charles felt compelled to count the footsteps. He figured he had only seconds before whatever was coming was upon him. He jerked against the straps; pressure accumulating in his head...four, five and six. Another soul-shattering shriek came from the stairwell, only closer. Blessed Anvil—it was skipping steps! Seven, eight, nine... Charles felt his heart would burst. Ten! Charles shut his eyes and stifled a yelp.

But, nothing happened. A few seconds passed, then Charles opened one eye. Everything was still. Everything was quiet. Relieved, Charles let out the breath he had been holding. Whatever it was, it must have gone back down the stairs.

Three loud knocks at the door shattered the silence.

"Charles?" It was the eerie, grating voice of the doorman. "Charles, are you in there?"

Charles lay motionless though he could feel his hammering heart pulsing in his fingertips. Maybe if he was silent and still—

62

The door handle creaked and turned. "I smell you in there."

Charles heard sniffing sounds.

The door squeaked open, just wide enough to show the doorman's pale, smiling face poking through the darkness. Once it saw Charles, its face twisted into a likeness of Charles' own face.

The thing sniffed again. "Hello, Charles. Something smells wrong. What did you do?"

Charles resisted the straps again in futility. The doorman scanned the room, moving only his eyes—his grin never fading. His gaze fell to the floor and there remained fixed, but on what, Charles could not see. Charles frustration turned to horror as the doorman's eyes distorted into sinking swirls and his grin turned into a toothy frown.

"What did you do, Charles!" The doorman's voice sounded ancient and feral.

The coin! Charles maneuvered his tongue for the coin, but instead caused it to stick to the roof of his mouth.

The doorman's mouth stretched to an oblong maw, armed with row after row of yellow, vibrating, shard-like teeth. His eyes had joined in a single, whirling vortex of red-tinged smoke and his head floated into the room toward Charles, like a dandelion seed on a fleshy, spindling stalk.

Charles bludgeoned the edge of the coin, over and over with his tongue, trying to free it. As he did so, he felt a pang of guilt for trying to save his own life. But he couldn't help himself. It was an automatic response. Besides, nobody deserved to die in such circumstances; not even him.

The door and attached wall exploded inward. Debris flew everywhere and Charles found himself engaged with the nightmare-vision in front of him: The otherworldly image of what used to be the doorman's head fixed by a mere wisp, to the body of an enormous and powerful mastiff, its shoulders the height of a man's. The creature shrieked, causing pain in Charles' ears, as it tensed its massive haunches for the pounce.

Agape with fear, Charles almost did not notice that the coin had dropped from the roof of his mouth and landed on his tongue.

The beast leapt at Charles, who just then negotiated the coin between his front teeth and open his lips, exposing it. This time, he heard his own screaming.

In a concussion of light, the macabre beast exploded and vanished in mid-flight—and save for the damage to the room it caused during its entry—there was no sign, anywhere. It was just gone. Exhausted, Charles rested his head on the cool stone and stifled the urge to cry, being both elated and disappointed that he still drew breath. Despite his efforts, the tears came. As he cried, he refused to move the coin from its current defensive position between his front teeth.

The Duke Atherton Kell, Grand Marshal of Zannistar, stood in the splintered debris of what was once the rosewood door to Gyldred's keep, at the north end of the Great Hall. He was sweating and breathing heavy from his assault on the wooden entrance. The remaining guardsman stood at a distance and watched in amazement, the strength of his commander. Atherton gathered himself. "What is your name, Guardsman?"

"It's Graham Buckles, Grand Marshal."

"Buckles?"

"Yes, Grand Marshal." The young guardsman was nervous.

"Ivo Buckles' son?"

"Yes, Grand Marshal."

"Good man, Ivo. There was no guile in him. And he was a rare voice of truth at court. I was sorry to hear of his passing."

"Thank you, Grand Marshal."

"Well, Guardsman Buckles, I intend to storm up these stairs, investigate the origin of those abominable sounds and kill whatever made them. We have no time to gather forces and we may soon forget all of it; the Effacer's sorcery is powerful."

Guardsman Buckles swallowed hard. "Yes, Grand Marshal."

"Now, given the inhuman nature of what may lie ahead, it would not be honorable to order you to follow me into such a deathly contract. But, I would welcome the selfless service of a true Zanni Guardsman at my back. The choice is yours."

The Guardsman summoned his composure and lifted his chin. "I do not believe a Zanni Guardsman has a choice, Grand Marshal."

Atherton nodded. He felt a genuine appreciation for this young man. "Very well. Just one thing—why did you not follow in your father's politicking and pursue the comforts of court? He was well-liked. Your place there would have gone unchallenged."

Buckles drew his long-sword and faked a pose. "Well, Grand Marshal, I am not a very good dancer!"

"Ha!" Atherton chuckled, striking Buckles' sword aside with his own. "Neither am I. To the task!"

The Grand Marshal burst into action, his companion close behind him.

CHAPTER 10

"GIVE ME THE SHARD and I will help you to your feet," said the man.

"No!" Aerion used his legs to throw his weight, moving into a kneeling position. From there he stood, the whole time keeping both control of the shard and his afflicted hand high in the air. He would not endure another melee with the faces above. Aerion figured those creatures could not advance as long as he displayed the coil.

"You are very strong," the man offered. "And wise." The stranger stood tall and lean, wearing a sleeveless, flowing robe of white cotton with a white silken cord at the waist. Encircling his forearms were bracers of smoothed alabaster or perhaps bone and his feet fit snug in white sandals. His short hair was pale and combed back. Strong cheekbones underscored dark, almond-shaped eyes. His complexion reminded Aerion of the color of acorns. This man hailed from a distant land. Aerion had never seen a person of this sort before.

"Who are you? What is this place?" Aerion did not trust the man.

"I am Vang. And this," he gestured at the tunnel. "This is the In-between." His voice was smooth but masculine.

"Between what?"

"Your world and the world-after."

"Then I am dead!" The conclusion was shrill and sincere.

"Oh, no," assured Vang, through an exotic smile. "You are alive indeed. The tunnel has trapped you. To return to your world, you need only walk to the end of it." Vang pointed along the tunnel with a finger tipped with a sharp and whitened fingernail.

"And you? From where do you hail?" Aerion pointed to Vang with the shard. He seemed a little disturbed by it.

"I am from a place called Rax, the world-after," answered Vang. "Like you, I am trapped here until you exit this tunnel. But you must understand, time passes different in this place. Already, in the few moments since your arrival, many years have passed in your own world. Everyone you care about has died. The longer you stay here, the more strange your own world will be when you return. You must act."

Somehow, Aerion understood Vang with clarity. Moments in this place were different from outside the tunnel. But he wondered where this tunnel came from? The ground in front of him and behind him was the same as it was when he entered the pit; snow covered dirt, stretching into the distance where he had come from. But there was a shimmering glamour, forming a kind of curved wall, surrounding him on the sides. His vision could not penetrate it to the forest outside, but he knew it must be there. Behind, the glimmering barrier formed a wall just beyond the deepest part of the pit. Of course, the sky was replaced with those faces. The ground was the only thing that made sense.

"And what of the specters? Are they from the world-after? Rax?"

"Yes," Vang took a serious tone. "They seek the coil. But they must kill you first to possess it, for they cannot confront the coil directly. Its power is quite coercive."

Aerion swallowed hard and stared at the undulating faces above, pondering the possibility of a gruesome death.

"If I die, will I go to Rax?

Vang's sparkling eyes narrowed even more and his voice softened. "Oh, yes. All with eternal purpose pass to the next world."

"What is eternal purpose?"

Vang became softer, caring even. He took the tone of a loving teacher. "Aerion, not all who draw breath have purpose beyond the three worlds. Some are bound for the Neverwall. Still, most are reborn over and over, their essence remaining in their world forever. These are the most tragic. They do not remember who they were.

"And others?"

"Some, through death and rebirth, can move between the worlds. You are such a person; a person with eternal purpose. Do you not feel special? You are special."

"How can you know? Are you in league with the Gastwyrd?" Aerion was hungry for the answer.

"I know all in my world."

Aerion paused, then scanned the tunnel's depths. "My father. Is my father there?" Memories of the burning funeral raft invaded Aerion's mind.

"He is."

"Am I able so see him? Can I go there without dying?"

"Find the tunnel's end, enter any world you want."

"But why you are here?" said Aerion.

Vang leaned in. "I came to find you, Aerion."

"Me? Why?" Aerion lifted the shard and furrowed his brow.

"You will understand at Stag's End. Besides, do you want to see your father or do you not?" Vang's eyes sharpened to slits.

Aerion stared at his surroundings. He dreaded tunnel's end, but knew he could not stay here. His hand would become tired and the evil faces would once again emerge.

"Yes, I do. But your strange looks frighten me and I do not trust you. This is like a bad dream. I need to understand what is happening."

Vang bowed his head, offering a generous grin. "Shall we converse as we walk?"

CHAPTER 11

A RECUMBENT CHARLES STUDIED THE IMAGE of the night-sky on the concave of the dome, unable to mitigate the tightness of the straps that bound him. The stars still shimmered as though real. It was mesmerizing. Again, a shooting star shot across the painting, then another a few moments later. He wondered what purpose the Effacer might have had with such a miraculous piece of art. Charles decided, he would trade it and all of Zannistar's treasures for a fresh set of clothes.

The sweat-dampened burlap he wore caused torturous itching he could do nothing to soothe. He felt a sense of distant familiarity with those stars on the ceiling; a genuine connection that went beyond his lonely, boyhood imaginings. He applied pressure to the coin in his teeth, just to make sure it was still there. The act helped him find a modicum of sanity.

Again sounds of footsteps on the stairs. Two people by the sound. Charles let the coin rest on his tongue, braced himself and waited. He would be ready this time. And, just as he had expected, two Guardsmen arrived with swords at the ready; sweating and looking confused. One was the Grand Marshal.

"What happened here?" Atherton asked, surveying the destroyed doorway. He pointed to Charles with his sword. "And why do I still remember you, Charles Warfield? I should have forgotten you by now. Where are Gyldred and the others?"

Charles trembled but said nothing.

"Speak up, traitor, or I'll rend you!" Atherton stooped to pick something up from the floor. It was Gyldred's robe. "What happened to the Effacer? Where is he? How did you best him?"

Charles shook his head and tried to shrug his shoulders. The straps denied him. Atherton picked up another robe; that of an acolyte.

"And, not that it pains me, but where did the large one go—the doorman?" Asked Atherton Kel.

Charles pleaded with his eyes.

Atherton furrowed his brow. "Why are you silent? Are you hiding something Charles? Perhaps you have engaged in more thievery on the way here, eh?"

In a burst of intuition-driven purpose, the Grand Marshal took his free hand and tried to force open Charles' mouth. Charles emitted sounds of desperate resistance through his teeth as he clenched them and tossed his head from side to side. The Grand Marshal could not gain a good grasp.

"Guardsman Buckles, aid me with this pathetic dog," Atherton said.

Their efforts were of no use. Charles was too slippery to handle with clumsy gauntlets.

Impatient, Atherton grunted in defeat. "Enough! Effaced or not, you are still a traitor to the crown and I hold the authority to end your filthy life here and now!"

Bellowing, Atherton swung back his shoulders and raised his sword high for the kill. But before he could thrust the blade, someone struck him from behind. He stumbled forward, slumping over Charles' midsection in a mass of metal and unconsciousness.

Blood flowed, staining Atherton's thinning, gray hair a spectacular shade of red. The young Guardsman, Graham Buckles, spun around in response and received the blade of an Aromite's halberd through one eye. The young Guardsman flew against the far wall on the end of the pole-arm and went limp, never knowing the truth of his last moment.

Charles kept his eyes closed, and he was again showing the coin in his teeth. Maybe it would destroy this murderous lot as well; whoever they were.

"Get him out of there, Veldic—quickly!" A familiar woman's voice.

Could it be? The shock of it caused Charles to lose control of the coin, which found its way to the back of his throat, further causing Charles to gag before swallowing it whole. He could feel the shape of the small coin as it slid into his gullet. He felt as if he had just done something terrible.

Charles opened his eyes, but it was not Nissa in front of him as he had expected. Charles squinted. The woman wore Nissa's face, though gaunt and somewhat sturdy looking. She had Nissa's black hair, but cropped short in back and long in front. She had Nissa's height, yet she seemed a great deal less nourished. The resemblance to his former wife was astonishing.

A tall, muscled, sun-beaten woman in a blackened leather shirt, bracers and skull-cap slipped the hook of her halberd under the straps that held Charles and severed them. She wore tan, oversized breeches cinched tight at the ankle, under which were feet shod in a blackened pair of leather sandals. She sported a shock of jet-black hair from the back of her head, out from an opening in her skull-cap and four large golden hoops in each ear, a feature Charles could not help but notice and count as the woman lifted the Grand Marshal off him, with one hand, and tossing him aside. Her wild, violet eyes burned with danger.

Intimidated, Charles looked passed the warrior. "Nissa, is that you?"

The much smaller woman leveled icy-blue eyes on him and held out her hand. "I am Dara, and we must leave at once! Do you have the coin?"

Charles stammered while rising to his aching, damaged feet.

"Where is it, Charles?" she asked.

"You murdered those two men," Charles was going into shock. "One of whom was the Grand Marshal!"

"Not so," said the warrior, poking Atherton with the blunt end of her halberd, "the older one still breathes."

"They would kill you," said Dara. "Besides, they and everyone else here is about to die anyway, and if you don't want to join them, you will come with us! The Beast of Sable Rock has arrived to usurp this place. Now, where is the coin, Charles?"

Somewhat embarrassed, Charles pointed to his belly and shrugged. "I swallowed it."

The large warrior rolled her eyes. "Bless the Venerable Spirit! He's an imbecile!"

Dara snapped. "Hold your tongue, Veldic! We will sort it out later. We cannot use the stairs. More men will be coming." She scanned the chamber and discovered the south window. "Over there! We leave now!"

"Where are we going? Is it safe?" Charles noticed blood on himself. "Might I change into decent clothing before we go?"

"I said, we will sort it out later! Move!" She pointed at the window with what looked like a crossbow bolt from her quiver as an extension of her gloved, index finger.

Yes, she was like Nissa, perhaps even a sister. But it was not her. The simple fact was that the Nissa he knew would never don such a utilitarian ensemble. Dara's clothing comprised a studded, collarless brown leather doublet over a tan shirt with black, leather gloves along with tan, cotton pants tucked into black, knee-high utility boots. She sported a plain, brown leather belt from which various tools and pouches hung. On her back, rested a brown leather quiver, with many bolts. To Charles, the image was as if his own Nissa had remained a Tertiary noble. The thought was interesting and absurd.

Charles did not know this person, but he felt a strong pull to her. Whatever lay ahead, it had to be better than staying here. Her presence intrigued him. Charles decided that despair could wait awhile longer.

Dara unfurled a length of rope given her by Veldic and attached an iron hook to its end which she pulled from a pouch at her belt. Veldic pushed the glass panes open with her pole-arm and, after catching the rope and hook Dara threw to him, secured it to the ledge, testing its stability.

Now at the window, Charles surveyed the palatial garden. It looked so different from this viewpoint. He turned back to Dara and motioned toward the window; a sentiment he knew must have looked ridiculous in his current state of attire: blood-soaked burlap and twine, such as it was.

She nodded and leaped through the opened window, spinning around to grab the rope in mid-air and sliding down the smooth, stone side of the keep into the bushes. Charles and Veldic followed in kind, albeit both doing so with less prowess.

Had they stayed an instant longer, they would have seen another shooting star arc across the painted sky on the dome above, and another, and another.

CHAPTER 12

THE KING WOKE HIMSELF with the sound of his own afternoon snoring. This was not an uncommon occurrence at court, but it was an awkward moment for everyone there, including the elegant Duchess Lydia Mirette, who had spent at least several minutes making her petition before she realized the King was sleeping and then several more minutes waiting for him to wake up.

The entire Grand Assembly pretended that nothing had happened, and the King summoned the Chamberlain over to him, who reminded him of what they had been doing.

"Yes," said the King. "The lovely Lydia Mirette of Virk! You were saying?"

Lydia's olive dress and curly chestnut hair remained in place as she bowed her head and cleared her throat. "Yes, Your Majesty, I hoped that His Merciful Highness would consider my request to return to the Southern Province through the end of the burgeoning season, that I may tend to some pressing matters in the hill-lands. There are reports of—"

The King lifted a hand and waved her off. "Duchess Lydia, you know well I must decline, for the third time, your petition to return to the Southern Province. Just as I did during the last Grand Assembly, I will remind you of our charter, which states that the highest noble from each area of representation shall live and operate here, in the Zanni Palace. Your predecessor understood this. She served ten happy and productive years at court before she succumbed to her illness."

"She would want you to stay, yes? Blessed Anvil, Duchess Lydia! Do you not have vassals of your own that can tend to this... pressing matter you speak of? Besides, what is so important that you risk arousing my disapproval? Trouble with brigands is it? Or perhaps your motives are more private." Lidig put a finger to his chin. "What was his name? Oh, yes—Bryndol Baylan—that's it, isn't it?" The King turned to Chamberlain Nolan Haspeth for confirmation, who nodded. "Besides, you are a Primary and he is a Tertiary—and half your age I might add. The relationship is inappropriate. You understand."

Anger was boiling just under the threshold of Lydia's polite manner. The King had no business judging the appropriateness of her relationships. She happened to know his own appetites were less acceptable than hers. Her large, brown eyes narrowed. "Your Majesty, my people grow restless and suspicious in my absence. It has been two years since I have appeared in Virk. It would be a short visit. I would return to court as soon as—"

"Enough! I have made my will known," yelled the King.

Jacent and the wig bearers jumped in their seats. "They are my subjects before they are your people, Duchess Lydia. Now I'll hear

77

no more of it. You have important work, here at court which requires your presence. It is our way. Send someone else."

The King looked to the ceiling, as if bored, and made shooing gestures at The Duchess of Virk who bowed and returned to her seat with as much dignity as she could muster. But on the way, she conceived of her escape.

The Chamberlain stood. "Now, if no more inquiries, His Majesty the King; the Sovereign of Zannistar and Supreme Authority before the Anvil of Ages closes this Grand Assembly of the Royal Court under the Royal Charter, to which all are beholden."

Nolan pointed to the south entrance. "King Lidig invites you to a special feast of roasted hind and grouse in the palace banquet hall. Wine shall flow."

The crowd clapped and congratulated one another. It was rare the King invited the entire court to dine with him. It was a great occasion! The nobles milled about and mingled.

Something still troubled Lidig. He doubted that an extravagant dinner and merriment were enough recompense to offset the decision to efface of one of their own. Yet he felt he had no choice. And as he regretted his decision, he realized that he should not be aware in the least that Charles had ever existed, much less harbor feelings of guilt for the boy. It had been a while since they had carried him off and yet the King still remembered him. He turned to the Chamberlain to inquire after Gyldred's tardiness, when a shrill scream from outside the chamber interrupted him. Everyone stopped and turned toward the south entrance, through which entered several large, armed men of a different sort.

Everyone froze speechless as the brutish men filed in, two-by-two, toward the Anvil of Ages. Though frightened, Tavist reacted according to his training. At his command, he and the palace guards drew their swords and rushed to form a line between the King and the Anvil. Once the invaders reached the Anvil, they spun and faced outward toward the audience on either side, creating a path in the middle.

They outnumbered Sir Tavist and his compliment. There were at least two dozen of these muscled savages, clad in massive hauberks of tarnished chain armor; some with metal or leather lamellar shirts. Wet furs from unfamiliar animals in various colors and shapes hung from their shoulders and legs, indistinguishable from their own unkempt hair and braided beards. Not a single one of these strangers was without disfiguring scars and not a single one was without an enormous weapon of battle-proven iron. Now in position, they held fast.

Overcoming his initial shock and now concerned for his own safety, the King sat up in his love-seat, closed his eyes tight, and tried to teleport out of the chamber. Nothing happened. He looked at the invaders and tried again, closing his eyes and concentrating. Still, nothing. The power of the chair was just beyond the grasp of his mind as if someone locked it in a box trapped under water.

The chair never denied him before. Fear gripped him. Like it or not, the chair trapped him here with everyone else. King Lidig sat in utter dismay and shock as the feral soldiers took their positions. He burned with questions. Who were these outlanders? Where did they come from? What happened to his throne? And where was the Grand Marshal?

Just then, a young lute player near the entrance attempted to sneak out backwards. He made it to the threshold, but someone ran him through with a sword from behind, sending blood and screeches into the air. All gasped in horror when the musician dropped his lute and fell lifeless to the floor, revealing his killer, who was standing at the entrance.

"I gave no one permission to leave," said the helmeted man, squatting down to wipe his bloodied blade on the musician's plush, velvet hat. He straightened, showing his build; muscled and tall, protected by a full suit of scale armor, the color of midnight and pitch. The visor of his black helm took the image of a snarling wolf's muzzle. A hooded cape of a black wolf's fur enveloped the menacing figure.

Another muscle-bound invader entered the chamber, taking bites out of the still-feathered carcass of a raw grouse from the kitchen. He had short, unkempt brown hair and wore no armor, only leather and a patchwork of furs. He carried a polearm topped with a massive, blood-stained, rectangular blade in his other hand. Deep wrinkles weathered his face.

"Look there, Thimgar," said the wolf-faced killer in a voice like silk, pointing to King Lidig. "There he is, as promised."

The fur-clad warrior's eyes widened, and he threw his dinner to the side. He had a ravenous look about him and a tuft of grouse feathers emerged from his smiling lips. The two invaders started toward the Anvil.

"Hello, Lidig," the wolf-faced warrior said, sheathing his sword. "We are so very pleased to see you—Very pleased. Aren't we, Thimgar?"

Thimgar grunted and nodded as he chewed.

The King stiffened. "And just who are you, that you dare defile an official Grand Assembly? How did you enter unchallenged?" They petrified him, but he had little choice. He needed to act like a king. Perhaps he could bluff his way to safety. "And killing my subjects! Are you from the Southern Province, come to usurp my throne? Are you in league with the Duchess of Virk?" Lydia scrunched her nose at the remark.

At the ready to fight, Tavist kept his sword trained on the two men as they neared the Anvil.

From behind the helm, the killer's laugh was tinny and muffled. "Well, well Lidig. Yes, I come to take your throne. But not from the Southern Province. I have traveled from a much greater distance than that." The man pointed to the north. "I've come all the way from Laedenor, in the Northlands beyond the Neverwall. Perhaps you have heard of it." Some other invaders chuckled.

"Impossible!" the Chamberlain protested, rising from his seat. "No one from the outside knows Zannistar even exists."

The wolf-faced man laughed again. "Yes. But I am one of you," he said. He lifted his helmet from his head and threw it to Thimgar who caught it with one hand. Sounds of disbelief and astonishment emanated from the crowd. Everyone at the Grand Assembly stared at the man in utter shock; The man looked a mirror image of Charles Warfield; a man they had just condemned to the Effacer's foul magic. And yet, here he was, except instead of a fist-beaten face and shaved head, his features were well-weathered but powerful, and he had a long head of straight brown hair; to the middle of his back.

"My name is Ember Driss," said the man with Charles' face, loosening the fingers of his right glove, removing it and throwing it on his helm. "And while I am many things to you, foremost, I am now your King." He tightened his bare fist and a thin wisp of crimson smoke escaped through his fingers.

Nissa grew pale, as did Osric. How could this be? It was Charles, but he was also very different. He was stronger, more confident—and King.

Infuriated, Osric pushed through the nobles like saplings and went around the back of the chamber and down the path toward the Anvil of Ages in a huff not unlike a child in a tantrum. One of the fur-clad warriors turned to stop him, but Ember signaled him to let Osric pass.

"I saw you humiliated and dragged away!" Osric approached the man who called himself Ember. "You are not King! You are a Secondary; and a traitor! If the Effacer cannot handle you, then I shall. I challenge you, sir, to a gentleman's duel! And this time, metal will pierce flesh!" Osric drew his rapier and put his other hand on his waist. "Nissa is my wife now, you worthless bastard," he said through clenched teeth.

Expecting the duel, the musicians played a celebrant piece of music, despite the absence of a breathing lute player. Some of the nobles huffed, but the Master Musician shrugged and continued on, making the best of a bleak situation.

Ember Driss smiled and stared into Osric's eyes for a long moment. "Nissa, you say?" He asked. "And where is she at present, Osric? Is she here now?" Ember broke his gaze with Osric and scanned the crowd.

Osric looked puzzled. "She is here with me, you idiot," Osric retorted. "You were here to see it! I do not know how you did all of this, Charles. I do not know how you escaped, changed your appearance and rallied these criminals to your cause in such a short time, or even where they came from, but I intend to see you bled out at the end of my blade. Then, I will take my wife to my bedchamber and bless her with a child of proper, Primary stock."

Unaffected, Ember's searching eyes found Nissa. She was looking back at him. But it was not fear that lived in her eyes—it was curiosity.

"Look at me, Charles!" screamed Osric.

"You never could control your anger, Osric," said Ember still taking in Nissa's beauty. "I remember that about you. I was always the attentive one; the diligent one. You were quick to boil, brash and ungrateful; a royal brat with no capacity for patience. Yet, despite your total incompetence, you still connived your way through life. Even in the treasury, you took credit for my work."

Ember glanced at King Lidig and frowned. "Your glut of an uncle would not address your flaws. Instead, the court celebrated you as his likely heir. But I happened to know you lacked the proper temperance required of a king. Still, your anger would be useful in the coming days. I had made plans to spare you, Osric— considering our shared upbringing. And despite your selfish antics, there was a time when I considered you as a brother. But for you, it would seem that you keep something of mine—something dear. And I cannot allow that transgression to go unanswered."

In a movement as fluid as a glacial river; as swift and frigid as a mountain wind, Ember snatched Thimgar's bladed polearm from his hand and scooped Osric up by his midsection, lifting him high overhead in a giant arc, then down on to the Anvil of Ages with the force of an avalanche, rending Osric and sending him in two different directions in a spray of nombits and entrails which struck the crowd on both sides of the Anvil with a generous portion of both. The music halted.

The details settled, and the nobility stared in shocked silence. Ember unhanded the polearm now embedded deep in the Anvil of Ages, and turned his attention to Tavist and the palace guards in front of him. He gave them a foreboding look that caused all, including Tavist, to drop their weapons and stand aside. Tavist cursed his own cowardice as two of the invaders moved in and held his group at sword-point. He had betrayed his oath as a Guardsman to die rather than surrender, an act not at all unexpected of him by his men. He wanted to tell them he had a plan; that he was not a coward, but the defeated looks on their faces told Tavist that words were useless at this point.

Arminius Morlund, the Scrivener, gathered up the nombits on the ground, placing them in his pouch as best he could, muttering and fretting under his breath. King Lidig, however, was sobbing and trying to hide under his enormous golden gown. The sight was pitiful. Nissa was breathing hard, Osric's blood on her face, adrenaline coursing through her veins; but this did not frighten her —it exhilarated her.

"Lidig, I have a surprise for you," announced Ember. He turned toward Thimgar, who was wrenching on his polearm, trying to free it from the anvil. "Thimgar, you may bring him in now."

Giving up on his current task, Thimgar nodded and left the chamber.

"My dear Lidig," began Ember. "Did you think this would not happen? Did you think you could make everyone forget the truth forever?"

The King continued to sob under his gown, shaking his head.

Ember turned and spoke to the room. "Did you tell them, Lidig, about how you convinced Gyldred to efface the entire kingdom for a second time, to make them believe you were the King, instead of my father? Did you tell them what it cost for such a selfish and dark favor? No, because you do not remember! You arranged their murders and those of an entire city so you could rule! How many met their end that day, Lidig?"

Lidig shook his head in genuine disbelief. Whatever evil he had perpetrated was as Ember said, no longer a part of his memory.

Though frightened, many of the nobles were interested in Ember's words. Whispers of the tragedy at Ganlis Bay resonated through the chamber.

Nissa stepped forward, realizing her opportunity.

"My Lord, "she began—always appropriate. "What is this cost you speak of, if I may ask? And, forgive me Sire, but you are the exact image of Charles Warfield, a traitor to the crown and my former husband. How is this possible? A brother? Or perhaps a cousin we were unaware of?" Nissa realized that she still remembered Charles. Something was wrong. Gyldred should have effaced him by now.

Ember smiled with endearment. "Nissa, Nissa. You are radiant!" He motioned her to him. "Please, come and let me see you."

She produced an awkward smile, mustered her composure and lifted the bottom of her dress so as not to touch Osric's grisly remains that lay at her feet. She turned and threw Osric's nombit back to his corpse before continuing. The armed invaders made way for her to slip by. Ember received her with a look of pride and adoration.

"Nissa, you are even more beautiful than I remember." Ember tilted his head, then reached up with his gloved hand and cradled her chin. "You and I have much to discuss, my love, much to discuss. I must know: where is your husband?"

Nissa basked in his presence and she felt trapped by the purr of his voice. He wore Charles' face, but he was nothing like the Charles she knew. She could not ignore him. He was alluring.

"My Lord, if you mean Charles, Lidig judged him a traitor and sentenced him to the Effacer's craft. And he is no longer my husband. " Nissa replied. "But I still have him in my memory. Something is amiss, My Lord. I fear the Effacer has failed."

Ember glanced at the former Duke Treasurer's remains then back at Nissa. "And Osric?"

"He took me as his own, only moments before you arrived. It did not work as planned." Nissa felt exposed. She had lost two husbands in one day. Rumors would come. Unacceptable.

Thimgar reentered the chamber, holding a heavy choker chain attached to a pale and obese mockery of a man that crawled on its belly. Its face was oblong, with a gaping-wet, sparsely toothed pit for a mouth and fleshy, black sinkholes for eyes and nose. It seemed confused or lost; and it was not until it sensed Lidig and smiled that everyone else realized that the hapless man-thing looked just like the sobbing sovereign himself; only twisted and evil.

It clawed at the ground to quicken its movement toward Lidig. It acted desperate—hungry even. Thimgar dropped the chain and pushed the abomination forward with his boot.

"Ugly, yes?" asked Ember, turning his attention to the frightened King. "It might interest you to learn that it is you, Lidig, who created it. In fact, you have created thousands-upon-thousands just like it over the years."

Lidig's expression morphed to confusion.

Ember pointed to the oversized throne. "Oh yes. Every time you have used the power of the Bekrot Chair to teleport, a copy of you appears in the Gearwood Thicket—where the magic chair originated—deep in the Nurdrayl forest."

"I do not understand," returned Lidig, looking into the audience as if they could somehow explain it.

Ember cocked his head and smiled. "Lidig, you have, at your command, one of the most powerful works of sorcerous labor ever achieved. And what do you use it for?" Ember waited for a response but received none. "To travel from your bed to the cook's table and back to bed again! It is no wonder you are now soft and unable to flee. How many times a day, Lidig? How many times did you invoke the power of the chair for such selfish gluttony? Ten, twenty or more? You are a fool!"

The King froze in horror; his open mouth receiving sweat from his brow.

Ember gestured toward the approaching creature with something close to pride. "I have learned much in my exile, Lidig. For example, Thimgar's people call these copies Dreka." Ember acknowledged Thimgar and collected his thoughts before continuing. Thimgar managed a toothy, feather-matted smile.

"The whole affair is astonishing. When the Bekrot Chair creates a Dreka, the creature has no real way of knowing it is a copy. Every copy thinks it is the original. Just imagine, Lidig, one moment you might be on your way to fetch one of your legendary suppers and the next moment, you find yourself in the middle of a snow-covered wood, devoid of clothing or explanation. It is a very disturbing experience, let me tell you."

Despite his overwhelming fear, Lidig looked at Ember, who smiled back. The ravenous pile of malicious flesh pulled itself across the silver tiles toward the anvil, drooling filth and dragging the iron chain behind, along with its useless, malformed legs. Ember made his way up the platform and squatted down next to Lidig, rubbing the back of the wooden love-seat. Red vapor escaped from his hand and coiled around the Bekrot Chair.

Jacent and the wig bearers attempted to seem unafraid. It did not work.

Ember moved close to the King's ear. "I speak the truth, Lidig. Oh, there are slight differences between each copy in temperament and such," Ember said. "Unlike this one, the first copies are almost identical to the original. The same intelligence, abilities and memories. But they are soulless outcasts; unforeseen constructs without part or purpose on the stage of eternity. Most of the time, the Dreka live out their lives, not even realizing they are copies.

They think the chair transported them, not created them. Well, until someone teaches them about their true nature or they run into yet another copy somewhere in the forest. The people of the Northlands say if a Dreka can consume the heart of the original person, that they will attain the living soul of their victim and a proper place in the annals of eternity, being allowed to pass into the world-after upon death. This is an enticing treat. There is no world-after for Dreka. Only the Neverwall."

As Ember spoke, the creature inched down the path. Its vulgar movements and groans repulsed all.

Ember sighed. "It would seem, however, that nature imposes the law of diminishing returns on as wicked a magic as this. So, over time, each additional copy becomes less and less like the original; nothing more than thoughtless, empty vessels for nearby spirits to fill—and in the Northlands, there are no shortage of arcane spirits, I assure you."

There was some agreeable laughter among the warriors at their commander's comment.

Ember continued, "Once a passing specter takes over a Dreka, such a fell creature becomes an agent of utter evil, part human and part malignant spirit. These Dreka are murderous abominations called the Ersatz, and unlike the other Dreka, they desire only one thing: the destruction of every living thing in creation. And above all, it seeks the originator of its tortured existence. I do not suppose I need to tell you it is just such a creature you now see before you, come to engorge itself on your flesh and your eternal purpose. This is a rare opportunity for Dreka and Ersatz alike!"

The crawling man-thing poured around the Anvil of Ages, leaving a trail of drool and foulness where it had been. Sensing its proximity to Lidig, it made excited noises similar to a starving infant expecting a meal.

Disgusted, Tavist Upland put his hand over his nose and stepped back.

Lidig whimpered. Ember patted Lidig's shoulder, stood tall and addressed the assembly.

"Today, everything changes. Today, I serve vengeance and a new dynasty begins! And today, bearing the status of Primary nobility will cost you your lives! Such is the way of shifting power."

Lidig mustered the last vestige of anything resembling courage. "And what about you," he bellowed. "Are you one of these Dreka? Were you also created by the Bekrot Chair?"

Ember turned to Lidig and regarded him with nostalgia. "I was born anew when you used the chair to take Charles and Nissa to their wedding sabbatical in the Gardens of Grynn. I suppose I should thank you. Had you not allowed it, I would not exist. And just like other Dreka, I also have no soul; a detail I intend to remedy just as soon as I locate Charles."

The Ersatz horror was drawing nearer. "That means there is one more of you," Lidig deduced out loud. "They teleported in the Bekrot Chair twice. Yes, once there and once back!" His whimpering worsened.

"Yes," Ember said turning back to Nissa. "There was another, yes. Two copies of Nissa as well. But, now only one copy of each remains—myself and another Dreka named Dara who wishes to see me destroyed."

"So," Lidig began, trying to buy time. "Why can I not teleport? Blessed Anvil, why does the chair deny me when I need it most?"

Ember chuckled. "Because, you shameful oaf, the Bekrot Chair's magic does not work in the hour of its user's death, which leads me to the fact that there is only one more thing you can do for me, Lidig."

Lidig hugged himself and sobbed. Making no sound, Ember leapt backwards, into the air above Lidig in a broad flip, landing behind the wig-bearers.

"Get out of my chair!" Ember screamed.

He thrust his foot into the back of the Bekrot Chair, causing it to tip and pour Lidig down the steps of the platform, like a giant, raw dumpling, into the clutches of the frantic Ersatz horror which forced Lidig's head into its mouth, exploiting the softer areas first. Lidig's struggling was brief.

Jacent and the wig bearers fled to each side while Ember lifted the Bekrot Chair to an upright position, brushing the dirt off it. With a primal roar, Ember threw his open hand into the air. Giant ropes of swirling smoke shot from a bloodless, spiraled wound in his palm, obscuring the stained-glass ceiling like great vermilion storm-clouds, blocking the light.

Having received their cue, the Laedenoran warriors engaged the attendees of the Grand Assembly with iron and hate. Most of the unpracticed nobles never even drew their jeweled swords before being dispatched.

In the fray, Tavist had dived to retrieve his sword after dodging a flying axe. But no sooner did he regain his footing when several Laedenorans were upon him, seeking his life. He blocked or dodged blow after blow, but could not find niche enough to attack. He was a good swordsman, perhaps one of the best, but he knew his limits. They were too many and too strong. In a final effort, Tavist dodged another strike and made for the south entrance, where he saw the old Scrivener, Arminus Morlund, also making an escape along with a few others, including the Duchess Lydia of Virk and Jacent, the former King's valet.

Nissa found herself trapped with the last group of nobles to the east of the platform. The sweaty, blood-drenched Laedenorans were closing in, proffering smiles of victory and the carnage to come.

"Stop!" Ember called out to his men, who complied.

Ember pushed through his men and engaged Nissa with questioning eyes.

"You have a choice, dear one," said Ember. "Fealty or death. There are no other options. I can show you a power you have never dared to believe possible. You would rule beside me. A king needs a queen." He held out his hand; blood-colored smoke wafted from a swirling vortex on his palm.

Nissa breathed heavy, staring hard at the vortex, then at Ember. "And if I refuse?"

Ember scowled, red vapor pulsing in his eyes. "Then your foolishness ends here and I mourn the loss of my dear wife for a second time."

Wasting no more time, Nissa drew a dagger from the belt of the man to her left and buried it deep in the lace-frilled chest of the very surprised Chamberlain Nolan Haspeth to her right. The remaining nobles cried out in terror and huddled close to each other. The Chamberlain laid bleeding at her feet, clutching at her dress; the haunted look in his eyes becoming empty. Once he was still, Nissa looked at Ember as a child seeking the approval of an elder.

"Good, good," cooed Ember Driss. He gathered Nissa to him and led her up the platform to the Bekrot Chair, leaving the other nobles to their horrid fates. Steel negotiated flesh and bone.

"My love, even now, hundreds of battle-thirsty Laedenorans make their way from the tower at Ganlis Bay across the countryside, liberating the people of Zannistar from their prior state of stagnation. And to the south, the city of Olix is under siege by sea-faring forces. And now with the fabled Bekrot Chair, we have the power to overthrow the Itinerants in Laedenor. Nissa, my heart warms that you shared this with me. Now, where did they take Charles? The Effacer's Keep? I will speak with them both. The world has forgotten Zannistar for long enough. The Effacer's immediate death should remedy that situation."

They sat together atop the royal platform, surveying the beginnings of a new kingdom. Nissa was alight with excitement. She could not ask for better. All of her diligence and sacrifice bore fruit, though maybe not as she had imagined. Nissa decided that her first official task would be to find and subjugate all those who had slighted her. She would enjoy training them and could not contain her elation. The new Queen turned her blood-speckled face to Ember and smiled.

Having finished most of its meal and once again restrained by a grim-faced Thimgar, the engorged Ersatz horror looked up at the new rulers of Zannistar and cackled in bliss. Nissa realized then that this strange and daring version of Charles seated next to her meant to kill her former husband and claim his soul. Her temperature rose as she imagined them battling one another.

"My Lord," Nissa probed.

"Not to worry, Nissa. My men will tidy up this awful mess."

"Not that, My Lord. It is about Charles Warfield. He may be awkward and meek, but he is no simpleton. I am worried that he may have escaped. That we are talking about him now means that the Effacer has either failed, is dead or is taking his time." Nissa scowled and clenched her teeth. "How I long to rid Zannistar of the name Warfield!"

Ember kept his gaze fixed on the disgusting revelry of the Ersatz horror. "And you shall be. If the Effacer has met his end, then his death breaks the ancient magic he used to hide this land. No longer will people forget Zannistar when they travel away from here. The world will know Zannistar once more!"

Nissa spun her head toward Ember. "I have never been this happy."

"This pleases me," returned Ember.

"My Lord?"

"What is it, Nissa?"

"Forgive me Sire, but what happened to her? The other Nissa. What happened to your wife?"

Ember stared ahead. "Do not trouble yourself, my dear. A Nurdrayl wolf tore her to tatters almost the instant she appeared in the forest. I arrived a few moments later, but because the beast had won its prey, it was not interested in me. She died so I could live."

Nissa found it difficult to hide her surprise. "I see. Tragic. How did you get away?"

"I did not get away."

"Oh?"

"I jumped on the beast. I took its eyes with my hands and I tore out its throat with my own teeth."

Nissa covered her mouth.

Ember leaned closer. "Watching her die changed something in me. I can not explain it. I became someone else that day. Someone better. But that was the past. Let it stay there. Besides, you are here now...the original Nissa; a gift for which I am grateful."

CHAPTER 13

THE THREE ESCAPEES HID THEMSELVES in the brush of the palatial gardens. The late afternoon sun made its way west, casting a golden light on the magnificent landscaping around them. Dara finished coiling the rope, returned it to her shoulder, then attached the hook to her belt.

"We need to reach the Geattor before it closes," said Dara.

"The Geattor?" asked Charles. He decided that his mouth tasted the way a funeral pyre smells. "Never heard of it."

Dara nodded while surveying her surroundings. "Yes, the Geattor is the Laedenoran name for the old obsidian towers that connect the three continents. Centuries ago, there were many. But most fell during the Sixteen Generations War. There are three remaining: one here, one in Laedenor and one in Arom."

Memories of the chilling dream of the tower and his mother flashed in his mind. Charles made a distressed face and shook it off. "Yes, I know of the tower here," he said. "But nobody has ventured into Ganlis Bay since the sea destroyed it. It is a forbidden place—a place of darkness. You should know this, Nissa."

Realizing his gross error, Charles blushed a shade of red reserved for only the most ripened of brierberries. "Your name is Dara. I—I must apologize. Well, you look so much like her. It is difficult to—"

"It is all right," Dara interrupted, trying to conceal the sting. "I possess all of Nissa's memories up to the point when the two of you used the chair to embark on your wedding sabbatical; including the memory of having her name." Dara took a deep breath. "I also remember that your parents perished that night at Ganlis Bay. Though you suffer, we must still reach the tower if we hope to survive the night."

Charles showed his confusion. "Excuse me Dara, but what is a Bekrot Chair?"

Veldic huffed. "The chair created Dara when you and Nissa used the chair to teleport. She is Dreka—borne of gearwood magic; doomed to a soulless existence."

Becoming uncomfortable with the conversation and eager to get on with business, Dara interjected. "As far as my own memories," she said. "We had used the chair to embark on our wedding sabbatical. But instead of traveling to the Gardens of Grynn in the Lurin Heights as planned, we arrived wearing only our nakedness, stranded in a strange and frozen wilderness. We did not realize, until much later, that we were copies of you and Nissa. Our lives became different from yours. The first hoarfrost was almost unbearable."

Dara stretched her arms and peeled through vegetation, hoping to reveal a path of escape.

Charles started after her and Veldic followed. "Copies?" He asked. "Dreka? And you said we. Is there a copy of me?"

"Enough questions!" Dara whispered as she motioned for her two companions to stay low. "Stay quiet, a sentry approaches."

Veldic did her best to make herself appear small; a considerable accomplishment. After a few moments, Charles could hear the footfall of someone walking on twigs. Dara reached into the quiver on her back with both hands—where several wooden crossbow bolts lived—and freed two of them; one in each hand. Charles could not help but notice she did not carry a crossbow, just bolts. The fact struck him as a curiosity because, even though Charles never once met him, Nissa's father was a well-known crossbow maker. That would mean Dara, this intriguing copy of his Nissa, was also the daughter of the same man; in a manner of speaking.

Like a determined predator, Dara tensed as the footsteps drew closer. Just when the sounds stopped, Dara lunged from the bushes and struck with great precision. Charles heard nothing except the thud of a body hitting the ground. After a moment, Dara poked her head back through the bushes and beckoned them out.

Charles complied to find that Dara had overpowered one of the Grand Marshal's sentries and was now removing his clothing and chain armor.

"Help me, Charles," Dara demanded.

"You murdered yet another innocent man," Charles noted with disapproval at the sight of the guardsman on the ground. "I know this man's family. His uncle is one of Nissa's favorite merchants. Sells fabric as I recall. He has been in my home. This is madness! What horror has found me?"

"I did not kill him, Charles," said Dara. "Disabled? Yes. Dead? No. Learn the difference."

Veldic shook her leather-capped head; her many earrings jangling like wind chimes. "I told you he was an imbecile, Dara. Why are we even wasting our time? He has no sense to speak of. Let us recover the coin from his belly and rid ourselves of him!"

Veldic made cutting gestures across her own mid-section with her hand.

Charles gave an open-mouthed look of outrage.

"Veldic," Dara warned, "You will do no such thing and you will keep your insubordinate thoughts to yourself! You know the coin is useless without Charles." Dara turned and glared at Charles. "And Charles, maybe you should wear something more appropriate for travel than that burlap sack, yes? Besides, he is about your height and you were the one whining about a change of clothes only minutes ago."

Both Charles and Veldic stood in silent indignation.

"Am I cursed to set out for Laedenor with two obstinate children in tow?" Dara asked. She gave a sigh of displeasure.

Charles felt wounded and foolish. Dara's belittling tone reminded Charles of Nissa. In a remote but shameful way, he felt comfort in it. "No," he replied and rushed to help Dara disrobe the fallen guard.

"Veldic, take the watch," Dara ordered.

"As you like," Veldic answered. She turned away, knelt down, planted the blunt end of her halberd into the soil and seethed.

CHAPTER 14

IN THE EFFACER'S PRIVATE CHAMBER, the Grand Marshal Atherton Kel woke from his slumber, roused by the repeating sound of his own name and the pungent smell of fermented herbs. The back of his head was aflame with pain; his vision reduced to the blurry operation of a single eye, but he was alive. He pushed himself up on his fists and tried to stand.

"Grand Marshal, you must not get up too fast," advised Templeton Kaid, the Court Healer, while trying to slather a generous amount of mending paste to the Grand Marshal's appreciable head-wound. "You have injuries, My Lord, and you have already lost a great deal of blood."

"My eye," Atherton complained through a groggy haze. "It no longer sees."

Templeton steadied the man and helped him up. "Yes, My Lord, this is sometimes the case with this injury. Your vision should return in a few days."

Atherton shook off the younger man with a grunt.

Templeton clasped his hands together, bowed and moved backward, his flowing green robes retreating with him.

"Where is he?" Atherton asked, pointing to the stone slab. "Others aided him. They struck me from behind. Where is Guardsman Buc—" Atherton turned around to find Guardsman Buckles body heaped against the wall. He was so young—so still.

Atherton felt rage brewing in his gut at a rate that threatened to consume the remains of his humanity. Shaking, he knelt before the young soldier and traced the edges of his mortal wound with his gauntleted finger, fighting back the waves of regret that spilled over him.

"Guardsman Buckles is no longer with us, Grand Marshal. He has taken the final path." The voice came from the darkened shadows across the room. It sounded to Atherton like Charles' voice. Spying his sword on the ground, Atherton picked it up and lunged in the direction of the voice with ferocious intent. However, the aged warrior found himself bound as if by a twine around his waist, unable to move further. Struggling only made it tighter.

"Pity," Ember Driss continued as he stepped from shadow and into Atherton's line of sight. Ember held his palm outward and red smoke spewed from its center in large cords that coiled around the Grand Marshal. "I remember Graham Buckles well. He was an adolescent when I last saw him." He regarded the corpse. "Who could have known this is how we would become reacquainted? No matter." Ember approached Atherton, open hand in front of him.

Atherton took a demanding tone. "Release me, from this foul magic at once!"

Ember looked at his hand. "Oh, this? There is nothing foul about this, Grand Marshal, I assure you. This is a blessing from the Holy Sojourner himself, and only the smallest display of the favor he has shown me, which—I might add—has bested the kingdom's most skilled and trusted warrior as if he were an afterthought. Is that what you are, sir—an afterthought?"

Atherton struggled and the veins in his head bulged; blood flowed from his scalp again.

"My Lord," said Templeton Kaid. "Things are different now. You need to understand, the King is dead, as are most of the Primary nobility. And I know this man has the look of Charles Warfield, but he is not." Templeton moved closer to Atherton and gestured toward Ember. "He calls himself Ember Driss, and he has laid claim to the throne. he has sacked the palace and his men move to occupy the Southern Province as we speak. My Lord, Zannistar has fallen."

Atherton shook his head in violent protest. "Lies!"

Ember lifted his free hand to silence Templeton from continuing. "It is true, Atherton," said Ember. "Zannistar is on the verge of something wonderful. No longer will the people of this land fester in decadence and self-indulgence while the rest of the world struggles just to feed itself. I am the instrument of judgment which has come upon you as retribution for five hundred years of crime against the Sublime Sojourner, to whom you owe your existence. However, some of you have a rare chance at redemption."

Ember leveled his unsettling gaze at Atherton. "It is why I have spared you, that you might blaze the Sojourner's Path and prove yourself worthy of restoration."

Atherton resisted his bonds again as was his nature. But he soon surrendered as thoughts of the young Buckles invaded his mind. With as much pride as he could conjure, Atherton lifted his scowling face to Ember.

"Sparing me is not enough!" Atherton bared his teeth; sweat and blood streaming down his face. "I can suffer many things. I can suffer the winds of war, and the changes that follow. I can suffer the humiliation of not being able to protect the King. I can even suffer the loss of my virility. But, even in my most merciful imaginations, I cannot even conceive to suffer a world that favors a worthless caitiff like Charles Warfield over such a just and promising young soldier as you now see hewn and lifeless before you!" With his head, Atherton motioned toward the corpse in the corner. "I thirst for justice!"

Ember smiled, narrowing his eyes to satisfied slits. "I see. You need a purpose. This I understand. Well, what is it you would propose then?"

"I only hope to see Charles Warfield—thief, murderer, and bane of all that this kingdom once stood for—held to account for his crimes. If you can assure it, then I will accept your terms. But understand, I carry little concern for religious nonsense or ancient legends promising salvation. I trust only in the cold, enduring justice of the Anvil."

"So you say," said Ember. "But I have high hopes for you, Atherton. The Sojourner's Path is set before you. Will you take it?"

"I will take whatever path leads to Charles Warfield."

"Then we have an arrangement," said Ember as he released Atherton from his bonds. The crimson vapor gathered in a large, turning swirl above and behind Ember. "See there? We are more alike than you think."

"What of my men?" Asked Atherton, regarding the magic smoke. "Do any yet live?"

Templeton Kaid stepped forward, wringing his hands. "My Lord, your men took up arms and fought well, but the ferocity of the Laedenoran forces overwhelmed them. None survived, you see." The surgeon's eyes darted back and forth between Atherton and Ember, trying to detect any signs of anger.

Atherton stared at Templeton, unsure of how to respond. He then realized the reality he now faced; a lifetime spent preparing for just such an event made no difference. Even as he lay unconscious in the Effacer's chambers, the kingdom fell to the hands of warriors better prepared than his. His heart sank into dread at the thought of his entire military force lying butchered; each one a testament to his failure as a leader. He was questioning if his life had any meaning at all.

Sensing he was about to lose Atherton to despair, Ember softened before interjecting. "I have taken much from you today, sir. And I have done so without consideration or respect for your loss. I am afraid the forging of destiny compels me. But today, I shall also impart to you much, for you are to be the champion of my cause. Kneel and receive the Sojourner's gift."

Atherton huffed and pointed a battle-hardened finger at Ember. "I will travel in your treacherous name but I will not kneel as long as you wear his face! It is all I can do to not rip it from your skull!" Atherton's bravado was genuine.

"Very well," Ember cooed, enjoying the warrior's outburst.

Sensing the menace in the air increase, Templeton backed to a safe distance behind Ember. Although he could not see Ember's face change, he saw a look of sheer horror in Atherton's eyes that told the story. Atherton swallowed hard and fell to his knees, unable to look away from whatever unspeakable visage stared back at him.

"Are you ready, my champion?" asked Ember; his voice being everywhere at once.

"Yes, yes," replied Atherton. "Lost! All is lost! Do as you wish!"

The red smoke and vapor moved forward and surged into Atherton's damaged eye. Atherton reeled in pain as the indwelling magic exacted its toll. After several terrifying moments, Atherton slumped over, with his hand covering his eye; some vermilion wisps escaping through his fingers.

Templeton stared at Ember's back, unwilling to investigate.

"Do you wish to see what fate the Sacred Sojourner reserved for you Templeton?" Asked Ember, as if he knew Templeton's thoughts.

Templeton rocked his head. "No—no I do not, My Lord. I never want to see. Never."

Ember chuckled from every corner in the room. "Pray to the Sojourner you do not."

Templeton took a step back and swallowed. Piercing the moment, Atherton stood with explosive resolve, uncovering his eye to reveal a glowing, red vortex in its place. "I see them, My Lord," reported an elated Atherton. "They make their way to the tower at Ganlis Bay; but for what purpose?"

Attention diverted, Ember nodded in approval. "They intend to use the Geattor before it closes, to travel to Laedenor," explained Ember. "You must stop them and bring Charles back—living. The final disposition of any others with him is at your discretion. But, you must not allow them to reach the top of the tower."

Atherton's bewitched eye surged a deep red and vaporous lines of crimson escaped the pores of his face. "I will have his blood!" His teeth vibrated in his skull, creating a low humming sound.

"His death is mine," answered Ember. "And I will not suffer any disobedience toward that eventuality."

Atherton considered the terms, being aware that he was no longer himself. There was something else—someone else perhaps —giving weight to his decisions; persuading, encouraging and fighting for control.

"Now, I trust you know your way to Ganlis Bay?" Ember motioned toward the window.

"I have no rope," Atherton complained.

"You do not need it," returned Ember. "Use your gift."

Atherton looked at the window, then at Ember, who nodded with encouragement.

"Very well," Atherton spoke through his vibrating teeth before vaulting through the window down into the garden, unharmed.

CHAPTER 15

DARA, CHARLES AND VELDIC MADE THEIR WAY
northwest, down the steep, overgrown hillside toward the mists of
Ganlis Bay where the Geattor loomed above, as if guarding the
ghosts of the city's long-dead citizens. By sight, it was at least
twenty furlongs from the palace to the city and most of the narrow,
seldom-used path comprising tedious switchbacks obscured by
time and neglect. Yet it was clear, by the many footprints going the
opposite direction, they were not the only recent travelers on this
slope.

"We must be mindful of Ember's men," Dara warned. "There
may still be stragglers on this path, heading up the hill toward the
palace."

"I hope there are," answered Veldic, thrusting her halberd
upward.

Charles was not accustomed to the cumbersome armor of the
Zanni August Guard. After several near misses, he tripped on an

unearthed root and stumbled forward but regained his footing. Veldic snorted with disapproval and Charles silently agreed.

"I thought you said this path was abandoned, Dara," said Charles. "Now you say they could assault us?"

"I will not allow any harm to come to you, Charles," Dara said. "You are too important."

"Yes, so people keep saying," said Charles. Reminded of the oubliette, he hobbled closer to Dara. "Who was it that spoke in the King's oubliette and gave me the coin? Was he real?"

Dara did not slow her pace. "Yes, Charles, he was real."

"How so? The place was empty. Who is he then?"

"Difficult to explain."

"Well then, try."

Dara sighed. "He is a friend which is everything you need to know, Charles. The rest will be clear in time. Now, just keep on the lookout for—"

"Excuse me please," interrupted Charles, causing Dara to stop and turn. "But since this nightmare began, my people have beaten, mocked, accused and imprisoned me. I have lost my status, my good name and my wife; not to mention you look just like her! And to top it off, it seems I am not me! Please tell me what is going on!"

Veldic shook her head, causing her earrings to clank. She leveled her halberd at Charles. "You complain too much. Dara has saved you from a terrible fate. Where is your gratitude? We are trying to help you."

Charles caught his reflection in the outstretched blade and shrank back. "Nobody can help me. Besides, I am not sure I want your variety of help."

Veldic puffed up, revealing the power in her frame. "Idiot!"

"Veldic!" Dara snapped as she resumed her walking. "Lower your weapon."

"Forgive me Dara," Veldic said. "But this will never work. He may look like Cenric, but he is nothing like him. He is weak and woeful! The people will never accept him. Look! He stumbles over himself like an infant. How can we trust him to lead an army?"

Veldic pushed the wooden end of her polearm into Charles' back, causing him to lunge forward and fall on his face. Peat and mud filled Charles' mouth.

With dizzying speed, Dara drew a bolt, sprung a backflip and landed on Veldic's back. She gripped the warrior's sides with her legs, pulled her head to one side by her earrings and pressed the head of the bolt against her stretched and exposed neck. A small bit of blood trickled down her collarbone.

Dara put her lips to Veldic's ear. "Would you care to be the first Aromite to bleed out on Zanni soil in five-hundred years?"

"Dara, I—"

"No, Veldic," said Dara. "He is the only chance we have. His life is more valuable than any other in existence, including yours, including mine. Do not abuse him again, do you understand Veldic?"

Chastened, Veldic relaxed her powerful muscles and softened her expression.

"Yes, as you like Dara. I am sorry."

Dara released her and returned the bolt to its quiver. "Let us tend to our task. Daylight is fading."

As she passed Charles to once again take the lead, she placed a tender hand on his shoulder. He was wiping dirt from his armor, still dumbfounded and awed by what he had just witnessed.

Veldic called from behind. "I still miss him, Dara."

Dara stopped but did not look back. "As do we all, Veldic; none more than I. But he is dead—assigned to the Neverwall. If you want to honor his memory, then protect Charles with your life. You will have many chances ahead. But Veldic, listen well. If you harm him again—friend or not, trusted companion or not—I will kill you."

Veldic hung her head. "As you like, Dara,"

Spent and in the grip of reflective silence, the three continued down the hillside, into the mist.

CHAPTER 16

TAVIST UPLAND HELD TO THE COACHMAN'S BENCH as the battle-damaged carriage hurtled south. Tavist had sought adventures on this road many times before, but never at such haste. Speeding toward an unknown future, Tavist felt the pain of what he had lost. He had been a promising member of the Zanni August Guard. Now, he was just a fleeing fugitive. All that suffering and sacrifice for nothing.

They approached his favorite spot of forest and memories of childhood flooded his mind of mock battles with wooden swords against trees he imagined were bent on destroying the palace. Even after he became part of the August Guard, he often returned to practice on these trees. Some still bore the marks from his sword. Now the trees seemed to judge him for failing Zannistar.

On the bench next to Tavist, the Duchess Lydia Mirette of Virk urged the four steeds to go faster with leather reigns and shrill wails; a clamor that brought Tavist out of his reverie.

"We are safe now!" yelled Tavist, competing with the sound of hooves and wheels. "We need to rest the horses and regroup."

Checking the sun's position in the afternoon sky, the Duchess Lydia considered Tavist's proposal then slowed the carriage to a stop with practiced efficiency. Tavist found the sight odd and unsettling. He wondered how a refined courtier was so adept at the work of a Tertiary noble, no less the coachman's craft.

Yet, Tavist felt grateful for her skill. Not long after their flight from the palace, a group of Laedenoran warriors had ambushed them as they attempted to board the carriage in the palace courtyard. They killed all of Lydia's attendants during the attack, including the coachman.

The situation degenerated, despite Tavist's martial skill. But, in the final moments, Lord Jacent Ferris engaged the barbarians and, at his command, bought the survivors enough time to escape. For this, he died. It would seem that the King chose Jacent for more than just his superior attentiveness. He had been an accomplished, honorable swordsman as well; a rarity among courtiers.

The only other survivor was the old Scrivener, Arminius Morlund. A Laedenoran spear had pierced him after he boarded the carriage. He was near death, clutching the Book of Nom and bleeding on plushy, gilded cushions. Duchess Lydia jumped from the bench, lifted her dress to avoid tripping, and rushed to open the side door, discovering Arminius to be lethargic and pale.

"Arminius!" cried Lydia. "You must stay awake! There are healers close by." Her voice was smoky; authoritative.

Arminius opened his eyes and smiled at Lydia. "My dear, I am beyond healing."

"No, you will not give in. There is still time!"

"Death approaches regardless, waiting just beyond the trees. I can sense his growing anticipation. It is how it must be. Lydia, I need to speak with Tavist. Quick, my dear."

Lydia had grown fond of Arminius over the years she had spent at court. She regarded him as her own grandfather. He always put her at ease when she was feeling homesick. He had also introduced her to the joys of storytelling over evening tea. Most of all, Lydia found his spirit humble and true; qualities deficient among most of the other courtiers. And she had to admit, his company was the only place she felt like herself. Blood relation or not, she cared for him and the thought of his passing was tearing her heart in two.

"Tavist!" Lydia called. "The Scrivener wishes to speak with you, now!"

Tavist rushed to Arminius, noticing the large stream of blood flowing from the old man's side, dripping out of the coach onto the dirt road. The young soldier's mood sobered.

"Yes," Tavist said placing a ginger hand on his shoulder. "I am here."

Arminius gazed at Lydia. "I need to speak to him alone, dear one."

Lydia did not mask her hurt feelings, but kissed Arminius on the forehead and cradled his face in her hands.

"Goodbye Arminius," Lydia said. She was shaking. "A hundred Effacers could not cause me to forget you. I will not."

The Scrivener only nodded with smiling eyes. It was enough. Lydia, turned and wandered ahead of the horses to cry in private.

"Young Tavist, I have tasks for you to complete," said Arminius with a weakening voice.

"Name it and I shall do it. I swear it!" Tavist's tone was desperate and dramatic.

"Do not be so quick to pledge. This is not a game you would play without cost."

Arminius' gaze was piercing, even in these final moments.

Humbled, Tavist hung his head. "I am sorry. Please continue."

Arminius patted Tavist's shoulder. "Good. Now, you must take this," Arminius offered Tavist a medium-sized, blood-stained book with a small, gold chain affixed to its spine. It was thin, perhaps fifty pages. "No matter where your life leads, you must never lose control of this book. To do so is to invite destruction."

Tavist hesitated then took the book. It was light. He knew it by sight as the Book of Nom. And as he regarded its plain, brown leather cover and binding, he could not recall a time seeing Arminius without it.

"It is the Book of Nom," Tavist said. "It contains the names of every family in the history of Zannistar. I realize it was important to the court but what possible value could it be to anyone now? Losing this book will not bring about destruction because Zannistar has already fallen! They have slaughtered most of these families! It is useless."

Becoming discouraged at the thought of not following through with his promise, Tavist attempted to give the book back to Arminius who shook his head in refusal.

"No, lad. You must take it. In moments, I will have escaped this world, but the book's power remains behind unprotected."

"Power. What power?" With a cavalier demeanor, Tavist opened the book and thumbed through its heraldic pages. He recognized a few names and their corresponding sigils. "There is no power here, Scrivener. Only the names of the dead."

Arminius placed his pale hand on the open book and gave Tavist a searching length of eye-contact, sizing up his trustworthiness.

"First close it," whispered Arminius. "Then flip the book upside down, toward you." He waited for Tavist to comply before continuing. "Now, rotate the book left, one-half turn. The spine is now on your right. Yes, that's it. Now, open it."

Tavist opened the back cover, expecting to see the unremarkable, last page of an old book. Instead, Tavist saw an illuminated title page to a different book—a hidden book within a book. The title intrigued Tavist.

"Bóctalu," said Tavist. The purple calligraphy shifted, as if alive, shimmering with a mesmerizing, star-like glamour. Around the title's perimeter, lay a border of woven wildflowers of every kind and hue—swaying as if blown by a gentle and intermittent wind. The air around the book seemed to become welcoming and warm.

"That, young Tavist, is a different book; a special book of names that must remain a secret. And it is now your task to safeguard its contents from unprepared eyes."

"These secrets are worth something, then?"

"The names of all in existence; even beyond this place."

Without looking, Arminius sifted through several pages, then pressed a finger on what was his own name, about halfway down the middle of the page. He showed it to Tavist.

Tavist could tell that the letters were fading, as were the many scenes of a studious life, each floating around the Scrivener's name like lazy fireflies. The smell of spiced tea leaves and parchment permeated the air. Tavist sensed a nurturing warmth, trust and truth. This was ancient magic, and it made Tavist nervous to be in its presence.

"This is sorcery! Your confidence in me is ill-placed. What am I to do with it? I am no Scrivener! I am a military officer—a guardsman. I know nothing of magic books or secrets!" An honest assessment.

Arminius waved off Tavist's protests. "You must take it beyond our borders, across the sea, to the land of Arom."

"Arom is a wasteland. There is nothing there. Only scars of war and anarchy. What good will it do there?"

"Listen, lad. The three continental Geattors have closed for another hundred years. You must make your way to Port Frailty, a city in the land of Arom by sea. There you will seek Charles Warfield. He cannot reach the Northlands without an Expanser which is why he will go to Port Frailty. There are few remaining Expansers and they all live there."

Tavist's eyes widened, and he rocked his head in protest.

"You must," Arminius whispered. "After your reunion, you will find and hire an Expanser, who will see you to the Islet of Abeodan within the Neverwall. You will then seek the Pit of Nihthelm where you will read aloud from the book. Doing so will make Charles aware of his true purpose. Then you will travel to Laedenor together."

Tavist reeled under the strain of so much information. "Madness! Charles Warfield, the traitor? I do not believe it! And you have been to Arom? I have heard of no Zanni citizens, other than banished criminals and foolish explorers, who have crossed the sea. None of them returned! Anyone who leaves forgets Zannistar exists!"

"Yes. And I have been there. I remember it."

"But why have you never spoken of your travels before?"

"Because, Gyldred stripped many of my memories. But they came back, lad. They came back!" a joyful smile spread across Arminius' face, cut short by a realization. "But that can only mean one thing."

Tavist leaned in. "What does it mean?"

"It means that Gyldred is dead. Charles must have defeated him." There was a hopeful tone in his words.

Tavist gave a puzzling look. "Charles Warfield could defeat no one much less a sorcerer like Gyldred. He is a buffoon. It is not possible."

Arminius smiled. "And yet it must have happened. Effacers destroy the memories they consume which remain gone even after the sorcerer's death. However, this is not the case for we Scriveners. Our memories are special, you see. An Effacer can not eat them. They can only hide them for a while." Arminius chuckled, coughing up a small bit of blood before continuing.

"Forgive me, but did you say Effacers consume memories?"

"Yes. The act prolongs an Effacer's life. But, once an Effacer meets their end, so does their wicked sorcery yield to a Scrivener's blessing of remembrance. And I remember many things, Tavist! Many things!"

The schoolmasters had always taught Tavist that Gyldred was a hero and the savior of Zannistar. If he had not hidden Zannistar, war would have obliterated everything in the kingdom. It seemed ludicrous that Gyldred would pilfer memories from the Scrivener without good reason. Tavist contemplated the possibilities.

"The book!" Tavist exclaimed. "By the Anvil of Ages! You remembered the secret of the book!"

"Yes, Tavist," replied Arminius. "I did at that. Just moments ago."

"Tell me! What other secrets have returned?"

"There is no time for stories. I am near death and it is you who must finish it here and now with your sword. Please." Arminius' eyes pleaded with Tavist.

It took a moment for Tavist to realize the weight of the Scrivener's dark request. "No! I will not!" Tavist attempted to retreat from the carriage but Arminius held him fast by the shoulders. Tavist flinched at the old man's strength.

"You must. They have spilled my blood. It will draw our enemy here. I must not be living when he arrives."

"Who is this enemy?" Tavist asked with a tinge of skeptical anger.

"Do it, lad. Before Lydia returns and stops you. It must be you! It cannot be him! Hurry!"

Arminius grabbed Tavist's hand and placed it on the pommel of his sword.

Though Tavist's rational mind protested against such a request, his heart told otherwise.

Arminius stared into Tavist's eyes. "Protect the book. I have always meant it for you. Keep it chained about your waist at all times. Remember, find Charles and get to the Islet of Abeodan. Take heart, Charles is no traitor. He is a king whose time approaches. Farewell, young Tavist. This task you must not fail."

Stricken by the absurdity of it all, Tavist resolved that it must be true. "I promise, I will do it." His vow sounded brave. However, inside he faltered under fear and doubt. He pushed them deep into the depths of his being.

Without another word, Tavist nodded, drew his sword and buried it deep in the Scrivener's heart, whose passing was silent and quick. Tavist had never imagined that his first lethal strike would be that of an honorable, mercy-killing. He perceived his innocence escape; like a house-guest no longer welcome. But he also welcomed peace. The old Scrivener wanted this.

Tavist sheathed his blade and arranged the Scrivener's body in a seated position in the corner. He regarded the corpse, then shut the door and made ready the horses and carriage.

After Lydia returned from her time alone, she peeked through the carriage window and verified the reality of her fears. She boarded the carriage and took the reigns next to Tavist, who had been waiting for her with Arminius' book on his lap. Speaking nothing, she snapped the reigns and the horses burst into a modest gallop.

As they moved away, the book grew cold, almost freezing Tavist's legs. Without thinking, he flipped the book and turned it, just as the Scrivener had shown him, and then opened it to a page about halfway through. He gasped.

The right page was blank. However, the left page undulated a reddish smoke that spewed unspeakable images of foulness and despair. In the maelstrom's center, hovered a single word; a word constructed of what Tavist somehow understood to be the substance of stolen innocence and dashed hopes. The sight of this word assaulted him and brought on thick waves of nausea. Even though he could not explain it, Tavist despised the word more than anything in the world and it also despised him.

Tavist slammed the book shut and placed it under his feet. He looked back. In the distance, standing in the puddle of the Scrivener's spilled blood, was a figure hidden under robe and hood.

It knelt down in the blood. A long tongue emerged from the figure's hood and lapped at the crimson fluid. The sight repulsed Tavist.

"Vang," said Tavist aloud, fear tickling his voice. The figure stood.

I promise I will do it! I promise I will do it! I have always hated you, Tavist. Here is my promise: I promise I will find you. And unlike you, I keep my promises. I like it when you fail. It feels wonderful. Make promises, Tavist. It feels good when you fail. So good. Bring the book Tavist.

"I defy you, most foul!" yelled Tavist, to thwart approaching insanity.

Startled, Lydia looked behind her, back down the empty road, and then shot Tavist a look of apprehension. "Who are you talking to, boy?"

Once Tavist realized the figure vanished, he shivered and turned toward the front. "None among the living."

"You are a strange one, Tavist. But keep your musings to yourself. Olix is three day's ride from here and I do not wish to add raving madness to the reasons I have for wanting to kill you."

"I am sure your point eludes me, My Lady."

"Just because I am adept at the lofty details of courtly business," explained Lydia, "does not mean I am blind to the obvious. I still recognize the wound of a merciful sword thrust when I see it."

"He wished it," said Tavist.

"Did he?"

After a long silence, Tavist spoke. "I need to sail to Arom from Olix. Arminius entrusted me his magic book and has placed me on a task to take it to a place called the Islet of Abeodan. I intend to see it to the end. I will need a ship. Can you arrange it, or do you intend to dishonor an old man's last wishes?"

Lydia huffed. She would do anything for Arminius even if it meant helping a brat such as Tavist. "Just like Ganlis Bay, Olix harbor is barren. But unlike Ganlis Bay, my people still live and labor in the city. We even fish the waters close to shore. But we must be very careful. No fisherman can venture more than a league or two beyond the shore before they forget where they started. The border of the concealing magic is close to the shore in the south.

As a result, proper seafaring is a lost art among my people. Most of the merchant ships fell into disrepair generations ago after Gyldred hid Zannistar from the world. There was no more need. You would know this if you ever bothered to travel outside the Northern Province. Still, there might be some old fishing boats around we could borrow."

"I rather like fish," said Tavist.

"It comes from us, as do many other foods and goods you privileged gluttons take for granted. You have forced us to serve the palace for so long that you have forgotten how to care for yourselves. And now that King Lidig has fallen, we may have a chance at freedom, but I fear for the safety of my people. If the current situation is any indicator, this Ember Driss character will invade the Southern Province next."

"My Lady, do you suppose what he said was true? Was he a copy? What did he say—Dreka?"

"Perhaps. One thing is certain—though he bears his countenance, he is not Charles Warfield. We must hasten south and warn my people before it is too late."

Tavist was eager to agree with any course of action that put distance between himself and that hooded figure on the road.

"To Olix, then!" Tavist sounded confident. He was not.

Lydia agreed, and they continued down the road toward the fertile pastures of the Southern Province.

CHAPTER 17

ALTHOUGH THE MIST WAS THICK, Dara decided she had a clear shot at both of the axe-wielding, Northmen standing sentry at the arched entry of the Geattor. The mist had allowed the band to get close enough to hide in and under the miscellany of a forgotten debris field near the tower. It comprised various household items, broken bits of wood from houses and carts. There were even human bones sprinkled throughout. Charles found the scene chilling.

They had been waiting for an opportunity to enter the tower, but large compliments of the invading forces filed out of the entrance, traveling in different directions, singing battle-hymns. Some took the main road south, some up the hill toward the palace. They saw no pattern. Timing would be difficult.

Dara turned and nodded to Charles and Veldic who lay beside her. Veldic nodded back, but Charles was far too preoccupied with the prospect that some of the bones around him could belong to his parents. Dara reached back, freed two bolts from her quiver and held one out, pointing it toward the guard on the left. Without further warning, the bolt catapulted from her gloved hand on its own, finding and tearing through the exposed portion of the guard's neck before striking and chipping the obsidian tower wall behind.

The sound startled the remaining guard, who readied his axe and scanned in all directions, even as his companion fell dead. He stopped when he saw the trail that the bolt had made through the mist, following its path. He took a few, battle-ready steps toward the debris field before another wooden bolt ejected therefrom, striking and destroying the fur-clad warrior's knee, causing him to drop as would a tree at the mercy of a woodsman's tools.

"Meddling spirits!" Dara cursed, not satisfied with her performance. She sprung from under the debris and made her way to the fallen barbarian where she encouraged his passing with yet another of her bolts; this time using it as a dagger. Crouching low, she glanced around her and motioned the other two to come forward, after which she retrieved the other two bolts and returned them to her quiver.

Charles stumbled at the sight. Not only was Dara a formidable and calculating warrior, but she also held sway over some unnatural power; a power that could end life. He realized why a muscled brute like Veldic feared her. Uneasy, Charles turned to the Aromite hoping for an explanation, which he did not get.

"We must go," Veldic said.

Overwhelmed, Charles considered running in the opposite direction, but remembered that he had no life to return to. "Very well," he said. Resigned to continue this course of insanity, he shimmied out from under the tangle of debris.

The three ran through the arched doorway and found themselves on a large, wooden platform in the middle of an even larger circular room. As part of a network of gears on the platform's perimeter, several massive lengths of iron chain ascended along the walls toward the top edge of the tower, which Charles discovered had no ceiling. It was open, revealing the sky at near-dusk. In the platform's center was an iron post and a simple crank handle.

"Brace yourselves," warned Dara, placing her hand on the handle. Veldic complied, widening her stance and crouching. Charles, however, was again too busy to pay attention; marveling at the height of the tower.

At the slightest turn of the crank, the platform shot up with alarming speed. The complex, unpleasant sound of rusted, salt-worn gears and pulleys echoed throughout the cylindrical interior. The thrust pushed Charles downward, forcing him to grasp hold of Veldic's arm in order not to fall. Not wishing another encounter with Dara, Veldic did her best to ignore the stowaway attached to her; a monumental effort that gained her an approving nod from Dara.

Charles never imagined the tower contained such a contraption. No one had been inside. Most considered it a colossal work of art more than anything else; a symbol of Zanni pride and the once prosperous city. Until today, he had assumed there was no way inside.

But now, as they rose toward the top, Charles became anxious. His thoughts moved to the nightmare he suffered whilst in the King's oubliette earlier. The remnant of his mother's cryptic words tickled memory and triggered feelings of loss. He could not have known he would later be in the place he had dreamed of—the old obsidian tower in the heart of Ganlis Bay; the City of Woe. He hated this place. He felt it more than a dream. It was where his parents were when the city fell to a wall of water caused by an unexpected storm out of season.

It swept thousands out to sea. Since that dark day, Zanni citizens kept their distance from the city out of superstition and respect for the dead. It was a place of national tragedy, and the people thought it offensive and irresponsible for a citizen to even consider paying a visit to its littered and mist-shrouded streets.

Dara slowed her turn on the hand-crank as they were near the top. And now that their upward movement had abated, Veldic gave Charles a quiet, consternating look letting him know it was time to let go of her arm, and Charles heeded.

"We are near," said Dara focusing on her task. "Are you all right, Charles?"

Charles opened his mouth to answer, but could not as he stared at the ghastly semblance of the Grand Marshal Atherton Kell, who appeared to have scaled the the outside of the tower under his own power.

Atherton bellowed with otherworldly timbre. "Traitor!"

Veldic, though startled, attacked the intruder with her polearm. Dara also burst into action, abandoning the crank and drawing two bolts on her way to engage Atherton, who seemed to have little problem defending against Veldic. The platform dropped a few feet before the gear system locked in place, giving all a jolt.

"Charles, you cannot escape justice," said Atherton, kicking Veldic in the midsection, launching the Aromite like a frail twig, backward and over the side of the platform. Veldic grasped the edge of the platform, preventing her descent to the bottom of the tower. Her polearm was not as fortunate, however.

Atherton spun around and swung his broadsword at Dara, who ducked and plunged two wooden bolts into the Grand Marshal's ribs. Blood and red vapor spewed forth, but they did not hinder Atherton. Instead, he grasped Dara by the throat with his free hand and lifted her off the ground. She attempted to wrench back and forth on to the buried bolts, but there was no effect.

"And who have we here?" asked Atherton. Vapor from his swirling eye took the shape of a skeletal hand and caressed her cheek. "Ahh, I see you have the likeness of Queen Nissa. Yet, I can see you are the same sort of creature as her husband, the new King —a copy; an empty abomination." He squeezed tighter. "Let us discover together how much that skinny, little neck of yours can take."

Dara attempted to protest but could not find air. Desperate, she raised her hands and commanded all the bolts in her quiver to fly free. They soared high above and paused. At the lowering of her arms, Dara's bolts dove toward Atherton with blurring speed.

They found their mark, piercing her attacker at multiple points. Again, she thrust her arms up and the bolts exited Atherton's body leaving behind spewing vermilion smoke. And again they penetrated the Grand Marshal. But he was unaffected and Dara was losing consciousness. Darkness had almost consumed her when she and Atherton's severed arm dropped to the wooden platform.

"I am the one you seek!" yelled Charles. The sword he held was shaking in his hands. The blade bore blood and wafting red steam.

Atherton turned to Charles and smiled. He seemed unaffected by his loss of limb. "King Ember wishes to see you, traitor. Come with me and I will spare this impostor."

"I will not!" Charles did not recognize his own voice. "What has happened to you? And who is King Ember?"

Atherton laughed and pointed at Charles. Blood was no longer exiting his wounds; only red smoke. The smoke took the rough-form of Atherton and mimicked Charles' movements in the air.

"They have not told you," Atherton said.

During the exchange, Veldic had pulled herself up onto the platform and labored to rise to her feet. She looked at Dara and saw she was coughing but able to hobble to the hand-crank. She turned it with all her might. The platform flew upwards, throwing everyone to their knees. It crashed to a stop at the top of the tower, launching everyone high into the air.

Shaken, but unhurt, they landed on the tower; all except for Atherton whose trajectory was beyond the tower's perimeter—a most untimely fate that found him plummeting down the west side of the tower into the mist. An arc of thinning red vapor showed his path.

"Quick!" yelled Dara in a panic. "We must jump off the tower's north side! The sun is setting!"

"What?" returned Charles, breathing heavy, "Are you mad?"

"Please, Charles. Trust me! If we jump, we go to Laedenor. The Geattor closes at nightfall for another hundred years! We must move now!"

Charles looked at Veldic who nodded in confirmation. But Charles had no time to consider it because several dozen snow-dusted barbarians appeared in a shimmering cloud of cold air at the north end of the tower. They noticed the three fugitives and hurled throwing-axes and spears as they advanced.

"It is too late! More have arrived from Laedenor!" cried Veldic, ducking under a flying spear. "And they are too many, Dara! We cannot go north!"

There came from the west a feral and desperate roar followed by reddened wisps of smoke in the shape of giant claws grasping the edge of the Geattor's west edge. It was Atherton returning.

Dara's eyes widened. "Veldic, it looks as if we will pay a visit to Arom!" She directed Veldic's attention toward Charles. "Please help Charles decide!"

"As you like, Dara!"

Before Charles could protest, Veldic grabbed him around the midsection, hugging him tight. She then sprinted to the south-eastern end of the tower where she jumped over the side. Dara could hear Charles screaming on the way down. With the Laedenoran forces close behind her, Dara ran after her companions, picking up Charles' sword on the way, and leapt over the edge just as the sun set.

Chapter 18

"FINISHED, YOUR MAJESTY," said the dark-haired, dark-eyed Templeton Kaid, removing himself from view.

Queen Nissa scrutinized the court healer's work on the three female servants she had spared from among the Primary nobility. Each servant sat erect, side by side on high-backed chairs in the middle of the King's chamber. They all looked the same: white maiden's bodices with matching powdered-white skin and nails. They each had straight, newly blackened hair, parted in the middle and reaching no further than the bottom of the ear; a condition that—for all of them—was a dramatic departure from their previous, illustrious state of grooming. Nissa stopped in front of each one, caressing the golden thread used to stitch their mouths closed. Blood dripped into the servants' cupped hands, waiting just below the chin, protecting such lovely, white dresses.

"To be my attendants, you must present yourselves with perfection," said Nissa. "I will not tolerate any mediocrity in your performance nor will I grant a clemency for even the smallest mistake." Nissa looked upward and placed a jeweled finger to her chin. "Do you not find it ironic that you were my superiors?" None dared attempt an answer—none, save the King.

"Well, I do," announced Ember, emerging from behind a changing screen in a silken, ebony doublet with paned sleeves of red and white, fitted over red trousers tucked in to polished, white knee-boots. He sported gloves of fine, red leather, and his hair fell, unrestrained over his shoulders to his waist. Nissa regarded him with pride and no small amount of desire. She longed for the evening to end in the quelling of her anticipation.

"Your Majesty exudes the essence of high kingship," said Nissa, bowing her head.

"Nissa, you flatter me," returned Ember. "It is a welcome treat to, once again, feel the caress of proper Zanni livery against my skin. I could never quite overcome the nagging discomfort of Laedenoran linens and furs. Such rustic folk, the Laedenorans. Still, in some ways, their simple society surpasses even that of the great Anvil of Ages."

Nissa nodded but kept her clear blue eyes fettered to his. "Will His Majesty be dining with the Queen this evening?"

"No," answered Ember, breaking gaze. "Kingdom business is pressing. There are petitioners we must receive and fates to decide. There are droves of Secondary nobility waiting to swear their allegiance and vie for a chance to fill empty positions at court. That is the smallest of our concerns. Thimgar reports that your former husband has eluded Atherton Kel and further traveled to Arom through the Geattor—an unfortunate circumstance that causes a change in plan. Beyond that, the next several days will find me steeped in something much larger than what you witnessed here today. My Darling Nissa, while it pains me to announce it, there will be time enough for proper reunions when we have assured our rule."

The thought of ruling over Zannistar gave her an enjoyable start. Despite this, Nissa did not weather Ember's rejection well, yet she proffered the expected response. "I shall count the hours as an agony, Your Majesty."

"Indeed you shall, yes," said the King as he, himself, inspected the three attendants in their chairs. He stopped in front of the middle servant and gave her a quizzical look.

"Does something displease His Majesty?" asked Nissa.

"No, no," replied Ember. "But, I am curious. Could this be Lavendra Norell—your childhood friend?" He looked harder. "I believe she is! Bless the Sojourner, it would seem that you have accomplished the impossible feat of making this woman even lovelier than before." Fear washed over the seated servant; her eyes becoming averted and wet as Nissa seethed.

Regaining her composure, Nissa turned to the King who made his way toward the bedchamber door. "Your Majesty, if I may ask; Who is this Sojourner you mention with such a reverence?"

Ember stopped his escape, looking ponderous. "Ah, forgive me. I seem to persist in forgetting that this kingdom has existed in isolation and spiritual darkness for the last five hundred years." Ember straightened his posture and gestured all around him. "The Sojourner, my Dear Nissa, is the reason we are all here."

Nissa regarded him with confusion.

"I will explain all in time," Ember announced. "You should know I expect you to appear at court tonight. Oh yes, bring your new attendants if you would like." With an admonishing look, he exited the chamber and disappeared down the hall.

Nissa boiled like a pot over a fire. Yet the ease with which Ember dismissed her also drew her to him. The ever-weak and trivial Charles would have jumped at the chance to experience a small crumb of the exclusivity she offered Ember. She could not imagine how they began as the same person.

Nissa screamed and clawed at the golden stitches binding Lavendra's mouth, ripping them out, causing ghastly and disfiguring wounds. Droplets of blood landed on the others. Nissa sneered at Lavendra and spoke as one to a disease. "You were never worthy, Lavendra! Never!"

Lavendra sobbed but dared not move her cupped hands to cover exposed teeth in her mouth.

"Templeton!" yelled Nissa. "Please see that this homely waif finds her way to the oubliette!"

"Yes, My Queen!" He answered, wringing his hands and rushing to the task.

"And as for you," Nissa said to the remaining servants, as a child to her dolls, "We cannot attend court with blood on our new dresses now can we? Now, I wonder what other delights hide in the palace wardrobes."

The floors of the palace were still littered with the morbid signs of battle. Ember gave only a passing attention to it, his eyes focused forward and legs moving at a brisk pace. His men were busy looting rooms, gathering together those few nobles who yet survived and disposing of those who did not. As he passed, all stood still, heads down and placing their right, open hand high, above their heads with palms skyward and the other hand on their hearts. Finally, he arrived at his destination: the kitchens.

He bolted through the door and startled Thimgar, who had the remnants of a brierberry cobbler on his face. His expression was one of surprise as he had never seen Ember wearing such fine clothes. Thimgar collected himself and gave the proper salute.

"Where is he?" asked Ember, stepping over a slain cook. "I must see him at once!"

"This way, Your Majesty" said Thimgar.

"You do not have to say that, Thimgar."

"I like how it sounds." Thimgar lead Ember through another set of doors into the bakery.

Ember stopped and placed his hand on Thimgar's shoulder. "I am still one of you, my friend."

Lying on its side on the stone floor, next to a large, brick oven, was the obese Ersatz horror, gnawing on the leg-bone of some unfortunate victim of the coup. They chained the creature to a rung on an overhead beam used to keep bags of flour off the floor and away from insects. The beast seemed oblivious. Ember studied it as it worked at the bone in futility with its few, flattened teeth, seeking to release the marrow within. Being a copy himself, Ember appreciated its resemblance to Lidig, despite its many, grotesque deformities.

Ember turned to Thimgar. "Leave us, Thimgar."

Thimgar grunted. He grabbed a loaf of sweetbread on the way out.

"That is the Thimgar I know," said Ember. He waited until he was sure he was alone before turning around to face the creature.

"I beg your forgiveness," said Ember. "Though my forces have driven much of the Northern Province to its knees, I have failed to capture Charles. He has escaped to Arom, and the Geattor has closed."

The creature stopped its feast, fixing its eyeless gaze on Ember. It shivered and quaked for a moment before calming. Something red pulsed deep in those eyeless pits and wisps of vapor escaped them. The Ersatz horror propped itself up on its hands—one of which still clutched the leg-bone—and dragged itself toward Ember, being stopped by the chain just in front of him. It looked up at Ember and smiled. Even Ember, the ruthless Beast of Sable Rock, found the creature's unnatural glee unsettling.

Its voice was low and grating, like rocks against rocks. "I forgive you, Ember. Who loves you more than I?"

Ember looked to the ground. "There are none, Vang."

"Am I not the Sojourner's Prophet, who has shown you the truth of your past—how they stole your life and destiny from you —how Lidig Branlin and the Effacer betrayed you all?"

"Yes, Vang."

"Then have faith, our time is near. Now you have the Bekrot Chair, and you must devote all of your energies to creating Ersatz. Once the horde is complete, we will descend on the Itinerants in the north and capture the Sojournic Stronghold. But we waste no time. Soon, the Sacred Sojourner will have completed his ancient journey to Stag's End. We—not the Itinerants—must receive him into this world."

Ember lifted his eyes. "These copies of me. Will you be able to control them?"

The creature swallowed a mouthful of sinew. "Yes, yes. When Dreka use the Bekrot Chair, all the copies are Ersatz like this body I am using now. Every last one is an empty cistern waiting for water. I am that water, sent by the Holy Sojourner himself."

Ember stared at his hands "And what of the soulmade Charles Warfield? He has already dispatched Gyldred and all of his acolytes, not to mention the Grand Marshal. As we speak, Charles forges ahead to Laedenor. If he should pass the Neverwall and on to the Sojournic Stronghold, they will accept him as their new leader and the bulwarks will be impassable. Since his predecessor's death, the Itinerants flutter with no direction. But, once they discover that the true, soulmade Charles Warfield lives, they will rally to him and we shall lose our advantage."

The creature changed his smile to a hateful frown. "Do not concern yourself with Charles Warfield. He will not last long in Arom. He is pathetic and useless; a frightened coward who runs from his own shadow."

There was genuine vitriol in the beast's tone and Ember could not help feel as though it was referring to him.

But the creature reassured him. "He is nothing like you, Dear Ember. It is you, not him, who deserves to rule." The beast smiled again, revealing rotting gums and a few remaining teeth.

It agitated Ember. "But, Vang, I yearn to own his eternal purpose. If he dies in Arom, his spirit will move on beyond my grasp and my life will have been meaningless. Tell me Vang, without his soul, should I be content to rule *his* subjects, survey *his* lands and bed *his* wife? Should the memories of a king—my memories—and all I will accomplish here in this place, go to the cold, deepening dark of the Neverwall while he leaves this world to join the Sojourner? I must have his soul!" Ember breathed hard and tightened his fists, causing red smoke to billow out from inside his gloves. Swirls of pulsing, crimson light appeared under the skin on his face and neck.

The Ersatz horror snarled. "Quiet! Your childish whining is ruining my meal! You only need do as I say. Once we secure the Sojournic Stronghold, the Sojourner will be pleased and will grant you a soul. And why is it you lust after another man's purpose when it is so feeble? Are you not a unique person? You deserve a soul of your own! A strong and brave soul. The soul of a true king. And you shall have it if you do not fail the Sojourner."

Ember conceded with his eyes, his agitation subsiding. "I will begin the preparations." Ember turned to leave.

"Wait. There is another matter that needs attention."

Ember felt his patience wane. "Anything for the Sacred Sojourner's Prophet."

"The familiar blood of an old acquaintance called from the forest. It led me to something very important; something hidden. It is a book, carried southward by an idiot named Tavist. He is bound to it."

Ember turned to the Ersatz horror and raised an eyebrow. "Tavist Upland. Yes, I know the name. He was a child last I recall; an orphan. He must have fled with the Book of Nom. It is priceless to the people. He could only have it if the Scrivener has died. I shall leave at once."

The creature cocked its head. "You will stay and produce my army of Ersatz. Besides, I wish the Ersatz horde to wear your likeness. It is my gift to you."

Ember bowed. "Then I will send Thimgar. He is loyal and—"

The Ersatz horror tossed its head to the other side as if nagged by memory. "This is no errand for Laedenoran savagery. Send your new bride, Nissa. She has a way about her that pleases me. She will not fail."

Ember furrowed his brow. "And what shall she do with the book when she finds it?"

"She will destroy it," the beast said with finality.

"Destroy it? Are the names of slaughtered families and deposed government officials so important to the Holy Sojourner?"

The beast propped itself on its empty hand and shook the leg-bone at Ember. "It is more than a history book, Ember—much more. Have her also kill the boy Tavist." It drew the leg-bone across its own neck, as though a knife. "And it is not for you to question the wisdom of the Sojourner's Path—only to walk it."

Ruffled but compliant, Ember bowed again. "Very well, Vang."

"Do not fret, Ember. You have found favor with the Sacred Sojourner. It is your destiny to have your own soul. But for now, just look at you! You are no common Dreka. You are a king! Just as I promised." The Ersatz horror offered a drool-soaked smile as it struggled to lift the leg-bone to Ember. "Now, be a gracious host and help me crack this open, will you? I love the taste of fresh marrow!"

CHAPTER 19

STILL SCREAMING AND RESTRAINED BY VELDIC, Charles swung his head around, desperately trying to get his bearings through the shimmering cloud that surrounded them. Only moments before, he and Veldic were plummeting to their deaths. Yet, they did not collide with the ground at the base of the tower as Charles had expected. And while he was grateful for that small mercy, his overall wellbeing was undecided.

Once she felt safe to do so, Veldic let Charles go and patted him on the back, disturbing the bright sparkles that floated around them. Charles was amazed and about to sit down when the cloud thickened and the small hairs on his neck raised. He thought the the cloud smelled faintly of sea salt but strongly of morning thunderstorms. Dara appeared slowly in front of Charles, like a specter through fog, holding the sword he had dropped. The sight chilled Charles and tightened his innards.

"You made it, Dara!" Announced Veldic in celebration, rushing to her and lifting her up to her level of vision.

"Yes, Veldic," Dara returned, "I did. Now, put me down!"

"As you like."

Once on the ground, Dara walked briskly to Charles, grabbed his shoulders and kissed his cheek tenderly before he could protest. He felt a wonderful shock course through his body.

"Thank you Charles," she said, "That was a very brave thing you did for me back there. There is a warrior within you, if only you would see it." She placed a warm, open hand on his chest and smiled.

Charles' face flushed instantly. The way he felt could not be explained nor quantified. How long had he waited for such a simple offering as this? It was wonderful. But she was not Nissa. He forced himself to commit that fact to his perception of the moment at hand. He mustered as much presence as he could. "Well, My Lady, I was only doing what anyone would—"

"Yes, but I personally would have chosen to separate his head," Dara interrupted. "but thank you all the same," She squeezed his shoulder and released him, signaling that the conversation was over, leaving Charles awkward and mute. She then knelt and scooped a handful of orange-tinged dirt in her hand. She pinched it, regarding it thoughtfully as the last bit of the shimmering cloud dissipated, revealing their darkened surroundings and prompting a blast of miserably humid air. The sounds of nearby crickets and slow-moving water overlapped the din of men and women cheering and singing in the distance.

"Where are we?" asked Charles, forcing the words through the evening heat that filled his lungs.

"I do not know," answered Dara, trying to discern the various moonlit shapes around them.

Veldic squatted and collected her own measure of dirt, her braid touching the ground. "This is Aromite soil we stand upon. It turns this color when fresh, flowing water is close. Nowhere else in the world does the ground behave this way." There was an audible pride in her assessment. "I also smell buttonwood leaves, which means we are a good distance from the city."

Dara looked up at the large, brightly yellowed moon, appreciating its fullness. "If this is indeed Arom, why here, instead of the tower?" Veldic shook her head, but had no answer.

"So you admit we are in the wrong place, then?" Charles goaded, discontentment skirting his voice. Veldic gestured toward Charles and expressed her disapproval to Dara with pleading eyes.

"That is yet to be decided, Charles," Dara said, acknowledging Veldic's concern. "However, we seem to be out of peril for the moment which puts us in exactly the right place. I say we follow the merriment and perhaps find information, food and rest. Let us seek to put this day in our past where it belongs. Tomorrow, we make for the tower in Port Frailty."

Dara stood, offering Charles his sword who accepted it but found difficulty in placing it in its scabbard. Veldic rolled her eyes and turned away so as not to be tempted to ridicule him, a courtesy that Charles appreciated. Once he finally managed the task, Charles nodded to Dara who slapped Veldic's sweaty, muscled shoulder, and the three travelers hiked along a lazy river, through the field of scrub and waist-high reeds, toward the soft glow of a village set against a partially illuminated treeline under a clear, star-stricken sky.

Chapter 20

DARA, CHARLES AND VELDIC WENT unchallenged as they entered the perimeter of the village; a transition marked by the sudden absence of vegetation in favor of dirt and orange-hued mud. Charles figured there were around two dozen wood and mud-brick buildings of a large size with bundled grass roofs clustered in the village's center surrounded by a smattering of dwellings of the same make, only much smaller. By the look, the only external fire-lights came from a line of tall torches next to a cooking pit outside a long, two-story building in the central cluster where most if not all the village's inhabitants were engaging in festivities.

There was a steady stream of flagon-wielding villagers moving in and out from the building in various stages of drunkenness. Some were conversing with others, some were dancing and some were even leaning over balconies on the second level, shouting and howling. The three travelers crouched behind a low fence of plain buttonwood branches and thatch, close enough to the celebration for a good view.

The throng of revelers wore modest attire, mostly in dark-toned farming garb and house dresses. There were a few villagers that sported finer clothing; perhaps that of merchants or entertainers, but even they showed signs of poor personal hygiene. King Lidig ensured Charles received a proper upbringing on the palatial grounds among Zanni nobility.

Charles had never seen such an uninhibited gathering of commoners. He felt as though he might contract a fever were he to venture any closer. Veldic, however, seemed to brighten up at the sight of what Charles figured to be a familiar scene to the Aromite.

"I am starved," complained Veldic, her mouth watering at the smell of wood-roasted meat that hung thick in the humid air.

"We will seek food and shelter there," said Dara, pointing to the busy, two-story establishment. "Let us hope these people are drunk enough to suffer our presence for a time."

Charles knew he was hungry, but fatigue and pain were resurfacing. Once again, he pressed the wound Atherton's men gave him just to make sure all of this was real. The pain was real enough. He could even wait until morning for a morsel in exchange for a nap now. Any bed would do.

"Reedsdrift Township," Veldic announced.

"Veldic, so you recognize this village?" Dara inquired.

"No, but I can read the sign," Veldic said pointing at the words, laid with a chisel and hammer on a buttonwood plank nailed to the back of a cart next to her.

Dara gave a thoughtful look. "I do not recall such a township in Arom, do you?

"I know of it," Veldic answered. "We are in Arom's Northwestern Region which means we are close to the city of Port Frailty, though by how many days journey I cannot say."

Charles huffed. "Days, did you say? Days away from something is close?"

Veldic's earrings jangled as she turned a sarcastic smile toward Charles. "I can carry you over my shoulder if you like."

Charles narrowed his eyes, which only made Veldic's smile grow larger.

"Let us go," ordered Dara. "Veldic, you take the lead. If anyone questions us, we are mercenaries from Eastern Arom on our way to find work in Port Frailty."

"As you like, Dara." Veldic grasped her braid and whipped it to one side, causing it to wrap about her neck once, the end resting on the back of her shoulder. "There is feasting to attend." With this last assertion, Veldic climbed over the fence and held out her hand for Dara, who furrowed her brow at the large warrior and jumped the fence with at least a foot of clearance

Unaffected, Veldic shrugged and offered her outstretched hand to Charles instead, hoping to humiliate him. However, believing the gesture to be genuine, Charles moved to accept; a prospect that caused Veldic to withdraw her hand and sigh before turning past Dara toward the festival.

"What was that all about?" yelled Charles. He negotiated the fence on his own. "You offered your hand did you not?"

"Please keep him quiet, Dara," said Veldic raising her hand without looking back.

With the high level of ruckus about, the three travelers had little trouble entering the Reedsdrift Hovel; so named by another buttonwood plank fastened above the arched entrance. The level of noise inside was louder than anything Charles had experienced. His head felt punished by it. He covered his ears with his hands to find relief, but Dara grabbed Charles by the arm and pulled him along to a filthy table cut from the stump of a massive buttonwood tree, upon which stood two drained flagons next to a short, crude wood carving of a figure holding up one hand in the sky.

After finding his seat, Charles realized that everyone in the place was holding one hand up above their heads as they danced about to the shrill cut of two fiddles. The dancers had circular marks on their palms which at first looked like blood, but Charles realized was paint. Those not dancing were cheering, those not cheering were drinking and those not drinking were motionless on the wooden floor; the wages of too much of whatever it was they had consumed.

After a brief absence, Veldic arrived at the table with a large platter in one hand of roasted meat—fresh from the roasting pit outside—steamed roots and simmered reeds, all spiced with a smoky glaze that smelled of apples and wildflowers. After sitting, Veldic poured sweet-smelling wine into the two waiting flagons on the table and ate. Charles made for the wine like a predator pounces but Veldic blocked Charles from the object of his desire with a meat-wielding fist.

"Not for you!" Veldic grunted through a mouthful of roast boar. "That river-bulb wine is for Dara."

Dara smiled and nodded, taking the golden wine from Charles' reach. "Why thank you, Veldic." She said. "It is not snow-berry wine, but it will do."

Dara explained that sweet snow-berry wine exclusive to the Northlands, that it was a favorite drink for an evening of revelry.

Charles reeled. "What? But, I am parched, Veldic! Have I not earned a proper drink?" He felt as though he was shouting to compete with the surrounding commotion.

He stood up. "Never mind! Your rudeness is astounding! I shall retrieve my own—"

Veldic smacked Charles' forearm. "Sit down, you idiot! I did not forget you. I am your protector, yes?" Veldic eye-balled Dara, who raised her eyebrows, expressing her curiosity at Veldic's game.

"Ah! Here it is," Veldic announced as Charles retook his seat. A grinning, gray-haired, elderly woman in a plain brown dress with a matching shawl offered Charles a small, wooden cup of steaming liquid, smelling of rot. Charles pretended not to see it, but the flaring of his nostrils gave him away.

"Take it, love," said the old woman. "It'll take care of your problem. Right fast! I should know. At my age, I use it quite a lot." The old woman laughed and placed the cup in front of Charles. "Go on! Drink!"

Charles noted that, besides a slight nasal quality, her speech was understandable and not at all representative of the unintelligible drawl he thought was characteristic of the outside world. In fact, he then realized that Veldic's speech was also discernible. They were not the savage cannibals that Zanni schoolmasters had made them out to be. He then reconsidered including Veldic in that concession and decided that, clear speech or not, Veldic was a savage.

With a nose-full of foul-smelling steam, Charles looked at the cup in disgust. "What problem would that be, Good Maid?"

The old woman laughed again, hobbling off toward another table. Charles shrugged and looked to Veldic.

145

"The coin, Charles," Veldic explained, failing an attempt to abstain from laughter. "This catch-moss tea will help you pass the coin in your belly! And it works quick, I am told."

Charles' dignity retreated like a turtle in its shell. "Oh yes, the coin. I had not thought about it." Embarrassment added a nice rose color to his cheeks.

Dara snickered somewhat, but hid her face in her flagon. She drank deep and slammed the vessel on the table. She widened her eyes, placed her gauntlet-covered hand to the side of her mouth and whispered. "Do not worry, Charles! It will not be so bad. Perhaps you could just let go of your troubles in a hot bath!" With that, both Veldic and Dara burst into belly-borne, mirthful laughter, sending roast-boar and roots across the table.

"Yes! Yes!" howled Veldic, near unable to breathe, flailing her brutish hands about. "And when the bath-maid comes to collect, you could tell her you left payment in the bathwater!"

At this, Veldic and Dara were inconsolable, their faces frozen in giant, painful-looking smiles, silent laughter keeping them prisoner. Veldic was hitting the table-top and tears streamed down Dara's face. And as beautiful as Charles found her to be, he did not appreciate the discomfort she and Veldic were causing him in the least.

The thought of retrieving the coin was distressing to Charles. Such bodily workings had always bothered him. His former wife Nissa had well known of his disdain for it. And, if Dara had Nissa's memories, then Dara should also know. Yet, she was making jokes at his expense. Nissa would never have done that. Belittle him in private? Yes, and with brutality. But turn his misfortune into a public comedy? No. It was improper. And Nissa had always been proper when caught in the public eye.

Wonder replaced the appall he felt when he realized he had never seen his Nissa laugh; not even when they were children. She had always been serious; always completing a task. She would finish one, and on to the next. She had little time to waste on matters of merriment. It was her way, and he came to accept and even respect it.

But in this land with strange dirt, music and even stranger company, he saw what Nissa might look like had she laughed. It was a discovered dimension to her beauty that filled the cup of his heart with the rich milk of adoration. It made him miss her and, in that moment, he realized it was his unquenched thirst for Nissa's love that caused him to follow Dara out of the Effacer's Keep into the unknown, not the lure of self-preservation.

But yet, as this beautiful, strong and lethal woman beamed with hilarity before him, he knew—despite sharing a haunting likeness with his former wife—Dara was her own person; a person that Charles was fast finding himself attracted to. The intensity of the feeling caused Charles to avert his eyes.

Returning to the business at hand, he did his best to scowl at the cup of medicinal tea on the table, but the sounds of the others' laughter seeped into his being, tugging at the muscles in his face. He redoubled his efforts to frown, an exaggeration that caused Dara and Veldic to point and laugh even harder.

Just then, a short, dancing man in gold silk, with the brightly painted face of a professional fool, noticed Charles' distorted expression and approached the table. The entertainer then nudged Charles with his elbow, and mimicked his face before moving on toward the stage, causing several customers at nearby tables to join in the jovial chorus. And that was that. Charles could only maintain his air of offense for so long. In a matter of moments,

Charles sprouted a spreading smile which formed into a chuckle, then a deep guffaw rivaling that of his companions.

For several moments, they laughed, enjoying the cathartic release it brought them. They raised their vessels and clanked them together. As if taking a cue, the surrounding patrons likewise made toasts to one another and drank, as friends often do. While Dara and Veldic drank theirs empty, Charles smiled, held his cup of catch-moss tea over the floor and poured it out. Dara and Veldic burst into laughter again, both choking on mouthfuls of river-bulb wine.

Neither the miserable humidity nor the provincial fiddle-music were all bad, Charles decided. And, as his eyes met Dara's, Charles felt for the first time since the day's surreal journey had started—no, for the first time in his life—that he was where he belonged.

The Reedsdrift Hovel remained to its capacity well into the night. Charles and Dara spent the rest of that evening playing dice with one another and listening to Veldic tell stories of her home, deep in the jungles of Southeast Arom where everyday life was a challenge. Veldic lamented over the loss of her polearm; an unfortunate situation that a tipsy Dara promised to remedy once they reached the city.

Several patrons introduced themselves and wished them well. Like Dara suggested, the three said they were mercenaries headed for Port Frailty in search of work. The three sensed no suspicion among the ardent merrymakers. The only bit of trouble they suffered was at the words of a single drunkard toward the end of the evening who kept pointing at Charles from across the room, shouting in slurred syllables.

He approached at last, stopping to bother other patrons along the way who pushed him away with unkind words. The man stood hunched and unsure, wrapped only in dirty cloth bound with twine. He wore a bearded face, his nose and cheeks red and puffed likely from years of wine and weather. A rotten smell settled around him like a fetid blanket. When he was close enough to touch, the man yelled at Charles, asking him where he found the armor he was wearing.

Charles shifted and shot his companions a knowing glance. "I purchased it. From a merchant."

The old drunk's words ran together. "No! Liar! This is from Zannistar. I know it."

The old woman who earlier brought the catch-moss tea interjected. "Don't listen to him. He has been talking about his imaginary land for years now."

The man swatted at her. "It's not imaginary!"

The woman snickered and hobbled off.

Charles figured the man a lunatic, but how could he know Zannistar? As far as Charles knew, Zannistar remained hidden. Or was it? He and the others should have forgotten all about Zannistar as soon as they arrived in Arom.

In that moment, Charles realized he still remembered his homeland which meant that Gyldred's sorcery was no longer in effect; perhaps by the strange power of the coin. But even if that were true, all lost memories stayed lost. That was the Effacer's craft. So, while the Effacer's defeat might explain why Charles, himself, still remembered Zannistar, it was impossible that this drunken fool could know Charles wore armor of the Zanni August Guard or that there was even a place called Zannistar. None of it made any sense to Charles.

Agitated, the man clutched Charles' shoulders and demanded to know where he had come from. This final intrusion caused Veldic to backhand the drunkard across the ear, sending him to the floor. As expected, he stumbled from the Reedsdrift Hovel into the night.

The ordeal cast a shadow on what would otherwise have been a perfect evening. But other than being unsettled, Charles dismissed the encounter and opted for another round of dice with Dara. They played and were content. Charles was a quick learner. If there was one thing he understood, it was numbers.

After a few rounds, Dara grabbed the dice and sobered her speech. "Charles, he was Dreka, like me."

"So who is he?" Charles asked. "How do you know?"

"I do not know him, but a Dreka feels another Dreka. It is not easy to explain. It is the ripple his emptiness makes. I can feel it."

"Why did he not recognize you?"

"Perhaps because he was focused on you or too drunk to care. Could be both. But he was Dreka. Dreka are made by the Bekrot Chair. That means he is from Zannistar.

"Well he is gone now, Dara. And I have no concern for Zannistar or its lost for I am among them. Good luck to us both." Charles lifted a flagon to the empty doorway in tribute.

At some point, the fiddles stopped and a troupe of entertainers dressed in fine, patchwork silk flooded the room. There were jugglers, fools and tricksters of all kinds. They dazzled onlookers with a blissful cacophony of movement and sound. Once they finished the performance, they walked about the room, holding out their hats for donations. Most everyone paid a copper or two at least. Even Veldic contributed several pieces of copper from her pouch.

Having their fill of food, entertainment and river-bulb wine, the three outsiders rose from their table and retired to the room upstairs that Veldic had paid for earlier. It boasted a large feather-filled mattress, a night table and a writing desk; all of simple, buttonwood carpentry. An opaque, glass-paned window invited a beam of moonlight which illuminated a large brass wash-basin on the floor.

Charles disrobed to his undershirt and sank deep into the feather mattress before anyone else could protest. Without undressing, Veldic rolled her eyes and took her rest supine on the floor, in front of the bolted door. And seeing that everyone had fallen asleep, Dara felt compelled to stare at Charles for a while, studying his face, before blowing out the wall sconce and taking the other side of the mattress, curling up with her back to his. Like Veldic, she remained clad in her studded leather, quiver resting on the floor next to her—ready for trouble should it call on them. And there in the safe, solitude of darkness, she quietly cried for a while, soon drifting into dreams of far off yet familiar places.

CHAPTER 21

THE NEXT MORNING, CHARLES AWOKE to the distinct sound of glass breaking. By the time he adjusted to the morning heat and found his senses, Veldic had already recovered the rolled-up reed parchment which someone tethered to a stone and hurled through the window. Charles sat up and wiped a layer of sweat from his bruised, shaven head. The act brought painful reminders of the previous day's peril. In fact, every joint and muscle in his body was sore beyond anything he had ever experienced before. Moving proved difficult.

"What is it Veldic?" asked Dara, who had burst from her sleep to her knees, grabbing a bolt from her quiver and scanning the room from the bed.

The leather-capped warrior unfurled the parchment and took several moments to read its contents. "It is over!" Veldic bellowed. "The coin has been stolen!"

"What? How? By whom?" Dara sprang from the mattress, swiped the parchment, took a breath and read aloud.

"*I must say I expected more than a single silver coin from a man wearing such fine armor.*" Dara glanced at Veldic with wide eyes before continuing. "*The coin may not be worth much in raw currency, but I now own it which tells it means something to you. If you wish it back, meet me at the lumber loading dock at the hottest part of the day, where we will discuss my fee for ensuring its safe return to your keeping. You will know me when you see me.*"

Dara lowered the parchment and ran to the window.

Charles grabbed at his midsection. "Impossible! How did they? When? I do not understand. I did not drink the tea! What is going on?"

"I wish I knew, Charles," said Dara, scanning for clues in the busy, dirt streets below. "But Veldic is right. If this letter is the truth, no matter how unlikely, then our situation is severe. We cannot prevail without the coin." she pointed at Charles' stomach. "Are you hurt?"

"I do not know. I do not think so," Charles muttered, searching for wounds.

"Wait!" cried Veldic, clapping her thick hands. "It was a Touchthief!"

"I am sorry?" inquired Charles, frustrated with his constant lack of what seemed like common knowledge to everyone else.

Dara turned to the others. "Yes!" She tapped her leg with the tip of the wooden bolt. "But who was it?" She snapped from a revelation. "Perhaps, that drunk idiot you pummeled! He grabbed Charles. That would be enough."

"No," Veldic griped, "he looked of many wine-soaked and wasted years on his face and the scars of a woodsman on his hands.

Those scars are from a lifetime of chopping trees for enough silver to stay drunk, not from writing prose on fine parchment. It was someone else."

Dara concentrated for a moment, then pointed to Charles with the bolt. "Then it was the fool!"

"I beg your pardon," Charles began, still clutching his stomach and becoming even more offended.

"Yes!" Dara continued. "The dancing fool that mimicked Charles last night." She made a jabbing motion with her elbow. "I remember that he poked him with his elbow. The fool is our Touchthief."

Veldic straightened. "Venerable Spirit! You are right! We must find him."

"Please excuse me," interrupted Charles. "but what is a Touchthief?"

Dara put the bolt back in its quiver and donned it. "A Touchthief is a sorcerer who can pilfer your valuables by touching you. They are uncommon but they exist."

"Ridiculous," Charles folded his arms and wished he was enjoying a proper morning meal of brierberries and oats instead of arguing such nonsense. "Stolen right out of my gut?"

Dara became irritated with his air of denial. "And just how ridiculous is it Charles? More ridiculous than meeting a created copy of your former wife, with whom you have been transported across vast oceans in the blink of an eye? More ridiculous than that? Or perhaps it is more ridiculous than the ghastly, unnatural soldier who beset us at the tower!" The quip caused Charles to look away and shrug his shoulders. Dara curled her upper lip in disappointment. She thought Charles petty just then.

"It is even worse than you think," Veldic interjected as she adjusted the gold hoops in her long-stretched ears. "Legend tells that a Touchthief's magic always knows the most valuable possession and takes it, but nobody knows where it goes. We cannot find the coin on our own. We must meet this thief and force him to tell us where it is."

Veldic thrust a fist into her other hand. Charles threw his arms into the air. "What is the purpose of this coin?" He pointed at Dara. "And do not dismiss me or tell me I shall know when the time is right. Now is the time. Now, or I go no further!"

"Well, Charles," Dara sat on the mattress and bade Charles to do the same by pointing to it with a drawn bolt. "What do you know of the coin?"

In a storm of words and emotion, Charles explained how it must have been the coin that somehow made Gyldred and his acolytes disappear, and the horrific creature that attacked him afterward, though he was not sure how. He again mentioned the time he spent in the oubliette with the unknown stranger who gave him the coin, who told him it would lead him to the truth and that people were coming for him.

Dara seemed unaffected by the details, a fact that bothered Charles, as if these types of events occurred in her life every day. He continued to voice his utter displeasure at the entire ordeal, going as far back as the day Nissa had betrayed him. As he unburdened himself, he again felt he sting of despair; the cold reach of a vast darkness caressing his sense of self. How could he have been so naive? So simple and unworthy. This reminded him of how insignificant his life had been.

155

The feelings grew, wrapping him in a blanket of self-hate and doubt. He ceased talking and fell into a state of apathy, staring at the floor. The three female voices from his dream rose into his consciousness and filled him, speaking in united malevolence.

Ah, there you are, Charles. You are in Arom! Yes. Hiding from me. But I have found you. I always find you, Charles. Always.

"Charles!" cried Dara, shaking him at the shoulders. "What traps you?"

At the sound of Dara's voice, the dark feelings faded and Charles came to his senses, pulling away. "I am fine. Now, why is this coin so important?" Charles folded his arms and tried his best to look authoritative.

Dara and Veldic traded concerned looks. Then Dara cleared her throat, composed herself and spoke.

"They say someone found a ball of pure silver near Mirlandis lake as large as a man's head, and from that, made the coin."

Dara shifted. "Nobody knows for certain just how long it had been there, but the Northern legends say it likely appeared after the Sojourner's arrival in the Nurdrayl forest, not far from where they found the object."

Charles' expression was empty.

Dara continued before Charles could protest. "Most believe the Sojourner is the Gastwyrd—the Great Spirit who connects this world to the world-before and the world-after. They teach us that, in this world, the Gastwyrd exists in the form of a boy who, for five thousand years, has been making a journey to Stag's End."

Charles threw his hands in the air showing his exasperation.

"He is a moving statue," Veldic explained. "Yet he moves too slow for our eyes to see. Only the Itinerants can see his movements."

"Yes, Veldic," Dara continued. "The Itinerants say he travels but three feet per year. Sometimes more, sometimes less. The Itinerants monitor him, interpreting the smallest details of his position, expression and movement as though they were signs and wonders. Most Northlanders worship the Sojourner and defer to the wisdom of the Itinerants, who they consider holy and wise. In the early days, they built a compound near Stag's End so they could study the Sojourner's movements at all times. Over these past one thousand years, it has grown to become a great influence on the world; the home of a compelling religion, strong and benevolent. The Sojourner became a god to be worshiped and the Itinerants his emissaries. But it does not end there. The Sojourner himself emanates a great and mysterious power which prevents most from approaching him. Many try."

"The Sojourner kills those who fail or sometimes turns them into living statues. Fortunate few can hope to harness this power. Yet this is the goal of all initiates. They spend their lifetimes attempting to master the art of Lucan—the Closing. Over time, they move closer and closer to the Sojourner, spending days or weeks sitting near him in meditation."

"For those few who can reach the Sojourner and touch the shard he carries are given powerful abilities. Some receive visions of other worlds, others can interpret dreams. Many times they become gifted with advising others; they can see the wisdom of choice. These special few become part of the ruling body of the Order. The Itinerants."

"More fell witchery," Charles surmised. "It all sounds so unnecessary. And his destination; this Stag's End. What is it?"

"It is the end of his journey," said Dara. "The Itinerants believe once the Sojourner reaches the edge of the cliff above the lake, he will emerge from his enchantment to unite all peoples in peace and plenty before returning to the sky to once again take the form of the Gastwyrd. The Itinerants have constructed a special courtyard and dais for his arrival at the cliff's edge."

Charles pointed at the bolts in Dara's hand. "This is how you let loose crossbow bolts with no crossbow? Are you one of these so-called initiates?"

Dara tensed. "They are not just *any* bolts."

"Oh," said Charles.

"And no," said Dara. "I am not an Itinerant." She held out her hand and opened it as if offering the bolt to Charles. The bolt rose from her upturned palm and spun in the air. "I am a Dreka Woodlock; soulless and borne of the occult procedures of the Cwalu Itinerants. I made these bolts from the flesh of a tree in the Gearwood Thicket. And like me, all Woodlocks command anything made of gearwood. The bolts know and obey my will. We have an understanding."

Charles examined the spinning bolt in disbelief. "A compelling story but why is it my concern?"

Dara grabbed the bolt and moved toward Charles, stopping just in front of him and stared into his eyes.

"Some believe the Sojourner is not who the Itinerants claim."

Charles caught himself appreciating Dara's features and blinked his eyes to vanquish the transgression. "So then who is he?"

"Just a boy," said Veldic. "A boy from an ancient tribe of hunters caught in a sorcerous trap. He is no Gastwyrd."

Dara turned again to the window. "Just a boy, yes. But the magic that surrounds him is real enough. Its source is the shard of black rock he carries in his hand. The Itinerant order of warrior-sorcerers known as the Cwalu teach us there is a powerful and evil being called Vang who seeks to defeat the Itinerants and destroy the entire world. The Cwalu believe the Sojourner walks to Stag's End to open a door for Vang to enter our world. If that happens, it will undo destinies. Even now, Vang's very own emissary, Ember Driss—your Dreka double—has invaded Zannistar and taken control of the Bekrot Chair; a tool he will use to create an army of Ersatz demons who will crush the Sojournic Stronghold and then everything beyond it."

Charles' eyebrows raised. "Gyldred, the Effacer hid Zannistar with his magic many years ago. How could this Vang fellow even know Zannistar existed?" When Charles said the name, he heard it whispered back to him in his ear, causing him to shiver. He waved it off with his hand.

Nissa moved closer still. "We know of Gyldred and his power. His name has sparked fear in the hearts of Laedenoran children since the beginning. But understand he is nothing compared to Vang. Vang is not of this world, Charles. The limits of his power are unknown. But I know he desires to corrupt all life. Charles, if we fail, then the world dies, perhaps all worlds."

Charles' thoughts flashed to his ordeal in the Effacer's chamber and Gyldreds apparent death. "Absurd," Charles said. "There are no other worlds."

"Wrong. There are many worlds," Veldic said. She took an admonishing tone. "You are blind to them, like all from your kingdom of cowards."

Charles raised his finger and opened his mouth to disagree but Dara cut him short.

"Veldic speaks the truth, Charles," said Dara. She stared out the window as if in a daydream.

Charles spent a moment in silence, pondering the possibility. "So then who fashioned the coin?" he asked, proud of his deductive ability.

"That knowledge is lost," Dara replied in a melancholy tone. "But we know what to do with it."

"And that would be what?" Charles returned to his posture of skepticism.

Dara's eyes intensified. "We take it to the north to raise an army."

"Oh, an army," Charles said. "Perfect. I suppose none of this would make any sense without an army." He folded his arms and stared at the ground again.

"But for now," resolved Dara, holding the Touchthief's note aloft, "we make our way to the rendezvous and retrieve the coin from that accursed thief! Then we find our bearings and travel to Port Frailty."

In the time that followed, Charles was only half-hearted in his enthusiasm as he allowed Veldic to help him with his armor. He had always wondered how the Zanni August Guard suffered such a laborious task each day. He decided that they deserved better wages, which he knew because of the time he spent in the counting house. The armor still felt large and awkward, but it would do for now. The purple-eyed Aromite slapped Charles' shoulder to signal the end of the task.

"Your sword, Guardsman Warfield," said Veldic through an impish smile as she offered the Zanni broadsword and scabbard to him, pommel first.

Charles stared at the coat of arms carved into the bottom of the brass pommel—a sheaf of wheat below the head of an ox. "Just as everything else in my life, this sword belongs to someone else," said Charles, reaching for it.

Veldic pulled it out of reach. "Though I might fail my duty to protect you by letting you anywhere near it."

"You are a terrible person, Veldic—terrible." Charles snatched the sword and fumbled with the strap as he followed his companions out the door.

CHAPTER 22

"I DO NOT UNDERSTAND," SAID CHARLES. "How will we recognize this thief?"

The three travelers leaned against the side of a large building near the docks, which Charles soon discovered to be a storehouse for lumber intended for shipment to the city.

The river docks, themselves, were teeming with lumber-workers and boat-hands, all busy at their various tasks. Most of the workers were loading massive flotillas with buttonwood logs and planks into high stacks.

Charles had never seen a more complex skein of rigging, pulleys and levers in action. Even the gargantuan gears of the moving platform in the Geattor were not as impressive. Charles puzzled at how the giant rafts supported such crushing weight. Charles was intrigued by this place. The smells, colors and noise all stimulated his senses, and made him feel brisk and alive. Most of the workers were violet-eyed and olive-skinned like Veldic, though none were as large or impressive as she. Charles marveled at the giant field of stumps and receding tree line, which suggested this was a most profitable operation.

He supposed that one might find such activity in his own country, perhaps in the city of Olix. But Charles seldom traveled south of Ganlis Bay. In fact, the only place that Charles had been in the Southern Province was the Gardens of Grynn during his wedding sabbatical. But this was a privilege reserved for Primary nobles and the occasional Secondary. Most in the Southern Province were Tertiary nobles without means to get there. Passage required magic or money—likely both. In every way that mattered, the Gardens of Grynn acted as an extension of Northern society.

Charles realized that his visit there did not count. He recognized the Southern Province as a place of industry where people produced goods but lacked social refinement. The Zanni schoolmasters taught that Tertiary society, aside from its needed goods and services, was with no appreciable social value. But being here in this fascinating place, he questioned his education on the subject. He wished he had spent more time traveling in the Southern Province. Perhaps he had been mistaken.

"Charles, look there!" said Veldic, pointing to a medium-sized boat tied to a small dock. Standing in it was a man in pants and shirt of gold silk. He had cleaned the paint off his face. He was beckoning them over to him.

Dara burst into a sprint, freeing a bolt from her quiver and let it fly from her hand. It struck the inside the boat, next to the thief's foot.

"Venerable Spirit!" yelled Veldic. "She will kill him!" Charles and Veldic started after her.

Before the thief could untie and push away from the dock, Dara was on him. She jumped from the dock into the boat with effortless grace, knocking the thief down with her boot. She straddled him, placed her hand at his throat and reached for another bolt, but she found none. She found no quiver at all.

"You touched me," said the Touchthief through a frightened grin. "Your little arrows must be very important to you."

Dara flashed hot. She jumped off the man and pulled the embedded bolt out of the bottom of the boat and pointed it at the thief, who was shielding his face with his hands.

"Where is the coin, dog?" The bolt in her hand was shaking as if trying to escape restraint. "And where is my quiver?"

"Not here! Not here!" the man yelled.

"Where then? Speak or die!"

"I can't think with that arrow pointed at my face!"

"It is not an arrow, idiot. It is a bolt. Arrows are larger. But this bolt can still end you. Speak!"

Veldic and Charles pushed their way through the growing crowd and joined Dara.

Charles drew his sword. "Dara! Are you alright?" Charles' own concern surprised him.

"Sheath your sword. I have the matter under control," said Dara.

The thief peeked from behind his hands. "Yes, your very fetching friend, here, was just lowering her bolt, which isn't an arrow. Weren't you darling?"

Dara looked around her at the many curious spectators whispering amongst themselves. She heard one man tell a younger one to hurry and alert the authorities. Beyond them, in the distance, Dara spotted the distinctive purple hue of several

Aromite military pennants whipping about in the brisk wind atop buttonwood poles. It was an outpost of the Nasaru Sentinels— Arom's governmental soldiers. Sensing Dara's concern, Veldic turned and grunted.

"Nasaru," Dara announced. "They approach."

Charles craned to see. "I do not suppose we are considering this a cause for celebration?"

"I'd say not," said the thief as he dropped his hands, revealing his face. "Since the Reedsdrift Provost forbids the use of unregistered weapons near the docks. I hear he treats such offenders with the utmost severity; even such lovely creatures as the lady before me."

Dara's face flushed. She scowled and feigned a thrust with the bolt. "Quiet," she said through her teeth.

Without his fool's makeup, the thief presented as a young man of a pallid complexion, short, uncombed dark hair and darker eyes, under strong, expressive eyebrows. He looked about two days without a bath and shave; a sight in odd contrast to the well-grown, white set of teeth that completed the handsome smile he wore.

"Dara," warned Veldic. "We must go. We will not win a fight with the Provost's enforcers."

"And a lovely name," said the thief. "Well, Dara, she's right. I'd be inclined to offer you refuge in my humble boat which, as it turns out, soon embarks for Port Frailty." He grinned even wider.

"I, for one, prefer the boat to more fighting," Charles admitted aloud. He was having trouble returning his sword to its scabbard.

The thief pointed at Charles. "There, you see? Even this skilled and brave warrior sees the wisdom in my offer!" Charles swelled at the sound of those words even though he knew they were not true.

"He is no warrior!" Snapped Veldic, her powerful arms folded in opposition.

"Not now, Veldic!" said Dara. "Tell me, thief, what do you expect for such a grand favor?"

The thief shrugged. "A simple apology," he answered.

Dara's face flushed. "An apology? For what?"

"For almost killing me with that nefarious bolt of yours. You were unkind."

"I can ensure I succeed the next time."

"Dara, that's not the apology I was looking for."

Veldic placed a hand on Dara's shoulder. "The Nasaru are coming, Dara."

Dara shook off Veldic's hand, assessed the situation and swallowed hard. The thief relaxed somewhat and grinned wider yet.

"I regret trying to kill you," conceded Dara.

"Well," said the thief, jumping up and clapping his hands together. "Was that so difficult? Now, let's catch the current and leave this place to its drudgery. Port Frailty and your precious property await. Oh, and we've terms to discuss!"

"On with it," said Dara, "But if you touch anyone you die."

The thief found his seat aboard the craft and regarded Charles' fumbling about. "Oh, I wouldn't dare. It's clear you three are much smarter than I."

"Watch your tongue, cur," growled Veldic.

"Get in the boat, Veldic," ordered Dara.

Veldic sighed and stepped into the boat. "As you like, Dara. As you like." The boat groaned under the Aromite's weight.

Dara boarded the boat, eyeballing the thief.

With some effort, Charles negotiated the sword into its scabbard and followed with his chest puffed out, still beaming with the thought of being called a warrior. He misjudged his steps and tripped on the iron bollard, falling face-first into Dara's back.

She flew forward into the thief's lap. She shouted something obscene and scrambled back to her feet. Embarrassed, she moved to threaten the touchthief with her remaining bolt, which was no longer in her hand. She searched her clothing, found nothing and shouted again.

The thief raised his hands and gave her an apologetic look. "That one wasn't my fault."

Dara spun and glared at Charles, who had fallen to his knees. After a moment, he collected himself, stood and crept in to the boat, careful not to look at Dara directly.

Veldic shook her head and grabbed one of the two oars on the bench. As they put out into the current, the thief grabbed the other oar and rowed alongside Veldic who gave no protest. They sped along the river, leaving the shore, and the Nasaru far behind. Dara placed one foot on the back of the boat and surveyed where they had just been. She seemed lost in thought.

"My name's Braden Bol," said the thief to Veldic.

"Do not touch me. My things are not for the taking."

"Don't worry, I haven't desire for golden earrings," the thief announced. "They're much too difficult to sell in Arom. Such superstitious people, Aromites. But you? You're from the jungles aren't you?"

"And I have no desire to converse with an honorless scoundrel," said Veldic.

"With your strength, you seem like you'd be quite a catch in your homeland."

Veldic snorted. "Best for you to remain quiet and row. Be sure, your kind would not survive one night in my homeland."

"My kind? And what kind's that?"

Veldic rowed and gave no answer.

"Ah, I see an interesting trip ahead." Braden Bol dropped the oar and produced a small leather sack from under the bench. "So who'd like some dried brierberries?"

"Have you stolen those as well?" Veldic asked.

Braden Bol smiled, shrugged and ate one, his teeth gleaming.

Charles raised his hand and looked about with a guilty countenance. "I would like some, sir." Then, sensing Veldic's disapproval, he lowered his hand out of sight.

"Pick up that oar and keep rowing, thief!" Veldic rolled her eyes and muttered obscenities under her breath.

The thief did as he was asked.

CHAPTER 23

THEY SMELLED THE FIRES long before they could see them. Tavist Upland and the Duchess Lydia Myrette of Virk had traveled for two days at least and the hour was late. Dusk had fallen across the hazy Southern Province, but the two escapees pressed on with great urgency. And when their carriage crested the hill, they confirmed their worst fears: the city was alight with flame. Lydia stopped the horses.

"No," whispered Lydia, "How can this be?

The conflagration lit the coastal valley, revealing the city walls were surrounded by a military force of great size and strength. Past the shore, Just beyond the city, Zanni fishing boats burned and smoldered. Giant galleons of foreign origin loomed over them like merciless, wooden mountains caught between smoke above and mist below.

The scene was one that Lydia had never dared to imagine. She had viewed Olix from this vantage countless times in her youth.

During her many trips home from the palace, the sight of its low-roofed buildings and planted foliage had always brought her a sense of contentment and familiarity. Now, she would never again remember Olix, the Southern City of Artisans, as anything but a burning pit of death.

Tavist tucked the small, tethered book under his arm and stepped down from the carriage. "They came by sea, Madame Lydia. It will pain you to hear it, but we cannot hope to make any difference here. The Scrivener was clear. We must press toward Arom. Perhaps we could—"

"Yes," said the Duchess Lydia. "It pains me, young Tavist, more than you know. But you are right. We will leave the coach here and travel east along the coast by horse. A kelp farm with boats lies a few hours from the city. They are friends and they have something there that may prove useful to us. But be sure, you need not mention Arminius' name to convince me of the situation. And as unlikely as it may seem, it is you Tavist, who now warrants the title of Scrivener."

"I knew Arminius enough to understand the book is more than it appears. I also know he chose you over me to keep it. He did that for a reason. And I shall honor him by respecting his faith in you." A Zanni fishing boat exploded in the distance. The two winced at the delayed sound.

Tavist turned and stared at her for a moment, wondering how she could maintain her composure in the face of such a horrific tragedy. He could see the reflection of the flames in her wet, stoic eyes. Even when they buried Arminius Morlund's body the day before, she stayed emotionless and focused. He wondered what the book would reveal about her.

"One more thing, Tavist," Lydia began. "I would prefer you address me as Lydia. First, your constant posturing makes you look foolish. Second, since I did not protect my Duchy, I no longer deserve the title."

Tavist prepared to protest.

"Tavist, you hold the emblem of your new office safe in your care, there under your arm. I, however, do not. My people are being murdered. Families, Tavist. I can do nothing to stop it. So should I not therefore be among them? I deserve death, but we must complete our errand first. If we succeed, perhaps you will grant me the same mercy you showed Arminius. Either way, Zannistar's legacy is at an end. We have been judged for our arrogance."

As Tavist considered her words, the book became cold.

"The book!" Tavist announced, flipping, turning and opening it. This time, it was instinct.

Lydia hopped off the carriage. "What does it say?"

"It is her."

"Who?"

"The Lady Nissa. She has been pursuing us with great speed." Tavist's face became ashen.

"What is wrong, young Mr. Upland?"

"Her heart is dark, Lydia. So dark. We need to leave at once."

CHAPTER 24

"WHERE IS YOUR LITTLE BOOK, ARMINIUS? Did you give it away?"

The Queen Nissa Driss, formerly Nissa Branlin, formerly Nissa Warfield, formerly still Nissa Kennard, daughter of master fletchers and betrayer most cruel crouched far enough to touch the peaceful, earth-laden face of the former Scrivener who lay still on the ground.

Two large Laedenorans exhumed him with unceremonious haste from his resting place under a sprawling oak. This was not something the pair of Northmen enjoyed but felt it better to disturb the dead rather than face the Queen's judgment.

Once satisfied that the book was not in or around the grave, Nissa stood and examined her long, white fingernails for signs of blemish or damage, then on to the rest of her ensemble; a hunter's pants, jerkin, boots and cape, all of softened alabaster leather. Even her once dark hair was now the color of fresh snow and set in tight, wound loops.

"My Queen," said the larger of the two warriors as he pointed east with his axe. "They will not escape. Our ships will control the shore and the city must be defeated by now. They have nowhere to flee but back toward us. We have only to lie in wait."

Nissa gazed down the road. She hated that Arminius escaped her wrath through death. He was a coward. "You Laedenorans are not well-witted are you? I am not sure why the King tolerates you."

The bearded brutes looked at each other. They both knew he had spoken out of turn. When this pursuit had started, the Queen had clarified that Laedenoran troops were never to address her unless asked to do so. Almost unnoticed, the shorter man slid back and away from his compatriot.

"Templeton!" The Queen called out.

Templeton Caid jumped down from his seat on the large, horseless coach in the road's middle and hurried over to Nissa, clasped his hands together and bowed. His own attire was likewise white leather pants, doublet, cape and boots. A milky-white cap of cotton covered his shaven head. Tassels hung from it like sideburns on his powdered face. "Yes, my Queen."

"We will go southeast. The good Duchess has many loyal friends and hiding places in her Duchy. We shall search every tavern, house and farmstead if need be."

"Yes, my Queen," said the chirurgeon, who now found himself a personal valet to the Queen rather than a healer. He did not mind. She saw him for what he was and appreciated his affinity for surgical art. No more would he have to hide in darkened chambers, practicing on rats and hounds.

There had been the occasional courtier who caught his eye and who, with the help of Gyldred the Effacer, became forgotten by all. All Gyldred asked in return was a steady stream of information about the King and Primary nobility. No longer would such obfuscation be necessary. He was now free from those former social constraints.

"Oh, and Templeton, why does this filthy brute address me? Am I a common chamber-wench, Templeton?"

"No, my Queen. You are pure and sublime."

"Yes," Nissa put her hand on Templeton's capped head. She inspected it for cleanliness. "How do you mean to correct the situation, Templeton?"

"I shall have him killed at once my Queen!" Templeton vowed.

The condemned Laedenoran tensed, assessed his chances and lifted his axe to the ready. He would not go easy.

"No, he should not go to waste," Nissa said. "I have decided that he will nourish the Calamity Engine" Her tone was matter-of-fact.

"Yes, my Queen," Templeton returned.

"Enough!" Spat the large Laedenoran, moving to strike Templeton unawares. But the other Laedenoran stopped him and wrestled him to the ground.

Nissa thought the act a rather surprising act of delicious treachery. She heard somewhere that they were brothers.

Inspired by the sight, she felt that perhaps there was hope for these barbarians. A calculated shift in loyalties against one's own family was a sign of higher thinking.

The trapped man attempted to escape his brother's grasp, but could not gain purchase. Templeton summoned three more

Northlanders to assist. None dared hesitate. Together, the four men forced their countryman to his feet and toward the carriage.

The unhorsed carriage was magnificent. Its proportions were three times that of anything Nissa had ever seen anywhere in Zannistar. Ember told her it was made of gearwood, the same enchanted wood used to create the Bekrot-chair. Its shape was that of a giant box of uneven sides and displeasing angles. Set into each of its corners were enormous carvings of demon-headed, winged men standing with arms folded across their chests. Each statue leaned out over the road, attached at the heels. Their wing tips touched, forming an enclosure around the carriage itself. Nissa thought the statues at once beautiful and terrifying.

The rest of the carriage was no less impressive. Banded with serrated, worked iron, each of the four wooden wheels were of a height that would exceed most Zanni buildings. This placed the belly of the machine higher than the tallest of men, allowing travelers to walk under it.

But its most peculiar feature was the hinged, wooden box, stood on end, atop the carriage like some misshapen coffin. The head of an unfortunate villager protruded from the top. He had been plucked along the way and chosen to nourish the engine. Red vapor rose from what were once his eyes, nose and open mouth, but he was gaunt and motionless. The Calamity Engine used the man up like a furnace uses wood.

"Prepare the engine," ordered Templeton.

A fifth Laedenoran climbed a ladder onto a platform in the carriage's rear and turned a double-handled crank. The coffin lowered, disappearing into the main enclosure of the carriage with deafening clicking sound.

After a few more disturbing audible emissions, the coffin emerged from the bottom of the carriage until the iron cradle that supported it was on the ground. Templeton disengaged the lock and opened the coffin, releasing the skeletal remains of the man trapped within. The corpse fell at Templeton's feet, red vapor rising from it.

"Brother!" yelled the prisoner. "This is madness!"

The men pushed the flailing, yelling Laedenoran into the coffin and Templeton slammed it shut, then he signaled the soldier at the hand-crank. The Northlander struggled in futility as the coffin raised off the ground, through the carriage to rest once again on the roof.

Someone brave helped the Queen up to a set of steps in the machine's front which led to several forward facing bench seats on a platform just below roof-level. Many of the more important members of the expedition took seats there, and the rest stood facing outward on the surrounding planks hidden between the carriage and the wings of the wooden demon statues.

The Queen bade the surviving brother to sit next to her, and she patted his knee as a friend might do.

"What is your name, you who honors your Queen regardless of cost?" Her smile was intoxicating.

The frightened soldier glanced at Templeton who nodded back. "Yeveryn, my Queen."

"Yeveryn, is it? Good. Well Yeveryn, I am pleased with you at present.

You seem to have a quality that so many lack; in my people and yours."

"Thank you, my Queen." The man trembled.

Nissa smiled with warmth and rubbed the arm of the seat. "You are quite welcome, Yeveryn. Could you have imagined such a marvelous machine as this?"

He hesitated. His brother's screams were distracting. "In stories of the old war, but I didn't know they were true."

"Oh? Well I suppose that could be since its maker is from the Northlands. His name was Gyldred; a special sorcerer. He hid it away all this time. And he was superb at hiding things, Yeverin. I excel at finding them. Do you know of Gyldred?"

Yeverin's eyes darted about. "Yes, My Queen. All Laedenorans know this name, but in the Northlands he is legend. A story."

She leveled her dangerous eyes to his. "When we again embark on our task, I would like you to tell me this legend, Yeverin."

"Yes, my Queen."

She placed a whitened nail to the tip of his nose. "But I am curious, Yeveryn. Will you again honor me? Your own brother calls out to you, awaiting such an unpleasant fate. Will you still choose me, your Queen? There, in front of you is the lever that gives life to the Calamity Engine. Your brother will feed it with his own life essence.

I must be truthful, Yeveryn, it seems very painful. Yeveryn, I want you to pull that lever. Will you do it? Will you do it for me?"

Yeveryn turned to the lever then to Nissa. He could hear his brother yelling obscenities and vows of revenge above him. Without breaking gaze with his Queen, Yeveryn reached out and pulled the lever.

The entire apparatus erupted in ghostly plumes of vermilion smoke that billowed out in all directions, followed by a dissonant chorus of screams coming from the mouths of the four statues. The Laedenoran prisoner screeched, adding accompaniment to the statues. A spirit-like column of flame engulfed his head and stretched upward above the trees. Yeveryn saw the enormous carriage was rocking, but the platform he was on was still.

Queen Nissa placed her hand on another lever in the bunch. "Well dear Yeveryn," she yelled over the noise. "Shall we continue on?"

Yeverin nodded. "Yes, my Queen!"

"Templeton, I want Yeveryn cleaned up and in the proper Zanni attire at the soonest opportunity," the Queen ordered.

"Yes, my Queen!" Templeton shouted.

Nissa smiled at Yeveryn and pulled a smaller lever. The Calamity Engine jerked into movement in a way most unnatural, careening down the eastern road at speeds never imagined by any Zanni citizen. Fading smoke and the faint echoes of screams followed behind. Had they waited a moment longer, they would have seen the discarded, desiccated corpse of the villager rise to its feet and walk down the road toward home.

CHAPTER 25

ATLI, THE BREATHLESS SENTINEL of the night-watch ran throughout the narrow, stone halls of the Sojournic Stronghold, offering no apology for the damages she caused to people or property on her way to the Watch Captain's quarters.

Atli wore a youthful face, her eyes green like pale emeralds and her straight, shoulder-length hair the color of rust. A freckled ear emerged from each side of her head. They were much larger than she would have liked. Her stature was less than most other Sentinels; a quality to her advantage since the Stronghold's corridors were so difficult to navigate at speed. However, Atli had been a Junior Sentinel for some time and knew these halls better than almost anyone.

As she ran, Atli realized she was not wearing her bear's-fur cap, a serious violation of the rules. She seemed to have no problem remembering to wear the rest of her uniform: fur tunic, pants and boots. But the cap had escaped her memory all too often.

Atli decided it was a small matter given the circumstances. Besides, she was sure that after tonight they would shower her with praise.

Sentinels bore a simple task: watch the Sojourner on the Sojournic Path Grounds for any signs of movement. And movement is what she saw; a great deal of movement. Of that she was sure. But, what was not so simple, she supposed, was how she would convince the Watch Captain that the Holy Sojourner, the Blessed Walker of the Ancient Path, had just taken more steps in a few moments than he had taken in the last three hundred years; three full steps. It was as if he was a normal person rather than a godlike statue standing still like a stone. If her eyes had not betrayed her, Atli knew she had just witnessed the most crucial event in Sojournic history.

Atli would never admit it, but she was close to dozing off when she saw it happen. They trained Sentinels to stare at the Sojourner for hours, blinking only in occasional, measured intervals so they might not miss the slightest movement. A Sentinel, if she were diligent and wakeful enough, could see the Sojourner's movements, however imperceptible they might be to the profane.

But Atli was not a well-regarded Sentinel by the others, more the demanding Watch Captain, who caught Atli sleeping on one occasion. She never recovered from the transgression and had since remained a Junior Sentinel though she was several years beyond the acceptable age for the position.

She often dreaded the thought of spending her entire life as a Junior Sentinel, preferring instead to one day become an Itinerant, but she knew it was unlikely. Either way, she would accept her fate as long as the Sojournic Stronghold protected her; as long as she could stay. And even if the Itinerants asked her to leave, she would never return to her cotlif village.

Her path in life seemed unchangeable now. Being so far from her family's lands and influence limited her options. Laedenoran society was not forgiving of young women with no attachment. She had lived twenty-one years, still unmarried. In the five years since she arrived at the Sojournic Stronghold, three separate men from her cotlif village in the northernmost reaches of Laedenor had traveled to seek her in marriage.

Her parents delivered her to the Itinerants for training when she was a girl of just fifteen years. Though they never told her why they did so, she knew it had something to do with the cotlif village Keeper's public desire to marry her. His name was Jorl and Atli's parents were among many in the cotlif village who regarded him as an unjust man, without patience and given to the wine skin. The cotlif village suffered under his stewardship, but he remained in power as his methods were persuasive and ruthless.

The Keeper Jorl was first among the three visiting suitors. This was no small gesture as it took sometimes weeks to travel south, through the dangerous, ice-covered forests of Northern Laedenor to reach the Sojournic Stronghold. Regardless, he was most unwelcome and Atli refused. She always refused. Atli had no desire for marriage or even the general company of men.

Experience taught her she did not like the way they looked at her. Safe in the Sojournic Stronghold, she could be herself. The strict Itinerants forbade much, but a young woman without a desire to marry was not one. They honored her request to send Jorl away. Not even the powerful Jorl could hope to stand against the Itinerants, the servants of the Holy Sojourner and the givers of light to the entire world.

No force, man or beast, had ever breached the walls of the Sojournic Stronghold. Many had tried. All were destroyed, not by the Sentinels who watched the Sojourner, but by a mysterious sect of Itinerants called the Cwalu who lived in the forest beyond the Sojournic Stronghold. They protected the walls and those within, including the Holy Sojourner himself. Their ways were dark and strange to those inside the walls but their protection was welcome.

Atli knew it was in her best interest to do well, so she could stay fed and housed. They cast out disobedient Sentinels who broke enough rules. But despite her best efforts she often found herself in trouble with the Watch Captain. Even the Sentinels who never made mistakes were inferior to the Itinerants in prestige and social importance. That was the life of a Sentinel.

Sentinels practiced their craft from afar, nesting in towers of wood, straw and pitch overlooking the Sojournic Grounds and beyond to the tree line. They watched while Itinerant Initiates spent their days meditating on the Sojournic Grounds, sometimes just an arm's length away from the Holy Sojourner where the magic was deadly and most efficacious.

These seekers of power placed themselves so close that the Sojourner might give them magic and favor, sometimes both. The Itinerants called this the Lucan and they called the brave Itinerants who sought such power Lucanites. But the art of Lucan was monumental in its difficulty and not for everyone. Such were the risks and consequences, most survivors of a mishap would consider death a better choice. Those Lucanites who could not bear the punishment that came with seeking the Sojourner ended up either leaving the Sojournic Stronghold or retiring to the less demanding —and less prestigious—ranks of the Sentinels.

As an aging, Junior Sentinel always in trouble, Atli started out and remained at the bottom of the Itinerant class system. She had always been invisible, but now the Itinerants would praise her, and perhaps even promote her to Senior Sentinel. The thought made her run even faster.

Atli turned the corner and, instead of slowing to knock on the Watch Captain's quarters, she ran into a wall of muscle, sinew and flesh. The event caused Atli to chirp like a distressed bird.

The Watch Captain stood tall, still rousing from his sleep. "Sentinel! Why aren't you attending the tower? And where's your cap?"

Atli backed away, wide-eyed and unable to articulate between heaving breaths. "Watch Captain, I—I saw something, Sir!"

"What is it Sentinel?" The Watch Captain said. "You aren't drawing me into one of your useless jests are you?"

"No, Sir!" Atli replied. "Sir, the Sojourner. He moved. I saw it!" She was pointing behind her.

"Sentinel Atli!" The Watch Captain barked. "You know well your skills are mediocre. So you've remained a Junior Sentinel. That, and you seem unwilling to wear your cap!"

"Yes, Watch Captain, I know, but I saw him move as plain as you or I. It was brief, yes, but it was real. I saw it!"

The Watch Captain's mouth slacked somewhat and his eyes became twice their normal circumference. "What?"

"Yes, Watch Captain. He moved three full steps then became frozen once more. I ran to report this to you."

The burly Watch Captain stared at Atli for an endless moment in utter disbelief.

"Watch Captain!" yelled Atli, but no response. "Watch Captain! We must act!" She wondered if this was the day they had waited their entire lives for.

The unlikely admonishment shook the Watch Captain from his stupor. "Yes, Atli. We must act." He thought for a moment then placed a heavy hand on the Sentinel's shoulder. "Atli?"

"Yes, Watch Captain?"

"Let's go see the Holy Sojourner, Shall we? Sound the alarm."

CHAPTER 26

THE BEACHES OF THE SOUTHERN PROVINCE were warm and wild, kissed by salt-filled gusts of air that brushed the tops of large swells of jade-colored water. Seabirds flew aloft in a stretching blue sky sometimes diving into the foamy wake of crashing waves then emerging with bright, hued fish for a meal. Tavist and Lydia walked east along the shoreline looking to the distance for signs of kelp farming.

Lydia had assured Tavist that the farms were no more than a few hours walk from where they had exited the forest but she did not convince him. The young swordsman resolved to keep moving without complaint in this beautiful place where the sun warmed the face and where, for the moment, they were free of the threat of blood-stained invaders.

It had not been easy. For two harrowing days, Lydia and Tavist traversed the wooded hills, evading the many groups of Northlanders that pressed inland from the coast. The pair had been careful to stay to those areas they figured might be difficult for armed men to negotiate.

The plan worked but brought them too close to provincial roads for comfort. On one occasion, they found themselves trapped in some thick, roadside brush, but an arm's length from an advancing contingent of grunting invaders trailed by enormous, wheeled war machines of curious design.

They were so close, Tavist could smell the malice of those men and taste their desire for destruction. During those tense moments the book at his side grew cold, tempting him to open it but after what the book showed him concerning the Queen, he did not care to know. For now, he felt grateful for the sand, the sun, the sea and for Lydia whose passion and knowledge of her duchy was deep and interesting.

He knew Lydia grieved much but even still, there were brief moments when she seemed to forget her anger with him over Arminus' death and explain features of the land or describe memories of her childhood explorations. Those moments gave Tavist a new perspective on Lydia and challenged the many rumors about her he had overheard at court.

There was something familiar in her mannerisms; a way of being that sparked distant knowledge long forgotten. Unlike the encounters with Vang and the Queen, the book did not become cold when his thoughts turned to her, but instead grew warm. Yet he still refused to open its mystic pages because he already suspected what he might find.

"How much longer, Your Grace? Tavist's youth came out in his tone.

"I wish you would drop the formalities, Tavist," Lydia returned. "That is all behind us now. All that matters is that we find Charles Warfield."

Tavist kicked at the sand. "Fair to say but you are still a Primary noble, I am still a guardian of the Anvil of Ages. And you still have not answered my question."

"Is that so?" Lydia stooped to pick up one of many large shells in the sand. It was rectangular, black with large red spots. She smiled somewhat as she examined it. Tavist had taken several steps ahead before he realized she had fallen behind. He spun around.

"What is it?" Tavist squinted at the object. "It looks like your family nombit."

"Superb, Tavist," Said Lydia. "Here, it represents you; or at least it is the sea-life equivalent of you. We call it a Shengmar."

Tavist added the scrunching of his nose to his squinting eyes. "A Shengmar,"

"Yes. In a world where not being seen by hungry enemies is important, the Shengmar has taken a different approach. It goes to great lengths to make sure it stands out and appears lethal hoping to traverse its way by sea to shore uneaten. And sometimes it works." Lydia cracked the shell in half and ate the fleshy interior in one bite. She savored it. "Other times? Well—"

"Are you mocking me, Lydia?"

"Well, I should think it obvious," said Lydia. She picked up another and threw it to Tavist.

He regarded its dimensions and texture, realizing the sting of hunger in his belly. It was easy to open and its meat was exquisite. "This is divine!" He picked up three more and devoured them. "I have never tasted such a perfect delight! I believe no one else in the Northern Province has either,"

"Should Northern socialites consume everything? We in the south must keep a few things to ourselves, yes?" Lydia watched the young soldier as he gorged himself on Shengmar meat. She decided that he was nice to look at, for an overgrown child with the accompanying manners. Still, he had a charm hard to ignore. "Tell me Tavist, what is your path in this life? Were you intent on attending the Anvil all your days?

"I suppose," replied Tavist through a mouthful of Shengmar. "I wanted to do something important; to be remembered." He pointed at Lydia with an empty Shengmar shell. "After my death, people would say 'Tavist was strong and true. He never gave up.' Yes, that is what they would say."

"Is it so important, that people think you strong in death? You are still dead. They waste the praise."

Tavist swallowed. "You know nothing of what it means to guard the Anvil of Ages."

"Nor should I," returned Lydia, smirking. "But I know something of what it means to be crushed by it. All here in the Southern Province do. Unlike you, our stated purpose is to toil to our deaths for the sake of the comfort of your people. Every convenience you enjoy, every object you use and every meal on your table is not possible but for the pain and suffering of our endless days of labor."

"Nonsense. You are exaggerating."

"I wish I were. You have not seen it because it is inconvenient. You are foolish, Tavist."

The poison took hold of him. His limbs grew heavy and a fog beset his thoughts. "You! You have killed me!"

"Never eat more than one," Lydia warned. "That is what we teach our children. Not an easy task considering how delicious they are."

"Why have you done this?" He was succumbing to sleep.

"The kelp farmers we seek have remained safe from northern exploitation for so many years because their location is secret. And as you have so noted, you are still a member of the Zanni August Guard. I am not sure my friends would appreciate you knowing their exact whereabouts."

Tavist formed a final thought before slipping in to sleep. "Duchess or not, I swear you will answer for this!"

"Have a good nap, my little Shengmar," Lydia said, ensuring his collapse was not too harmful.

CHAPTER 27

ATLI, THE MEDIOCRE, JUNIOR SENTINEL and Jeth the Watch Captain were the first to arrive at the at the Sojourner's site. Jeth noticed that the Holy Sojourner was not in the same position as before but had moved forward at least three steps. The footprints in the snow behind the Holy One's feet were further evidence of the event. The Sojourner's position was different. For one hundred twenty-three years, he had maintained the Sibb-gewealc, the Walk of Peace.

Every denizen of the Sojournic Stronghold knew it well and none lived who could remember a time before the Sibb-gewealc. It was a well-studied and well-interpreted position: the Mystic Coil in the Sojourner's right hand held high, but the Shard in his left hand held at his side pointed down. It meant that the Itinerants were to travel the world offering help to all in a posture of tolerance and deference. That would change.

The Sojourner now held the Shard with both hands above his head as one about to strike an enemy with a dagger. His expression had turned from calm, curiosity to determination, perhaps anger. The Itinerants would likely interpret this as the Wyrsa-gewealc; the Walk of Battle which had not been seen since the Sixteen Generations War.

But added to the intrigue was the Lucanite adept who lay at the Sojourner's feet, shielding himself with his hands as if a Nurdrayl redbear were about to trample him. This adept, only moments ago, was making his way closer to the Sojourner over several days. When Lucanites survived this process, they emerged with new abilities or insights giving them the right to join the ranks of the Itinerants.

It was the dream of every Initiate to achieve this momentous feat. Few had managed it, and Jeth was among those who had failed; unable to handle the raw power of being so close to the Holy Sojourner of Laedenor. He, himself, had only lasted for two days before he could stand it no longer. The experience blinded him for several weeks. That was twenty years past. The Itinerants resigned him to the ranks of the Sentinels and there he toiled for years until he achieved the highest rank possible: The Captain of the Watch.

Watch Captain Jeth knew the motionless Lucanite before him. He was called Amarl. Amarl joined the Lucanites one year ago and had since exceeded every expectation of his elders and even caught the eye of the Father Prelate himself. Jeth and the other Sentinels liked Amarl and often made wagers concerning his progress.

This time, Jeth would lose his money. He wagered one of the daywatch Sentinels that Amarl could master the Lucan, get close to the Sojourner and emerge a mighty Itinerant. Instead, Amarl was as still as stone; frozen in position on the snow-covered ground. Once the Sojourner cursed a Lucanite in this way, they remained unmoving forever. None had escaped this fate.

The path behind the Sojourner teemed with failed Lucanites from the depths of Laedenoran history, all frozen in various positions; the consequence of approaching too close to the Sojourner too fast. The Itinerants named them the Shard-Fallen. Many wore the blue and white striped Sojournic robes expected of Lucanites. These failed Lucanites were well-known among the Itinerants as the names of all Lucanites, Itinerants and Sentinels had been recorded in the Sojournic Rolls since the beginning of the Sojournic Order a thousand years ago. Such administrative accuracy was a matter of pride for the Itinerants.

But there were other Shard-Fallen who did not wear Sojournic garb. These were further down the path and further back in time going all the way to where the Holy Sojourner's journey began in the Gearwood Thicket five thousand years since. Those doomed ancients predated the order and nobody alive knew who any of them were, though there had always been local legends and speculation regarding their identities, origins and purposes. These stationary unknowns were a testament to Laedenoran history. The Itinerants referred to them as the Elder Shard-Fallen, or sometimes Shard-Mothers and Shard-Fathers.

It was common, if not expected, for Itinerants and aspiring Lucanites to study the Shard-Fallen to gain insight into their own journeys. They hoped for clues to help them understand the past. But unlike the Sojourner, aspirants could approach the Shard-Fallen and touch them, although doing so—even with a stick or gauntlets—was not a wise idea as it resulted in instant death. This meant that studying the Shard-Fallen came with great personal risk.

Amarl, the Lucanite was now one of the many Shard-Fallen, forever still and forever unfulfilled.

"Oh wondrous night!" Came an elderly voice from behind Jeth. "The Sojourner travels a great distance before us! He favors us!"

At the sound of the Prelate's voice, everyone on the Sojournic grounds dropped to one knee and held their open, right hands aloft. Atli lagged behind the others. The Prelate motioned all to rise by waving his hand.

The Prelate wore flowing robes of a blue only found in the deepest of frozen lakes. His frame was slight and sinewed and his features were grandiose. Uneven tufts of grey hair sprouted from his brow, atop icy blue eyes. A ring of grey, unrestrained hair fell to his waist around which a cord of white, braided silk was tied. In the center of his chest was a golden, embroidered emblem of five conifer trees in the formation of a square; one tree in each corner and one in the middle.

"Watch Captain," called the Prelate. "You have witnessed the Astyr; the Moving Fate! The Sojourner chooses you to see his path. You have found your place among the Itinerants. Jeth, tell us of your experience and you may seal your entry into our order. It is long deserved!"

The idea was tempting. Jeth toiled at the watch for twenty years, always observing, always seeing the blessings of others. His heart longed to be an Itinerant and seeing the Astyr was the only way a Sentinel could transcend their station—the only way. He could accept the offer. Nobody would dispute it. The Sentinels loved Jeth. And if Atli disputed it, nobody would believe her. They thought Atli a jokester, a reprobate and a fool. But Jeth was a just man; a Sentinel, chosen by fate and bound to it. He was proud and resolute. His honor would survive this test.

"Father Prelate," belted Jeth, gesturing toward Atli. "Atli was at the watch. The Sojourner showed her his steps. She alerted me."

The aged, blue-robed Prelate seemed to deflate in posture, leaving only his opened eyes as evidence of his previous enthusiasm. He turned his head toward Atli with measured slowness. "Sentinel Atli, is this true? Have you witnessed the Astyr?"

Atli looked at Jeth who encouraged her with a quick nod.

"Yes, Father Prelate," Answered Atli. "I did." She winced and shrank away expecting a thrashing.

The Sojournic Grounds grew silent while the Prelate considered this unforeseen complication. Then, a thunderous laughter cut through the cold night, startling everyone. The Prelate's mirthful chortling subsided, and he approached Atli with his arms outstretched. He embraced Atli. She was confused, but she allowed it to happen.

"Atli, I do not know what strange purpose this serves, but it is not for me to challenge the Sojourner's choosing." The Prelate smiled as a father, his eyes meeting hers. His voice was loud and celebratory. "On this day, Atli, the Sojourner claims you and enters you into the ranks of the Itinerants; we few who court his holy path. And though you have no known powers, your particular gift is much more precious. You have seen the Sojourner's steps and are, by our tradition, given the right to interpret them. I welcome you as a Daughter of the Path, Atli. You should know, however, that it is my duty to inform you as your Prelate you are now, at this point in time, out of uniform."

A tall, stoic, female Itinerant in the crowd ran inside the compound and after a few silent moments, emerged holding light blue, folded Itinerant's robes. She presented them to a surprised Atli. All cheered and closed in on Atli, including Jeth who for all of his frustration with Atli, was still glad for her. Congratulations were cut short. An intense hissing sound that overlapped waves of discordant singing interrupted the celebration.

Several dozen figures appeared all over the grounds, emerging from a colorful glamour that, in force, illuminated everything in sight. The figures were clad in armor of black chainmail under thin plates of black rock that seemed to swallow the surrounding light. They wore no helm, showing thin, hairless scalps and pale faces with black orbs for eyes. Black, moving tattoos of varying design covered their heads including many spirals and circles. Each had a black long sword at their side and wore a single, black gauntlet on their right hand. They had an air of death that made the attending Lucanites, Itinerants and Sentinels exchange nervous glances with one another.

"Father Prelate Quincunx," began the figure closest. The female voice was otherworldly and altogether unsettling. "We also welcome the chosen as an Itinerant and we look to her insights. The Sojourner's movements called us from our tasks and our patrols. This is most unexpected."

The Prelate grinned, his tone took on an edge of caution. "Yes, yes it is! Is it not splendid, Dohtor Yuun?"

"I know not of splendor, Father Prelate, but I serve the Shard and the choosing of the child who wields it." She bowed toward the Sojourner, right palm raised to the sky. The other dark figures followed her in kind. Yuun turned her ghostly gaze to Amarl, the Lucanite, frozen in time, forever still.

"But the interpretation is clear, Father Prelate."

"Dohtor Yuun, it is not for you or I to say." Prelate Quincunx placed his hands on Atli's shoulders and nudged her forward. Atli felt exposed like a human shield just then.

"Yes," said Yuun. She moved toward Atli like lightning, leaving a trail of wispy black vapor in her wake, stopping only a hand's distance from her face. "And who wins such favor from the Holy Sojourner?"

Atli had never seen a Cwalu Itinerant so close before. They kept to the Cwalu encampment outside the walls of the Sojournic Compound where they could practice their unnatural, magically enhanced battle tactics without being disturbed by their less macabre counterparts inside the walls. Sometimes at night during the watch, Atli could hear their discordant singing coming from the Nurdrayl forest. It was distracting and made it difficult to concentrate on detecting the Sojourner's movements.

That singing somehow made the land itself more menacing to Atli than it already was. Shadows were darker, winds were colder, and the watch was lonelier. Like most Lucanites, she did not trust the Cwalu. But the only reason the Sojournic Compound still stood after a thousand years was because of Cwalu's sworn protection.

As cold and lightless as the other Itinerants thought them, the Cwalu were likewise Itinerants, if but a different sort. They were ethereal, secretive, bizarre and lethal. Facing in battle was a committed decision to visit the world-after.

Their power came from touching and tasting the blood that dripped from the Coil in the Sojourner's hand. The inhabitants of the Sojournic Stronghold found it disturbing the Cwalu started out as all Lucanites do; attempting the Lucan. But during their journey, each of them used their will to move closer to the blood that hung, frozen in the air in a crimson column that emerged from the Sojourner's hand, hoping to touch it with their right hand so they could then imbibe it giving them terrible power.

A Lucanite who succeeded in this way left the Sojournic Grounds to join the Cwalu Itinerants outside the compound who would complete the process through a series of secret rituals meant to alter the new Cwalu's body and mind.

For the rest of their lives, the Cwalu would wander the Nurdrayl Forest, searching for threats to the Sojournic Compound, awaiting the day that one of their own, a Cwalu Itinerant, would become Prelate and wage war on the world once again. But that could not happen until the chosen interpreter made their determination. The Cwalu had waited for so long.

For sometime now, the main task of the Cwalu had been clearing the forest of the strange, obese Dreka that appeared at Sable Rock. The creatures had stopped appearing, which was just fine with the Cwalu but made the Father Prelate nervous for he knew it was the lost and fabled Bekrot Chair that created them. Had the chair found a new owner? Had the user of the chair perished?

"My name is Atli, Dohtor Yuun," She could see ashen spirals appear deep in the distance of Yuun's black eyes, causing her to look down. It terrified her.

"Atli? An odd name for such a beautiful girl." Yuun seemed to envelop Atli with her presence. "You know, I was beautiful like you once," she reached out with her gloved hand to touch Atli's cheek but a look of warning from the Prelate stopped her. Touch between the two sects of Itinerants was forbidden. "But now I am much more that; I pursue much more than the temporary glory of beauty. But it is not beauty you desire Dohtor Atli, is it?"

Atli looked up at Yuun who smiled in as feminine a way as she could feign, showing blackened, receding gums and blood-tinged teeth. The swirling pulse of her tattoos mesmerized Atli.

"I desire only to walk the Sojourner's path, Dohtor Yuun," She lied. She wanted more.

"As do the Cwalu," Yuun backed away in a specter-like movement, causing all in blue robes to relax somewhat. "It appears our time to serve is at hand. You see it, Dohtor Atli," Yuun pointed to the Sojourner. He was still, but vibrant, powerful callings beckoned her soul to his blood.

The Prelate could stand for no more. "Enough! No more of this! Atli will make her interpretation known to all in the tradition of our ancient order one day from now when the sun is at its peak. Until then, we will allow her to ponder this event in peace," His voice echoed through the compound.

"Yes, Father Prelate," Yuun and the other Cwalu bowed. She turned to Atli and gave a venomous smile. "Again, welcome to the Itinerants, Dohtor Atli and we await your wisdom."

The Cwalu faded out of sight, one by one, leaving small wisps of red vapor behind. The Prelate Quincunx placed his arm around the dazed Atli and led her toward the complex. "Come Atli, tomorrow the world as we know it may change forever. But tonight we celebrate!"

She turned to see the Sojourner once more, but the Prelate redirected her inside the complex.

CHAPTER 28

THE BOAT DRIFTED NORTHBOUND on the River Kem toward the city of Port Frailty. It was warm, humid and though they rowed all day, there was little discussion. Dara napped while Veldic maintained a watchful eye of both Charles and Braden Bol; Braden Bol because Veldic mistrusted thieves and Charles because he was an idiot.

Charles often said if there were just one food to eat, it should be brier-berries. They were not the most expensive food as they grew just as wild in the Northern Province as they did in the south. He loved their versatility. They went well in dumplings, tea, bread and by themselves. And until now, Charles could not think of a single flavor or aroma combination that suffered by adding of some measure of brierberry goodness.

Veldic stifled her laughter as Charles leaned over the side of the boat and gave his lunch of stolen brier-berries to the river. It turned out that the smell of sulfur and filth was an exception to his brierberry rule and did not compliment them well, not to mention he was still a little affected by the previous evening's festivities. He had been baking like a buttered squash inside his armor and had removed pieces over the course of the afternoon. Only the leggings remained.

At least the sun was setting soon. The stench had been its worst a few hours earlier when the air was still hot. With luck, they would end the day in a warm bed after a good meal.

The Touchthief Braden Bol chuckled. "Looks like your friend does not approve of the stench of our great city. Do not worry. You will get used to it." He stopped rowing and looked down river as far as he could. There were many boats of varying size and speed, traversing to and from Port Frailty; the majority buttonwood barges. The distant city rose from both sides of the banks of the river over the trees and into the sky.

From this far, Port Frailty looked like some massive mountain made of worked stone, metal and wood, spewing smoke and vapor in all directions. And even though he had seen it before, Braden Bol still marveled at its overwhelming presence.

"Why have you stopped rowing," Asked Veldic, herself gawking at the city. "We haven't much time. We're almost there. Let's finish this!"

"There, look!" Braden Bol pointed forward and to the right bank of the river. About one furlong away stood a waving figure on one of the many private docks extending into the river.

Dara yawned, waking from her nap at the sound of Charles' retching. "Who is that?" she said.

"That, good people is my brother," said Braden Bol. "We will stay with my brother in Ultshome Manor tonight and you can enter Port Frailty by waterway tomorrow."

Dara, now awake, turned. "Does your brother have our property?"

"I hope so," said Braden Bol. "And after we agree to terms, We shall return your coin to you."

Dara's tone sharpened. "What do you mean? I am warning you. If you think—"

"Keep your head, my sweet. Your coin is probably safe."

Dara, reached for her missing quiver.

"As are your quiver and arrows," added Braden Bol. "My brother can be impulsive but in my reply to his message I admonished him not to sell your belongings."

Dara shifted. "Bolts. They are bolts. So, you used messaging terns? That explains how you knew it was a coin you had stolen. Your brother sent you a message by flight. Messaging terns are not cheap. You must be wealthy. Thieving has treated you well."

Braden Bol grinned. "Not messaging terns, my delicious truffle, but messaging bees. And no, I am not wealthy. I am just clever, charming and available. Did I mention before that I was available?" Dara grimaced at Braden Bol's daring words and Charles winced with jealousy. It was obvious to Charles that Braden Bol enjoyed their discomfort.

Veldic grunted her acknowledgment. "I have heard stories. I thought they had all died off. How did you happen to find one?"

Braden Bol wiggled his fingers in the air at Veldic. "Touchthief, remember?" He pulled out a necklace from inside his shirt that ended in a small, open locket. Inside was a small, glass sphere inside which sat thick, golden liquid. "My brother holds its counterpart. This, friends, is a honey-charm."

"And it attracts the messaging bee to it I assume?" asked Charles.

"Correct!" spat Braden Bol. "Each messaging bee makes honey from rare blossoms which grow only from the corpses of murdered innocents. For the rest of its life, the bee seeks this honey no matter where or how far it might be. So, when the beekeepers cultivate them for service, they also destroy the hive except for one bee and all the honey except for a small amount which the beekeepers split between two lockets. Both people keep the lockets open at all times.

The messaging bee will stay near the closest source of the honey. When someone wants to send a message, they attach the message to the bee, close their locket and the bee will fly to the other honey-charm. And no hives produce the exact variety of honey, eliminating confusion. Brilliant, I think!" Braden Bol snapped his fingers and tucked the locket back in his shirt.

With Veldic at the rudder, Braden Bol again rowed, and the boat moved toward the dock. Charles was still nauseous but did well in keeping any further retching at bay. The smell was terrible.

"Ho, there!" yelled the waving man on the dock. "Braden! You've guests!"

"Yes, Ganeth, indeed I do!" Braden Bol shouted. "And they are interested in negotiating!"

"Wonderful! Let's get you moored and on your legs, brother!"

By his features and gait, the man had the look of Braden Bol and was about the same age, though he boasted a thick shock of yellow hair that hung the length of his back and a full, matching beard cropped short. His attire alluded to a man accustomed to comfort although not unfamiliar with hard work. His billowing shirt was low cut and made of varying shades of green cloth, his black pants tucked into tanned, hard leather knee-high boots adorned with three silver buckles. At his side was a thin dagger set into a silver ring that pierced a brown leather belt. He reached for Braden Bol's outstretched oar to guide the boat in. Charles could see Ganeth's honey-charm hanging from his neck.

Braden climbed up to the dock. "Our friends here have never seen a messaging bee."

Ganeth smiled with genuine warmth and hospitality, holding his hand out to help the others. "They are a few among many, brother."

None of the others dared take his hand, for fear of losing more of their things.

"Ah!," announced Ganeth. "You are right to mistrust me. I understand. I am not a Touchthief like my brother, I assure you." He reissued his hand while Braden finished tying off the boat to the dock. The three travelers gave each other curious glances.

"I have supper and wine waiting at Ultshome Manor," offered Ganeth. "Shall we retire there and begin our negotiations?"

"You mean extortions?" Dara asked.

Ganeth smiled, raised his eyebrows and again offered his hand.

Slow, but with decisiveness, Charles grasped Ganeth's hand. He wanted wine; if only to quell his disturbed stomach.

"Charles!" Dara protested. "They're scoundrels! You wish to deal with scoundrels?"

"No Dara," replied Charles while climbing out. "I wish to leave this stinking river and out of the rest of this armor."

"Good," added Ganeth. "We will be much happier inside the Manor when night falls. Swarms of rats and Shamblefolk will soon beset the entire area outside the city. Neither of them are very pleasant. But my guards are well-paid and well-trained. It is safe inside. Come!"

The three travelers followed Ganeth Bol up the path cleared through the tall grass toward Ultshome Manor, a giant estate-house of considerable taste and cost. Veldic noted aloud the beauty of the house's Aromite construction; the first level made of white marble rounds and orange mud under which the second level sat resplendent in its construction of exposed, lacquered buttonwood planks and plaster.

Several bay windows of beveled glass and diamond-shaped, lead trim protruded at odd angles on both floors. The roof was of river grass set between buttonwood trusses and gables. On each side, like Sentinels, two white marble chimneys rose high above the river land. Despite his haste toward refreshment, Charles could not help but notice and count the guards, each in a different tree, following their movements with their weapons.

There were four. He turned to warn Dara.

"Yes, Charles," Dara said. "I see them."

Charles decided the river lands were a dangerous place.

CHAPTER 29

AERION AND VANG PROCEEDED through the magic tunnel which had darkened in its hue to the color of drying blood. He looked to the snowy ground; the only part of this place he had seen before. But Aerion found it hard not to turn his eyes back to the ceiling. The malformed faces, now framed in black, swirled about, waiting for Aerion to drop his hand. Aerion found their expressions to be puzzling. Some seemed in pain, others worried. All looked desperate.

A choice few were cleverer than the others, attempting to smile and curry Aerion's trust. They only intensified Aerion's terror. Such creatures could not feign happiness. As if they sensed Aerion's disbelief, they returned to their murderous expressions, only to once again grin with glee.

"Vang, why do they hate me so much? I've done nothing to them."

"Not yet you haven't," corrected Vang. "But you will. I have seen it. Remember, they exist in your future; in the world-after. They know you though you do not yet know them. At least not this version of you."

"You sound mad," said Aerion. "But none of this makes much sense anymore does it?"

"It is not very far now. I will make all clear at Stag's End."

"Stag's End?"

"The cliff where your quarry escaped you."

The statement antagonized Aerion's sanity. "That just happened, Vang. It was only moments ago. I'm still wet and filthy with mud. How? Who could have known? It's not been long enough to be given a name!"

Vang spun around to face the boy. "It has been far longer than you can yet comprehend, hunter. And I've explained this to you."

"I'm not a hunter," returned Aerion. "And since you seem to know everything, you should know I'm disgraced."

"Just because your cotlif village didn't choose you to bear the title of Huntsman doesn't mean you are not a hunter. Oh yes, Aerion. You are a hunter. And besides, everyone you know is long dead, remember? There's no one left to argue."

"What happened to them?" Aerion stopped walking.

"Well, this did, Aerion," Vang's almond-shaped eyes glinted like gold.

"You mean this catastrophe from the sky? The animals that swarmed to their deaths?"

"Yes."

"I don't understand."

"Aerion, all of this you see around you interrupted your eternal purpose. On that day everything changed."

Aerion pointed to the ground with the hand bearing the coil. "Stop! What day? It is still this day!" The faces and clawed hands from above pressed in to the tunnel, moaning as would wounded beasts of burden. Vang motioned toward them with his eyes and Aerion raised his hand again with a start. The terrible things receded.

"For you it is, yes. For the world outside, it's not. I've already explained this to you."

Aerion let out a yell of frustration and as they continued walking, he noticed that Vang's footsteps made no noise in the snow, mud and plants.

"None of this was part of my plan. And the existence of this entire world upsets the balance."

Aerion shook his head with confusion. "What?"

Vang winced, wiping away the thought with a bony hand. "You were supposed to go back to to your cotlif village triumphant in the hunt. You killed the rock stag with your father's spear and you became a revered huntsman; the best in all memory. Then you became the cotlif village Quarrymaster, took a wife who bore you many children. You grew old together, and you died in your sleep, satisfied at a life of renown and plenty. Isn't that nice?"

It was everything Aerion wanted. "Liar! How could you know?"

"Because Aerion, after you died you left this world. I met you in the world-after."

Aerion puzzled at the idea. He understood at face value, but such things were impossible. He indulged Vang. "Did I look as I do now?"

Vang chuckled. "No, no. On Rax, each person is born anew as an infant. When we reach adolescence, we come to remember everything about who we were in the world-before."

"The world-before? What about this world?"

"No. Only you knew of this world. Until you came, two worlds mattered to humanity: Vel and Rax, the world-before and the world-after. But you are special. You called this world Myn. It is between Vel and Rax. And before you told me, I didn't know it existed."

The thought intrigued Aerion. "Do others in Rax know a person's past as well?"

"Not unless you tell them."

"Are bad people always bad?"

"Sometimes, not always. But you would want to be. Who we are in previous worlds has influence, but it does not decide."

"There are more?"

"Yes, there are more. Many more. But this world, Myn, only touches Vel and Rax."

"Unthinkable! Who was I in the world-before? Who were you in the world-before, Vang?"

Vang stopped as though impaled on sharpened ice. "I was a murderer." He said it with malice, ensuring every syllable was deliberate and rich.

Startled, Aerion tensed his sore muscles and waited for Vang to walk again. "Then are you here to murder me Vang? You might. If all of what you say is true, you have stolen away my perfect future. I care for nothing else save to see my father again though by your account I would not recognize him, anyway."

Vang nodded. "I am not here to kill you, but to help you. For what I can offer you in the world-after, you would trade your perfect future a thousand times over. Rax is a land of riches and plenty beyond anything here in Myn."

Aerion scowled. "I don't trust you, Vang. Your words are empty but I trust those creatures around us even less. Lead on, then. Your company is preferable to theirs. Let's start with that. But walk ahead of me. So far as I can see, I'm armed and you are not."

Away from Aerion's view, Vang smiled. "You are a clever hunter, keeping your quarry ahead of you. Shall we continue on?"

"Continue on." The two drudged forward. "How do I know you are telling the truth?"

Vang snorted. "I know things about you, Aerion. You told them in the world-after. Things no one else knows; choices you made in this world and betrayals you committed. Aerion, believe or don't believe. But we will become good friends you and I."

Aerion raised an eyebrow. "What kinds of choices? What betrayals? And you have interrupted all of that. There is no guarantee those events will happen now since you have ruined my life."

"Enough. It is not so simple and we must be quick. We cannot hope to stave off these demons forever. Whatever questions remain I will answer at Stag's End. In a short time you will understand everything." Vang flicked his white hair with his hand and increased his speed.

"Can we fight these things, Vang?"

"No. We are too weak in this place and they know it. but I'm working a plan."

CHAPTER 30

CHARLES HOVERED ALOFT IN THE DUSK SKY, *seeing below untold numbers of drowned beasts awash in tumultuous and putrid seas. To the north, the clouds separated revealing a great horror of unimaginable size in the shape of a rotted face, disembodied and surrounded by wisps of blackened ghost-light. Its mouth shambled open and siphoned the fetid sea into itself. The bodies of the dead creatures came awake and begged for peace. Their cries went unheeded. A massive column of corpse-laden sea water stretched upward into the terrible maw.*

"Stop!" yelled Charles. "They are innocent!"

Bright, crimson eyes appeared in the decaying sockets of the thing and fixed on Charles. It stopped siphoning the water, sending it crashing back down.

"They are not for you!" Charles was sobbing.

"All are mine!" The thing boomed. "Even cowards. Even you!"

"Who are you?"

The face shrank into a woman's distant form. The woman flew toward Charles with arms out in front.

"You know who I am Charles. I love you." The voice was Nissa's.

Charles turned to run but in front of him stood Nissa, devoid of raiment. Before Charles could react, she pressed to him, grabbed his face and kissed him. Charles surrendered but soon realized something was wrong. Nissa giggled as they kissed. Charles tried to pull back but was powerless as Nissa vomited rotten seaweed into his mouth, filling his lungs. The influx of plant matter muffled his attempts to scream. Charles felt himself fall toward the open ocean below.

"Charles, it is time for you to remember what you are." Nissa's laughter rang into the distance as Charles plummeted.

"Wake Charles! You are dreaming!" It was Veldic looming over him. "It is morning. We have much to do."

Charles stirred with a sudden kick, launching Veldic across the room into Dara, who was dressing for the day. Before Veldic could recover, Charles was upon her, his eyes a deep, ancient green and his teeth bared. Veldic tried to collect her wits as Charles pummeled her with his fists, but the act caught her off balance. She misjudged Charles' strength. Through bursts of pain, Veldic subdued Charles in a headlock. Charles writhed and spat, making feral noises. It took all of Veldic's strength to hold him. Dara leaped forward and slapped Charles in the face. The sound was bright and final. Startled, Charles stared at Dara dumbfounded. Veldic breathed heavy, but relaxed her great and powerful arms as Charles became himself again.

"What in the Gastwyrd's name?" Dara yelled, scanning the room.

Charles heaved and stared at his scraped and painful hands. "I do not know." He turned up to Veldic. "I am sorry Veldic. I did not mean to—"

"Ha!" Veldic spun Charles around "You hit like an Aromite vine-beast! You were hiding your strength all this time! I cannot wait to see your skills in action, boy!" Veldic's elation was genuine, as was the blood that colored her lip.

Charles stared at his hands. "I do not understand what just happened."

Dara relaxed her tense muscles and resumed dressing. "Now that we are awake, let's find some food."

"Agreed!" Veldic smiled and slapped Charles' shoulder.

Ganeth Bol burst into the guest quarters with urgency. "Friends! Good, you are awake! Come see!" The others followed him.

The previous evening had been festive. As hosts, Braden and Ganeth were gracious and entertaining. Their food was delectable, and the wine was effective. There were several scoundrels who inhabited Ultshome Manor; their affect akin to thieves and footpads.

It was quite the operation. Ganeth explained to them that small teams of thieves would foray into the city and surrounding areas for three or four days at a time, to return with whatever they could liberate. The three outsiders expressed their relief to know Braden Bol was the only Touchthief among them though not for lack of effort on his part. Over drinks, Ganeth told of how his brother Braden tried to teach others and failed.

No one could teach this kind of magic; a curse meant for those few chosen to bear it. Ganeth spoke how Braden had made the most of a bad situation. Yet no matter how much wine flowed or how much Charles pestered him, Ganeth refused to speak regarding the details of how it started. He only admitted it an embarrassing family matter.

During the evening festivities, the conversation had turned to the coin and its disposition, along with Dara's quiver of bolts. Dara even let slip their need to get to Laedenor and traverse the Neverwall; that an Expanser could guide them across. Ganeth assured the safety of her things; that he had not yet sold them. Throughout the night, the band of travelers and their hosts made many claims through wine-stained teeth. There were promises of fortune and of revenge and many rounds of storytelling besides.

When asked, a talkative Charles tried to explain Zannistar to what had become a very large and interested group, a task met with many puzzled looks since no one there had ever heard of such a place. Charles knew this was because of Gyldred's sorcery. Charles pondered how Dara and Veldic could know Zannistar existed at all. He also wondered why the Effacer's magic was not affecting them at this very moment.

He surmised this meant that Gyldred's death somehow negated the magic and stopped people from forgetting Zannistar once they had knowledge. There were questions from inebriated privateers and mercenaries about Zannistar's location. Sensing their enterprising motivations, Charles changed the subject.

The evening progressed, filled with much bragging and dancing about. At the end, Ganeth promised to return the coin to Charles in exchange he and his companions complete one simple task: the death of the Minister of Port Frailty, Surek Taben. He offered no other information or reason. They would either accept or refuse. That was the deal.

The thought was shocking and left the three travelers in varying states of emotional turmoil. They were not assassins. Warriors at the most, sniveling nobles at the least, but not assassins. They retreated to a less crowded corner of the main hall and debated their options into the night. No closer to a decision than when they had begun, they slept off the wine and resumed when the sun came up.

Having just risen to magnificent hangovers and Charles' odd and violent outburst, they followed Ganeth Bol over the sleeping revelers and out of Ultshome Manor into the misty, morning humidity of the river lands beyond the towering walls of Port Frailty. Ganeth ran to the dock where the row boat was.

He pointed upriver where a giant wall of mist lay on the calm waters. "Come! Listen!" he yelled. "Do not worry, friends, the Shamble Folk crawl back to their holes with the sun. You are safe. Quick!"

Charles, Veldic and Dara caught up and paused in place. Charles' stomach protested the morning.

A slow thrumming emerged in the distance like a massive, beating heart. It blended with the other sounds of the river, then overtook them. As it grew louder, it became more percussive. Charles' hunger pangs disappeared as his focus heightened. He noticed that the mist moved with the pulses.

"What is this?" asked Veldic

"That, my wine-soaked friends, is the sound of the Jaibok." Ganeth gathered the others to him, his voice reduced to a quiet rasp. "It returns with a bounty from the Eastern Arom mountain lands; medicines, metals, exotic creatures and much more!"

"I've never heard of such a thing," said Veldic. "At least not in the jungle-lands. Is it a beast?"

"No, but a machine. An amazing, sorcerous machine! And it is how you will enter the city. Each time it returns from its travels it waits outside the great doors for a few hours while the gate opens and the city's guards inspect the hold. During that time, you will gain your entry."

Dara put her gloved hands on her hips. "And would you have us swim into the city once the gates are open? If so, your plan is stupid. Why not enter through the main gate? Why must we sneak at all?"

At this, Veldic and Charles both turned to Ganeth with wide-eyed indignation.

"Because readers watch the gates." It was Braden Bol, Touchthief and Master of Ultshome Manor, adjusting the buckle on his belt as he joined the group on the river bank. "They can see your intent. They would capture you and hang you before you could do anything."

"Good morning brother," said Ganeth. "You are just in time for the Jaibok's arrival."

"Good!" Braden inhaled the river air through his nose with audible delight. "I trust you dreamed of yesterday's lovemaking and tomorrow's riches. Tell our associates the time is near. The Jaibok approaches!"

"Aye then." Ganeth chucked and patted Charles' back as he sauntered toward Ultshome Manor, fists raised in victory.

Dara pointed at the gargantuan river gate that lay at least five furlongs down river, difficult to see through the mist. "So how do we gain entry, then?"

"Ah, good morning to *you*, Dara," said Braden, taking a step toward her. "Your beauty improves the river's magnificence, if even such a thing were possible."

Again, Dara reached for bolts not there. She folded her arms and stewed.

"You will reunite with your weapons soon," Braden promised. "You will need them for the task at hand." Braden pantomimed shooting a bolt from his hand and made a whooshing noise with his mouth. "But again, you will get caught if you try to enter the city by any normal means."

"So how is it that the thieves of your household can enter unchallenged?" Dara was skeptical. "Wouldn't the readers catch them too?"

Braden grinned. "The minister allows for a certain amount of underground industry to take place; thieving, gambling, prostitution and the like. I don't think there is a pure soul in Port Frailty. But an attempt on his life? They would know at the gate, which is why nobody knows of it save for my brother and I."

Charles shrugged. "So are we going through with this? Will we murder an innocent person? I will not do it. He has done nothing to us."

"Perhaps not to you," said Braden, "but I assure you he is no innocent. All know he is responsible for the untimely disappearances of hundreds of citizens, many of them children. What he does with them is unclear, but there are rumors that Surek Taben is not human; that he consumes those he captures."

"He is a relic of a war fought long ago between Arom and Laedenor; a creation most unpleasant. No, of his qualities prominent and otherwise, innocence is not among them. And while my own chosen profession may be below the line of general morality, the minister's machinations are nothing short of true evil."

216

"Why us?" Veldic interjected. "You've access to people more qualified than we."

"Yes, many scoundrels haunt Port Frailty and the Riverlands, but none of them can do what she can do." Braden pointed at Dara with both index fingers.

Dara winced. "What, mastery of gearwood?"

Braden snorted. "Well, yes. You are Dreka are you not? And not any Dreka, no. A Woodlock besides. I knew it as soon as my brother described the arrows, sorry, the bolts in your quiver. I thought your kind to be a legend. Soulless and able to command the mysterious gearwood from the Northlands. I have never seen one of you in person. Interesting. I see no difference between you and a normal woman."

Dara showed he wounded her.

"Again," Braden continued. "The Minister of Port Frailty is inhuman, or at least that is what most believe. He is swift and has thwarted all attempts to harm him. The Minister discovered even the best, highest-paid assassins before they ever got close. No arrow, sword or poison has worked. But you? You are special. And though you are without a soul, you are gifted which gives you the best chance of success. Besides, unlike your soft-bellied friend Charles here, you and Veldic do not strike me as those who would shy away from dispensing bloodshed, if it were necessary."

Veldic straightened. "We're on an important errand. Our purpose extends beyond you and this accursed place. The Itinerants sent us. You interrupt a holy task."

"It is the truth," Dara said. "I am Dreka, doomed and soulless. But you know I am dangerous and I answer only to the Itinerants. Our task more important than you can imagine. More important than one city. If we fail, all of existence will suffer. And Charles is the only one who can stop it, soft belly and all. So yes, I will kill to see him to Laedenor. But I beseech you, give us the coin and let us be on our way. Your life is also in the balance, Touchthief."

Braden pondered Dara's plea for a moment, but his face hardened. "You will steal into the city by the Jaibok and kill the Minister of Port Frailty. There are no other options. You have one day." Braden Bol had a terse side to him.

Dara leaned in. "And what if I kill you instead and take back our property by force? Remember I have no soul and no cause for concern over eternity."

Braden smiled and likewise leaned in, almost touching Dara's face with his own, an act that caused a twinge of jealousy in Charles. Braden noticed. "Because, lovely, if you do that you will never find your coin. I have taken steps to ensure its safety. One day."

Fire flashed in Dara's eyes. "I am sure I can find it without the help of your corpse."

Braden's toothy smile widened. "Go ahead. Call your bolts to you. Do it."

"Dara, no," interrupted Veldic. "We do not have enough time. He has the upper hand. Like it or not, this has become part of our mission."

"Listen to the outlander," coaxed Braden Bol. "Anyway, you'd have retrieved your bolts already if it were possible. But you can't. Can you? Not even the legendary power of a Woodlock can penetrate a Touchthief's treasure hold."

Dara's eyes softened. "Fine. But once we complete this, we have no ties and you are my enemy."

Braden nodded his understanding. "I look forward to it."

"Then give me my quiver and let us get on with it," ordered Dara.

"Good, we have an agreement!" returned Braden. He snapped his fingers.

"Ganeth will see to it."

Charles looked terrified at the prospect. He had gone from counting house nobility to fugitive and now an assassin. He felt adrift.

On cue, Ganeth and some men approached with rope, hooks and provisions for the three insurgents. Ganeth threw a large burlap bag to Dara, who caught it. Inside were her quiver and bolts. She counted twelve.

They were unmarred and in order. She donned the quiver and stood defiant. Dara and Charles were each given leather armor of the correct size. Charles realized he liked the armor he had been wearing but understood it to be heavy and not at all good for sneaking about.

Veldic wore her usual gold earrings, leather breastplate and skullcap, black pants and sandals, only she now carried a new spear which made her glad. She felt naked since she lost her halberd over the edge of the Geattor at Ganlis Bay. It was a good weapon, sturdy and straight. Charles brandished his own broadsword with growing familiarity and secured it to his side. They were ready.

Ganeth bowed to them. "You look magnificent! Make ready! The Jaibok approaches! When you have entered the city, find the Fountain of Remembrance at the north end of the city and wait there. Surek Taben makes a morning pilgrimage each day with the sun. End it there. It will be your only chance. If the Minister finds you out, you will die. But if you complete your task, you will meet me back here on the river banks, south of the city where I will return to you your property."

"Why go to the trouble to kill this Surek Taben? What is in it for you, Braden Bol?" asked Dara. "I have a hard time believing you to be altruistic in this case; defender of lost children, liberator of the innocent and such."

"Never you mind, my sweet," answered Braden Bol. "You want the coin, you kill Surek Taben. Either way, and as much as I would love to spend more time entertaining your beautiful personage, your destiny lies to the north as you have said."

The thrumming grew in loudness and the ground shook in kind. The waters were choppy. Men and women from Ultshome Manor moved away from the river-bank which prompted Charles, Veldic and Dara to do the same.

A mass of wood, gears, metal and rope crashed out of the mist into the water, sending spray in all directions. It was as tall as a young fir, twenty persons high and half as many wide at least. Red mist shot from a ring of glass tubes that encircled the giant structure. The sound of chains and wheels clanking and spinning was deafening. There was a symphony of groans, clicks and clacks that played behind it all; the music of some unnatural construct.

A second, identical object emerged from the mist plunging into the water near the opposite bank. Then a barge emerged from the mist, enormous in its width. From its top, dozens of iron columns shot into the air to a platform out of which four giant, articulated legs radiated out. The four giant legs, two in the front and two in the back, like lumbering vermin, pulled the barge in its center along the top of the river. The three had never seen a moving object so large.

Charles gasped. He realized that there were people inside the glass containers on the legs. He also realized that amid the sounds, were human screams.

"Quick," yelled Braden. "The lines!"

One thief threw a hooked line with an attached pulley that found purchase high up the side of the leg. He drove a spike into the ground and attached a contraption to the line that looked like a platform big enough for the group to kneel on.

"Get on," said Braden. "Go! There is time between the steps. Once there, climb to the ledge above, near the soul chambers and open the hatch. Climb inside. You will be safe. No one will think to look there. When you get inside the city, wait for night and make your escape. Hurry! Go now! Hold on to the platform!"

The three crawled onto the platform and grasped it. The complement of thieves from Ultshome Manor, including brothers Braden and Ganeth Bol, heaved on the line, sending the platform soaring into the air at dizzying speed.

They traversed the expanse and thought they would crash into the side of the thing, but they slowed enough to grab onto the platform. They climbed up onto the ledge and realized what they were looking at. Inside the glass containers were people; some of them desiccated corpses.

Others were on their way to becoming the same, only they were screaming while a red mist shot from their eyes and mouths. It horrified Charles. As he tried to collect himself, one corpse turned its head toward him and opened its eyes. Smiling, it opened its mouth and red smoke poured out followed by a sea crab that crawled onto the corpses face.

Charles the Coward! Where are you going? You cannot win. I am coming Charles.

"Charles! Wake yourself!" Dara pulled at Charles' shoulders, thrusting him into the opened hatch in the structure's side. "It is moving!"

Dara and Veldic jumped in after.

CHAPTER 31

TAVIST UPLAND'S HEAD THROBBED WITH PAIN. As he regained his consciousness, he felt the fullness of that pain and he remembered what Duchess Lydia Mirette had done to him. It was a delicious betrayal; at least he lived to taste the Shengmar, which he decided was both his most and least favorite food.

"It is time to wake, Shengmar," Said Lydia. "You have been asleep for two days and we are at our destination."

Tavist grumbled but sat up, realizing he was on a ground of stone bricks. He panicked as he felt for the Bóctalu, which was safe, chained to his hip. "Where are we, Lydia?"

"Good, you have dispensed with formalities. Well, young Tavist, we are in Port Frailty. We are here to meet Charles Warfield and to find an Expanser. You spoke in your sleep about it quite a lot. And you spoke of other things."

"Port Frailty? How? What other things?"

"Well, you talked about me," Lydia smiled. "I did not understand you were so descriptive. It was nice. And yes."

"Yes, to what?" Tavist's cheeks reddened.

"That is for you to figure out. Now we must find Charles Warfield."

"How did we get here?"

"Remember when I told you the kelp farmers had something useful to us?"

Tavist squinted and rubbed his temples. "Yes."

"Well, my little Shengmar, the famous kelp farmers of the Southern Province have a Geattor of their own, hidden within a giant undersea cave. It is not as tall or as magnificent as the other Geattor are, but according to the writings on its walls, they used it during the Sixteen Generations War to move people and supplies to 'The City of Frail Peace'. It must be Port Frailty. The farmers told me that many used it, never to return. And unlike the Geattor at Ganlis Bay, they say this one stays open. The good thing is, I still remember Zannistar, which means something or someone broke the spell. We can go back when our task is complete to liberate Olix, Virk and all of Zannistar."

Tavist looked as though in a trance. "We have to find Charles, Lydia."

"I know, Shengmar. We must move now. We are exposed here. There is no guarantee he will be alive when we find him."

"He is alive."

"How can you know?"

"Because the Bóctalu knows."

"I hope you are right." Lydia stared at Tavist, her eyes wary.

Tavist and his pounding head rose to see they were in the middle of a giant city in the night. It was like nothing he had ever seen. The buildings sat crowded and were so high he could not see many of their tops. The moon hung high and lit buildings upon other buildings, roadways and alleys; so many it made him nauseous. This city seemed built in levels and layers. The air felt warm and humid but smelled foul, which did nothing to help his souring stomach.

A few cloaked and cowled people moved about the streets. None stopped to question them, but went on about their way in a hurry. A few of the buildings hinted at candlelight through darkened windows, but they were all shrouded in shadow. There were no accommodations; no places of rest here. This was a dark and dangerous area. Tavist could feel it. Even the buildings themselves held menace. Tavist, clutching the Bóctalu and Lydia clutching hope, moved even deeper into the heart of Port Frailty.

CHAPTER 32

EMBER DRISS STIRRED from a bothered slumber to find himself drenched in sweat. Tired and frustrated, he rose and robed himself, then walked to the west window of his palace chambers to stare at the stars. The sound of the ocean was soothing, just like he remembered as a boy. There was no other sound like it. He had missed it so much.

He remembered the common belief that waves in Zannistar were nurturing to the soul, curative even. But Ember had no soul. He was Dreka, born without eternal purpose, created by the cursed Bekrot Chair and doomed to rot in the earth, save for a remnant of his memory that would become a specter, roaming the borders of the Neverwall, looking for escape.

Ember's soulless life meant nothing in the world-after. His memories of these waves belonged to another person. In fact, none of his memories of this land before the Bekrot Chair created him were his alone. He shared them with Charles Warfield, who squandered them, learning nothing from the lessons they taught. Ember's anxiety increased at the thought.

But there was one chance; a chance to continue on, a chance to matter. Vang said the Holy Sojourner blessed him with power and would grant him a soul if he were victorious, a new soul of his own. Ember wanted to end it; to kill Charles and absorb his eternal purpose for himself. But Vang forbade it. And Vang treated him well, cared for him. Vang showed him how to master the magic inside him and regain control of his own thoughts. Vang showed him a better way to live. Ember did not always agree with Vang's methods, more so lately, but he delivered on his promises; unlike the Itinerants. Ember had no reason to mistrust him. If he wanted Nissa to find Charles then that was his decision. Still, something distant nagged at Ember's thoughts and he wondered if Vang had other plans.

Restless and brooding, Ember turned to the Bekrot Chair at the other end of the chamber. With ceremonious intent, he walked to it and sat, running his hands along the arms. The Bekrot Chair was a work of art unmatched by any in the palace, fit for a ruler. Despite its hardness, gearwood was a forgiving wood. It honored the artist's chisel and aged well. This chair was four thousand years old; it's magic potent and persistent. Ember thought it strange to touch the object that created him.

And now he would use it to create more of himself, only they would be Ersatz, soulless like him but devoid of human reason, being instead ravenous ghouls bent on consuming everything in their paths. Ember was not thrilled about the idea but it was necessary to overcome the Itinerants. Vang was powerful and could control the Ersatz to that end.

He closed his eyes and saw in his mind the places he could go.

Nobody quite understood the mystery of the Bekrot Chair. It showed what it wanted to whom it wanted. The chair showed Ember two places: opposite sides of the chamber. The fact angered him. It was just one more reminder of how he was inferior, how he was less. He allowed the magic of the chair to infiltrate his flesh and he felt warm. Then a soft light overtook his field of vision and then he was on the other side of the chamber, facing where he had just been, a wisp of red vapor hung in the air. Again, he allowed the Bekrot Chair to take him back to where he had been. Over and over, he teleported back and forth, his speed increasing as he melded with the chair until he was going so fast he was sure he could see himself in both places at once, looking back.

In the cold darkness of the Nurdrayl forest, hundreds of hollow-eyed, Ersatz copies of Ember Driss appeared one after another, each more hideous than the one before, and each searching for something or someone to destroy.

CHAPTER 33

THE ROOM WAS HUMID AND DARK. It was just large enough to fit them. The deafening sound of competing mechanical impacts and movements drowned out any attempt at verbal communication. This was fine with Charles since it also overpowered the sound of the screaming corpses in the glass chambers. He also didn't mind the dark so much, having spent several days in the oubliette back home. Charles, Dara and Veldic sat in a circle, back-to-back as the Jaibok thundered downriver to the city gates.

After what seemed like an eternity, the Jaibok stopped. There was a distant clamor. The three travelers assumed it was the inspectors looking through cargo for contraband. The three chose silence, not for fear of capture, but to savor this respite. Just when Charles thought he might find his way to a nap, the mighty Port Frailty river-gates opened. They could tell by the sound of thousands of tons of wood and metal pushing water aside.

Again the giant Jaibok moved forward. Once inside, the Jaibok found moorage close to the inside the gate which closed behind them. They succeeded in their plan to enter Port Frailty. Now they would wait until nightfall to debark to avoid detection and capture. Charles would get his nap after all.

CHAPTER 34

ATLI SAT CROSS-LEGGED ON HER NEW BED, in her new quarters, pondering the strangeness of her new situation. The moon was half-full and bright. Atli had a perfect view of its splendor through the circular window on the wall. As she supposed the nature of the heavens, she also felt immense gratitude for the day's happenings. The Holy Sojourner blessed her, despite her misgivings and penchant for trouble.

She was an Itinerant now, worthy of all the rights of that office. If she desired, she could travel across Laedenor, or even beyond, bringing light and wisdom to people in need, she could study in the great library of the Sojournic Stronghold or she could attempt the Lucan. But best of all, they would never ask her to stand watch again.

Tomorrow was an important day. Her task was to interpret the Holy Sojourner's new position. But how could she? She knew little about the Holy Sojourner; something she now regretted. She had been too busy having fun to pay attention to her studies. She felt anxious, a feeling heightened even further by the thought of that wretched Cwalu, Dohtor Yuun. Atli wanted to escape to that moon in the sky.

There was a knock at her door.

"Are you in there, Atli? May I come in?" It was the Father Prelate Quincunx.

Atli made sure she was decent and answered the door "Come in, Father Prelate."

"Thank you, Dohtor Atli" The Prelate smiled warmly and entered the room gracefully.

Atli gathered the cloth of her new attire in her hands, exposing her gangly ankles.

"The robes are lovely, Father Prelate," said Atli.

"Yes, they are quite blue, I think." His smile endured as he sat on a small wooden stool near the matching desk. "But the robe does not make the Itinerant. Neither does the Lucan for that matter."

Atli seemed puzzled by this. "But Father Prelate, all the most worthy Itinerants attempt the Lucan. It's—"

The Prelate raised his hand and shushed Atli gently. "It is one part, but not the most important part."

"What's most important?" Atli focused on the old man's face.

"Compassion, Atli. Feeling the plight of another. Taking your energy and using it to ease suffering. You do not need the Lucan for that."

Atli shifted her gaze again out the window. "But if I don't have the Sojourner's blessing, how can I be a true Itinerant?"

"You have his blessing enough. He chose you to see his movements. That is a great honor. Nobody has ever seen such a movement; none but you, Dohtor Atli. You are greatly blessed indeed. And tomorrow you will interpret that movement according to your own will and whim. Everyone will respect your interpretation and abide by it."

"Even the Cwalu?" Her light emerald-colored eyes intensified.

"Yes, child. Even the Cwalu. You know, the Cwalu have their place on the Sojourner's path, just as we do."

Atli turned to the Father Prelate. "I understand. But they frighten me."

"They are different, yes. But without them we would have been destroyed long ago. They are our sisters and brothers, bound by the will of the Sojourner and to our well-being. None would harm an Itinerant. Especially you."

"Yet they seek war. Why?"

"They believe the Sojourner is a messenger of the end of the world, instead of its savior. They believe that the wickedness of the world must be cleansed, especially Arom. They fought the Aromites and Zanni in the Sixteen Generations War. Their ranks were much larger then. They mean to finish what they started."

"I know of Arom. Who are the Zanni?"

"The High Kingdom of Zannistar ruled over all, but the great war cost them much and created unrest within their own borders. A civil war threatened to destroy them from within. Fearing destruction, the high King made a deal with a powerful Effacer named Gyldred who enchanted Zannistar, hiding it from the rest of the world and from all memory. He succeeded."

"If it was hidden then how do you know, Father Prelate?"

"That is a story for another day, Atli,"

Atli momentarily grumbled but then resumed her energetic prodding. "So the Sojourner forbids the Cwalu from spreading destruction?

"As interpreted by the chosen Itinerant, yes," Quincunx assured Atli. "They wait for the one whose interpretation will release them to visit terrible judgment upon the world. Dohtor Yuun believes you to be that Itinerant."

She felt somewhat better but a question pushed its way to the surface. "But instead of studying in the library, what if I want to attempt the Lucan?"

His demeanor became authoritative. "Then that is your right. But be warned, you are a rambunctious sort; given to folly and mischief. You have had problems as a Sentinel. Harnessing the power of the Lucan requires dedication, discipline and long periods of stillness. I worry that you may not be able to pay attention for long enough. It would be dangerous, maybe fatal. And besides, you already have a long life ahead of you as a worthy Itinerant. But yes, you can do as you wish."

Atli looked back at the moon and sighed. "Thank you Father Prelate. You're kind."

"Nonsense," The old man rose and made for the door. "Get your rest. We all have much to look forward to. Goodnight."

"Father Prelate?"

"Yes, what is it, girl?"

"Do you think my parents are proud of me? In the world-after?"

The Prelate seemed pensive for a moment, then approached Atli and kissed her on her forehead. "Yes of course, I am sure they are. Atli, we are all proud of you. Your life begins anew. Now good night."

"Good night, Father Prelate."

The Prelate left shutting the simple wooden door, leaving Atli to her thoughts and the moonlight. She lay down and thought of the possibilities until she slept, but her sleep was disturbed by dreams of war and suffering from long ago.

On the edge of the Sojournic compound, a dozen Cwalu lurked unseen, whipping about anxiously in anticipation of tomorrow's news. They pulsed and twisted in and out of physical form, hissing curses. Yuun was there also. But she sat quiet and still in the snow, her black tattoos undulating slowly on her face and scalp as she stared coldly with her black eyes in the direction of Atli's room.

She was in a state of deep rest and contemplation. Yet, something began to infiltrate her thoughts; something was infecting the forest, something ancient and terrible. The feeling broke her trance. She hissed causing two Cwalu to follow her into the forest toward the Nurdrayl thicket at the speed of wind.

CHAPTER 35

DAWN WAS NEAR. Dara the Woodlock chose the tallest building overlooking the plaza and the so-called Fountain of Remembrance. She lay against the steep rooftop on the side opposite the plaza so she could poke her head over. From that position, she could see the entire area.

Ready for anything, she held a gearwood bolt in her hand. Charles and Veldic waited, perched on separate rooftops on the other side of the plaza. They prepared to help Dara; the bulk of this unpleasant assassination business belonging to her.

Dara could also see that Port Frailty's Geattor was near, a short walk. Just then, she felt frustrated that they did not appear here in the city instead of near Reedsdrift. Their journey may have been less complicated. The magic of the Geattor required precision. The Geattor would remain closed another hundred years. She was tired and about to slip into sleep when she saw them approach.

From the edges of the plaza emerged three hooded figures, one of them much larger than the other two. They snuck to the plain, circular fountain and knelt. Dara couldn't be sure which one Surek Taben was, but she brought the bolt to bear on the larger figure and concentrated on the gearwood, building power. She would have to take her chances. She had since made peace with completing this dark task. She would not turn back.

The bolt launched from her hand at blinding speed but to no avail as the cowled man caught it in mid-flight with his hand without looking.

"Dara! Behind you!" Screamed Veldic from the rooftop across the plaza.

Dara spun to see a brutish man in furs looming over her in mid swing with a heavy axe. She relaxed her body and slid halfway down the roof between the man's legs. His axe split the rooftop where it hit.

"Northlanders!" Dara yelled.

Dara ran back up the roof and shoulder-rammed the warrior in the back, sending him over the rooftop to his death in the plaza. There were more of them scaling the buildings to reach them.

Three Laedenorans with swords beset Veldic. She worked her new spear beyond their defenses and into flesh, dispatching them with ease. She ran across the rooftop and jumped to the next building, and the next to reach Charles.

Charles noticed dozens of combatants moving to surround the three figures in the plaza. He recognized the attackers as the Laedenoran invaders that sacked Zannistar. The three figures faced outward and closed their formation. The large, hooded figure burst into movement, bringing death to the bearded assailants, rending them with his hands. Another of the hooded figures drew a sword and joined the fight. The other produced a book which they flipped around and opened.

Veldic reached Charles. "Charles, we must get to safety! Dara will kill me if you die!"

"No Veldic," Charles said. "I will not run. I will fight. I must fight." His resolve was genuine.

Veldic looked into Charles soul and nodded. "As you like, my warrior friend." She reached out, and they locked forearms.

A bright, ripping sound destroyed the moment. Veldic's headless body crumpled down the side of the rooftop, breaking Charles' grip. Charles watched it drop off the eaves to the ground.

"Hello, Charles." It was a familiar tone. "What are you doing with that sword I wonder? Can you use it? How exciting!"

Charles reeled and fought nausea as his mind tried to reconcile this horrific moment.

"No!" Charles agonized as tears flowed. "It is you! What have you done?"

"Are you not happy to see me? I expected to find Tavist here but not you, Charles. What a treat! The world outside is so intriguing! I wonder what will you do Charles? Will you strike me? Will you take me by force?" Her eyes flashed murder and lust.

Standing in front of Charles was the former Nissa Warfield, the current Nissa Driss and Queen of Zannistar, holding a curved knife in one hand and Veldic's severed head by the braid in the other. She had made changes. Her hair, her adornment, everything was white; white and stained with fresh blood. She looked happy.

Charles' head pounded, and he felt his heart would explode. He could hear the blood of the fallen call to him. He fell to his knees.

Nissa sighed. "Oh, Charles. You are such a disappointment! To think I wasted so much time on you and your constant sniveling."

Charles dropped his sword and grasped his temples. The pain was intensifying. Something was happening he could not control. He approached a horizon in the landscape of his mind he always knew was there but never dared to reach. As he turned toward Dara, he could feel his rational being fighting to remain. He saw Dara running in an unnatural slowness toward him, leaping from roof to roof, pulling bolts from her quiver and shooting them from her hands at Northlanders who had made it to the roof in front of her. She was becoming slower every moment. Her expression was one of horror and desperation.

Charles saw the hooded figures engaging the contingent of attackers with ferocity and deadly skill though it looked as if they were close to being overrun. They, too, were slowing down until everything around him stopped. Charles felt his grip on his identity fading but he knew time had stopped. The man who he then understood to be Tavist was on his knees near the fountain, holding an open book and staring back at him. Unlike the others, his movements were normal. He stood and pointed at Charles.

"You are Furtyr!" yelled Tavist.

Charles' consciousness fell into a cold darkness; a void. He felt his body thicken as a sack filling with millet. Pain bit into his spine as it stretched him. He put his hands up and saw he had a rich, brown fur on his enlarged, clawed hands that moved up to his elbows. He felt his sense of self retreat and then remain just above the point of no return. His instinct carried him at blinding speed from the roof to Tavist below, whose expression was absolute terror. He loomed over the boy by half a person or more. Charles wanted to rend him.

"You are Furtyr!" Tavist screamed again, showing Charles the pages of the book, using it as a shield.

What remained of Charles shrieked with the voice of a thousand birds and beasts of the wood. The surrounding ground shuddered.

Tavist stiffened and mastered his fear though the mere presence of this beast caused him great physical pain. "Protect us this day! Your enemy has reached out to stop you from your task!"

"You are my enemy," Charles said in a language long forgotten. His voice was ethereal; his mind joined to another intelligence, ancient and vast.

Tavist had a complete understanding and spoke in kind. "No! I am your herald. The Bóctalu confirms it. And you, Charles, are the Furtyr, with a destiny beyond this place. Your spirit survived many ages, but the time has come."

Charles' voice emerged as low thunder. "How can you know this?"

"Because your name, like all names, is in the pages of the Bóctalu, as is your eternal purpose." Tavist softened. "Also because I remember you."

The creature looked to the sky. "And I you Tavist. All is not agreeable between us. You would take Nissa from me."

Tavist shrank back. "No, Charles. I meant I remember you from Rax, the world-after. Your future is in my past. Please understand. There is much at risk."

Charles cocked his antlered head and his beastly visage intensified; endless black pits for eyes and a grin of large, jagged teeth, leaving only his cheeks, nose and ears to resemble humanity. He pulled morsels of some distant truth from his mind, but not all.

"You are the Scrivener. Arminius has died."

"Yes," replied Tavist. "The Bóctalu has awakened me to the truth."

"Tell me, Scrivener, why do I not remember more?"

"You will, Charles. For now, your enemy surrounds us."

"Vang." Charles could not conceive of how he knew the word.

"Yes."

"I am here for the coin. I need it." Charles' memory pulsed with images.

Tavist raised the book. "No. The coin has great power, but the Itinerants sent it only to wake you from your dormancy. You no longer need it because I have read aloud your name from the Bóctalu. You have been joined to your true self and will remember more in time. You need only complete your task to the north."

"You make many claims," said Charles. "Scrivener or not, you are yet a boy."

"I keep the Bóctalu." He proffered the book. "I have learned from it much in these past days. Things are different now. I am changed; a creature of a great burden. The Bóctalu showed me things forgotten and yet to come. I remember the world-after as my past and I see the world-before a future vision. The book reveals to me the nature of people and places. It showed me how to wake you."

Another bit of truth floated into Charles' mind. "The coin. It can change me back; return me to myself again."

"Back into Charles Warfield, a condemned traitor? Yes, it can. But is that what you really want? This is who you are. More than Charles Warfield could ever imagine. You are death, come for any you deem deserving."

"And do you deserve it, Tavist? Death? Your eagerness to steal my wife in the Zanni palace was public and undeniable. Both you and Osric Branlin; filthy wretches. Should I suffer to allow such a dishonor to go unanswered? Shall I join you to the everlasting shadow?"

"I have liberated you; given you your name," Tavist said, aware this was a dangerous moment. "Osric is dead; murdered by Ember Driss, a dangerous Dreka who wears your face. And Nissa is lost to darkness. Through marriage to Ember, she belongs to Vang. And to be sure, she was never your friend, just as the Warfield family was never your true family. Your family lies to the north. This I know."

"You are wrong. She was my friend once." Charles scanned the motionless battle. He looked upon Veldic's body and turned to Tavist. "I will tell you what I know. I have a great capacity for destruction; more than I had ever realized. I remember happenings. Distant things but only parts. My thoughts are countless and turbid, like a storm stretching across creation. Yet as I look on you, my feelings are clear. You did something in the world-before; something terrible. The Furtyr was there. He has shown me this. Tavist, I want to kill you."

Tavist pleaded, feeling Charles' irresistible malice wrap around him like a wool blanket soaked in icy, lake-water. "No! Events in the world-before are my future, Charles. I can only see glimpses of possibilities. For me, they have not yet transpired. Perhaps there is another way. Perhaps I can change it."

Charles' massive, feral form closed in on Tavist, his black eyes revealing a promise of despair unknown to mortal minds. "I will not kill you this day. Some part of me knows you speak the truth. Instead, you will live for now." Charles looked up at Dara.

"And her. I will protect her." She looked picturesque, determined to reach her fallen companion, not even yet aware that

Charles was no longer on the roof.

Tavist pointed to Lydia and Surek Taben. "Them," Tavist said through his fear. "Save them as well."

"I will protect the Duchess Lydia. She is worthy." said the Charles-Furtyr beast. "But not the Minister. He dies."

"No," Tavist retorted with care. Small fissures began to erupt on his skin. He could feel something crawling just under them. There was more pain. "You must trust me. Please, Charles. He is an Expanser, able to navigate the Neverwall. We need him! Not even you can traverse it on your own!"

Charles snorted, reached out with one, black claw and placed it over Tavist's mouth. "No more talk, Scrivener. You are starting to decay."

A large, black insect of many legs pushed its way through Tavist's palette onto his tongue before escaping his mouth. His right eye fell into the cavity made by the small vermin. It scurried across the beast's claw and Tavist screamed a word of undoing through pain and horror. The insects subsided and still screaming, Tavist fumbled around his face and in his mouth for wounds no longer there.

"A warning, Tavist," said the creature. "Today you live, but we have unfinished business."

The world snapped back into sync, the bedlam regaining its frenetic pace. The thing that Charles had become shrieked and ploughed through the Northlanders, sending them aloft, limbless and hapless. Swords, axes and spears bit into Charles' body, but only seemed to enrage him further. Small spikes of bone emerged from where the wounds were. They pulsed with a dark shadow, having movement and a mind of their own.

Without pattern, they shot out from Charles' muscled body on the end of translucent appendages and impaled several enemies through the back of their heads. A visible black line of liquid traveled from Charles, through the flexible spines and into the dead or dying Northlanders. After what looked like a brief struggle, the victims became limp, then fought their own brethren with ferocity, like puppets on strings. In a matter of moments, the Furtyr reduced the contingent of skirmishers to a few, retreating deserters.

Charles turned his head to face Nissa on the roof. All the impaled Northlanders did likewise as insects erupted from their bodies. Nissa grinned and nodded back. Charles turned to the fountain and took refreshment from its bloody waters. With a disturbing sound of bones breaking, a pair of black feathered wings with grey tips emerged from his back. The other spiked appendages retracted back into Charles' body, leaving the Northlanders' corpses to fall motionless to the ground. Again shrieking, he took to the sky and flew south over the city.

Having dispatched a dozen more opponents along the way, Dara reached her rooftop destination to realize that Charles was not present, but instead the Queen Nissa stood, observing Charles' exit with glee, still holding Veldic's head at her side. Red vapor escaped Nissa's eyes. Dara stopped and aimed a bolt at Nissa. Dara could not fathom the truth of her companion's death nor her proximity to Nissa, her soulmade counterpart. She was looking in a mirror and loathed herself.

"What have you done, demon!" Dara yelled through pain. "Where is Charles?"

Nissa pointed to the sky with her blood-stained knife. "There, and he has abandoned you to your death!"

244

Dara glanced up. The beast in flight was a small dot over the city; too small to make out.

Nissa held up Veldic's head. "Oh, I met your friend. She was a big one."

Dara launched the bolt with a scream of rage. It lodged in Nissa's ribs but brought no reaction of pain or surprise. Nissa brought her wicked countenance to Dara. "So, it is true," said Nissa. "The resemblance is curious. Yes, you are thin and your hair? Well, I can remedy it! Tell me, do you have all of my memories?"

Dara made a fist with her open hand, causing the wooden bolt to rip itself out of Nissa's body and fly back into the open wound. Again, there was no reaction.

Dara pointed to her enemy. "Well, I remember everything, including the darkness inside us. But I am different now and I fight you every sunrise! I am not you!"

"No, you are not. You are a shadow; a fake. You have no soul. Sad."

Dara let fly the bolt once more. It embedded in Nissa's side below the first wound. Nissa winced the tiniest bit. She brought Veldic's severed head to her face and licked her lifeless, open mouth as a lion licks a paw, then made a hooting sound as she tossed it off the roof down to her body. "Shall I show you how to be beautiful now? I know you want to be beautiful. Oh, has he begged you yet? Has he pleaded for your touch? No, I suppose not. Why would he? You are nothing."

Enraged, Dara extended both her hands outward, calling on her strength and every spent bolt flew back to her. Blood covered her hands. She released them toward Nissa who jumped out of danger, landing in the courtyard near Tavist.

Nissa's voice became shrill. "The Book! Give me the Book boy!" Red smoke billowed from her eyes and mouth.

Tavist drew his sword whilst clutching the Bóctalu. "No!"

"Come back with me," continued Nissa. "You can be the Grand Marshal! That is what you want, yes? Give me the Book."

"I will do nothing for you!"

"Do you not seek me for a wife, Tavist? Do you not wish to relish in my comforts?" She rubbed the blood oozing from her side over her breast. She smiled and her teeth were vibrating in her gums. A humming sound like wasps escaped her mouth.

Tavist took a step forward. "Enough! Engage me or flee!"

She gazed into him. "You are spent, boy. I will take the book and bathe in your blood!"

Nissa's face twisted into a window of pure malice. As Nissa lunged toward him, Surek Taben's fist caught her in mid-air. She folded around it and was flung against the fountain with force enough to destroy it, releasing bloody water into the plaza. She arose but became still when a volley of a half-dozen gearwood bolts from the rooftops found their home in her chest.

Dara descended the side of a building and ran toward the courtyard. She crawled onto Nissa who was awake but near death and looked her in the eye.

"He will hate you for this," said Nissa through blood. "He will never love you. He is mine, even in death."

"You loved him once too, Nissa. I remember. He made you better; made you feel."

"Quiet, false one. We are not weak, frightened children anymore. I have seen power. I know things dark and forbidden. I have no fear. End it. Unlike you, I am eternal."

Dara was in agony over the death of Veldic. She spoke with care. "No, you are not eternal. But I will be. Are you ready to release your eternal purpose?" It was the ultimate opportunity for Dreka, facing one's soulmade counterpart. "Did you think I had forgotten? Did you think I wouldn't do it?"

Nissa's eyes widened releasing more vermilion smoke. "I hope you choke on it! And you will! It is of darkness and so shall you be! I will meet you in the Neverwall!"

Dara raised her hands, closed her eyes and screamed to the sky. The bolts disappeared into Nissa's chest and then they burst part way out of her neck, radiating like some macabre necklace, pointing upward.

Dara brought her hands down hard and the bolts cut to the left in unison, releasing Nissa's head from her shoulders. A column of crimson vapor and smoke billowed from the wound with a deafening hiss. It gathered above the scene then dissipated. Dara grasped one of the exposed bolts and with it dug out Nissa's heart.

"No! You mustn't," yelled Tavist. The Bóctalu grew cold. He performed the motions and thumbed to Nissa's page. Some ink in her name dissolved from the page and formed a twisted tendril that hovered in place.

It was too late. Dara ate Nissa's heart with ravenous desperation. She forced it down. She steadied herself and waited, surprised at her own wild instinct.

The blob of ink floating in the air vanished, leaving the page blank where Nissa's name used to be.

Dara stiffened and waited for something to happen. She closed her eyes, held out her hands but there was nothing; nothing but the tang of blood in her mouth. She felt nauseous. "Where is it?" she asked. "I don't feel any different."

Tavist looked down at the book. "I do not know."

"Nonsense," said Dara. "The legends say I must consume the heart. I've done that."

"Dara, I do not know what to say," Tavist thumbed through pages. "Perhaps you must wait."

Frustrated, Dara rose from her ordeal to see that Tavist, Lydia and Surek Taben were at her side concerned for her wellbeing. Surek Taben had removed his cowl, revealing the face of a veteran warrior. Green-eyed and strong of jaw, burn scars mottled Surek Taben's face. He was in an oversized suit of full armor that was also a contraption or a machine of some kind. She could hear the whir of an apparatus within the armor when he moved.

"Are you harmed?" Surek Taben asked.

Dara wiped blood from her mouth as she stood and walked toward Veldic's severed head. "No. I don't think so."

Surek Taben followed her. "We must hurry. There will be attention and soldiers. For now they will not intervene and they dare not cross me but we must hasten to prevent panic among the people. When they arrive, my forces will tend to the fallen."

"They sent us to assassinate you," said Dara. "They accuse you of terrible crimes."

"Lies," offered Surek Taben. "Lies of the Shamblefolk. Their agents have fooled you. Who was it?"

She crouched at Veldic's head and caressed her face. "Braden Bol of Ultshome Manor—"

"Stop there, you needn't say any more," said Surek Taben. "The denizens of Ultshome Manor are all well-known Shamblefolk criminals not of this world. They have been attempting to kill me for many years. They wish to destroy me and take the city as their own. I have used Readers to find them out and keep them from entering the city. They would say anything to convince you to kill me."

"But he warned us of the Shamblefolk," said Dara. "Protected us."

Surek Taben roared. "Girl, you are a dupe."

Dara furrowed her brow and unclasped Veldic's many golden earrings. "Why not sack Ultshome Manor and arrest them? You are the leader of this city! It is minutes from the river gate!"

"Because we cannot find them. Shamblefolk make their dwellings inside an unreachable place in between this world and the next. They move there and back at will. Only Shamblefolk can find Ultshome Manor. We know the door is outside the city near the banks of the river but we cannot find that door."

"He speaks true," interjected Tavist who had approached them.

"Why do I know you?" said Dara to Tavist.

"Because you carry some of Queen Nissa's early memories. I was younger then."

Dara raised an eyebrow and plucked the last earring.

"I am Tavist Upland, a former member of the Zanni August Guard, now become the Scrivener and guardian of the Book of Nom in the wake of Arminius Morlund's untimely death. The Queen was searching for me and the Book to destroy it. We knew you would come to Port Frailty looking for an Expanser. Nice to meet you."

Dara turned to Tavist. "Yes. I think I remember something. You were a small boy last I saw you. You have grown."

The Duchess Lydia Mirette pushed her way into the conversation, pointing at the sea. She bled from a wound on her hand. "We are on an errand from Arminius. We travel for the Pit of Nihthelm on the Islet of Abeodan, within the Neverwall. Tavist must read from his book there. Surek Taben is an Expanser and can see us through the Neverwall alive. He has agreed to take us."

Dara winced. "Charles? He is lost! And Veldic! I have failed the Sojourner! I have failed the Itinerants!" Dara glanced at Veldic's corpse and placed the earrings in her pouch. She fought back tears and replaced them with anger.

"No," said Tavist. "He will return soon. The Furtyr has awoken."

Dara's eyes widened. "How do you know? The Father Prelate, the Cwalu, Veldic and myself were the only people alive with any knowledge of the fabled Furtyr."

"No," said Tavist. "There are others." Tavist remembered Arminius' words about Effacers; that they could not consume the memories of a Scrivener but could only hide them for a while.

"Friends! Time is short. A fishing vessel awaits us at the docks," said Surek Taben. "We sail now! This way!"

"Shouldn't you stay and see to the city?" Asked Dara.

Surek Taben stood tall. "There are others trained and ready to stand against anything. They will know what to do. Besides, only I can navigate you through the Neverwall. This is more important than the city. More important than anything."

"Yes I know! But what of Charles?" screamed Dara. "Without him we will fail!"

"He will find us," said Tavist, interrupting them. "I am sorry about your friend. But we must leave her. Now we run!"

Dara called all of her gearwood bolts back to her at once. "She was not my friend, she was my family. Lead the way."

The four sped through the alleys toward the northern seaside docks. As they ran, Dara turned to Surek Taben and hollered through heavy breathing. "So how'd these two Zanni travelers gain such quick audience with the Minister of Port Frailty?"

"Simple," Surek Taben called back over the thundering footfalls of his mechanical armor. "The young Scrivener approached my guards and requested to meet with Thadelon Bask.

"Who is that?" Dara returned.

"Me. It is the name my mother gave me at my birth. I took the name Surek Taben upon going to war nine hundred years ago. No ordinary, living person would know me by my given name."

"Are you saying you fought in the Sixteen Generations War?"

"I am."

"Impossible." Though she knew it was possible. because she held some of Nissa's memories, including those of Gyldred, himself a relic of that ancient war.

Surek Taben moved through the streets with ease. "The Scrivener Tavist told of a kingdom named Zannistar. I do not remember it. He claims an Effacer hid the place from all memory, from all of us. It would explain certain mysteries. I suspected something amiss all these years."

Dara pressed in. "What mysteries?"

Before he could answer, they had arrived at the docks and the Minister's fishing vessel, though it was larger than any of the others had expected.

The Minister of Port Frailty took the lead and approached the guard at the brow.

"Sergeant, send word to the council there has been an attack by outside forces at the Fountain of Remembrance and inform them of my temporary departure by sea. I will return as soon as the Neverwall will permit and they are to act with honor in my absence."

"Yes, Minister." The sentry ran into the city.

The ship was no fishing vessel, but a war galleon. It boasted three masts and twenty seven cannons on both sides. It was constructed of dark, almost black button wood with trim painted bright yellow. Its sails were likewise yellow, each with the embroidered image of a black bird's head inside a black circle.

Tavist somehow knew it to be the sign of the Expanser's craft. The masthead was a massive raven in flight extending beyond the bow, made of buttonwood and painted to represent the creature's true nature. There were a hundred sailors at work preserving the ship and taking on stores. This was a full complement, ready for a long journey. The traveling outsiders recognized soon that much of the crew were blind. Others covered their eyes with rags.

Surek Taban sensed their curiosity. "Yes, most of them are blind, either by birth, by disease or by choice." He pointed to one sailor with no eyes at all.

"Why?" Lydia asked.

"Because it keeps them safe from what lurks in the Neverwall."

Surek Taban smiled and gestured toward the ship's brow, his armor whirring. "You may board the Corvax at your pleasure; the most ready and capable fishing boat in the world."

Lydia Snorted. "And what type of fish are you trying to catch? Sea serpents?"

"Some days, but those are the easy ones," Surek Taben replied. "The ship's healer can see to your wounds. After you, good Duchess."

The four boarded the ship.

CHAPTER 36

AERION TRUDGED AFTER VANG, trusting him less with every passing moment but likewise relying on him more and more. Though he held the coil high, the craven faces pressed around the edges of the tunnel, looking for a way in. The situation tired Aerion.

"Where are we Vang?" Aerion asked.

"We are near to where you found the shard," answered Vang without turning around.

"I wish I could see beyond the tunnel," said Aerion.

"You can. If you want to that is."

Aerion stopped and huffed. "And you've not mentioned this for a reason, I am guessing?" Blood from his hand continued to drip.

Vang turned and approached Aerion with speed. "Look there. Concentrate on seeing past the tunnel. Use your senses as though they were fingers searching about in the hollow of a tree at night. Feel your world form in your mind.

Aerion did as instructed and dropped the hand holding the shard to his side. The young hunter concentrated for several moments. There was pressure from the sides of the tunnel causing him nausea. He looked down at his hand to see that the blood disappeared from mid-air as it dripped from his hand. There were invasions into the tunnel on both sides in the form of blurry streaks.

"What is happening Vang?"

"The people of your world are worshiping you as the savior of their existence. They believe you are a god. They are trying to touch you. To them you are moving slower than the seasons. They see you as a statue. And some of them are eating your blood. These activities give them power; our power."

The constant streaks and colorful incursions mesmerized Aerion. The moment was beautiful if absurd. For a moment he forgot about the faces above. But only for a moment. Aerion faltered.

"Aerion," Vang began, "Concentrate harder. I have an idea."

Aerion again did as Vang said. He squinted to see beyond the tunnel, twisting his own stomach and gritting his teeth. He walked again, pushing his will on a spot in the tunnel wall. The wall disappeared there. A man flew into the tunnel, falling in front of Aerion. Aerion yelped and moved to avoid trampling the man.

"It is a demon!" yelled Vang, pointing. "Kill it now!"

Frightened, Aerion brought the shard up high over his head.

You are a hunter. You are worthy, brave and strong.

Aerion plunged the shard into the man's chest, killing him. He removed the shard and found the wound to be identical in its spiraling redness to the coil on his hand. The faces turned their wanton leering away from Aerion and toward the twisting wound in the dead man.

Aerion stared at the man he had killed in disbelief. But he also felt relieved.

"Quick, Aerion," warned Vang. "We must go. They will discover the truth soon."

For once, Aerion felt in control. And he harbored no remorse; only curiosity. "You are clever, Vang."

"I thought you did not trust me."

"I don't. I only said you are clever."

"Yes, we are." Vang continued down the tunnel, almost at a lighthearted pace. "Come, Aerion."

Aerion embraced the new boldness he felt and continued after Vang.

CHAPTER 37

SILENCE FELL ACROSS THE SOJOURNIC GROUNDS as Atli approached the carved, frost-laden lectern. She steadied herself then looked out and marveled at the numbers in attendance: Itinerants sat to the left, Lucanites and Sentinels to the right. She scanned the multitude for the Cwalu Itinerants, but they had not yet arrived, a fact that left Atli both relieved and disappointed. She surveyed the aisle that led from the lectern, through the crowd, ending at the Holy Sojourner himself. Soon she would walk the aisle and decide the future of the world.

A quiet, chilling breeze pushed through the Sojournic Compound. The snow on the ground had receded somewhat, revealing bits of the wet, greenery underneath. It would continue melting in the coming months, but this far up some snow always remained. Atli liked it when the green was out though it only lasted a month or two. Laedenor never saw warmth of any kind, only varying levels of cold.

The Father Prelate Quincunx and all the Itinerants were in full Itinerant regalia comprising blue Itinerant's robes and tall hats of brown, snow-bruin leather. Each held at their sides a ring of gearwood with a small bell attached. Unlike the others, Atli wore a plain, white smock with a likeness of the shard embroidered on its front. Her new attendants had washed, oiled and combed her cropped, chestnut hair.

Atli was the only Itinerant who slept the previous night. The other Itinerants had flocked to the Holy Sojourner through the night to observe his slow, but perceptible movement. Every Itinerant knew how to do it; performing the Lucan, unblinking and alert. This was an unprecedented and holy event. Overnight, the Sojourner had gone from holding the sacred shard overhead to plunging it into the heart of the Lucanite Amarl. Amarl lay displayed on the ground, his widened, terror-filled eyes turned towards the lectern where Atli stood. A red, swirling spiral replaced the wound. A motionless arc of blood emerged from it, still as a statue. This was a miraculous occurrence. It had to mean something profound.

The crowd's visible breath bellowed up like steam from a pot. There was a palpable energy among the attendees, a mixture of fear and excitement. None had ever seen such a Sojournic movement as this Astyr.

Atli saw the Watch Captain Jeth among the Sentinels on the right side in back. He seemed proud and adoring. This made her nervous, terrified even. She had grown accustomed to being treated like a fool. This was a new feeling.

A somewhat saddened Father Quincunx locked eyes with Atli and nodded. "Once the Cwalu arrive, we'll be ready, Dohtor Atli. You're free to interpret the Astyr as you wish. None will oppose you. However, remember that your interpretation must be true to your inner inclination." He shook his finger at her.

Atli nodded in return though even as she did, the discordant aria and hissing of the coming Cwalu broke the silence. A sparkling opening formed in front of Atli, electrifying the cold air. Dohtor Yuun and two other Cwalu emerged from the opening which closed behind them. Dohtor Yuun descended on the Sojourner with visible, ravenous interest at his current state and let out a scream of victory.

"Where are the others, Dohtor Yuun?" asked the Father Prelate Quincunx.

Without using her muscles, Yuun's body shifted its direction to face Quincunx. Her voice was ethereal. "They are doing their best to contain the Ersatz horde that lay at the farthest reaches of the Gearwood Thicket, only days away from your doorstep, Father Prelate. My brothers and sisters have erected a field of repulsion. They must tend to it else it will fail but it will not last forever. A few days."

Jeth the Watch Captain spoke out of turn. "Sable Rock? Dribble. The Dreka there are useless piles of flesh. Many have no bones at all. They are of no threat. Not for many years now. You most of all should know that."

"These are different, Sentinel," said Yuun. "Twisted and strong. They wear the face of Ember Driss. There are thousands, naked and mindless. They congregate at Sable Rock, waiting. For what I do not know. But I do not have to be the chosen interpreter to understand the Sojourner's message. We are to go to war!"

The Father Prelate Quincunx reacted as though punched in the stomach. "No, Yuun. It's for Dohtor Atli to say." Yuun shrank in her presence.

Quincunx rubbed his eyes. "An army? That means the Beast of Sable Rock's captured the Bekrot Chair. He's created an army to take the Stronghold and the Sojourner."

Atli and many others reacted as though confused. Some in the crowd called for Atli to make her interpretation. A general humdrum broke out to support it.

"Enough!" yelled Quincunx. "Atli, It's to you and the Holy Sojourner to decide our course of action." All eyes returned to Atli.

Sweat ran down Atli's face. She was not frightened of invasion or bedlam. She was frightened of making the wrong choice, of failing the Father Prelate. The gathering fell quiet once more. Atli looked east to the walked path, its edges and the Shardmothers and Shardfathers who remain motionless there. She wondered why, of all the Lucanites in history, had the Sojourner taken Amarl. He was unremarkable, even among Itinerants.

Atli sensed Yuun at her side. She turned, looked deep into Yuun's timeless black eyes. She knew what she had to do.

"They threaten us," Atli announced with surprising authority. "So I will not waste your attention with practiced words. The Sojourner's actions are clear. We must answer the call of the bearer of the Shard. The Holy Sojourner shows us the Wyrsa-gewealc, the Walk of Battle! The time of peace has lapsed! We will defeat this army and any other that would destroy us!"

The crowd erupted in cheers and applause. The Father Prelate Quincunx was not among them. He appeared hopeless and wounded. He approached Atli and embraced her.

"It's as you say, Dohtor Atli," Quincunx began. "But I wish it weren't so. Our end approaches. We must make preparations. The Cwalu are strong allies, but they won't hold the Ersatz army for long."

"What is an Ersatz army, Father Prelate?" asked Atli.

"They're little more than empty husks for evil spirits to work through. It appears they remain empty for the time being. But if I were to give a guess, I would say they won't remain so forever."

"Yes, Father Prelate," said Yuun. "which is why the Wyrsa-gewealc demands that one of the Cwalu be the Prelate of the Sojournic Compound. This is the law!"

"I know the law, creature!" Quincunx barked. "We've until the sun goes down to prepare! You'll have your wish and you'll be Prelate. I pray the Sojourner you don't destroy all we've built since the ancient war ended."

Yuun burst into mocking laughter. It chilled everyone within earshot more than the receding snow. "No, no old fool," Yuun said. "It is not my destiny to be Prelate, but hers!" Yuun drew her black sword and pointed it toward Atli who looked dumbfounded.

Dohtor Yuun, the leader of the Cwalu Itinerants slid her black sword across her own palm, releasing a dark line of steaming blood to the snow below. All the Itinerants took a step back. "This will not make you Cwalu, but it will allow you to approach the Sojourner's blood without delay. It will not last long, child, and if you do not taste the Sojourner's blood after having tasted mine, you will die within the hour."

Atli knew this was her destiny. As much as she rationalized to decline, the Sojourner's blood beckoned her. It always had. She looked at the Father Prelate, who, with his eyes, pleaded with her to refuse. She would not.

Atli ran from the lectern and knelt below Dohtor Yuun, collecting the blood with cupped hands then bringing it to her mouth to sip. Yuun fixed her dark gaze on Quincunx who sobbed quietly. The blood from Yuun's hand stained Atli's face, smock and hands. Atli looked at her hands then rose to her feet. The crowd gasped as they watched her tiptoe toward the Sojourner.

Without resistance, she penetrated the invisible boundary that kept others at bay. Closing her eyes, she knelt and accepted a single drop of the Holy Sojourner's blood into her mouth. Atli forced herself away from the Sojourner and fell to the frozen ground.

She was overwhelmed with images of lands elsewhere. Her mind perceived a gleaming city over which flew great beasts. Its residents were grey-skinned people of immense power and intellect. They held truths unfamiliar to Atli. Her consciousness floated into the air from that place and flew at speed many weeks' journey away toward a silver, mountain palace with hundreds of needle-like towers.

Shafts of black lightning struck their tips in unpredictable waves. Hundreds of feet below, surrounding the mountain was a battle of unimaginable size. Swarms of men and women in a strange, living armor and wielding stranger swords besieged the mountain.

Gargantuan living machines moved by dozens of insect-like spines beset them. The creatures' many arms tore at flesh and delivered blackfire which rotted all it touched. Fighting alongside the towering machines, were hordes of what Atli could only guess were demons of human form with a single, swirling pit where features should be. They could change their shape at will, sometimes into grotesque, fleshy weapons for impaling, strangling or cutting. They even joined, forming new and lethal creatures before separating again. Clouds of large, biting insects harassed the human forces, entering eyes, mouths, ears and nose and emerging from their necks, coated in blood.

Atli's mind found a particular man in the fight who she felt connected to. He was strong in jaw and dark in complexion. He had rich, short and curled black hair. His silver eyes glinted as though lit with fire. She watched him fight, taking many enemies down until one of the giant, living machines impaled him through his stomach with a chitinous spine. It spewed blackfire from an orifice on a ropy arm-like appendage onto his sword-arm which rotted.

Some shape-shifting demons stopped to laugh and mock him. One demon picked up the fallen man's sword and examined it. The creature then transformed itself into the image of the warrior on the ground, only its eyes remained spiraling pits. It stabbed the man many times and laughed. As the insects entered him through his decomposing arm, the fallen man looked up with his silver eyes and recognized Atli's presence above him. The mental connection separated him from the physical pain of his body being destroyed. He reached out with his own mind.

"Atli. I am glad you are here with me. Thank you for this gift."

They reached a mystic understanding between them. She knew they shared the same spirit. They were the same person, only in different worlds.

"Thank you, Nikiru." She knew his name as she knew her own. She could not help him.

Nikiru smiled and closed his eyes, succumbing to his murder in peace.

The demon with Nikiru's sword stopped stabbing and turned its borrowed face toward the sky. It recognized Atli. Its face morphed into a perfect representation of Atli's own likeness this time, again with pits for eyes. It beamed at Atli as it resumed stabbing Nikiru's half-rotted body over and over. Though her mind was viewing at a distance, Atli saw the demon's teeth vibrating.

As quickly as she had come, Atli's consciousness retreated away from the carnage and back into her body. Atli regained her bearings to find Dohtor Yuun cradling her while the other two Cwalu kept the other gatherers at a safe distance. Atli's forehead stung. She put her finger to it and found more blood, but it was her own.

"Dohtor Yuun," Atli said. "What have you done?"

"I have brought you back from Vel, the world-before, and I have given you your first Aydward. It will keep your mind and body safe from intrusion. Your new power is like a beacon in the forest that calls out to the darkness, searching for those who crave it. There are many. And with precious few exceptions, you do not wish to meet them."

Atli knew most of the others were staring at her forehead. "Is it a marking like yours?"

"Yes. It is a wound, made with my knife. Soon it will cure into a proper Aydward, the first of many. Its power lives in its truth. Anyone who wields sorcery can give it though few know of it and fewer still would bear it. Now, we would take you to our encampment and prepare you in the way of our tradition, but there is no time, Dohtor Atli. I must ask you a question."

"A question? What is it?"

"Did you see anything? Anything in the world-before?"

"Yes."

"What did you see? Come, child! It is important!"

"A battle. A terrible battle." Atli was shaking.

"Did you meet anyone, or were you drawn to anyone?"

Atli looked at Yuun with horror. She noticed that Yuun's knife positioned at her throat. "Yes."

"Who? Speak child!"

"A fighting man," Atli found trouble saying the words. "He was strong, dark of skin and he fought well. I watched him die, killed by evil creatures or demons, perhaps." Atli grimaced.

"Good," said Yuun. She removed the knife from Atli's throat. "What was his name? Did he tell you his name?"

Atli became calm. "No, but I already knew it. It was Nikiru. His name was Nikiru and I believe he is me. We are one."

Dohtor Yuun smiled and embraced Atli. "I knew it. You are one of us, Atli. You were there as was I; as were all of us. We fell during that battle in the world-before."

Atli seemed puzzled. "But have not others attempted the Lucan through consuming the Sojourners blood? Not everyone could have been there."

"You are wrong, Atli," said Yuun. "All Cwalu have experienced the darkness of battle on Vel and only those who have been there feel called to the blood. It repels all others."

"So why the knife at my throat?" It was a reasonable question.

"Because, child," revealed Yuun. "Some who consume the blood connect with the creatures you saw."

"What do you do with those people? Kill them?"

Yuun got closer and whispered. "We take them to the Gearwood Thicket and bury them to their necks. We force them to swallow a gearwood seed, which is toxic. If we find them alive the next day, we remove them from the ground and train them in the ways of the Woodlock. These few are useful to our cause but they are not true Cwalu. If instead we find them dead, which is most of the time, we leave them and a gearwood tree will grow from within their body, absorbing the power from them and imbibing the tree."

Yuun stood and helped Atli to her feet. "Brother and Sister Itinerants! We have found Atli to be true Cwalu! In time, we will prepare her in the ancient ways, but today will end soon and when the sun dies, we will see her take her place as Mother Prelate. This is the common law of both our sacred orders!"

The gathering remained quiet for several moments. All were looking at one another. Father Prelate Quincunx motioned for an Itinerant in the crowd to surrender his bell loop. Quincunx then rang the bells and the other Itinerants joined in. It was a show of finality and acceptance. Quincunx stopped after a time as the others continued. He approached Atli and kissed her bloody cheek.

"I'm glad it's you, Atli," said Quincunx. "It's good, yes." He held her gaze before leaving the gathering to prepare for his resignation.

Atli stood silent, bloodied and different. She found it distasteful that she would need to bathe for yet another ceremony. She rather hated baths.

"Look there!" yelled one Itinerant. "The Astyr continues! The Holy Sojourner moves quicker still!"

All in attendance approached the Sojourner, many prostrated and sobbed as his movement became fluid and perceptible. He was still slow, but moving at a pace. The Itinerants analyzed the new information. They determined he would now reach Stag's End in a week's time. There was rejoicing and elation. They would see it within their lifetimes. It was the event of the ages.

CHAPTER 38

EMBER DRISS SURVEYED THE CAVE where the secret Geattor lay hidden from the people of Zannistar and the world. It lived deep underground, several minutes from the shoreline. The path to the bottom area was almost vertical. Someone had fashioned stairs in the rock through a narrow passage which opened into a massive chamber, large enough to conceal the Geattor. Its top was only a few feet from the roof of the cave, low enough to touch if one jumped.

Ember was very disappointed in the lack of cooperation from the kelp farmers. He was one of their countrymen, in a manner of speaking. They refused to answer his questions or even speak at all. This precipitated their gruesome deaths one after the other until only one remained.

King Ember along with the chirurgeon Templeton Kaid, and the fratricidal Northlander Yeveryn, all stood at the top of the Geattor. With them was Yorn, a seasoned kelp farmer. Templeton had cut his face several times with surgical blades during an earlier encounter. He did not capitulate, so they tied his hands behind his back and positioned him at the west edge of the tower. On the ground below, were the bound and broken corpses of Yorn's friends.

At the mouth of the cave entrance above, a small group of Laedenoran Northlanders tended the Calamity Engine, the great, sorcerous coach that brought the Queen here. It fed on the souls of people, one of whom was Yeveryn's own brother. When he had heard of it, the story raised Ember's eyebrow.

The Queen Nissa had discovered this secret Geattor and taken a contingent of men through it to Port Frailty. She left Templeton, and her personal attendants and the others behind to secure the Geattor and the rest of the kelp farmers in the surrounding area. However, once they went through, the Geattor closed and ceased to function. Ember arrived with his own men after the fact, having traveled by horse.

"Yorn, is it?" Ember asked. "Yorn, would you refuse your King?" Ember doffed his gloves.

"You are not my King," defied Yorn. "You murdered my King."

Ember sighed. "Well, are you such an idiot? I have conquered your land, Yorn. And when that happens, kings and queens die and new ones replace them. This is common in the world, Yorn."

"But I suppose it is foolish to expect you to know, because you and everyone else in Zannistar have been hiding for so long, without care or responsibility. I offer you this: tell me what I require and I will spare you. Come now, your dead friends litter the floor of this cave. Will you be so eager to join them?"

"I will tell you nothing," said Yorn. "Kill me if you must."

"Oh, you are a brave one. Yorn, how do I activate the Geattor?"

Aside from Yorn's heavy breathing, there was silence.

"Yorn, soon Templeton here will push you off the edge. If you tell me what I need to know, I will activate the Geattor. I will then test your words. If you are telling the truth, you will transport to Port Frailty and to your safety. Perhaps start a new life and forget all about Zannistar. How does that sound?"

Yorn hung his head. "No."

"Templeton," said Ember.

"Yes, Majesty," returned Templeton, hunched over and wringing his hands.

"Please cut this faithless man's face from his head and feed it to him."

Templeton smiled, nodded and advanced on Yorn, knife in hand. He may have been salivating somewhat.

"Oh, Templeton, please leave his vocal chords intact. I still need to speak with him afterward."

"Yes, Majesty" Templeton could not contain his dark excitement.

With a final act of defiance, Yorn shifted his weight and threw himself from the tower top to the cave floor below, joining his companions in death.

"Oh my!" exclaimed Templeton, disappointed.

"I had not yet released him," said Ember. With thunderous speed, Ember ran to the edge of the tower and thrust his hands downward. Crimson smoke and vapor shot from his hands and entered Yorn's dead eyes and mouth. Ropes of reddened sinew hoisted Yorn to Ember's line of sight, suspending the corpse in mid-air. Yorn's carcass shook, its back broken and head crushed from the fall.

"Not yet, Yorn," commanded Ember. "Tell me what I want to know and I will release you."

Gurgles and spittle were all that emerged from the returned Yorn.

Ember huffed. "Templeton, can you repair this?"

"I would need my laboratory and tools, Sire."

"Good. Bring him back with you and do what you must. We may need him yet. In the meantime, leave him at the bottom of the tower to contemplate his options. Do not fret, my twisted friend, he will go nowhere nor will he die without your say so." Ember released Yorn who fell to the ground a second time, breaking more bone but keeping his consciousness.

"Yes, your Majesty."

"The Queen will discover a different way to return with the book. In the meantime, Templeton, secure this place and continue your efforts to activate the Geattor. Feel free of use as much of the local citizenry to test your adjustments to the tower. Just clean up your mess. Once you have succeeded, return to the palace."

"Yes, Majesty," Templeton bowed.

Ember made for the stairs. "I must now leave you to your creeping and fidgeting. Vang is not one to keep waiting."

Templeton winced. "I will alert your men."

"No," Ember interrupted. "I will return alone. I seek solitude. My men will answer to you."

"Yes, my King."

Exiting the cave mouth, Ember mounted his horse and made north at speed. Now he had been to the legendary kelp farms of the Southern Province, and he could use the Bekrot Chair to return there at his leisure. As he rode, he contemplated much: his existence, his growing mistrust in Vang and a life separate from him. He rather liked the thought of ruling Zannistar with Nissa alongside him. But she was an ocean away, unable to use the Geattor to return until it opened once more.

He was Dreka and soulless. He either needed Charles' eternal purpose, or he needed to get his own. Ember decided he would wait a little longer before taking a drastic course of action, but his patience was waning. He had doubted Vang's authenticity as the Sojourner's chosen for some time but felt too weak to oppose him. What is worse, he could tell that Vang knew how he felt. Sometimes, Vang could infiltrate his thoughts, dreams or even his actions. Vang told him it was the Sojourner's will. But Ember knew that if he had his own soul, he could stand on his own.

Ember shook his head to banish the thoughts and he focused on his surroundings. He wished he had traveled more to the Southern Province when he—and Charles—were younger. He realized he loved Zannistar and he doubted the soulmade Charles felt the same. In fact, he knew it.

The soulmade Charles never knew the cold justice of life in the north. Zannistar was far more comfortable than Laedenor. No wolves, Nurdrayl redbears, Cwalu or frostbite to deal with. Zannistar was a beautiful place, and it belonged to him. He was thankful to the Sojourner for its deliverance into his hands. The people would see it soon enough. They needed faith and discipline. He would provide both. Maybe then the Sojourner would award him a soul. He did not need Vang for that.

CHAPTER 39

THREE DAYS AT SEA and the morning was crisp, gulls were calling and for once the water was calm. Dara Warfield emerged from her very comfortable officer's quarters at the stern of the ship to find Lydia Mirette, Surek Taban and Tavist Upland, along with a smattering of sailors, surrounding Charles Warfield on the main deck of the transport ship Corvax. He was naked and stirring from sleep. Frantic, Dara ran down to meet them.

"Is he all right?" Asked Dara. "How did he get here?"

Tavist squatted down and held out his hand to warn her. "He is fine, Dara, but he is weak."

Lydia looked puzzled. "How did this happen?" she demanded.

"He flew right onto the ship!" announced one sailor. "In the middle of the cursed night."

Dara spun to identify the voice.

Glass eyes of green filled his eye-sockets and sparkled in the morning sunlight. His wrinkled face and head were shaven, and he wore the dirty white tunic over a sailor's brown trousers. Across his chest, was a black sash embroidered with a black raven's head. A broadsword and marlin spike rested at his hip, his boots of brown leather rose to his knees, trousers tucked in.

"Who saw it?" asked Dara.

"Well, no one saw it," answered the sailor. He drew his marlin spike and with it tapped his left eye. "We Brymróc are blind, or haven't you noticed? We heard it though. It flapped and flopped, making noises. Then it landed. One of my mates found stomach enough to check on it and discovered this naked man."

"His name is Charles," said Dara. "And how do you know he is naked?"

The sailor snorted. "How do you think? Naked or clothed, there's something off about him. Men don't fly."

"He is important," said Dara.

"So you say," said the man. "Well, my name is Gervin. Gervin Tackelbrot and I lead the Brymróc." He gestured to the other blind sailors who moved below decks to rest.

"I'm glad your naked friend lives," said Gervin. "Off to my flea-ridden bed for a spell." Gervin left confident, giving no indicator at all he was blind.

"Good dreams Tackelbrot!" yelled Captain Surek Taben.

"Oh they will be, Captain!" returned Gervin as he went down the hatch ladder.

"I am famished," said Charles, groggy and hoarse.

Eyes still closed, Charles made a groan as he tried to sit up.

"Charles! You are awake!" Dara pounced on him, hugging him to her and kissing his forehead. She turned his head, looking for damage. "I thought you were dead, or worse!"

"Nissa, is that you?" Charles drawled. "I smell brierberry dumplings."

Dara stopped, her throat tightened and tears welled in her eyes. "No, it is Dara."

She dropped him and stood. "I am glad you are all right, Charles. I was, I mean, you worried us. Where have you been?"

"Retrieving this, I think," Charles opened his hand and revealed the silver-colored coin.

Tavist's eyes widened. "Yes, Charles. You mentioned the coin when you were in the other form; the form of a beast. The coin changed you back, just as you said. Do you remember Charles?"

Charles rubbed his head. "I remember something, but it is a fog. You called a word. You said Furtyr—"

"Yes," said Tavist. "And until you find your heart, only I can call the beast into you."

"I already have a heart," Charles said with a snotty tone. "Nonsense."

"Do you, Charles?"

Charles strained to remember what he had done after he changed into the beast. He could not grasp its fullness.

"What am I, Tavist?" Charles anguished. "What terrible things have I done? I remember blood and flesh. Tavist, I killed them. I killed them all for the coin."

Tavist nodded. "I am grateful you changed back."

"You did what you had to do," interrupted Lydia. "As have we. Our country lies in the hands of invaders and our people suffer. Tavist says you can help. Arminius believed in you. So then I believe in you. Whatever you are, and whatever it is you can do, you can do it for Zannistar and our people."

Charles looked at his hands and panicked. "Zannistar? I can no more protect Zannistar than I could protect Veldic. She is dead. I saw it. Nissa killed her." Charles' eyes widened and became wet as he remembered. "I am sorry Dara, I could not protect her. I only knew her for a short time but I respected her."

Dara softened. "Charles, it was not your fault. She was supposed to protect you and she knew the risks. We both did. And she was my friend too."

Charles jerked away from her. "Where is she, Dara? Where is Nissa?"

Dara looked down. "I killed her." Her words sounded small. "I thought I would win her eternal purpose, but nothing happened."

"I feared it," Charles said. "You had no right." He wept.

"She killed Veldic, Charles. Her forces attacked us! She was a threat to you; to this mission!"

"She was my wife, Dara. I loved her."

"No, Charles. She used to be your wife. Wake up and stop being a child! Nissa betrayed you to your exile and effacement, stripped you of your nobility and tossed you away. She was evil, Charles! Evil!"

"And what of it? Did you not hear me? I loved her, Dara! But you are Dreka. How could you understand love?" Poison words.

Dara froze. She wore a shocked expression. "What did you say?"

"I said, how can you understand love? You are a shadow; a copy." Charles stared at the deck.

Dara said nothing.

Charles looked disgusted. "Neither you nor your fallen Dreka husband could experience love the way a normal person could. Even if you could take her soul, it does not belong to you. Both of you are accidents."

Dara slapped Charles' face. The sound was bright. He continued to stare at the deck.

"Look at me!" Dara yelled. "Coward!"

Charles would not. Wounded and angry, Dara left toward the forecastle where she could be alone.

"You earned that, Charles," said Tavist.

Charles turned away. "I do not care."

"Well you should," continued Tavist. "Charles, though you lack tact and basic decency, you have a great destiny. The Bóctalu has revealed it. You are more than you can imagine. You can set things right. All. But you must finish it."

"Young Tavist, I should like a brierberry dumpling," returned Charles, his expression shifting to indignation. "I can smell them cooking." Charles made sniffing noises.

Tavist shook his head. "Charles, we must prepare for the Neverwall."

"What is there to prepare for Tavist? We pass through it and on to Laedenor. We have a ship and an Expanser I assume. Let us concern ourselves less with the details of travel and more with filling our stomachs!"

"Charles, I am no longer a Guardsman but the High Scrivener of Zannistar. Arminius bequeathed me the Book of Nom at his valorous death. It is by his last words we found you. You would do well to remember that. But yes, we have an Expanser," Said Tavist, nodding at Surek Taban. "First, we sail to the Islet of Abeodan. There, I will read from the Bóctalu at the Pit of Nihthelm. Then you will remember your true self."

Charles snorted and mumbled something about the High Scrivener and rose to his feet. He was still rubbing his head and moaning. He turned his naked back. He seemed to not realize he had no clothes on.

"What will that accomplish besides put us in more danger?" asked Surek Taben.

"Captain," began Tavist. "In order for Charles to beat his opponent, he must remember who he is. The Pit of Nihthelm hides a window into the world-before, called Vel. It will show him all. Then he will be ready."

"The risk is great, but I accept," said Surek Taban.

"Thank you, Captain," said Tavist, staring at Charles. "We need something special; we need Charles, or all will die. Everyone."

Charles folded his arms. "Well I for one, will die if I do not find a fucking dumpling!"

Lydia rolled her eyes and ushered Charles toward the ship's galley. "Let us find you breakfast and some clothes."

"We reach the borders of the Neverwall tonight," said Surek Taben.

"I hope Charles can do what is necessary," said Tavist. "I hope he survives."

Surek Taban approached Tavist with grace. "Scrivener, does that book of yours show you the future?"

"Not as yet, Captain," said Tavist. But I can feel it working on my mind, changing me. It is a thinking and living creature. But it is not from this world. It is not explainable, Captain. Its truths are inescapable and terrible but I cannot say how. It is a heavy responsibility. And deep in my heart I know that it shows me only those parts I can understand. Its true nature is incomprehensible. We are nothing to it. Yet it concerns itself with our existence."

The captain gave a long stare to Tavist, then slapped him on the shoulder. "Well, let me express how fortunate I feel it is your task and not mine. The Neverwall is perilous enough without having to deal with thinking books. Besides, my old mind is tired. Good day, Scrivener."

"Good day, Captain." Tavist said.

Captain Surek Taben left for the helm. Tavist sat, watching Dara lean against the railing, as she looked out to sea. The Bóctalu grew cold at his side.

Forming in the distance, he could see what looked like a shimmering curtain of darkness stretching into the sky.

CHAPTER 40

THE HOLY SOJOURNER, THE WALKER OF THE PATH, had been the foundation of the world's faith since the ancient days. The Itinerants had interpreted his movements for a thousand years since the founding of the order. In following years, all lived by those interpretations without question. It was the one thing that tied the different lands together; the one good thing they shared.

Choosing the life of an Itinerant meant a lifetime of selfless service to the Sojournic Order and to the world. Not only was a candidate expected to know the details of the Lucan, of the Sojourner's walk and of every manuscript written concerning the same, they were also expected to travel the world at the whim of the Prelate, offering alms and help to all. This was the Sibb-gewealc, the walk of peace. These days, there were more Itinerants traveling across the Northlands than south of the Neverwall.

Expansers were scarce, and the Geattors opened for a single day every hundred years. As a result, there were precious few Itinerants in places like Port Frailty, where they were most needed. Quincunx had no stomach for travel. His was a lifetime of study and reflection.

Quincunx had been a model student in his youth. His particular specialty was in Interpretive Arts. He had spent many years in study going over the decisions of the past major interpretations whether by the presiding Prelate or the seldom fortunate Lucanite who could get close enough to see the Sojourner move. Never in the history of the Sojournic faith had a Sentinel witnessed the Astyr. Yet, it happened. And no one had ever seen an Astyr so dramatic; so obvious.

It had taken millennia for the Sojourner to walk the distance he had. The Sojourner's wisdom had always guided the faithful through the most difficult times; even the Sixteen Generations war. Now, the entire epoch of the Sojournic journey was about to come to a close in the next several days. Atli interpreted the Astyr as the Wyrsa-gewealc. After tonight's ceremony, she would be Prelate and all the Itinerants would trade their bells for swords. The Walk of Battle would begin under the new Cwalu leadership.

The afternoon was late. Stripped to only his undergarments, Quincunx looked at his own reflection in his bedroom window and considered his lifetime contribution to the Sojournic faith. He had been the best Itinerant he could be. He made life altering choices based on that faith.

Some of those decisions affected others in sometimes painful ways. But he was the Prelate. That was his burden. And as long as he believed in the Sojourner's truth, it justified him. But he did not believe. Not anymore. Not for some time. Not since he met the evil one during the dreamsight, one of the rarest of Sojournic gifts.

He called himself Vang. He was a virile, well-spoken, white-haired young man in white robes. His message was simple: the Sojournic faith was a lie. At first, Vang identified himself to be the specter of a long dead Itinerant. Quincunx was at first suspicious, but indulged the entity.

Nightly, Quincunx would enter the dreamsight and Vang would be there, ready to debate the finer points of Sojournic theology and eschatology. Vang made the case that the Holy Sojourner was not the worldly incarnation of the Gastwyrd at all, but instead was a child caught in a magical trap, many years ago. It was an absurd thought. How could an entire civilization's faith be a mistake? And yet, night after night, Vang chipped away at Quincunx's belief. But soon after, Quincunx learned Vang was no ghostly Itinerant at all, but something very different. He was dark and ancient beyond measure, with desires and words following.

Vang seemed to care only for the diminishment of Quincunx's faith as though it amused him. Eventually, Quincunx fell into a darkened melancholy, unable to escape Vang's prophecies of despair. Searching for relief, he ceased entering the dreamsight, but he was never again the same as some part of Vang remained a part of him. The ordeal had destroyed his faith. He questioned everything. Nothing made sense anymore. All seemed lost. He continued for nearly five years in mental anguish, fighting off intermittent waves of despair. And despite sometimes maddening thoughts, he never told or showed anyone what he had been dealing with.

Then one night, Quincunx found courage and chanced the dreamsight a final time. He intended to confront Vang once and for all. But instead of finding Vang waiting for him, he found something or someone else. The creature presented as a large man with the antlers of a stag, wings of an eagle and bottomless, black eyes.

The creature showed him the ancient cataclysm when the great fireball from the sky crashed to the ground and burned the Nurdrayl forest. He saw the child run to it and lift the shard from the pit. He saw the animals jump to their deaths. Quincunx asked the creature's name. It said it was the Furtyr and pointed across the Great Sea to a land hidden from memory. Zannistar. Quincunx saw a man counting coins in a counting house. The Furtyr said Vang would destroy the world and that the man in the counting house held the key to stopping Vang.

The Furtyr also led Quincunx's mind to a small, abandoned dwelling near Mirlandis Lake. Inside was a trunk that housed a small, silver coin. The Furtyr told Quincunx to give it to the soulmade Charles Warfield. The Furtyr mentioned many other arcane things, including how to use the Geattor to reach Zannistar, the hidden land. Quincunx asked the Furtyr if Vang was lying about the Sojourner.

The Furtyr looked him in the eye and told him that Vang spoke the truth. He said the Sojourner was a boy under an ancient magic. He was not supposed to be here. Then he told him something too terrible to say aloud, and too terrible to share.

In a single moment, after a lifetime of false religion, Quincunx knew the truth. The Sojourner was a false god. This knowledge was worse than death. Even the Cwalu believed the Sojourner to be divine; a destroyer, not a savior. The Furtyr told Quincunx to wait for the opening of the Geattor. He was to send someone to Zannistar to find and bring Charles Warfield to the north.

Not long after, the Cwalu brought a naked man and woman they had found in the Gearwood Thicket nearly dead from exposure. After being taken in and nursed back to health, they told their story. They were a newlywed husband and wife who had mysteriously ended up in the forest when they were supposed to be teleported to the Gardens of Gryn in the Lurin Heights. Their names were Charles and Nissa Warfield.

Charles Warfield was the name the Furtyr had told him about. Quincunx knew, based on their description of the throne, that it was the lost and accursed Bekrot Chair of Mirlandis Lake. It was likely the two outsiders were Dreka, created by the Bekrot Chair. Quincunx would take no chances.

From that point forward, the two refugees enjoyed Quincunx's favor and protection. Eventually accepting their existences, Charles and Nissa took new names. Nissa became Dara, which meant star, and Charles took the Laedenoran name Cenric, just because he liked the way it sounded.

In time, under the tutelage of the Cwalu, Dara would become an accomplished Woodlock and Cenric would become a skilled warrior. Though unlike his wife, he never took for himself the blood of the Sojourner. The Cwalu came to respect his bravery and eventually counted him among them.

Life flourished in the Itinerant Stronghold for a while under Quincunx's leadership. Quincunx had come to terms with his apostasy, and decided that worldwide order took precedence over the struggles of one, lonely Prelate. So he went through the motions, blessing things, admonishing acolytes, granting audiences and providing hope, even though by then he harbored no faith in the Sojourner whatsoever.

Eventually, the Dreka Cenric Warfield became so well liked by the populace and so proficient at martial combat, Quincunx gave him command of the Sojournic forces, which included the Cwalu

Itinerants, the Sentinels and the volunteer regiments from the many cotlif villages in Laedenor; mostly those along the coast and near Mirlandis Lake.

This was timely since another Dreka with Cenric's likeness had been discovered. He had been raiding cotlif villages all over Laedenor for supplies and troops. He called himself Ember Driss. He raised an army of people sensitive to his plight. These were mostly folk from the extreme north.

Many of his converts had been previously without religion. He sought to liberate the Sojourner from the Itinerants, convincing his growing army that the Itinerants were evil. He taught that the true emissary of the Sojourner was not the Father Prelate, but a prophet named Vang whom Ember served.

In return for fealty, Ember taught them new ways of fighting, planting food and making medicines. The most loyal to him were blessed with strange powers. In a short time, he had united the whole of remote Laedenor to his cause, under one name: Vang. Thus started the conflict between the Itinerants and Ember Driss.

A year after the conflict began, a decisive battle played out at Sable Rock, seven days walk east of the birthplace of the Sojourner's long journey. Ember Driss leaked false information tricking the Cwalu into traveling to Mirlandis Lake to the west. He then lured the Itinerant forces to concentrate in the furthest reaches of the Gearwood Thicket, where he and his forces ambushed them, slaughtering the majority of the Itinerant forces.

Without the Cwalu present, there was no chance of survival. Cenric Warfield was among the dead. Defeated, the remaining Itinerant forces retreated to the compound and have since fortified there under the diminishing protection of the Cwalu and what little remained of the Itinerant Forces, chiefly the Sentinels.

Shortly after that defeat, Quincunx realized that the Geattor's one hundred year sleep would soon be over. Quincunx traveled to Mirlandis Lake and found the silver coin that the Furtyr told him about. Upon his return to the Stronghold, he plotted with Dara and Veldic to go to the fabled land of Zannistar and bring back the soulmade Charles Warfield. He told them that only Charles could save the world from the destruction that lay ahead.

Quincunx assumed that because Ember Driss was Dreka that he must also have memories of Zannistar. It was vital they get there before Ember Driss did. Then, on the first hour of the Geattor's open day, he sent them. Quincunx then entered the dreamsight and, according to instructions given by the Furtyr, could open a tiny magical doorway to Zannistar through which he sent the coin and through which he could briefly speak with Charles Warfield who had then been rotting in the King's oubliette. That feat nearly cost Quincunx his life. He spent many days bedridden, almost drained of his own life force. It was a price he had been willing to pay.

Thoughts of the past slowly faded from Quincunx's awareness. He continued to stare out the window, only now his vision focused on the many Itinerants who flocked to the Sojourner. He was moving quickly now; enough that interpretation of his positioning would be difficult. But none of that mattered now. The Sojourner would reach Stag's End soon. Quincunx thought to pray that Charles Warfield would arrive in time, but he knew there was nobody listening; at least nobody that loved him.

Quincunx turned, making sure the note he had written was still there on his desk. It was. He could see the large words he wrote: 'The Sojourner is Vang'.

With a final will, the Father Prelate Quincunx stepped off the chair and hanged quietly to his death. As his consciousness shrank, Vang's voice rang out in the darkness.

You made the right choice, old man. It is better this way, Quincunx. So much better. We will meet soon.

CHAPTER 41

THE SOULLESS EMBER DRISS THUNDERED through the Great Hall in the Zanni palace, his brow sweaty and his expression cross. He pushed past courtiers, returning none of the greetings he had received. The new King stopped in front of Charles Warfield's quarters and regarded the space above the door where the coat of arms used to be. Reminded of etiquette, he wiped his brow, straightened his doublet and slowed his breathing. He knocked on the door, then entered.

The quarters were in shambles. The furniture broken, the wardrobes tossed, the bed torn apart. At the west window was the creature, inside whom lived Vang. The creature leaned against some linens and silken pillows so it could look outside at the Western Sea. The quarters smelled of rot.

"Vang," began Ember. "I can not find Thimgar."

"Come in, Ember," said the grotesque thing. "Look with me, it is beautiful out."

"Vang, the men say they last saw him with you. Perhaps you could—"

"Silence! Come!"

Ember walked over to the west window and stood beside Vang.

"Can you believe how beautiful this creation is?" The creature chuckled. "Is such a thing possible?"

Ember looked out at the sea. He remembered it well. "The Sojourner is mighty."

"It turns my stomach!" Vang spat the words.

"I do not understand," said Ember.

The thing nodded downward, out the window. "There is your friend, Ember,"

Ember moved closer and looked out the window. He saw Thimgar, dashed against the rocks below in a twisted position. Feelings of anger welled up.

"Oh do not start so!" said Vang. "I know well you doubt me, perhaps you even plan to slay me."

Ember looked surprised. "You are mistaken, I—"

"Enough," Vang returned. "I am after all a forgiving sort. The Sojourner demands it. But I required a small retribution for your indiscretion. Consider yourself absolved and your debt paid. You may go."

"He was loyal, Vang—a friend."

"I am your friend, Ember. Your only friend. Now go."

Ember swallowed his hasty words and replaced them. "Yes, Vang." He turned, seeking the door. Vang enraged him but he needed to be clever.

"Oh, Ember," said Vang. "I forgot to tell you. Your new wife Nissa is also dead. Decapitated." The thing made a chopping motion on the side of its neck with its useless appendage. "The

Dreka Dara Warfield killed her. Isn't that interesting? I suppose she now owns Nissa's eternal purpose. The Sojourner showed me in a vision. No matter. You have no time for a wife. It is as it should be."

Ember froze. He thought it a game at first; an attempt to rattle him. Then the truth of it pushed into his being. He had lost her again. Ember continued for the door but he was no longer willing to grovel. He turned and approached Vang. "I want a soul, Vang. I want a soul and I want it now! No more lies and no more promises!"

The creature looked puzzled. "Do you intend to kill me, Ember? After everything I have done for you? You are pathetic and no different from the others." Vang made his best approximation of a pout.

"You are no emissary of the Sojourner but a fraud! And yes, I will kill you." Ember drew his sword.

Vang's few jagged teeth vibrated. "He killed himself, Ember! Thimgar killed himself! And you will do the same. You will all do the same! I do not need you anymore. My army awaits me in the north! It's the Neverwall for you, Ember Driss!"

Ember swung at the creature and found purchase, spilling blood and bile. "You can not kill me Ember! This body is but a vessel. But you are right I am not the Sojourner's emissary, because I am the Sojourner himself and I come to destroy all of you!"

"Lies!" Ember swung again.

"You will never have a soul!" screamed Vang as Ember reduced him to tattered oblivion.

Ember's anger took over. He struck the creature numerous times until there was no more to strike. Ember dropped his sword, fell to the blood soaked floor and sobbed.

As the sun set, so did Vang's power leave Ember. Red wisps of vapor emerged from Ember's tearing eyes. He was empty and without power. He was ordinary. But the absence of Vang's darkened power did not change who he was inside.

He was still the same, pathetic shell that emerged from the Gearwood Thicket those many years ago. Ember was not heroic, just or kind. The world had no place for him. Vang had been his focus and his purpose. Now he was nothing again. Ember felt the bleak despair of utter solitude and began walking to the window. He thought he would end it here. It was proper. The pain would be temporary.

"No!" Ember screamed into the empty room. "No, Vang! I will not!"

Yes, Yes, Yes!

Ember grabbed his aching head. Something nagged at him. It was something he needed to remember. Then it hit him.

Ember ran from the room and down the Great Hall into his own bed chamber. He stopped in front of the Bekrot Chair and regarded its artistry.

"I will go to Laedenor myself!" yelled Ember into the air. "I have no need of the Geattor. Vang, you are no longer my master. The Bekrot Chair is mine and I will to do with it as I please! I will take Charles' soul and I will take Dara for my wife as payment for her murdering Nissa."

I am murder.

Ember shook his head. "Leave me! I am free of you!"

He sat in the chair and envisioned the many places he had been in the Northlands. The Bekrot Chair only showed him one place: the cotlif village on Mirlandis Lake. It was half a day's journey to the Itinerant Stronghold from there. Ember tried again to envision the Sojournic Stronghold and again only the lake appeared. The chair showed what it wanted to whom it wanted.

"So be it," said Ember. He closed his eyes. He and the chair vanished leaving behind a wisp of red smoke.

CHAPTER 42

THE SOULMADE CHARLES WARFIELD SAUNTERED across the deck of the Corvax, with a bottle of snowberry wine in hand. He had found it in the ship's store where he had been snooping for brierberries. He remembered she mentioned she had a taste for it when they were in Reedsdrift where a person could find river bulb wine but not much else. The Corvax had many kinds of wine in the store; the spoils of frequent travel to the Northlands, he figured.

The sea was silent, and Charles saw it was nearing dusk. Charles quickened his pace and noted the sightless sailors called the Brymróc had emerged from their slumber to assume the watch from the day crew. They began preparations to enter the Neverwall. Their movements were precise and quick. Charles wondered how they avoided running into people or things. He spied Dara who was on the starboard side, staring at the horizon. He called out.

"I brought snow-berry wine," said Charles. "And I brought your hoodwink."

Dara remained silent, the small ocean breeze pushing at her cropped hair.

"It is your favorite," Charles said. "I remembered that."

The silence made Charles anxious. "Dara, I wanted to apologize, for what I said."

"I am not sorry I hit you," Dara said without turning her head. "You are wrong, you realize."

"About what?"

"About Cenric, my husband. You are wrong. He was kind, brave, loving and merciful. Cenric always took care of others before himself. He gave us hope, Charles, and he loved me with all his heart. My husband never let me think any less of myself for being Dreka. He even turned Veldic around after he caught her stealing food from the Lucanites. Instead of having her prosecuted, he taught her to believe in something other than herself. She became Cenric's most trusted soldier. My husband died a principled man, protecting us. Is that not love?"

Dara's face hardened. "And about Nissa's eternal purpose. I thought I would feel something, but I do not. I thought I would *be* different. But I am not. I fear the legends were false. I am just Dreka, an impostor, doomed to spend eternity in the Neverwall. At least I will see him again."

Charles felt terrible. "I am sorry, Dara, I do not understand why I said those things. I was different. But I am sorry."

Dara turned to look at Charles. "And yet, here you are. You look like him and you have similar mannerisms." Dara moved closer. "You even smell like him. When I found out I was to come find you, I had hoped that I would find him in you; that somehow in death he would find his way to you. Instead of him I found you, arrogant and selfish; afraid and undisciplined. You have a precious soul, yet you are in my husband's shadow."

Charles looked at his feet. This was a familiar view and a familiar feeling. He despaired at his inadequate attributes.

Then Dara lifted his face with her hand. It felt warm. They locked eyes. In that moment anything was possible.

"But, I know his essence is in there somewhere." Dara touched Charles' chest.

Charles' heart skipped a beat.

"On some level you two are the same person," said Dara. "You share a past. And I want to be near you. Do you not wish to be near me?" Dara's eyes promised deepening bliss. She pressed in. "Do you find her in my face?"

Charles gulped and pulled away. "Dara, I am not sure I—"

The fire in Dara's eyes retreated, replaced by cold indignation. "Forget it, Charles." She did her best to hide the rejection, breaking their proximity.

Dara snatched the glass and raised it high. "Thanks for the wine. Did you say this was snowberry wine?"

"Yes, I did."

"Well then, apology accepted!" Dara drank it down in one swig and threw the glass overboard. "Come, we must prepare for the Neverwall." She glided past him, hiding her tears.

"You forgot your hoodwink!" yelled Charles, stumbling after her.

The sun was setting. Captain Surek Taben emerged from his quarters in a special coat made of black wool, over a black doublet and black slops. Atop his head sat a black, woolen tricorn with a single opal on a leather strap affixed to the brim. Knee-high, black boots and black buckles finished the uniform of a proper Expanser.

"Lookin' sharp, Captain," said Gervin Tackelbrot, himself in black raiment.

"How do you know, Gervin?" replied Surek Taban. "You are blinder than a cavern fish."

"That I am," Gervin returned. "Call it intuition. The crew and the ship are ready, Sir."

"Good," announced the Captain. "Passengers?"

"Gussied, hoodwinked and snug in their quarters."

"Fine. Join me at the helm. Let us enter the Neverwall smartly."

"Smartly, aye."

"We sail for Abeodan," ordered the Captain. "Alert the passengers."

Gervin made a clicking sound and a nearby sailor sprung to the task. Within a few minutes, the ship entered the borders of the Neverwall.

Surek Taben looked up to the sky and as was the norm, the stars disappeared, one by one. An immense pressure developed affecting everyone's ears. It made hair stand on end and put butterflies in stomachs. After a moment, it was over. Then nothing. No sound, no water, no sky and no sense of safety.

Surek Taban concentrated his thoughts on the opal on his hat. Like a beacon, it erupted in light. A sphere of white light grew from its center and engulfed the ship. He gave the wheel to Gervin.

"The ship is yours, Tackelbrot," ordered the Captain. "Make my heading per my adjustments,"

"My ship, aye," Gervin took the wheel. "Awaiting adjustments. I assume, Sir, you are well-rested and alert?"

"I hope so, Gervin." Said the Captain; his voice foreboding.

The Captain stepped back and sat in a great, wooden chair just behind the piloting area and focused on keeping the sphere aloft, which was itself, keeping the ship aloft.

It took longer than normal, but the forlorn faces of the Nihtgessa appeared against the convex of the sphere. They pressed against it with spectral hands, testing its strength. They looked distressed, in need of help. Soon, Nihtgessa of all types beset the entire outside of the sphere. As their numbers grew, so did their presentation of malice.

"Ahead true, Tackelbrot," warned the Captain. "We will see more than this tonight. Well, *I* will anyway."

"Ahead true, aye, Captain."

The Duchess Lydia Mirette and the High Scrivener Tavist Upland lay facing each other on the overstuffed, silken pillows that made up Lydia's bed in her quarters. They were both dressed in black pants and tunic and had also donned their black hoodwinks. They had their hands lodged between their knees and so close were they that each felt the other's breath.

"Shengmar?" asked Lydia.

"Yes Lydia," answered Tavist.

"Is my name in that book?"

"Yes. I have not looked, but I know."

"How? How can you know?"

"All names are in the Bóctalu."

They sat quiet for a time. The only sounds they heard were of Brymróc movements about the ship. No waves. No birds.

"Where did it come from? The book."

"It came from another world. A world called Vel. Some call it the world-before."

"And this idea just came to you?"

"Yes. Every day, more knowledge grows in my mind. I can not explain it."

"You differ from when we first met. You have wisdom."

"I had not noticed."

"Shengmar, speak to me about the other world, Vel."

"I can not."

"Why?"

"Because I have not yet been there. But you have."

"Have I?" Her tone was playful.

Tavist took her hand and folded her thumb and pinky, using her three largest fingers as examples of the three worlds. He touched them as he explained. "Yes. Most people start their eternal journey in Vel. When they die, their souls travel here, to Myn, then on to the world-after, Rax. Not me. My soul started its journey in the world-after and it moves in the opposite direction."

"Absurd," said Lydia. She smiled, though none could see it.

"Yes. It is. But it is true."

"Then do you remember the other world? Rax?"

"Some of it, peoples' faces. Sometimes I recognize someone here in Myn that I knew in Rax."

"Who for example?"

"Well, for example, I think I knew you."

"How did you know me?"

"I believe we were in love."

296

Lydia laughed. "In love? Well that is a grand story. I would think a delicious morsel as yourself would not need to create such nonsense to coax women into bed. Did we have little ones as well?"

"I do not recall."

"Is that so?"

There was silence again. Tavist was still holding Lydia's warm hand. He traced the contour with his own. She laced her fingers with his, testing their strength.

"Tavist?" asked Lydia.

"Yes?"

"Thank you." Her voice was softer.

"For what?"

"For giving Arminius a merciful death."

Tavist did not know how to react. He placed her hand on his chest. "He meant much to you."

Lydia stifled the urge to cry. "Is he like you? Does his soul travel backward between worlds?

"Yes. It has been so for all Scriveners throughout the ages."

"He is in Vel?"

"Yes."

"Why can I not remember him? Or You?"

"It does not always work that way. The worlds are vast. And time is unpredictable between them. But there are methods to wake a person to their other selves. We sail for one now."

"The Islet of Abeodan." Lydia said it slow and deliberate.

"Yes," said Tavist almost a whisper.

Lydia felt for Tavist's face and cradled it in her hands. Tavist did the same. They touched foreheads and waited in silent consort.

CHAPTER 43

CHARLES LAY SUPINE AND MOTIONLESS on the floor of his quarters. Ever since they entered the Neverwall, his stomach had been churning. Being on the deck helped a little.

He hated the clothes the Brymróc had put him in. The hoodwink was most uncomfortable. Not being able to see was torture. He could not conceive of how the Brymróc could live without sight, much less operate a ship. It took great concentration and self-control to not rip it off his face as waves of panic washed over him every few minutes. He could not shake the feeling that someone was near him; watching.

As he tried to forget his predicament, his mind wandered back to Port Frailty, when he turned into that creature. He still only remembered fragments. This entire mission had been one unbelievable disaster after another. How was it possible he, a low-ranking member of Secondary nobility, be privy to such raw power? But yet, it felt right and familiar. He admitted to himself that it felt more proper than his life in Zannistar.

And there was Dara. He knew she cared for him and he for her. As strange as all of this was, he was beginning like her and he felt bad for how he had treated her. She deserved better, and he knew it.

He could not let Nissa go. Despite all of her cruelty and betrayal, he loved her. He had since they were children. He could remember their first summer together. Their parents introduced them pending their future betrothal. They spent many days together exploring the palace grounds and the surrounding woods. They had even made a hovel out of fallen sticks and pretended it was their own palace. They made crowns of flowers for one another and pretended to be Primary nobles: he the King and she his Queen. They acted out all the many facets of a royal family, except for kissing. That was repulsive. That did not, however, stop young Charles Warfield from chasing her around making horrible kissing noises.

This ended in pain for Charles as she was faster and stronger than he was. She was a precocious child. She taught him manners and noble conversation as he was not great at it. He was not great at most things. But she did not seem to care so much as she appreciated his endless willingness to sit and listen to her.

It continued that way as they grew into maturity. When his parents perished at Ganlis Bay, and the King took him as his own, she was supportive. They married as planned. For reasons only known to him, King Lidig Branlin liked Charles very much. So he took them to the Gardens of Grynn with the Bekrot Chair. After a happy month together, the King returned to bring them home. That was when she changed.

Charles was feeling the stress of recent events saturate his awareness. There were many things he could not explain: The creature that attacked him in Gyldred's laboratory, the man in the oubliette who gave him the coin, the strange and terrible voices in his head, his own transformation into a ravenous, flying demon. His head throbbed. He forced himself from the ground and felt his way for the cabin door. He opened it and poked his head out.

"Dara," he called. "Dara are you there? Dar—"

"Here, Charles, this way!" The voice came from the left passageway.

"Where are you? Keep talking so I can find you." He ventured into the passageway, hands on the bulkhead.

Dara kept calling until Charles reached her.

"There," she said. "I have you." She grabbed his hand.

"I do not wish to be alone, Dara," said Charles.

She pulled him to her. She smelled sweet. "I know, Charles," she said, stroking his hair. "But you *are* alone. You are alone because you are a filthy coward."

Charles' mind flew from sanity. "No!"

The sweet smell turned sour.

Yes, yes yes!

Charles thrashed but he could not pull away. He was suffocating. He clawed at his hoodwink, yet something stopped him.

"Charles!" yelled Dara. "Wake up! What is wrong?"

Charles came to his senses. He had fallen asleep. Dark imaginings faded as he put his mind back together.

Dara put her hand on his shoulder then to his face. His hoodwink was still there. "I heard you screaming down the passageway, so I felt my way here."

"I am fine," said Charles. "Thank you." He was not fine.

Dara sat with him, back to back.

"Dara, do you remember playing with me in the woods when we were children?"

"Yes, Charles. I do. Why?"

"I was happy. That made me happy."

"Me too."

"Was that you? Was that Nissa? Does it matter?"

"I remember it, so it was both of us I imagine."

"So, I suppose you also remember the Gardens of Grynn?"

"No. I remember going, but we never arrived. Instead, Cenric and I appeared in the Gearwood Thicket, believing we had become lost."

"So, the others: Ember Driss and the other Nissa; the one that died. The Bekrot Chair created them when Nissa and I went back to Zannistar."

"Yes."

"So they would have remembered our wedding sabbatical. But not you and Cenric."

"It stands to reason, yes." Charles intrigued Dara. "Why?"

"Well, that means you have not yet experienced the delights of my excellent kissing," said Charles, making obnoxious kissing noises. He could not believe he did so.

"My husband kissed well, thank you. And he too remembered playing in the woods those many years ago." Her tone was at once playful and serious.

"Yes, but I would wager I am better," He made more kissing noises. "I must be better at something."

"Yes, I believe you are better at complaining," said Dara.

Their belly laughter tore apart the brief silence, and the release drew them closer. In what way, neither of them could explain but closer, nonetheless. In that room they sat hoodwinked, back to back and heart to heart, waiting out the rest of the trip, reminiscing of childhood innocence and happy adventures.

CHAPTER 44

THE CORVAX FLOATED through the Neverwall; the sphere surrounding it covered with the writhing forms of Nihtegessa. The Neverwall was enveloped in eternal night; an unnatural darkness penetrating everything, even the bones. There were many dangers for those who sailed its waterless waves.

Torchlight was half as effective and burned half as long. Time meant nothing here, impossible to measure. There were stories from the early days of ships which had emerged from the Neverwall years after entering though it was only several days for the crew. There were also stories of the opposite: ships exiting only moments after going in, but the crew having aged many years. There were even ships still missing. Those unfortunates braved the Neverwall without an Expanser.

Captain Surek Taben was an Expanser, and therefore immune to the power of the Neverwall and the Nihtgessa inhabiting it. It had something to do with the magic that flowed in his blood, put there by the Cwalu during the Expanser preparation process. It enabled him to look at the Nihtgessa, to know them and to keep them at bay. He had traversed the Neverwall so many times, more especially during the Sixteen Generations War, that he recognized some of them on sight and they him. Were he an ordinary person, looking on them would prove deadly.

The Nihtgessa were notorious for leading ships in circles while they slowly devoured the minds of the crew. Just making eye contact gave them permission to interact with a person in whatever way they wanted. They were powerful. Even the sphere's protection lasted only as long as an Expanser could stay awake. If sleep came, so did the Nihtgessa.

No matter how many times he had been through and back, he never grew exactly accustomed to the quiet. Gervin, the coxswain and leader of the Brymróc, knew this of the Captain, so he learned songs to keep the Captain feeling comfortable. If the sphere were to drop, the Nihtgessa would immediately accost them. The Captain was also responsible for navigation through the Neverwall. This required concentration.

Captain Surek Taben was enjoying Gervin's song when he spied the formation of water and the features of a small island with a low profile. He looked to the sky and stars appeared, densely situated and bright. They had arrived at the protective sphere that surrounded the Islet of Abeodan. As they passed through the sphere's boundary, the ship's sphere blended with it, then formed again once they were inside. The Nihtgessa horrors transferred to the outside of the larger sphere surrounding the island and became smaller as the ship left them behind.

The Captain had been to the islet once before, during the war. It was small; a few hours walk from one end to the other. The beaches were made of coarse sand, with a few larger rocks about. The islet showed no evidence of a single beast or tree. A rock jetty stretched toward the ship from a small bay. The Captain gave Gervin directions, and they found themselves alongside the jetty. The Brymróc secured the vessel to bollards on the rocks. All was well. Surek Taben was happy to hear and feel waves again.

The passengers gathered on the main deck. The Captain explained to them they could remove their hoodwinks once they reached the Pit of Nihthelm in the islet's center. He instructed them to hold the shoulder of the person in front at all times. So they went, in a single-file line toward the center of the island. It was about an hour over fairly easy terrain and they came to a low-lying cave mouth containing rock stairs. Surek Taben ushered them down the stairs.

Once at the bottom, they removed their hoodwinks. The company shielded their eyes from the bright light that filled the round cave. In the space's center was a hole, as wide as a person is tall, its edge lined with a sparkling metal of unknown origin. Inside the hole seemed to stretch down forever in a spiral of black and gray liquid. Suspended by a heavy chain above it, was a massive, uncut opal of a yellow hue larger than a steed. It was the source of the light. There were many divots in the opal as though someone had chipped away smaller pieces. Around them were strange markings on the walls. When considered all at once, they resembled the night sky, but more complex and somehow alive with movement.

Charles immediately felt an uneasy familiarity with this place. He looked around at the others. Dara and Lydia were already walking around the room, attempting to understand it. As they touched the wall, it responded by glowing under their touch.

"I will wait atop the stairs," announced Surek Taben. "This place does not agree with me. Put on your hoodwinks and call when you are ready to leave. And be quick." He bounded up the stairs.

The Bóctalu grew very warm. The large opal seemed to respond to its presence. It pulsed. Tavist flipped the book around according to Arminius' instructions and opened it somewhere in the middle. He heard and felt a low rumbling in the chamber.

Tavist cleared his throat and said aloud the word that appeared on the page. "Vel."

The opal emitted a high-pitched sound and the dark, thick liquid in the pit spun faster.

"Charles," said Tavist. "That is the Pit of Nihthelm. Are you ready?"

"No," said Charles. "No I am not. What will happen?"

"I do not know," said Tavist. The sound was growing louder. "But I think we must move closer."

"Closer to *that*? How do you know these things?" Charles was competing with the growing sound.

Tavist turned the Bóctalu toward Charles. Stretched across both pages of the open book was an image in wispy, undulating ink of the four of them sitting at the edge of the pit with their legs crossed. He showed it to Lydia and Dara who looked at each other. The sound continued to grow and a second sound began, creating a dissonance that assaulted their ears.

"We have to do it now!" yelled Tavist as loud as he could. The opal was pulsing in a rhythm and gaining speed.

Not understanding their fear, the four scrambled to get into their positions according to the book. The sound grew in such intensity they could hear nothing else. The pulsing had become a solid wall of white light.

Charles put his hands to his ears. He looked across and saw Lydia doing the same but screaming silently. Dara shut her eyes and remained still. Charles and Tavist both peered in the book and saw four appendage-like ropes of ink exit the pit and attach to all their faces.

Charles and Tavist exchanged looks but had no time to react. The spinning liquid took the form of four appendages and stuck to their faces.

Charles was floating high above the world, amongst clouds of spectacular density and size. He was drifting forward; the wind playing at his ears. Above him was the ominous presence of two moons, one small and one very large, each a different shade of rust red. They were so close that even in the daylight they were visible.

Below him and stretched into the horizon was a lush green wooded valley with hills on either side. In the distance was what he thought to be a city comprising hundreds of gleaming spires of metal. As he got closer, he realized that there were gargantuan beasts of shifting color with unrecognizable feature and quality floating in the air above the city. He caught the glint of sun off the surface of a crystalline lake nearby. Floating on its surface were vessels of wood and metal in shapes he had never dreamed of. He floated over the city like a ghost, unaware he was entertaining a guest.

"Charles," an ancient voice, low and soft filled his mind and resonated through him.

Charles turned around to face upward, his back to the valley below. Flying with him, looking down at him was the Furtyr. It had its fur-covered and clawed hands at its side. Antlers shot from its head, ending in points of immense, destructive power. It brandished razors for teeth and its black eyes were forever. Great eagle's wings sprouted from its back; the feathers ending in razor tips. The rest of its body was a man's. They spun together in a lazy spiral, facing one another.

"Where are the others?" asked Charles. For once, his heart was not beating fast, nor was he sweating.

"They are more or less asleep. They are safe." The voice electrified Charles' spine.

"I am in the world-before. Is this Vel?" Charles felt ideas and memories probing his consciousness like little hands with daggers, looking for soft places to bury them. "We know each other?"

"Your mind is here in Vel. And yes, I am you and you are me."

Charles knew it was true. "You are a frightful monster. I am a shell of a man; a useless coward and a burden. How is it we are the same?" It hurt to say it.

"I created you, Charles. I created your entire world and hid it from him."

"Vang," The word was decay in the mouth of Charles' mind. His ability to comprehend what was happening stayed just ahead of the revelatory words of the Furtyr. As the Furtyr spoke, the environment itself was pouring itself into Charles, as if he had always known.

They glided together past the city, between it and the immense floating beasts overhead. Sometimes, the beasts blocked out the sun. Their groans were gentle but powerful.

"Vang is the oldest evil," said the Furtyr, "A being of pure malice. His countenance is not conceivable by your kind. You lack the senses to recognize it. Vang was there when all things began. He sat in an endless void, forgotten and hungry. With sheer force of will, he created this world called Vel and also the world-after, called Rax. He took the essence from a dying realm far from here and with it, he created all the beings in both worlds, people and beasts. He did not do this for love or out of loneliness or even detached curiosity, but to quell his desire to create suffering.

"The product of suffering feeds his reach across the stars and gives shape to his existence. He subsists on the failure of what you call a soul. He revels in the experience of loss. Base acts of cruelty and vulgarity quench his thirst. He suckles the sweet dew of an innocent heart choked by hopelessness. And betrayals are his alms."

Charles anguished at the implication. His mind cried out for relief.

"He also created me, the Furtyr, a demon of dashed hopes, crafted from essences taken from that realm beyond the borders of the great dark. He gave me the simple purpose of ruling over Vel, causing suffering for all. For untold millennia, I did just that. Vel was a place of eternal war and tragedy. Vel's plight was to never know peace. So many lost. How many fell to my claws alone?"

"To be born in Vel was a condemnation to despair and suffering under my rule. Every time someone perished, their essence, their soul would bleed into Rax where they would be born again in a different form only to live another life of cruelty and depravity. Once they could endure no more, Vang collected and consumed their bodies and souls in a final death. Those were the fortunate ones."

"The most tragic were those who remembered. During their adolescence on Rax, these few unfortunates would wake to who they were here in Vel. The despair generated by this was the honey of ecstasy to Vang. It crushed hope beyond repair. These few were a sweet confection to Vang who glutted on their hopelessness and fear. I am part of this cycle. I too am responsible."

"But this is my given purpose, Charles; my reason for being. There are seven others like me, demons of indescribable construct. Each of us oversees a world. Some resemble Vel, others are much different. Vang created us for the same purpose: to ensure the suffering of all those he created; to prepare them for passage into Rax, the world-after, where he would feed on them at his will and pleasure. With each soul, his reach across the universe becomes longer. He seeks more to consume; always more. Vang blots out goodness and light."

Charles was numb. He could never describe the overlapping, macabre images that violated his mind's eye. He tried to focus on his surroundings.

"But I see no evidence of war here," said Charles. "Are you telling lies? This land is beautiful. I have never seen such colors; such brilliance."

The Furtyr moved closer. "I grew dissatisfied, Charles. I questioned the skies and the stars. I needed more. My suffering was unbearable as was proper to please Vang. I searched the vastness until I found a tiny light alone in the great dark. It called. I captured it and nurtured it in the high places of my domain. After lifetimes, it was strong enough to have form and give all in Vel hope. It brought light and life to what were once greying wastes and sulfur pits. I used its power to create all you see. People sought the promise of love and light. Families flourished, and the people forged histories, pursued noble pursuits and reached for the height of human potential."

"What of Vang?" Asked Charles.

"I was an abomination to him," said the Furtyr. "He could no longer enter Vel himself to destroy me. By the time he had learned of my activities, too much hope and goodness had taken root for his physical form to bear. He was no longer allowed. But all was not safe. He sent the demons and their armies from two nearby feeder worlds to destroy Vel. They came from the sky in waves. And once again, war enveloped the world."

"However, the people had changed," the Furtyr continued. "They no longer resigned to despair and faceless death. No, there was hope among the fighting. The people became joined and fought together for purpose and righteous cause. They fought for a future. They fought for the love of one another."

The two glided over the distant hills. The landscape had changed into one scarred by the constant battle. There was fighting in the distance.

"Vang could not dispatch me and the people fought well for their land. However, the souls of this world were still traveling to Rax where they were met with torment and final destruction. I could not allow it. So I took the source of that light and created a hidden place in another existence called Myn; your world. I placed it between Vel and Rax. It was there I hid the light."

"Vang's power is vast, Charles. I was far from victorious, but neither was I defeated. From that moment forward, souls passed from Vel to your world first, not Rax. This gave them another lifetime to pursue goodness and happiness before being forced into Rax. I had altered the course of Vang's conquest. Souls would arrive in Rax, born to people with something they never had before: hope. This angered Vang and diminished his power."

"For many millennia there was peace and plenty on Myn. Its existence crept its way into the legends of the people of Vel somehow and they regarded rebirth on Myn as a reward for a righteous and upright life. The people of old times needed a benevolent host; something to guide them to the light and to prepare them for the darkness of Rax that lay ahead. That was when I created you."

"Me?" Charles had almost forgotten that detail.

They were aloft, over a battle between grey-skinned men and women in brilliant armor with strange swords against giant, spider-like creatures with smiling, metal faces where leg joints should be on each of ten appendages. The creatures were fading in and out of view, obfuscated by living, red smoke.

"Yes, Charles. You." The Furtyr's eyes pulsed. "I am evil, created by evil for evil. My passions take me. My justice is without compassion. I am the fiber of hopelessness. I am base and murderous. You cannot conceive the numbers I have condemned. Yet, I found that small light alone in the vastness. That light had touched me, Charles, somewhere else a long time ago. For the first time, I knew love. I had to protect it, nurture it."

The images pressed into Charles' mind of him running free, and powerful in the great forests of Laedenor. He leapt over logs and through meadows and came to a lake's edge wherein the water, his reflection showed him the face of a massive rock stag with chocolate fur. More of his kind beckoned him back into the wood and he bounded after them.

"I was a rock stag?" The thought swelled Charles mind to the point of bursting.

"That and more. You were the spirit of the wood; a symbol of hope to the people. They regarded your image as the balance; the Great Spirit. You were an aspect of me I had lost when the stars were young. Myn was paradise, and you were its heart where I could not be."

Charles looked surprised. "Then Vang found us."

"Yes, Charles, he did."

"How?"

"I became emboldened with the idea that if there was a part of me out there somewhere awash in light, then it also had to be true of Vang."

"Did you find it?" Asked Charles.

"I did. It was a dangerous game, Charles. But I found a fading memory on the outskirts of reality that tied him to a single soul, floating in a stretching blackness. I took that soul and placed it in Myn. It came as a child who grew strong in the knowledge of the hunt. His given name on Myn was Aerion Gwyndol. He lived out a perfect life of hunting and oneness with his clan and the land. But as with most, when he died an old man, his soul traveled to Rax."

On Rax, Vang's lost essence was born into the body of a girl who, like so many, was a slave. During the fifteenth year of her life, she realized her prior existence in Myn. She remembered being Aerion Gwyndol. This drew Vang to her as Rax is his world. His mind probed hers and knew the truth of what I had done; that I created Myn and hid it away from him. He also discovered that I found an aspect of his essence he had forgotten and he knew I placed it in the world I created. After he searched the memory of the girl's soul and saw Aerion's life, Vang probed deeper until he found Aerion's most defining moment. He connected to Aerion with his mind at that moment and could breach Myn."

Charles struggled to talk. "So he went back in time? Is that possible?"

"There is much to explain, Charles. In one sense, yes he did."

"What happened to the boy?"

"He almost made his first kill; an act that would earn him acceptance by the hunters of his village. Then Vang arrived from the sky."

"It was me. He was hunting me," Charles said.

"Yes."

"How do I know that? This is all absurd! You are me, I am the Stag. That makes you the Stag. Stop. Just stop!"

"Charles, you ended your own life rather than face Vang. You jumped to your death."

Despair welled up in Charles' being. "It was my fate to die!"

"Was it?"

The truth of the Furtyr sank into Charles and took hold. "I was full of fear."

"In your despair and hopelessness, you left the world to its fate. You abandoned your domain, taking with you the natural order. Beasts and birds knew your great emptiness and damned themselves to the depths of the lake. Myn would have no hope. In time, the land recovered, and the beasts returned. But not you. No one would see a rock stag in Myn again."

The battle below was long behind them, they had come to a great ocean, turbid and deep blue. A gargantuan column of seawater twisted into the clouds on the horizon.

"I was hiding," Charles' tone changed to a monotone near whisper as he remembered images of distant stars. "I went somewhere else. But I came back. I came back as me." Charles looked at his hands.

"Yes, Charles, you did."

"But why?"

"I do not know. Perhaps, Charles, you came back because you are hope."

"But I am a coward. I will fail. He is the end of all light. I know it."

"You can still choose. He is right now trapped with Aerion Gwyndol."

"How?"

"When you ended your life, the boy Aerion fled to the Gearwood Thicket where Vang crashed into the ground after entering your world. Aerion injured himself on a Voidclaw, a talon of one of Vang's most deadly physical forms. This created an impossible relationship between the physical objects of his world and yours. The world encapsulated them as a defense and slowed him down to almost stopping, but not quite. Not quite." The creature chuckled.

Charles reeled. "The Holy Sojourner!"

"Yes. In searching for the lost hope you corrupted with your selfish death, the people of Myn found it in a frozen child who is the essence of the evil come to destroy them."

Charles could bear no more.

"Charles, the boy Aerion, imbibed with Vang's dark energy, is the creator and source of all magic in your world. His body and blood are the means by which Effacers erase, Expansers travel, Scriveners see, Cwalu fight, Itinerants dream and Touchthieves steal. Before the Sojourner, there was no willful sorcery on Myn, only the Great Spirit's blessing—My blessing, through you."

Charles Warfield and his demon counterpart and creator, the Furtyr, twisted over the sea ever closer toward the spinning column of sea water. Its width was unthinkable; perhaps as wide as Zannistar is long.

Charles furrowed his brow. "Why did Vang not discover Myn sooner? Other people died in Myn and traveled to Rax before Aerion did. Did they not remember their own lives in Myn once they were of age?"

"Some did, Yes. But Vang could not see Myn. I hid its existence from him. He only saw their lives in Vel, the world-before, yet he could not account for the delay in their arrival in Rax, their erratic thoughts of Myn, nor could he explain their strong, newfound will to fight back. Even though I changed Vel's nature, Vang knew there had to be more; another, brighter source of light he could not find. It vexed him. It was not until Aerion, a piece of himself, entered Rax that he could see Myn and he caught me."

Charles feared the water and contemplated the Furtyr's words. "What can I hope to do? I am not strong. What choice do I have?" The questions were pure.

The Furtyr reached out and pulled Charles to him and they embraced. Here in Vel, the Furtyr's body was larger than in Myn. Charles looked as a nuzzling child. "You can forgive yourself and face your life, Charles."

"I do not know how."

"Go to Mirlandis Lake. Find the cabin on the south bank. It is there you will find your heart."

"How do I kill Vang?" Charles felt cold.

"You can not kill Vang. But you can prevent him from destroying Myn and Vel. It is hope he hates above all. Hope is bitter in his mouth. Should he make it to Stag's End, he will destroy all hope. But you must go now, Charles. You are dying and Vang is coming. Once he is free of his prison, he will end your world and then he will try to enter Vel through the Neverwall. A portal exists on the Islet of Abeodan. It will grant him passage if he finds it. You cannot allow that."

Charles could not breathe. He grabbed at his throat and faded away from Vel like a shooting star.

CHAPTER 45

CHARLES WAS CHOKING TO DEATH. He thrashed about, grasping at the black and gray appendage attached to his face. He opened his eyes and saw the other three writhing on the floor trying to pull the eldritch things off of their own faces. Charles could feel spindled ropes of flesh stretching down his windpipe into his lungs, testing tissue and filling all space there.

Lydia had lost consciousness and Dara was seconds from joining her. Charles tried to scream. The act made the thing shoot additional tendrils into his sinuses and pushed behind his eye. While he tugged at the rubbery appendage, he could see a dark red line being drawn on the wall by itself. It was spiraling around and making strange patterns. In anguish, he noticed that Tavist's book was open, on the ledge of the pit and red ink was spilling from it into the swirling liquid. He then saw that the book was open to a page with Vang's name across it and the ink was coming from the letters.

He motioned to Tavist with his eyes who had pulled the thing away somewhat and was looking at him in frozen fear. Tavist looked down at the book, jumped on it which closed it. In an instant, the grotesque things on their faces and in their lungs retreated into the liquid in unison. There was blood and a great deal of heaving from all as they regained their senses. Tavist yelped and jumped back, revealing the frost that had grown on the stone around the Bóctalu.

The line on the wall receded backward the same direction it had come. Charles knew they had just averted disaster.

"Tavist!" said Charles through heavy breaths. "What happened? Was that—"

"Yes," Tavist said, also winded and still heaving. "I saw him. In a dream I think. Somehow he made me open the Bóctalu to find his name. I had no control over it."

Lydia gave a blank, horrified stare. "I also saw him," she said. "I do not wish to remember the things he said. He is too powerful. We should not be doing this. We need to turn back."

"What did you see Charles?" asked Tavist.

"I was in Vel, the world-before," said Charles. "I saw the creature that overtook me at the Fountain of Remembrance; the Furtyr." Charles became sheepish and let the next words come out slow. "We share a soul or some such."

"Yes," Tavist stroked his chin, then opened the Bóctalu, per the prescribed method, to Charles' page. This gave everyone a start.

Charles threw his arms in the air. "I am supposed to prevent Vang from entering the world somehow," he said. "I must visit a cotlif near the lake. Something about having a heart? No, taking a heart? Some other thing? I do not know."

"Some other thing, yes," said Tavist. "According to this, you must find your real heart."

Charles squinted. "Sorry? I have one already."

"Yes," said Tavist. "And yet, the Bóctalu says you must find it."

"Are you certain?"

"Scrivener, remember?" Tavist lifted and rattled the chain that connected his hip to the book.

Charles looked unconvinced.

Tavist showed Charles the page, revealing a detailed drawing of a small cotlif on the southwestern shore of a lake. The cotlif door was open. An image of Charles stood in the doorway holding the heart with both hands and smiling. In the background, a cotlif village sat snug against the cliffs on the opposite side of the lake. The ink on the page wafted out of the chimneys.

"That is Mirlandis Lake," said Dara. She was holding her stomach. "A dark place. It curses the people. The light is scarce in its streets. High cliffs surround the lake and the cotlif village. Few live in the cotlif village and fewer visit. Even the Cwalu avoid it. There is a wide break in the cliffs to the south, facing the sea. It is the only way. Stag's End overlooks the lake from the cliffs. The Sojournic Stronghold is close to there."

Tavist slapped the Bóctalu shut. "Well, curse or not, let us be on our way to Mirlandis Lake, shall we?"

Wide eyed, Lydia looked at Tavist, then the rest. "And then what? Fight that infernal thing in my dream? We are nothing to it, Tavist!" She shuddered and held back tears. She gestured toward Charles. "Charles, if you can become such a creature as you did before, then we can just go back to Zannistar and oust that false King Ember and the invaders to save our people! Then we can plan something more worthy of the risk. Remember the Anvil?

Remember your oath? You may be Secondary nobility but you are still a Zanni courtier. Your duty is to Zannistar! Be reasonable!"

Dara stood then doubled over. "Lydia if we do not stop Vang, all will perish. Stay here if you would like, but we continue on."

Tavist took a soft tone. "Lydia, remember Arminius. He gave me this task. I promised. You said you believed in him. You said you would go with me. I want you with me."

The look in Lydia's eyes was one of absolute fear; the fear that takes a lifetime to erase. After a moment, she squinted and rubbed her right eye as if something infected it with vermin. She shook it off. "I know Tavist. And I want to be with you. But what awaits us there is unspeakable. If I go with you, I will die."

"If you stay here you will die, fair Duchess," said Surek Taben. He was standing in the doorway, not at all winded from running down the stairs.

"We must embark, pull lines and get underway," Surek Taben said. "The opal is failing. We have a few hours, maybe." He pointed to the opal on his hat and it was flickering as was the large opal over the Pit of Nihthelm. He nodded toward the larger opal. "We have less time with that one. Something has happened."

They all looked at the large opal and back at Surek Taben as though caught in mischief.

"Well there is no time for hoodwinks!" yelled Surek Taben. "Just shut your eyes, grab the shoulder in front of you and do not stop moving! Follow me!"

They obeyed the Captain and ran single-file with their eyes shut, up the stairs and out of the cave. Surek Taban guided them back the way they had come only much faster. Charles stumbled a few times, but the others kept him moving.

At last, they reached and boarded the Corvax; afraid but unharmed. Surek Taben ushered the four passengers into the galley. The blind crew took to sea even as the sphere around the Islet of Abeodan failed. With a thunderous sound, all the Nihtgessa that had been clinging to the larger sphere slammed against the smaller sphere around the Corvax. The Captain moaned in pain, trying to maintain his concentration. He barked course corrections to Gervin.

Soon after, the ravenous Nihtgessa fled the protective sphere a few at a time, then in droves. They were flocking to the Islet of Abeodan and the cave. Surek Taben gasped when he realized that the Pit of Nihthelm was unprotected. He felt for the opal in his hat. It would last long enough. It had to.

In the Galley, the four travelers sat at a nailed-down long table sipping warm, Aromite spiced tea. A grim member of the Brymróc arrived and gave them new hoodwinks. In a few hours, they would exit the Neverwall and enter the frigid North Sea. Judging by the sound, Charles surmised that Tavist was comforting Lydia.

She was holding her hand over her right eye and shivering. She did not care to retell her ordeal, but she agreed to listen to Charles tell of his own vision, which everyone concluded was a strange tale. After he had answered many questions, he realized Dara had been silent.

"Dara, you saw something," Charles said. "When we were dreaming."

"Nothing, Charles. I saw nothing." She was lying. Charles saw her scoot away from him.

CHAPTER 46

THE ITINERANTS VALUED SIMPLICITY. Most of the grounds, architecture and furnishings of the Sojournic Stronghold were basic and functional.

This was not true of the ceremonial refectory in the central area of the compound. Alternating squares of gold and red obsidian comprised the floor. Great columns of polished dark wood lined all four walls of the massive, rectangular space.

Besides the great, blazing fireplace on the wall opposite the stage, were dozens of braziers of iron secured to the walls, bathing the hall in light. Two rows of carved, wooden long tables lined the room lengthwise. Upon them was a feast for hundreds. Itinerants, aspirants and off-duty Sentinels sat together at the tables, but positioned themselves toward a large stage at the end of the cavernous room.

The Cwalu lined the walls between the columns. They held their black swords in their left hands, blade down and they positioned their right hand above their heads palm up. Itinerants at the tables sang the ancient hymn of the Wyrsa-gewealc. Their harmonies were rich and practiced. Sounds of low, rhythmic pulses from the Itinerants' bells echoed along with the music. It was an auspicious feast. Excitement and anticipation electrified the room.

In the stage's middle, Atli stood facing the room. Dohtor Yuun and the Watch Captain Jeth were both facing Atli, their backs to the assembly. The wall behind Atli presented several bas-relief sculptures of red obsidian depicting each of the eleven major interpretations of the Sojourner since the Itinerants had formed from a loose group of simple pilgrims so long ago.

Atli stood upright with her shoulders back. She wore her new Prelate's robe of deep blue with five green conifer trees embroidered on its front. Her attendants had used pine nut oil to slick back her short hair. On her forehead was the wound Dohtor Yuun had placed there only hours before, but it was already healing. It was three circles of different size arranged and connected by a vertical line.

All the Cwalu shared this Aydward somewhere on their bodies; many on foreheads. However, theirs moved, sometimes spinning, sometimes pulsing, other times fading and reappearing. Atli's had not yet started. She hoped it would soon.

The Itinerants finished their hymn. Atli held her hands out as the Watch Captain Jeth placed in them the emblem of a Prelate's office: a spyglass found in the Gearwood Thicket at the heart of the Nurdrayl Forest a thousand years ago.

The small device represented a single piece of silver; an abundant but prized metal in the Northlands. The first Itinerants taught that the Sojourner placed the spyglass there to mark the beginning of his journey. It represented humility and reflection to the Itinerants; a reminder of the importance of beginnings. She placed the spyglass in its holding strap tied about her waist and held out her hands once more.

Jeth stepped behind and beside Atli, then turned to face the Itinerants. Dohtor Yuun approached Atli, unsheathed a black sword and lay it across her open arms. Three feet long, its straight, dark blade led from an unassuming guard and tapered to a point. The grip was a hand and a half, ending in a tear-shaped pommel, all black metal. The pommel bore an engraving of the same Aydward healing on Atli's forehead.

This gift was emblematic of the fact that a Cwalu Itinerant had become the Prelate. Were Quincunx's successor a regular Itinerant, the highest ranking Itinerant would have given Atli a special bell symbolizing the walk of peace.

These were ancient artifacts, ceremonial but functional. The Itinerants treasured them. But a Prelate could only choose one. Sword or bell. War or peace. The choice would be the final ratification of the Sojourner's will. The unchosen implement would be placed in a special chamber until needed. It was time retire   the   bell   in   favor   of   the   sword. Yuun gave a satisfied expression before retreating behind and to the side of Atli opposite Jeth to face the Itinerants.

"Brothers and Sisters of the Path," Atli yelled, still cradling the sword. "It is with great honor and yet sadness I accept this burden."

The Itinerants rang their bells once.

"The Father Prelate Quincunx left this world on his own terms. We honor him for his life and his leadership."

The Itinerants rang their bells twice.

"As your new Prelate, I will do everything I can to bring the Sojournic Order to the will of he who walks the Path. The Sojourner shows us the Wyrsa-gewealc. Today we trade the bells of peace for the sword of war. The time for kind counsel has passed. Today, we bring righteous destruction to the face of the unclean!"

The Itinerants rang their bells three times.

"You have feasted. You have communed. You have pondered your newfound purpose. Look at your brothers and sisters around you. The Holy Sojourner has found them worthy! They, like you, enter the Walk of Battle! Do not fear for your lives or the lives of your friends! For you are blessed by the one who sends you!"

The Itinerants rang their bells four times.

"The Holy Sojourner has hastened his walk to Stag's End. For a thousand years, we have watched and waited. Well, no more! He moves faster! We have found that he will reach Stag's End in just one day. One day! And when he arrives, we will be ready. Go, brothers and sisters. Make ready! Prepare your swords and prepare your souls!"

The Itinerants rang their bells five times, stood and cheered. After a while they dispersed, then formed a line out the door. On the way, they were throwing their bells into the great fireplace and each accepting a black sword from several Cwalu at the door, handing them out.

The Watch Captain Jeth bowed to the ordained Mother Prelate and made off for the Sentinel's quarters. The Mother Prelate Atli looked on, but she could not banish the images of Quincunx's lifeless corpse. She cursed his name under her breath for leaving her. And what of the note? Atli was lucky to have found it before anyone else.

She showed it only to Yuun, who reinforced its message, contending the note was true; that it was an ancient Cwalu secret. The Sojourner was a terrible enemy come to blot out all life and his name was Vang. It is why they took the Aydwards. It protected them from his control. Atli's entire perception of reality had been turned on its head in a single conversation. But she was strong in mind and her wits made sense of it somehow. She was responsible and burdened to lead.

"Mother Prelate," said Yuun. "Remember what I have told to you. The Sojourner brings destruction to all. This a Cwalu secret. The Father Prelate Quincunx learned of it somehow and was trying to warn everyone."

"Well it is a blasphemous secret, Dohtor Yuun," Atli found herself still affected by the strange timbre of Yuun's voice. She also tried to maintain a happy posture for onlookers. "The occult teachings of the Cwalu are just legends. All Itinerants, Aspirants and Sentinels accept and tolerate them. Even I found them interesting during my studies. But they are just that: legends. Why would the Holy Sojourner walk the Holy Path for thousands of years just to destroy us? It makes no sense, Yuun."

Yuun's magic sigil tattoos moved faster.

Atli softened. "Dohtor Yuun, forgive me, but the regular Itinerants and the world see his arrival as a day of salvation. Yes, we are in the Wyrsa-gewealc, which you seem to desire, but that could mean his arrival brings death to his enemies, not to us, his faithful."

Yuun's eyes flashed. "You, too are Cwalu, Mother Prelate. Do not forget that. You have taken the blood and the first Aydward. You should urge the other Itinerants to take the Aydward. It will protect them. This is not a game. Death will come."

"We have already discussed this, Yuun," Atli became more authoritative. "If they choose it, then so be it. But I will not force harm on the brothers and sisters based on an old rumor. Everything will be just as it should. The Sojourner will come and he will lead us in the Walk of Battle to first eradicate the Ersatz horde in the forest, Then, together, we will bring light to the rest of the world. I will hear no more of it."

Yuun said no more on the subject. Another Cwalu warrior glided up the walkway to Yuun. He put his mouth to her ear.

"What is it Dohtor Yuun? What is happening?" asked Atli.

Yuun grimaced and her dark eyes sparkled. "The Ersatz have broken the line. They are loose, and they approach the Sojournic Stronghold."

CHAPTER 47

AERION AND VANG WALKED SIDE BY SIDE along the path to Stag's End. Aerion struggled to see beyond the tunnel, but it looked as though there was something taking shape. Trees? A building? He could not be sure. However, whatever was out there it was moving with great speed.

Aerion held the coil high. He lifted the shard so he could see it better.

"We are close, Aerion," said Vang. He was walking next to him but could somehow stretch to be in front of Aerion at the same time. "Stag's End."

Aerion looked up at the faces above them. They caught up with them after being fooled earlier. They offered saddened expressions. Somehow, Aerion preferred the faces when they seemed angry.

Aerion looked forward. "Vang, what happens once we get there?"

"Your followers will greet you," said Vang. "They adore you."

"Then what?"

"Well, I imagine they will gather to worship you."

"They think I'm the Gastwyrd. But I'm not."

"No?"

Aerion furrowed his brow. "But you are, is that right?"

"You are clever, Aerion. How did you know?" Vang touched the tip of Aerion's nose.

Aerion shrugged away. "I don't know. It's more of a feeling. If you're the Gastwyrd, then I'm dead." Aerion's eyes formed tears.

"Do not cry," Vang stopped, knelt and grabbed Aerion's chin, holding up his face. "You are not the Gastwyrd. You are my vessel in this world."

Aerion looked in Vang's eyes as the reality set in. "I'm you. Is that it? My guts tell me so."

"Yes," Vang said. "We are of the same origin. But I did not create you. Neither did I create this world. Another of my own creations did. He has hidden its existence from me for a long time. But because of you, I found it." He smiled at Aerion as an elder would.

Aerion remembered back to earlier in their talk. "You said you met me in Rax, the world-after."

"Yes. When I saw you I realized you did not belong. When I looked into you I knew the truth."

"If that's true, then who created it?"

"A fool. He worked behind my back when I was not looking. I named him the Furtyr; a lying coward and a traitor. I believe you already know him."

"Now you're telling lies," Aerion continued walking and returned to his untrusting disposition.

Vang caught up with Aerion. "Remember your quarry? The stag that escaped you?"

"Don't remind me of my failures, Vang."

"Well that is him. Or rather, it is one aspect of him. Now he exists as a man. His name is Charles. We will kill him."

Aerion flared. "You said I could go wherever I wanted! That I could see my Father!"

"And you can," Vang's tone was condescending. "After we kill Charles and destroy your entire world. It will not take long, I assure you."

"Wait, you want me to help you destroy my world? Even if this nonsense is true why would I help you destroy everything?"

Vang's spoke louder, tensed his muscles and red mist escaped his eyes. "Because this world should not exist. Its presence upsets my design. I am starving, you see. Your world delays my satiation."

Aerion stopped then backed away.

Vang calmed his menace. "Aerion, the Furtyr created you from a piece of me floating in a long-forgotten place in the universe I can no longer reach. We are the same, you and I. You can not hide from who you are, Aerion. I know you will do it because I know myself. Besides, I have many places and things to show you Aerion."

"How do I survive this destruction?"

Vang motioned to the shard. "You do not. After we have completed our task, your body must die. Then your essence will travel to Rax."

"No."

"You have no choice!" Vang flashed with anger, his almond eyes spiraling in and his teeth vibrating. The faces over them retreated then floated back. "Small price to pay for traveling the universe with me."

Aerion contemplated the absurdity of it all. He somehow knew Vang spoke the truth. He pondered that his entire family was long dead. Aerion had nothing and no one left.

"I'll still see my Father like you said?"

"Yes, Aerion. You will meet in the world-after. He will look different. But you will know him."

"What of my Mother?"

Vang stared ahead. "Your Mother is not there. She has served her purpose and moved on."

Aerion was about to protest when Vang stopped walking. The faces stopped. They hovered.

"Here we are," said Vang with an enormous grin. "Stag's End."

The tunnel had no visible end that Aerion could see. But the veil had thinned. Through it, he could see snow, trees and people; lots of people. There were people dressed in blue robes, some looked strange in black armor with one red gauntlet. Still others had regular clothing, more of what he was used to.

They were moving fast, but Aerion could make out their movements. They looked to be cheering and celebrating. In front of him was a raised platform at the edge of a cliff. Aerion recognized the place where the rock stag escaped him earlier. He could not be certain, but it looked as if there was a young woman standing on the platform with her arms outstretched toward him.

Aerion turned to Vang. "How do we do this? They're many! As you said they are here to worship me. Is this necessary?"

Vang smiled. "There is an army waiting on the edge of the Nurdrayl forest. They are under my control. As soon as we leave this place, they will storm the Sojournic Stronghold. But that is only the start. All in your world who have partaken of our combined essence will feel my influence. My power will confuse some and others will be under my control. So you see? There is nothing to worry about."

Vang stopped and grabbed Aerion's shoulder. "This is it," he said. He sniffed. "Yes, I can smell it. This is where he threw himself off the cliff rather than face me. Coward. He comes. You will get a second chance, Aerion. You will kill him."

Aerion thought of that tense moment with the rock stag. To him, it had just happened. Here was another opportunity to prove himself. He made the mental decision to join Vang. Vang sensed it and chuckled.

"Vang, you're here with me or am I imagining all of this?"

Without looking, Vang pointed to the coil on Aerion's hand. "I am there." He then pointed to the shard "And also there."

"So you're inside me?" Aerion looked terrified.

"Well yes. I am in many places. Try to keep up."

Aerion sighed. "Let's finish this."

Vang smiled. "Ah, there is an opening here. I thought so." Vang clapped his hands. "When you are ready, step onto the platform."

CHAPTER 48

THE CORVAX WAS ANCHORED off the coast of Laedenor in the North Sea. The ship ebbed with the lazy flow of the waves. The Captain and his crew were more than elated there had been no Laedenoran war vessels to contend with, but an oddity leaving the seafarers unsettled.

Before Lydia and the others debarked for the seashore, she had suggested that the Laedenoran fleet was likely at or en route to Zannistar. She explained how she had seen many vessels at Olix during the invasion. Surek Taben decided he would keep the ship on a state of alert, regardless. The crew outfitted the travelers with food, water and warm clothes to wear, comprising black pants and shirts, black leather seafaring armor, black half-boots and black fur capes. Those who served aboard the Corvax wore only black. This was tradition.

The ship's Master at Arms gave Charles and the others their choice of weapons from the ship's armory. They were old and given to the corrosion of salt air. Charles chose a sword but had trouble holding it, even with two hands. The Captain snuck up, grabbed it with one hand and put it back.

The battle-hardened Captain chose a smaller sword and gave it to Charles, handle first. It was a foil with a covering hand guard. Charles swung it about and smiled. The others opted to keep their own weapons.

The Captain Surek Taben then bid them all good luck and made them promise to come back in one piece. They said their final goodbyes and boarded the short boat. As Charles was heading for the ladder rope, Gervin, the leader of the Brymróc, proffered a small burlap sack to him.

"What is this?" asked Charles.

"Dumplings," said Gervin. "The lady said you had a thing for them, so I told the cooks make a few extras for your trip."

"Well that is decent of you," said Charles in genuine gratitude. He went for the sack.

He pulled the sack back. "So, I was thinking," continued Gervin. "If you turn into that thing everyone keeps talking about, you remember your old friend Gervin, yes? You remember Gervin has dumplings. You remember that."

"I will, Gervin. Thank you." Charles went for the dumplings again.

"Dumplings." said Gervin again. "Say it."

"I am sorry. Say what?"

"Gervin has dumplings."

"Fine. Gervin has dumplings."

"Good! Here you go, youngster." He gave Charles the sack, patted him on the shoulder and wandered off.

"Hurry Charles," yelled Tavist.

Charles almost made it down the ladder without falling.

Dara and Tavist each took oars and rowed toward shore. The four could see the entire length of the Laedenoran shoreline in both directions. To the extreme east, perhaps two day's journey by foot, was the lofty spire of the Laedenoran Geattor. Dara knew unlike the other Geattors, they had not built this one in a city, but on a lonely beach, like a giant lighthouse. It was under the control of Ember Driss and his band of followers. It was luck she and Veldic could get to it before they did. That seemed a lifetime ago.

"Dara," said Charles. "Are you all right?"

"Yes, Charles. I have to be."

A few hours journey inland from where they emerged ashore, and a whole sack of dumplings later, the four travelers came over the top of a forested ridge to find a lush, deep valley below. The southern end of the valley was meadowland and the rest of the valley was forested, partially consumed by a very large lake.

The land was mottled with patches of snow. Breathtaking cliffs surrounded the lake in all directions save for south, whence they came. Down and west, perhaps an hour's journey on foot, was a cotlif village nuzzled against a cliff. Smoke rose from fireplace chimneys.

Charles, Dara, Tavist and Lydia all stole this moment to catch their breath, taking in the beauty of the Northlands. Dara knelt down and picked up cold earth and felt it in her hand, just as Veldic had done when they arrived in Arom.

She thought of Veldic now, how she had spent many years in Laedenor even though he came from the deep untamed lands of

Southeastern Arom. She took to the north when she was a young warrior to make her fortune on silver and other metals she had heard were in abundance in Laedenor.

She soon discovered the work did not suit her. She ended up thieving to keep her belly full but could never raise enough coin to charter a ship with an Expanser back to Arom. That was before Cenric Warfield caught her stealing. By the time Veldic had learned all there was to learn about how the Itinerants and Cwalu fought, Veldic turned down the money Cenric offered her to return to Arom. But she was dead now. They both were. She threw the dirt down.

"Let us be on our way," Dara said with authority, wiping her hands.

They wandered down switchbacks until they came to the southeastern shore of Mirlandis Lake. The sun was high, but the clouds were thick, denying the lake warmth. Heavy mist clung to the water in most areas. The vegetation here was very dense, dark and wet as many of the plants and trees grew right up to the water's edge. The water lapped at the pebbled shore. Somewhere aloft, the echo of a bird's call carried for a long time against cliff faces.

"There it is," said Tavist pointing to a large, covered rock outcropping on the Eastern shore, just before the cliff.

On the flat of the outcropping it was a small cotlif, dilapidated and overgrown with moss, weeds and tall grass. It shared its side wall with the cliff face. They recognized the front door through the moss.

Tavist had the Bóctalu open and was making sure. "Yes, that is it," he said.

Lydia rubbed her right eye and then folded her arms. "Tavist there is a cotlif village over there, not one hour's walk. They have fireplaces, likely food and wine. There is plenty of daylight. Should we not first refresh ourselves before tending to this terrible business?"

"No, we must carry on," said Dara. "We must get whatever is in that abandoned cotlif and then get Charles to Stag's End."

"Not this again, Lydia," said Tavist. "You are allowing your fears to cloud your judgment. It is unprofessional. You refuse to tell us what was in your dream but yet you expect all of us to be as afraid as you are. You had great mettle when all this began, but you have become scared of everything. Come to your senses. You are a Primary Noble of the Anvil of Ages! Act like it!"

Lydia shot Tavist a murderous look. The words that followed were harsh and violent. Dara did her best to not listen but Lydia was a font of vulgarity. She turned to usher Charles away and noticed his absence. She turned her head this way and that realizing he had wandered off toward the abandoned cotlif by himself. He was at the rotted door. She called out.

"Charles," she yelled, speeding toward him. "Wait, what are you doing?"

He opened it, then turned to answer. "This is where I find my heart, Dara!" He looked excited, almost happy.

"Nobody goes off on their own!" Dara felt sick. She increased her speed.

"I am fine, Dara." Charles said.

The blade burst through Charles' abdomen from behind, sending blood into the receding snow and dirt in front of him. Charles looked at the blade in utter confusion. A hand gripped Charles' right shoulder, a face appeared over his left. It was Ember Driss.

"No, Charles," Ember whispered into his ear. "This is where I find my heart."

Ember Driss bared his teeth and withdrew the sword with violence. He pushed Charles to the ground with his boot.

"Let us have a taste of that heart, Charles," said Ember.

"Charles!" screamed Dara. "No!" She drew four bolts from her quiver and let them all fly at once. Ember moved sideways, attempting to dodge, but one hit him in the arm. He sheathed his sword and pulled out the bolt but Dara focused her mind and it pushed back in. Ember let out a painful noise.

Ember laughed. "Have you come to avenge your husband's pathetic death?"

Dara screamed. The sound alerted Tavist and Lydia. They sprang to Dara's aid. They ran toward Ember and drew their swords. Dara leapt in the air as she fired two more bolts. Ember drew his sword and deflected both of the projectiles in one smooth motion, snapping them in two. He may have had Vang's power removed, but he was still an excellent swordsman.

Lydia and Tavist were upon Ember. Tavist held the Bóctalu with one hand and swung at Ember with the other. Ember dodged with ease and kicked Tavist, sending him to the ground.

"You can not beat me with Zanni sword dancing, brat," Ember said as he turned to block Lydia's sword with his own. Lydia attempted to roll to the side for the kill, but Ember countered her, meeting her sword with his.

"Not bad for a Duchess," said Ember. "But you give away your intentions."

Lydia tried to kick Ember but Ember sidestepped and elbowed her in the face. She fell back stunned. Blood flowed from her nose.

Ember went for the kill raising his sword above his head, but Dara howled, sending the bolt in Embers shoulder deeper still.

Ember yelled and dropped his sword. He reached out his hand at Dara to call on Vang's magic but nothing came. He looked at his hand and cursed.

That gave Tavist time to get to his feet and charge Ember, sword high. Ember ducked and thrust upward, flipping Tavist over him and on to his back, knocking the air from him. Ember kicked his head, rendering him unconscious.

"You cur!" yelled Lydia, swinging again with her sword. Ember moved close enough to avoid the hit and grappled her. He threw her into Dara's line of sight. Dara dodged and shot another bolt at him. It hit him in the chest. He staggered back and looked at Charles on the ground. He reached for him.

"No, it is mine!" Ember yelled. "Mine!"

Dara hit him in the chest again with yet another bolt. This time he flew backward through the door into the cotlif before she could finish it. She gave chase, jumping over Lydia who was coming to her wits. When she entered the small cotlif, Dara could not find Ember. Aside from an empty room with a wooden table, the only thing Dara found was presence of red vapor and the smell of burning pine needles.

Dara remembered Charles. She rushed out of the cotlif and scanned the area. Lydia was several yards away kneeling next to Charles who had dragged himself to the lakeshore. He lay on his stomach, his right hand and the top of his head submerged in the water. Blood coated the pebbles around him and seeped into the lake water. His eyes were open. His breathing was shallow.

"He is alive, but near death," said Lydia.

"No, no," said Dara. She knelt next to him. "Listen Charles. You must stay with us!" She sobbed.

Charles groaned. "Dara, is that you?"

"Yes, you foolish bastard!" returned Dara. "You must be still. You are wounded."

"I am sorry. Dara, I have failed you. I always fail you. I fail everyone."

Yes, Charles, you do. Now come. I will receive you now.

"Nonsense," Dara rebutted. "You will be fine."

"I am not fine and I am not stupid," Charles groaned in pain. "That was him. That was Ember."

Dara grimaced. "Yes. It was him. He escaped, but I wounded him."

Lydia ripped some of her underclothing and attempted to stop Charles' bleeding.

Tavist ran up to them, still somewhat stunned. "Charles, no!" He fell to his knees in the bloody pebbles next to Charles and opened the Bóctalu to Charles' page. "Quick," he mumbled.

The name Charles Warfield appeared in a strange language that only Tavist could read. The words bled into a single drop of red blood which spun in the left page's middle. Once it was circular, the drop of blood expanded to cover the entire left page. Then the circle morphed into a nautical compass. Tavist recognized it right away. He showed Dara and Lydia. Dara likewise recognized it.

"That is the symbol on Charles' nombit," Dara said. "Exactly."

"What do you mean?" asked Lydia. Zanni heraldry was not her best subject. She knew her own, a black-spotted shengmar.

Dara stroked Charles' hair. "Well, his family arms are a nautical compass on the left side of an open book. I suppose they were my arms as well; for a brief time."

The compass showed the cardinal directions, but north was facing the wrong way. The compass was pulsing to a rhythm.

"I believe I have slowed the bleeding," said Lydia, having placed more of her clothing in the wound. "But he is growing pale."

"What about the Mirlandis Lake cotlif village?" Dara asked. "We can take him there. Maybe someone can help him."

Lydia shook her head. "There is not enough time."

Tavist stood up and ran a few feet into the lake. "What does it mean?" He yelled and kicked at the water. The sound of his voice echoed against the cliffs. He turned, noticing the compass' needle in the Bóctalu was pointing toward Charles. It had pointed toward a different direction before.

"What is this?" Tavist whispered. He walked in a circle around Charles and the needle stayed trained on Charles. As he moved closer, Tavist realized the needle pointed toward Charles' submerged hand. It was closed in a fist.

Tavist reached in the water and pulled it out. He opened Charles' hand and found in it the silver coin. Tavist plucked it from Charles' palm and held it up. As if pulled by an invisible string, the coin shot from Tavist's hand to the Bóctalu and hovered there, just over the north point of the compass. The coin flickered with a blue light. Together, the coin and the north aspect of the compass swung toward the abandoned cotlif.

"What is happening?" asked Lydia.

"I do not know," answered Tavist. "I did not see this before. He was meant to enter the abandoned cotlif. But he is now near death."

Angered and fearful, Tavist ran into the abandoned cotlif with the Bóctalu open. Inside the one-roomed cotlif, there was a disintegrated table and an old chest of rotted wood. Time had put holes in the floor exposing the rock of the outcropping underneath. Moss and vegetation had weakened the roof, caving it in somewhat. The entire room smelled of peat and mold.

"Show me," said Tavist.

The pulsing coin and the compass spun toward the east wall. Tavist saw no wood, just vegetation growing on the cliff face. Someone had built the cotlif right up to the rock, using the cliff face as the wall.

Tavist cut away the vegetation with his sword and he gasped at what lay underneath.

It was a complex, painted mural depicting a story comprising five, connected vignettes. The first image showed a large symbol: a central circle from which seven, equidistant lines radiated. At the end of each line, was another, smaller circle. In between the central circle and the top circle on the line, was another even smaller circle. Near the top circle was the word 'Vel', in a language that only Tavist knew. The larger, central circle was labeled 'Rax'.

Between those circles was a much smaller circle labeled 'Myn'. Stretching between Vel and Myn, was a painted image of a man with short black hair running, reaching for Myn. The other circles were not labeled.

The second image was the same man leaving the Isle of Abeodan on a boat. There were spirits chasing him. The ship's sail contained the same symbol as in the first picture.

The next image revealed the same man learning the ways of the Cwalu. A teacher was showing him how to use effacing magic. Another Cwalu was using a knife to carve a symbol onto the man's back. It was like the symbol in the other pictures. Instead of seven circles, it was only the three, labeled circles: The large middle circle, the smaller outer circle and the tiny circle in between. A vertical line connected them.

The next image showed the man in a room creating a loveseat out of gearwood. There was a woman laying on a table near him holding a bouquet. Her eyes were crossed-out, as if she died. The next depiction was a battle between Aromite, Laedenoran and Zanni forces. The man was floating above them.

Deep in Tavist's gut, he knew the man was Gyldred the Effacer, and he knew the chair was the fabled Bekrot Chair. As Tavist contemplated the images, he noticed that the small circle in the first picture, representing Myn, was a depression in the rock.

He looked down at the Bóctalu and decided he had no time to second guess himself. If he could save Charles, he had to try. He reached down, grabbed the coin and placed it into the depression in the rock. It fit.

The Bóctalu grew ice cold and shut on its own. The entire room shook.

"Tavist! Tavist!" Lydia's screams came from outside.

Tavist ran out of the room and saw both Dara and Lydia, each grasping one of Charles' legs, trying to keep him from being pulled into the lake. Charles was floating on the water unconscious, his arms outstretched. An invisible force was pulling his body.

Tavist rushed to their aid and tried to hold him around his waist, but there was too much blood and he could not gain purchase. Inch by inch, he slipped further out until all at once, the invisible force pulled him away with a violent tug. They all lurched into the water.

At blinding speed, Charles' body skipped along the top of the lake out to the middle, then vanished under water.

"No!" screamed Dara. She fell to her knees and wept in the lake. Lydia went to her side and held her while Tavist stared at his hands and then back to the abandoned cotlif.

The water was motionless where Charles went under.

Tavist tried to open the book, but it froze shut. He pried it with his sword and he beat it on the rocks. It became so cold he could no longer hold it. Giving up, he let it drop to his side. Tavist found himself in a state of grief. Both Lydia and Dara were kneeling in the water, sobbing. They had lost all.

"Dara," said Tavist. "We must still complete the task."

Dara kept looking at the blood in the water. "Why, Tavist? Why should we? Charles is dead as is all life. We are ruined."

"Because we said we would. Yes, we may die, but we die on our terms, Dara. All we have left is our will."

"I have something to show both of you," said Tavist.

Tavist led them into the cotlif and showed them the drawings. They all agreed that it was likely Gyldred depicted. Tavist pointed to the symbol being drawn on the man's back and asked Dara if she knew what it meant.

"It is an Aydward," Dara said. "The first Aydward. The Cwalu use it as a protection against being controlled by evil spirits. The other Itinerants and the Outside Order can choose it, but the Cwalu must receive it."

Tavist looked intrigued. "Outside Order. You mean people like you, Woodlocks."

Dara nodded. "Yes, Woodlocks, Effacers, Expansers. Anyone the Cwalu train in any of the sorcerous arts. The Cwalu believe the source of all magic is evil and that it can control them. So they use Aydwards to protect themselves."

"And it protects them from being controlled by evil spirits?" Asked Tavist.

"Yes. That is what they believe."

"Do you have one?"

"No, I declined. The gearwood protects me, Tavist. I am no Cwalu. Everyone knows Aydwards are bad luck. I would leave them to the Cwalu and so should you."

"I think you should have one, right now." Tavist pulled a small dagger from his belt.

"Why?" Dara's eyes widened. "Am I so weak?"

"Because Vang is a real evil that is coming and you are a Woodlock. You have partaken of his power. You are compromised. True, every person is different. Some can resist. But why take the chance?"

Dara shook her head. "No."

"Well, I am giving myself one," Tavist said. Without thought of the pain and to the best of his ability, he carved an Aydward into his left hand. It was excruciating, but he could not think of a worse fate than being controlled by an evil spirit. Not after everything he had experienced on this journey.

Just as he was finishing, he heard the echo of a howl against the cliffs. It was chilling, but only because it sounded like a person. Satisfied with his handiwork, he ran outside.

CHAPTER 49

THE SUN HAD JUST PASSED THE HIGHEST POINT in its daily arc. Dusk would be upon Stag's End in a few hours. Stag's End was perhaps the most beautiful section of the Sojournic Stronghold. It derived its name from the legends passed down from the Laedenoran tribes of old. It was a kempt garden of fountains, conifers, wildflowers and ferns of various types.

The Itinerants established it as the end of the Sojourner's journey long ago before the Sixteen Generations War during the third of the Great Interpretations by a prominent Lucanite named Urlan Hyb. During his thirty subsequent years as Prelate he sanctified Stag's End and had the wall extended to the cliff so it would enjoy the Sentinels' protection. While it was the most beautiful of the Sentinel's posts, it was also the most frightening, since the turrets extended somewhat beyond the cliff's edge.

Urlan Hyb also had a platform of gearwood built at the edge of the cliff to receive the Holy Sojourner. It was three yards wide and fifty yards long, running right up to the cliff's edge. He ensured they engraved the names of all Itinerants in the wood; even the Cwalu. It was the greatest honor one could receive.

The day had come, by some estimates several hundred years too soon, when the Sojourner would at last complete his journey. Itinerants lined both sides of the Sojourner's Path. Until now, they had been celebrating, dancing and prostrating before the Sojourner.

Once the Mother Prelate Atli made her way onto the platform, they became silent. They each drew their swords with their left hand, blades down and held up their right hand in the air. Some of them had taken the first Aydward as Yuun had suggested, but most did not as they were superstitious about the ward turning them into Cwalu.

Dohtor Yuun and the Cwalu were invited to attend, but could not. Instead they were out in front of the Sojournic Stronghold awaiting the Ersatz horde almost upon them. In their midst was a smattering of the once great army decimated at Sable Rock, a few Woodlocks and militia from surrounding cotlif villages.

The Sojournic Sentinels stood on the walls of the Sojournic Stronghold as a last defense in case the ground forces failed.

Atli stood in the platform's middle facing the Holy Sojourner. For the previous hour, the Sojourner had been moving faster. She couldn't believe he had ever been still.

This was history's most important moment. As was proper, Atli held out her hands to receive him. She trembled. In mere moments he would arrive.

Dohtor Yuun and hundreds of Cwalu Itinerants along with the assembled volunteer fighters held formation outside the gates of the Sojournic Stronghold. Down range a hundred yards, the edge of the Nurdrayl Forest stretched for miles. Dohtor Yuun looked beyond the trees. She and the other Cwalu could see the Ersatz, waiting and watching.

The Ersatz were idle all along and just behind the tree line. Some had weapons and clothing, likely pilfered from their victims on the way but most had no clothing or weapons, only an insatiable lust for destruction in their eyes. There were thousands, and to varying degrees of similarity, each was wearing the face of the fallen Cenric Warfield. This would be perhaps the toughest test the Cwalu had ever faced.

As Dohtor Yuun contemplated her fate, the Ersatz horde crashed through the wood, running toward the Sojournic Stronghold, all of them smiling, screaming and laughing with unnatural glee. Yuun cursed to herself the ugly task of having to kill so many with the face of such a Laedenoran hero as Cenric Warfield.

"Now!" yelled Dohtor Yuun.

Sanctified by the Wyrsa-Gewealc, the black-armored Cwalu drew their swords and charged the Ersatz using their unnatural and vaporous speed. Trails of black vapor followed them. The volunteer forces cried out and likewise ran toward the oncoming demons.

CHAPTER 50

ATLI HELD OUT HER BLACK SWORD in offering, as the Holy Sojourner stepped foot onto the platform. If he accepted the sword, it would be his blessing on the Wyrsa-Gewealc. She swallowed hard. The Sojourner finished pulling himself up to the platform, and he stood there, shard in one hand and his right hand in the air. He was an adolescent boy. They stared at each other for a moment. The sound of battle cries and metal hitting metal shattered the moment. The battle outside the gates had begun.

The Sojourner looked at the Itinerants along the sides of the path. He looked at his hand in the sky and pulled it down. As if ordered, the Itinerants dropped their hands. He looked at Atli and walked toward her. Atli likewise walked toward him. She was sweating and wary. As they grew closer, Atli noticed that his eyes were not normal. They were deepening pits, spiraling red into oblivion. She became more frightened and doubted this as a wise course of action. She could see that some Itinerants in the crowd were also concerned.

The Sojourner smiled, but it was too wide; impossible, inhuman. At that, Atli stopped walking forward. Her fear escalated to where instead of offering the sword to him, she brandished it with both hands as a weapon against him.

"Hello Atli," said the Sojourner who had also stopped. His face twisted. "I have been waiting for you. This world has delayed you and I am hungry." He looked around again. "All of you are delayed! But I am here now. My name is Vang and you belong to me!"

The Itinerants stirred. This was not right. Atli braced herself and held fast.

"Come, Atli," said Vang. "Let us embrace in this holy place. Let me help you find your purpose!"

Vang's face contorted though his voice remained that of a boy. Blood and rot spilled from his mouth. "You resist me!"

Atli remembered the Aydward. She felt it with her hand then put her sword at the ready again.

Vang howled with the child's voice but it tore through the Sojournic Stronghold like a diseased knife. Atli heard chopping noises and screams. She looked to the Itinerants and some of them had attacked one another with their black swords. She looked back at Vang who was inching toward her, but his countenance was no longer recognizable as a child. It was indescribable. Only part of her mind could accept what she saw.

"I know you, Atli." Vang moved closer. "You are a special and delectable soul. Do you remember being that insufferable crybaby Nikiru?"

Atli took a step backward. The image of the demon stabbing Nikiru in her vision after she took the blood flooded her mind. "Stay back!"

"My children killed you that day, fair and without guile. You are mine. Come to Rax with me, Atli."

Atli continued to back away. The gathering was a bloodbath. The possessed Itinerants had finished carving to pieces the others who had taken the Aydward and were now climbing the walls to engage the Sentinels.

Outside the gate, the Ersatz horde beset the Sojournic Stronghold and the Cwalu, tearing flesh from bone with gleeful irreverence. The Cwalu teleported in and out of the blood-soaked skirmish; striking with their black swords and claws. The sounds of many dissonant choir voices heralded their arrivals and departures.

With each strike, black electricity arced from Cwalu weapons into the Ersatz invaders' bodies; stopping some, provoking others. The Ersatz were mighty. They swarmed in waves by the hundreds; all with the face of Ember Driss, the Beast of Sable Rock. The Cwalu were outnumbered.

Dohtor Yuun teleported to the front of the gate, facing the oncoming horde. The remaining Cwalu teleported to her side, forming a black wall of death. The sounds of wicked laughter and screaming permeated everything.

Yuun brandished her sword and shifted her footing. "This is the moment! This is our purpose! This is the walk of battle!"

The other Cwalu warriors howled with a ghost-like quality as they were overtaken by the Ersatz horde. The Cwalu fought with strength and without mental reservation but after only moments, the enemy overwhelmed them and pressed on to the gates. Yuun was among the Cwalu still living. She and the others continued to fight.

At the walls, the Sentinels on the battlements engaged the invaders with arrows and oil, but the creatures were too powerful. The Ersatz rammed the doors with their bodies over and over. Some perished from their wounds and others took their place.

Many of the Ersatz had armed themselves with the black swords of fallen Cwalu and struck their corpses over and over until nothing remained of them. The doors buckled under the weight and Ersatz spilled into the grounds of the Sojournic Stronghold.

CHAPTER 51

TAVIST HELD OUT THE BÓCTALU as though a shield, his other hand on the pommel of his sword. His eyes had widened to their limits.

"Dara! What are you doing?" Tavist yelled.

"I want to you hear your promises, Tavist," Dara said in a voice that was hers but also not hers. "You make such good promises."

Dara held Lydia in front of her. Her arm was cradling her head, and a bolt was just piercing the flesh of Lydia's neck. Dara had taken Lydia hostage.

"Vang." said Tavist.

"What is that on your hand, Tavist?" asked Vang. "Did that filthy little book teach it to you? It will not protect you forever. I made you! I will sup on you even if your soul moves away from me. Myn traps you, but soon you will be in the world-before. Do you not know you are my servant?"

"I am a Scrivener. My soul began in Rax, meant for Vel. I move against nature; against time. But I decide my true fate!" Tavist was speaking in authority.

"All with your condition are constructs of my deception, meant to infiltrate Vel. You are as dark as I."

"I am not such a thing! I choose right! I will choose right!"

"More oaths, more promises," Vang said with loathing. "Do it!" Vang screamed. "Promise her you will save her, Tavist! I like it! I like it when you fail!" Dara's teeth started to vibrate and blood trickled from her gums. In control of Dara's body, Vang moved Dara's hands from the bolt but it hovered in the air, still pressing against Lydia's neck. Vang forced open Lydia's eye and licked her right eyeball, making satisfied cooing sounds.

Lydia grunted with disgust.

"I promise," whispered Tavist.

The bolt spun in place, drawing blood.

"I promise!" Tavist yelled. "I promise I will save you!"

"But you will not save her, Tavist!" shouted Vang. "You have failed again! You are a liar! You break your promises Tavist! Break them all for me!"

With no warning, the earth shuddered to an extent that knocked everyone to the ground. Dara struck her head on a large stone and became disoriented. The bolt also fell and Lydia took her opportunity. She drew her own dagger and jumped on top of Dara.

"I do not need saving!" Lydia shrieked. She was about to strike when Tavist stayed her hand.

"No, Lydia. Hold her down!" Tavist grabbed Lydia's dagger and, looking at his own, carved an Aydward in Dara's skin near her collarbone. Dara's face contorted. Vang whispered profane sayings, looking at both Tavist and Lydia. She thrashed for several moments then relaxed. Vang left.

The earth quaked even more. The waters of the lake were restless and choppy. Tavist and Lydia helped Dara up, and they all staggered back away from the water. Lydia cried and wiped her eye with the remnants of her tattered underclothes. She wiped it until it bled.

Tavist realized the Bóctalu was growing hot. He unhooked it from his hip and tossed it to the ground. It opened to Charles' page, showing a stag's head. Then the quaking stopped but before anyone could think on it, there was a deafening, booming sound followed by the emerging of a giant, twisting column of water that shot from the middle of the lake up into the sky. The shock wave threw them again to the ground.

Tavist lay on his back, staring at the massive, spiraling wall of water. "Charles, you are the Furtyr." he whispered.

CHAPTER 52

ATLI POSITIONED HERSELF as far back on the platform as possible. The boy that was both Aerion and Vang was upon her. He brandished the shard as a blade and was stabbing at the air. The ground had been quaking, and she struggled to keep her balance, yet she knew she had to stay focused if she were to escape alive on this most terrible of days.

She could see behind Vang that the Ersatz horde had entered the grounds and were overrunning the remaining Sentinels. It was not long before they dispatched the last Sentinels The Ersatz swarmed up the path and, one by one, came to a stop behind Vang. They were swaying and silent, their greedy maws and hands dripping with blood.

Their expression was of a darkened lust. The surviving Itinerants under Vang's control joined the forming crowd. Atli even recognized several of the Shard-Fallen in attendance. Vang stopped.

Atli looked around the compound. Everyone was dead or injured. There was no sign of Dohtor Yuun or Jeth. She was on her own.

Someone had started a fire in the rectory. Smoke billowed out the door and Atli heard screams inside. She could see several self-immolated Ersatz demons dancing in the flames through the double doors. They had defeated her.

Vang cracked his neck side to side and smelled at the air. "Ah, such pure hope in this world. It tastes so sweet as it dies. So tell me Atli, how does it feel knowing it is I who you pitiful insects have been worshiping for so many years? You vermin made quite the fuss over me." He smiled at Atli. "Well this is the end of the path. Are you ready for me, Atli? No? You are not ready. How could you be?"

Vang took a sadistic tone. "Atli, In the next life during the time of your budding adolescence, you will remember this day. One day you will mind your own business doing the things that young people do, and it will hit you, all. You will remember how it felt when I tore into you and ate you alive. You will remember that your only purpose in the whole of existence was to satiate me at my will and pleasure. You will remember that you lost, with no hope of redemption.

You will know that it was you who let it happen. And Atli, when you remember and wake into a living nightmare on a scale you can not imagine, I will know it too, and I will come find you and consume you for all time. You will cease to be. I will use the darkness that comes from that and corrupt others to the same fate. That is your eternal purpose."

Atli was sobbing. "No. No."

"After I have murdered you, I will find Charles. And then perhaps I will go visit the Nihtgessa in the Neverwall. Did you know the Neverwall protects a doorway to Vel?" Vang laughed. "A doorway! Oh this is a great day! Once I destroy this world, I will destroy that one as well and start over. I have needed a change in leadership there for years."

All the Ersatz horde tensed in unison. Vang smiled at Atli and cocked his head. "It is time, Atli. Time to go."

The entire Sojournic Stronghold shuddered and an earth-shattering booming sound sent a shock wave that knocked every standing creature to the ground; everyone except for Atli who was knocked over the side of the cliff. Her sword fell to the platform.

Vang and the Ersatz horde steadied themselves. Vang spat bile and shrieked to the sky. Then a distant rumble became closer and closer. Vang ran toward the edge of the cliff, but before he could get far, a vast and spinning column of lake water emerged in front of him, shooting high. Soaring just above it, the Furtyr held Atli in his arms.

"There you are!" yelled Vang, his head tilted upward. "You have been very, very disobedient! However, I have to commend you. You have done a delightful job creating all of this."

The column of water stopped ascending and turned downward, twisting in place. Inside its tubular maw, were the churning bones of untold thousands of forest animals along with lake creatures and endless types of lake vegetation. The Furtyr flew down to Stag's End. He placed Atli down. The shock wave had stunned her, but she collected her sword and moved beyond the side of the platform.

Vang danced a little. "And this young man you have created, this Aerion. I find him promising. I would think so, considering he is me in a manner of speaking. I am now thinking I might spare him the final death in Rax that he may become your replacement in Vel. He would make a splendid overseer. What do you think of that?"

The Furtyr's body morphed into Charles. There were still antlers, black eyes, eagle's wings along with claws and teeth like razors but they were smaller than before. He approached Vang.

"I am the Gastwyrd here Vang, not you." Charles' mouth did not move.

Vang leaned in and spoke with venom. "The coward speaks. I made you. You are mine. They are mine! You kept them from me, made me wait!"

Charles pointed at the dead bodies of the Itinerants. "They deserve to hope and a chance to remember what they are. They deserve to roam the cosmos in their former splendor. We all do. Vang, we yearn for the lost and forgotten light. Even you. It is not too late."

Vang's eyes sank deeper. "I am the eater of light!" he shouted. The Ersatz horde mimicked Vang, screaming it at the same time. "You used to understand that and revel in it." said Vang. "I made you base and foul. Your task was to honor me with your suffering and the suffering you caused. Now you speak of light? Now you create it? You are a traitor and you will pay the price."

Vang struck at Charles with the shard but Charles rose his hand and grasped Vang's arm. A sound, like crystal in the wind rang out and Vang flew back along the platform and crashed into the Ersatz horde, head over heels.

"No, Vang," said Charles. "I am the Gastwyrd here. My power is greater."

"You forget, coward, I came here in a physical body."

Charles squinted.

Vang let out laughter and threw the shard into the air. It shot to the east, down the path. "You remember now, yes?"

Charles, looked to the east. He knew what it was. It was the thing he fled from five thousand years ago. It frightened him to the point of suicide rather than face it.

"Yes, I am here. Not even you can defeat me in the flesh." He pointed at Charles. The Ersatz horde burst into action running for him.

Charles' eyes flashed and the twisting column of lake water crashed down past the platform into the Sojournic grounds. Chest-high water surged into the Stronghold, bowling over all in its path. It flowed out the gate into the forest, carrying many dead and wounded with it. The water that stayed in the compound receded back over the cliff. Charles was hovering over the water as it passed underneath him.

The water level shrank. Emerging therefrom was a swarm of skeletal forest beasts covered in skin of lake plants, crustaceans and sea life. The throng of animated creatures trampled and destroyed the remaining Ersatz horde. There were none remaining.

Having finished their task, the skeletal mob returned to the lake over the cliff.

Atli had avoided the flood by getting to high ground near the west barracks. Once the beasts left, she ran down to the platform. Charles landed and received her. They embraced for quite a long time.

"Thank you," said Atli.

As they held one another, Charles returned to his human form.

A distant rumbling emerged toward the Gearwood Thicket, deep in the Nurdrayl Forest. The sound reminded Charles of the remaining peril. He broke with Atli and turned toward the east.

Standing at the end of the platform was Vang. He was wet and holding a spear he had collected from a dead village fighter.

"Here we are once again! Will you flee? Will you deny me?" Vang shifted his footing.

Charles looked at Vang. His eyes flashed, and he morphed into a giant rock stag with chocolate fur. He moved in front of Atli, shielding her.

A voice came from everywhere "Today I face you, Vang."

Vang yelled and sprang into a sprint toward Charles. Charles lowered his antlers and charged Vang. With only a few yards remaining, Vang launched the spear. Charles parried it with his antlers and impaled Vang through the chest with them. Vang screeched then lay still. Charles flung Vang off his antlers and morphed into the Furtyr. The child was once again Aerion Gwyndol, lifeless on the platform, eyes open and blank.

Atli caught up with him. "What now?"

"Vang's essence has left this shell. There is still a danger," said the Furtyr. "We must stop it."

"How," asked Atli.

"Look away," the Furtyr said. "This is disagreeable but necessary work."

Atli might protest, but she knew in her heart what was coming could not be forgotten.

The Furtyr turned to the corpse of the boy named Aerion and removed a femur from it. He broke it in two pieces. He kept the more jagged of the two, throwing the other piece to the ground.

"I will return," said the Furtyr.

"I wish to go with you and I will not relent."

"Will you? You are like Nikiru after all, though he was nicer than you. It is good to see who you have become."

Atli did not understand, but let it alone. The Furtyr picked her up and flew east. They soared high over the Nurdrayl forest. Atli took it all in, she was awash as in a dream, but she knew it had all happened. The image of Nikiru being stabbed over and over invaded her mind. She shuddered at the memory.

The sun was almost down, but enough light illuminated the hulking creature attempting to pull itself from a frozen, overgrown pit in the ground. The creature, trapped waist-deep, was man-shaped, but made of rock and semi-transparent flesh. It had no facial features, only a spiral of red smoke twisting inward into the void.

Though its legs were buried deep, Atli thought the creature had to be three people in height. Inside the transparent parts of the creature, were small spheres that were glowing red. It had claws the exact shape and size of the shard the Sojourner carried.

It groaned, causing the world to sigh, as all the nearby vegetation died and putrefied before their eyes. It seemed to struggle somewhat in freeing itself and tore at the frozen ground with its claws. The Furtyr and Atli arrived and landed a short distance from the thing.

"What is this accursed thing?" yelled Atli.

"We call it the Ellengæst," said the Furtyr in Atli's head. "It is the Ersatz embodiment of Vang's power in the world-after. It is a construct of utter decay and destruction. If allowed to roam free, it can corrupt all life in but a few weeks. I can not stop it, I can only delay it."

Atli saw that where the Ellengæst's claws touched the ground, a network of small, red and black, rotting lines grew outward like cracks in a frozen lake. Tiny swarms of spider-like creatures poured from the cracks. They overtook the rotting vegetation and consumed it somehow, leaving behind a black, viscous tar. They appeared to gain in size as they fed.

"Atli, you must run now," The Furtyr warned, brandishing the bone shard. "I will slow the abomination."

"No, this burden is mine alone," said Atli. "All of this is my purpose. I knew it when I saw Nikiru die in that battle in the world-before."

"Are you certain?"

"I am."

The Furtyr handed Atli the bone shard. "Strike where it is soft."

Atli nodded, took the bone shard, and they embraced again.

"Forever the brave one, Nikiru," said the Furtyr.

Atli looked into the Furtyr's black eyes. "Never stop searching for the light in us. There is much hope for Laedenor and we are worthy."

"When you do this, you must run. The Ellengæst is slow but irresistible. Run as fast as you can to Stag's End. It is the only way out."

"What then? What will I do?" Atli glanced back at the Ellengæst.

"I do not know, Atli. But this buys the world time to stop the Ellengæst; to send him back. But everyone you know will be gone.

"They are already gone. Where will you go?"

"I cannot say. The Furtyr's presence in me wanes. Farewell, Atli."

"Farewell." She regarded the abomination.

It had freed one leg. She mustered whatever raw and unpracticed Cwalu power she could and willed herself to run toward it. She ran between the forming cracks and dodged the spiders until she was in striking distance. She brought the bone shard down, plunging it into a transparent area of the Ellengæst's free, bent leg. The crystalline skin though transparent was soft. It gave way like the skin of a fruit. Everything became still. Atli, the Ellengæst, the cracks and spiders; all motionless.

The Furtyr morphed back into the likeness of Charles. "Thank you Atli," he muttered. He sat and stared at the scene for some time before he set out to meet his friends at the lake.

CHAPTER 53

SUREK TABEN, CAPTAIN OF THE CORVAX and Minister of Port Frailty, had set sail as soon as his new friends were back aboard. Seas were rough and the journey back would take longer. There would be time to rest; to ruminate.

The four travelers unanimously decided they would travel back to Port Frailty where the Captain could help them organize an offensive to take back Zannistar from Ember Driss and the Laedenoran invaders. Perhaps then, they could later return to Laedenor and secure the dark magic now brewing deep in the Gearwood Thicket region of the Nurdrayl Forest. One thing was certain: they had plenty of time to prepare for the doom of the Ellengæst; lifetimes.

Joining with the Furtyr forever altered Charles' mind. He did not understand how it worked or how to manage it. It was as if he was himself, but also he could sometimes feel the mind of the Furtyr pressing into his own.

Neither could he explain what happened to him in the lake. He remembered being dragged to the bottom and fighting to stay awake. He had nearly passed from the world when he noticed the tip of something shiny buried in the sand and muck. It was pulsing with light. With all his might he reached out and freed it. It was a small sphere of silver-like metal with a disc-shaped divot in it, the size of the coin.

He felt himself being imbibed with energy. With each pulse, the sphere poured life back into Charles' body. He felt his wounds heal, which he now realized was rather unsettling. The surging had been so intense, he could not hold on the sphere and dropped it. It was then that the Furtyr overtook him. The rest was like watching a dream. He was the Furtyr and Charles, sometimes more one than the other. It was like he existed in two places simultaneously. As the feeling subsided, his thoughts and words were clearer, which suited everyone else just fine since he had made little sense since they left Laedenor.

But now, days later, he knew the Furtyr was fading from him, though he still felt somehow different from before. He was so much more than the orphaned, frightened Secondary noble who spent his days assessing the wealth of the kingdom. He had much to consider. His eyes opened to many things he could have never imagined possible. But no matter how he rationalized, no matter how he pleaded with the possibilities, he knew there was only one course of action to take.

That next day, while traversing the Neverwall, everyone sat together in the galley, wearing hoodwinks and sipping tea. Tavist and Lydia were discussing the finer points of how to invade a country and Dara had been talking to Charles about the journey they had just endured.

Charles and Dara were holding hands across the table, with the coin laying between them, a gift from Tavist who remembered to remove it from the mural in the cotlif at the lake when Charles returned. Tavist had shown Charles the mural. He had agreed with Tavist the man in the vignettes was Gyldred. It would seem that Gyldred was much more than a Laedenoran Effacer who defected to Zannistar.

"Does it hurt?" asked Charles referring to the fresh Aydward on Dara's shoulder.

"A little. Charles, I want to tell you something." Dara said.

She and Charles scooted to the end of the table. He fell off but re-situated himself.

"I love you, Charles. I always have. Ever since we were children."

"But you are not in love with me," The words were true. "You are in love with your husband, Cenric. I can never be him."

Dara paused then squeezed Charles' hand. "Yes, but you are special. I want you to know that."

Charles gave a puzzling look. "Dara, this is right. I am in love with *my* wife Nissa. She was cruel, true. But it was my choice to endure it. I am in love with her still. I always will be."

"You must hate me; what I did."

"No, I understand. You had to. I know that now. But you are proof that the Nissa I remember could still be inside her somewhere."

"She's gone from this world, Charles."

"I know."

Dara squeezed his hands again and for a while they sat quiet, not being able to see but being connected. Charles broke the silence.

"That is why I will be leaving."

"What? What do you mean?" Dara whispered.

"Dara, I am changed. I know things I can not explain. I did not find my heart at the cotlif in Mirlandis Lake, but I did find my purpose. My destiny lies beyond this place in Vel, the world-before. The doorway to Vel on the Islet of Abeodan is no longer protected from the Nihtgessa. I aim to join the Furtyr there and help fight Vang's forces. We must protect Myn from them. Maybe I can find who Nissa was in Vel before her soul entered Myn. Cenric Warfield is what this world needs. It should have been him that the Furtyr created first, not me."

"I do not understand. If you go to Vel, will things in Myn change?"

"I am not sure. Maybe. There are many possibilities. I know we will both continue on. Dara, I am unable to explain it, but I can go anywhere in the universe. That is how the Furtyr created me. I cannot control it, but in time I will. For now, I choose Vel. There are matters there that concern me. Gyldred is there. Arminius Morlund is there. I must seek them out. Nissa will not remember me but the Scriveners will. Their souls and their awareness moves backwards through the worlds. I must go now."

"Charles, wait. What are you saying?"

"Your love for each other is real. That makes you real, and it gives you purpose beyond yourselves. Myn is a bright spot on a vast darkness. It is hope. You and Cenric are part of that hope. And we must protect hope and ensure it continues. Goodbye, Dara."

There was silence. Charles hands grew cold and Dara gasped. Some minutes passed. She could not see what was happening. Dara was about to alert the others when his hands grew warm again.

"Charles? Do not scare me like that ever again!" Dara scolded him.

"You have not called me Charles in quite a long while," said Cenric in his usual tone and cadence which differed greatly from Charles'.

Then she understood. It was her husband, returned in Charles' body.

"Is it you, Cenric?" Dara was in near hysterics.

"Yes, it is me." They gripped hands. "The Neverwall trapped me. I missed you so."

"But how is this possible? Am I dreaming?" She was sobbing.

Tavist and Lydia were silent.

"Charles and I have an accord. He promised to give me his eternal purpose and his flesh but in return I had to promise him that I would take back the throne of Zannistar and that I would love you for whatever time we have in this world."

They embraced. It was him. She knew it.

"I think we can accommodate both things," said Dara.

Lydia and Tavist had overheard and fumbled over to Cenric and Dara. There were questions and answers, stories and lessons. The Captain came down to alert them it was acceptable to remove their hoodwinks, which they did.

They all looked at Cenric, perhaps expecting Charles to be there. But it was not Charles anymore. His eyes gave him away and the way he stood. Cenric and Dara touched their foreheads together, held each other's faces and cried. Tavist and Lydia approached them and hugged them both.

"What did I miss?" asked Surek Taben. But they did not answer. There would be time enough later. Surek Taben shook his head and went back up the ladder to his duties. Now clear of the Neverwall, the Corvax set a course due south for Port Frailty.

They talked late into the night, about Charles for the most part. They talked of his bravery, his sacrifice and his less flattering qualities. They vowed for as long as they lived, they would remember just how special he was.

Just before they turned in, Cenric found the Brymróc berthing and descended the ladder.

"Gervin?" Cenric called out.

A voice resonated in the dark. "Who wants to know? We are out of the Neverwall and off duty!"

"Forgive me sir, but I am Cenric, a friend of Charles' and I am told that you have dumplings."

A burlap bag hit Cenric square in the chest. He cradled it, opened the bag and smelled blessed comfort. He smiled.

"Thank you, Gervin. Good night to you." He turned on his heels and ascended the ladder to find his beloved Dara who was waiting for him on the aft deck staring at the stars. He joined her there and together they marveled at the night sky, laughed, kissed, ate dumplings and sailed into what would soon become a very different world.

EPILOGUE

FOR MANY WEEKS, EMBER DRISS LAY IN BED, recovering from the wounds he suffered near Mirlandis Lake at the hands of the Woodlock Dara Warfield. He had been staying in Charles' and Nissa's quarters. He liked it there. Templeton Kaid, the Royal Chirurgeon was tending to his stitches.

Once finished, he retreated and wrung his hands. "Your Majesty, your wounds are healing well."

"Are they?" Ember returned with a bored tone. "Perhaps I should have died there."

"Nonsense, Majesty," said Templeton. "This kingdom is greater under your rule than it has ever been before."

"Perhaps," said Ember. "I no longer have Vang's power."

"You have your wits, Majesty."

"Is it enough, Templeton?"

"You also have the Bekrot Chair and the Calamity Engine."

Ember grinned, his eyes sparkling. "Yes, I do."

"I have other news," Templeton announced. "Your old enemy Cenric Warfield is alive. Someone has spotted him in Port Frailty."

"Impossible! I killed him myself! Where does this information come from?"

"Someone named Braden Bol. He is staying in one of the guest-chambers. He arrived from Arom this morning by boat."

"Well, Templeton, that means we must also find ourselves in Port Frailty. Have you been?"

"To Port Frailty? No."

"Neither have I, which means I cannot use the Bekrot Chair, at least not yet. Send word to ready my ship. We leave tomorrow. And bring me this Braden Bol fellow. We have business.

"Yes, Majesty."

GLOSSARY

Aydward: A type of magic symbol carved into a person's flesh. Once healed, it starts to move around on that person's body. Meant to protect the wearer against certain kinds of attacks depending on which symbol is used.

Bekrot Chair: A magic loveseat made of gearwood. It can teleport users to places they have already been to at least once. However, sometimes it will limit a user's options or refuse to teleport at all. It was brought as a peace offering to Zannistar from Laedenor by Gyldred the Effacer.

Bóctalu: A secret book of names.

Brierberries: A well-known, versatile and highly sought after food berry that grows worldwide.

Brymróc: A contingent of blind sailors.

Buttonwood: Wood taken from the fast-growing buttonwood tree; an abundant resource in Arom. Central to Aromite culture.

Calamity Engine: An oversized, horseless carriage powered by human souls. A relic of the Sixteen Generations War.

Cotlif: A very small, single-roomed dwelling, usually in clusters. A cultural mainstay of Laedenoran society for millennia.

Cwalu: A reclusive, mystical branch of the Itinerants who live in the forest, who possess unique abilities and who are adept in matters of battle.

Dreka: A soulless copy of a person who uses the Bekrot Chair to travel. The copy appears in the forests of Laedenor. Each successive copy becomes less and less like the original.

Effacer: A sorcerer who can eat the memories of others. Effacers were common during the Sixteen Generations War. They were outlawed after the war.

Ersatz: A creature with no soul or mind of its own; an empty husk which attracts malevolent spirits who can inhabit it. Created when a Dreka uses the Bekrot Chair.

Expanser: A sorcerer who can safely navigate the dangerous region known as the Neverwall.

Furtyr: A demon of immense power.

Gearwood: Hardwood taken from a very special type of magic tree that only grows in the Gearwood Thicket; a densely forested area in Laedenor on a plateau overlooking Mirlandis Lake.

Geattor: A tower that can transport people to another tower somewhere else in the world. Users jump off the tower to activate it. Where users end up is dependent on which side of the tower they jump from. Most were destroyed during the Sixteen Generations War. There are three known Geattor left which only function for one day every one hundred years.

Itinerant: A member of a religious order in Laedenor whose purpose is to study and interpret the movements of the Sojourner as well as to provide spiritual guidance to the world.

Jaibok: An enormous river ship with spider-like legs. It is a remnant of the Sixteen Generations War.

Lucan: The art and science of gradually moving closer to the Sojourner in order to gain power and favor.

Lucanite: Someone who is attempting the Lucan. They can be anyone the Itinerants allow onto the Sojournic Compound.

Nihtgessa: Disembodied consciousness' trapped in the Neverwall. Some are benevolent and some are malevolent.

Nombit: A coin with a person's family symbol embossed thereon. Unique to Zannistar.

Reader: A sorcerer who can detect specific types of intent in others.

Sentinel: An internal mercenary force who provide protection to the Itinerants and who also assist the Itinerants by watching the Sojourner for movement.

Sibb-gewealc: The Walk of Peace. A specific interpretation of the Sojourner's movements and position. If this interpretation is made, then the Itinerants are expected to maintain peace in the world at all costs.

Shamblefolk: Creatures of Aromite folklore who are reported to come out at night near the city walls of Port Frailty to terrorize any people who are out and alone.

Shengmar: A special type of shellfish, known for its unique coloring, exquisite flavor and sedative properties.

Sojourner: A statue-like boy in the forest near the Sojournic Compound who is walking so slow, he only moves a few inches every year. He is worshiped as a God throughout the world and studied by the Itinerants. Those who get close to him and survive sometimes receive powers or visions. He is considered the source of all magic. The Itinerants have built their compound near a cliff which they believe to be the end of the Sojourner's journey.

Wyrsa-gewealc: The Walk of Battle. A specific interpretation of the Sojourner's movements and position. If this interpretation is made, then the Itinerants are expected to go to war.

Woodlock: A special type of sorcerer that can control the properties and movements of gearwood.